Praise for Road Ends

NATIONAL BESTSELLER

"If the part of Ontario west of Toronto is Munro country, then the area . . . where her fictional towns of Struan and Crow Lake are roughly located . . . may well end up being dubbed Lawson Country. . . . Fiercely readable." *National Post*

"Mary Lawson finds gold in the hard landscape of the Canadian Shield." *Ottawa Gazette*

"Like all great writers—and Lawson is among the finest— she tells her story in a deceptively simple and straightforward way. . . . Lawson's writing is clean, clear and accessible. Her descriptions are strong, and her dialogue believable. Like Alistair MacLeod, Lawson writes of bone-searing tragedies without shrouding her novels in impenetrable darkness. She leaves room for light—and hope. Reading *Road Ends* was like getting the favourite book I wanted for Christmas; my only regret was when I finished it and had to leave Megan, Tom, and the rest of the residents of Struan." Laura Eggertson, *Toronto Star*

"*Road Ends* is the type of book you can curl up in and read in a day: it's beautifully written, never dull, and the best enjoyed with a steaming mug of cocoa." *ELLE Canada*

"Every Canadian student should be reading Mary Lawson's novels—starting with *Crow Lake,* and now including her newest accomplishment, *Road Ends.*" *Toronto Star*

"This is a very readable book, its narrative compelling, its setting richly drawn, its characters sympathetic." *The Globe and Mail*

"From whatever well her muse is drawn, there is no denying the compelling draw of her prose." *Manitoulin Expositor*

"What sets Lawson apart is storytelling so matter-of-fact (in the best possible way) that readers are able to feel the emotional intensity of the characters' situations without succumbing to moroseness. . . . Admirers of Lawson's previous novels will not be disappointed with the author's latest effort. The same easy grace and economy of language that drew readers into those earlier stories are employed to full effect, and the setting, along with the welcome reappearance of a few familiar characters, imparts a sense of homecoming. . . . Complex and satisfying." *Quill & Quire*

"One of Lawson's gifts is her ability to bring her characters to life without judgment. . . . In Lawson's gentle, skilled hands, we watch this family change and find reason to hope for them. *Road Ends* is an engaging book." *Guelph Mercury*

"*Road Ends* deals with the life within families and the push and pull between responsibility and individual desire." *Zoomer*

"Subtly funny, touching in ways that are at time shockingly true, awe-inspiring for its use of language." *Montreal Gazette*

Praise for Crow Lake

"The kind of book that keeps you reading well past midnight; you grieve when it's over. Then you start pressing it on friends." *The Washington Post*

"Lawson is a brilliant storyteller . . . [and] an elegant stylist. . . . The depth, honesty and feeling throughout are superbly wrought. *Crow Lake* is a wondrous thing . . . a new Canadian classic." *The Hamilton Spectator*

"Deep, clear and teeming with life. A lot of readers are going to surrender themselves to the magic of Crow Lake. . . . This is the real thing." *The Globe and Mail*

"A tribute to the power of old-fashioned storytelling. . . . Lawson's narrative gift, voiced in quiet, unselfconscious prose that never distracts from the story, is immense." *Maclean's*

"Darkly unpredictable and compelling. . . . It is a wise book too, saying as much about how we deny our capacity to hurt as about how we deny our ability to help." *The Financial Times*

"Beautifully written, carefully balanced, [in *Crow Lake*] Mary Lawson constructs a history of sacrifice, emotional isolation and family love without sounding a false note." *Daily Mail*

"Impossible to put down." *The Edmonton Sun*

"Full of blossoming insights and emotional acuity... a compelling and serious page-turner. Turning points and consequences are outlined with unusual sharpness, allowing the reader to dwell on painful might-have-beens as if they were one's own." *The Observer*

"*Crow Lake* may be one of the loveliest novels you almost ever read." *The Telegram*

"Lawson delivers a potent combination of powerful character writing and gorgeous description of the land. Her sense of pace and timing is impeccable throughout. . . . This is a vibrant, resonant novel by a talented writer whose lyrical, evocative writing invites comparisons to Rick Bass and Richard Ford." *Publishers Weekly* (starred review)

"Spellbinding. . . . The language is subtle but beautiful. . . . A marvelous story." W. P Kinsella

"A compelling, slow-burning story of a fractured family in the rural 'badlands' of northern Ontario, where hardship is mirrored in the landscape and tragedy is never very far away." *The Economist*

"Compulsively readable." *The Globe and Mail*

"A remarkable novel, utterly gripping. . . . I read it in a single sitting, then I read it again, just for the pleasure of it." Joanne Harris

"[*Crow Lake*] that looks back to a young woman's harshly beautiful childhood in rural Canada. . . . A simple and heartfelt account that conveys an astonishing intensity of emotion, almost Proustian in its sense of loss and regret." *Kirkus Reviews* (starred review)

"A touching meditation on the power of loyalty and loss, on the ways in which we pay our debts and settle old scores, and on what it means to love, to accept, to succeed—and to negotiate fate's obstacle courses." *People*

"Every so often, a novel is so beautifully structured and rivetingly told you want to collar everyone you see and tell them to read it. Mary's Lawson's *Crow Lake* is just such a story." *Newark Star-Ledger*

Praise for The Other Side of the Bridge

#1 NATIONAL BESTSELLER
Longlisted for the Man Booker Prize
Finalist for the Rogers Writers' Trust Fiction Prize

"A beautiful read, on every level." *The Independent*

"I could not put it down, but perhaps better to say that I could not let it go or that it would not let me go. . . . Lawson transported me into a place that I know does not exist by taking me deep down into the story of a family whose fate is inexorable and universal. Her reality became mine." *The Globe and Mail*

"This is a book you will be driven to share with friends." *The Gazette*

"An enthralling read, both straightforward and wonderfully intricate." *The Guardian*

"Page-turning. . . . A tension-filled plot with enough twists and turns to keep the reader up at night unwilling to put the book down." *Calgary Herald*

"Like her fellow Canadians Alice Munro and the late Carol Shields, Lawson is a master of the quiet moment made significant." *The Scotsman*

"Eloquent and thoughtful. . . . Not only has Lawson fulfilled the promise of her first novel, she has surpassed it in a layered, complex story about emotional power shifts. Storytelling, not showmanship, dictates the honest, serious art of Mary Lawson." *The Irish Times*

"Lawson's gifts are enormous, especially her ability to write a literary work in a popular style. Her dialogue has perfect pitch, yet I've never read anyone better at articulating silence. Best of all, Lawson creates the most quotable images in Canadian literature." *Toronto Star*

"The author draws her characters with unobtrusive humor and compassion, and she meets one of the fiction writer's most difficult challenges: to portray goodness believably, without sugar or sentiment." *The Washington Post Book World*

"Lawson clearly knows and loves her terrain—the countryside, its people and their way of life—and she tells this story without sentimentalizing anything about it. . . . She writes vividly of the joys and hardships of rural life, the harsh but sublime beauties of the natural world, as well as the threads connecting one

generation to the next and the depredations wrought by the flow of man-made history. By the time you've come to the end of this deftly restrained yet intensely dramatic book, you'll have been taken out of yourself into a world most of us have never known."
Los Angeles Times

"Tragic and haunting—get the Kleenex for the final page." *Daily Express*

"Like the great nineteenth-century novelists of provincial life, Mary Lawson is fluent in the desperate intensity of the small, individual dramas of respectable people—and she paints an eloquent picture." *The Sunday Telegraph*

"Evokes beautifully the big joys and sorrows of most people, no matter how small their town." *The Times*

"This is a fine book—an enthralling read, both straightforward and wonderfully intricate." *The Guardian*

"A subtly wrought affair of complex relationships, hard times and shocking events." *The Independent*

"Beautifully observed with characters who are all realistically flawed." *Scotland on Sunday*

"In this follow-up to her acclaimed *Crow Lake*, Lawson again explores the moral quandaries of life . . . [in] a world . . . where beauty and harshness are inextricably intertwined." *Publishers Weekly*

"A note-perfect tale of coming of age in northern Canada, as beautiful as the landscape is stark. . . . A deftly interwoven story of love and loss." *Kirkus Reviews* (starred review)

"Lawson beautifully skirts the clichés of sibling rivalry embedded since Cain and Abel, with a story that aches with its inevitability and yet suggests hope." *New York Daily News*

"Lawson's writing is much like that of the late William Maxwell. She is patient, never flashy, and her virtuosity never calls attention to itself. Her characters are ordinary, decent people, living out the dramas of everyday life in a place that is beautiful and demanding. Through them she reminds us that old-fashioned storytelling is the best kind and the hardest to do, and that simple themes often touch us most." *Arizona Republic*

Road Ends

MARY LAWSON

Road Ends

VINTAGE CANADA

VINTAGE CANADA EDITION, 2014

Copyright © 2013 Mary Lawson

All rights reserved under International and Pan-American Copyright Conventions.
No part of this book may be reproduced in any form or by any electronic
or mechanical means, including information storage and retrieval systems,
without permission in writing from the publisher, except by a reviewer,
who may quote brief passages in a review.

Published in Canada by Vintage Canada, a division of Random House of
Canada Limited, Toronto, in 2014. Originally published in hardcover in Canada by
Alfred A. Knopf Canada, a division of Random House of Canada Limited, in 2013.
Distributed by Random House of Canada Limited.

Vintage Canada with colophon is a registered trademark.

www.randomhouse.ca

This book is a work of fiction. Names, characters, places and incidents either are
the product of the author's imagination or are used fictitiously. Any resemblance
to actual persons, living or dead, events or locales is entirely coincidental.

Library and Archives Canada Cataloguing in Publication

Lawson, Mary, 1946–
Road ends / Mary Lawson.

ISBN 978-0-345-80809-7

I. Title.

PS8573.A9425R63 2014   C813'.6   C2013-901559-0

Text & cover design by Kelly Hill

Image credits: (street) Sandra Cunningham/Trevillion Images;
(figures) Fuse/Getty Images

Printed and bound in the United States of America

2 4 6 8 9 7 5 3 1

In memory of my parents.

Road Ends

Struan, August 1967

The road was heavily overgrown and they had to stop the car half a dozen times in order to hack down shrubs or drag fallen trees aside. Once a sizeable beech blocked the way and they attacked it with a cross-cut saw. Simon had never seen a cross-cut saw before, far less used one, and he was predictably useless, but ridiculing him was part of the fun.

"Would you look at this city-slicker," Tom said. "Keep your leg there and you'll cut it off. Okay, that's better. Now pull the saw straight towards you . . . don't let the blade bend or it'll jam."

Simon took the saw handles and pulled. The blade jammed.

"As I was saying . . . ," Tom said, repositioning the saw. Simon pulled again. The blade jammed.

"Back home we have *real* saws," Simon said. "Flick a switch and *bam*! You could deforest this whole state in ten minutes." He was American, from Alabama, and had a long slow drawl. Tom had been afraid he would be bored up here in the middle of nowhere for a whole week but he was game to try anything and seemed to be having a great time.

"Province," Tom said. "Not state. And I can just see you with a chain saw. Give me plenty of warning okay? I'll emigrate."

He drew the saw back again, then paused, noticing the angle of the sun slanting through the trees, and glanced at his watch.

"Actually, no offence, but I think Rob better take over or we won't make it down into the ravine and back while it's still light. Okay, Rob?"

Robert was standing with his hands in his pockets, looking off into the woods, and seemed not to hear. Each time they'd had to stop to clear the path all three of them had climbed out of the car, but each time Robert had then merely stood and watched as if lost in thought. Tom was starting to find it both annoying and embarrassing. Rob was still not in good shape, anyone could see that, but given that he'd agreed to come with them he could at least make an effort to join in. He'd hardly said a word since they set off.

"Could you give me a hand here, Rob?" Tom said. No response.

"Rob? Could you give me a hand?"

Finally Robert looked around. "Sure," he said. His face was a waxy colour as if he'd been shut in a dark room for a long time. He came over and took the saw handles and in less than a minute they'd made the first cut.

"That was so *impressive!*" Simon said, overdoing the awe a little. "Were you guys *born* knowing how to do that?"

Tom snorted. He and Robert took the saw to the other side of the road and made the second cut. No longer supported at either end, the log thudded to the ground. The two of them picked it up and heaved it off the road.

"Right," Tom said. "Let's go." He went back to the car and dumped the saw in the trunk.

Robert was looking past them, down the road.

"Rob?" Tom said again, not making much effort now to hide his annoyance.

"There's a lynx," Robert said quietly.

Tom turned and sure enough, there was a lynx not more than thirty feet away, crouched at the side of the road, watching them.

"God!" Simon said in an undertone. "Look at him!"

"You don't see many of those," Tom said. He was absurdly pleased, as if he himself had arranged for the big cat to appear. "They're night hunters, mostly. Consider yourself honoured."

"I do!"

The lynx watched them for a moment, tufted ears angled warily. Then it turned and was instantly gone. The three of them stood, peering into the woods, trying to make out the shape of the animal in the shadows, but it had vanished.

They got back into the car and carried on, the car jolting over the uneven ground, the woods closing in behind them. Finally they rounded a curve and up ahead the road abruptly came to an end, nothing in front of them but forest.

"That looks kind of final," Simon said. "What do we do now?"

"We get out. We're there."

Tom edged the car up until its fender was almost touching the sign that stood between the road and the nearest trees and switched off the engine.

"What's the sign say?" Simon asked, leaning forward, trying to read it.

"You need to see it," Tom said. "It's great." He opened the door and got out.

It was an ordinary road sign, black and white enamelled metal, bolted to a stake that had been hammered into the ground. There were scabs of rust breaking through the paint and it was covered in dust and mud, but when Tom wiped the surface with his sleeve you could still make out the words.

Simon came around the car to join him. "ROAD ENDS," he read aloud, and gave a whoop of laughter. "Did they think you might not notice? Did someone put it there as a joke?"

"I don't think the Department of Highways is known for its sense of humour," Tom said. "The ravine's right here; I guess they wanted to warn people."

There was a sound behind them and he glanced over his shoulder. Robert was getting out of the car.

"The ravine's here?" Simon said. "Where, exactly?"

"Just there, through the trees. The bushes hide it, so be careful. In fact, maybe I'll go first."

He picked his way through the trees and undergrowth, going slowly because it was possible that there had been some erosion since the last time he'd been there and he didn't want to walk out on an overhang by mistake. Suddenly the ground ahead disappeared, just fell away, a sheer drop of two hundred feet to the river below. Instinctively he stuck out his arm to stop the others.

"Christ!" Simon said, hastily stepping back.

Robert joined them and the three of them stood looking down. The ravine was narrow, not more than thirty feet across, and the rock face on the other side glistened grey and green in the rising spray from the river below. As it rose into the air the spray caught the sun and a rainbow arced up and across the gorge, fantastical and unreal. From somewhere in the background, somewhere unseen, there came a sound like rumbling thunder.

"I'm getting soaked," Simon said, wiping his face with his sleeve. "Where's all the spray coming from?"

"There's a waterfall just around to the left. A big one. That's the sound you hear—the thunder. If you go down to the bottom you can get right around behind it—there's a cave. I'll show you."

"We're going down there? Are you kidding?"

"There's a path. It's steep, but it's okay."

He glanced around. "You coming, Rob?"

He and Rob had been down to the falls countless times when they were kids. It had been one of their favourite hikes. They'd cycle as far as they could up the road and then abandon their bikes and go the rest of the way on foot. They'd kidded themselves that no one else knew the cave was there, though of course all kinds of people did. The road had been put in by a hydro company, who'd thought it was a good place to build a dam. But in the end they'd found somewhere better and moved on, leaving the road to be absorbed back into the woods.

Robert nodded. "Sure."

"Good," Tom said. "Let's go."

The old path, when he found it, was overgrown but still passable. For the first hundred yards it ran parallel to the edge of the cliff, then started to descend down a gully carved by millennia of rainwater and spray, rapidly becoming steep.

Tom said, "Better go down backwards from here on. It's slippery, so watch your step. There are good handholds." He looked past Simon, up the path, but he couldn't see Robert.

"Rob?" he called. "You coming?"

"Sure."

From the faintness of his voice he was still back at the top of the cliff.

"Is he okay?" Simon asked, keeping his voice down. "He seems kind of . . . quiet."

"Yeah, he's fine," Tom said dismissively. "He's been through a bit of a rough time recently. Nothing serious."

Nothing serious.

The truth was he was embarrassed by the state his old friend was in and didn't want to have to explain. Didn't even want to think about it, in fact, because he'd been very sympathetic for a long time now, over a year, and he was just plain tired of the whole thing. Today was a perfect day, the sun flickering through the trees, the spray drifting gently in the air around them, beading every leaf, every frond of every fern with silver light, and here he was with a friend from university, a great guy, funny and smart, from a different background, who knew things Tom didn't know but who rather against expectations was prepared to be impressed by the things Tom did know. So in every regard, except for Rob's behaviour, it was a perfect day. And the past is the past, after all; what's done is done and you have to move on. Robert had missed the final year of his degree but he'd be able to make it up, and for Simon and Tom the university years were behind them and the future was out there waiting.

They were more than halfway down now. The thunder of the falls filled the air; you could feel the reverberation inside your chest like the bass notes of some great and ancient instrument. Tom looked up at Simon, who was cautiously climbing down after him. No sign of Rob yet, but he knew the way. Tom waited until Simon was close enough and then reached up and tapped his shoe.

"You okay?" The thunder of the waterfall was so loud he had to shout.

"Yeah!" Simon yelled. "It's fantastic!"

The two of them grinned and carried on down.

———

He listened as their voices faded into the rumble of the falls. He was thinking about the lynx. The way it had looked at him, acknowledging his existence, then passing out of his life like smoke. He was very grateful to it. It was the first thing—the only thing—that had managed, if only for a moment, to displace from his mind the image of the child. He had carried that image with him for a year now, and it had been a weight so great that sometimes he could hardly stand.

Until this moment the fear that it would accompany him to the end, enter eternity with him, had left him paralyzed, but the lynx had freed him to act. He thought it was possible that if he focused on the big cat, if by a great effort of will he managed to hold it in the forefront of his mind, it might stay with him long enough to be the last thing he saw, and its silence the last thing he heard above the thunder of the falls.

CHAPTER ONE

Megan

Struan, February 1966

Two weeks before Megan left home she began a clear-out of her room. She put her suitcase (the biggest she could find, purchased from Hudson's Bay) on the bed and a large cardboard box (free of charge from Marshall's Grocery) on the floor beside it and anything that wouldn't fit into the one had to go into the other. She was ruthless about it; she intended to travel light. Out went any items of clothing she hadn't worn for a year or more, any shoes ditto, any odd socks or underwear with holes in it that she had saved for days that didn't matter, in full knowledge of the fact that none of her days mattered, or at least not in a way that required respectable underwear. Out went the debris left in the bottom of drawers: safety pins, bobby pins, fraying hair ribbons, a beaded bracelet with half the beads missing, the remains of a box made of birch bark and decorated with porcupine quills, ancient elastic bands looking so much like desiccated earthworms that she had to close her eyes when she picked them up and a quill pen fashioned from an eagle's feather, made for her by Tom when he was at the eagle's feather stage.

She threw out a bottle of perfume the twins had given her for Christmas one year, the name of which—Ambush—had made her father laugh out loud, an exceedingly rare occurrence, and followed it with a hideous blue plastic brush and comb set (a Christmas present from Corey), a pink velvet jewellery case containing a mock-diamond ring that had turned her finger green (a Christmas present from Peter), a black velvet Alice band (from her mother) and a fluffy collie dog she'd won in a prize draw at a fund-raising day at school when she was much too old for such things.

Out went a large part of her childhood, in fact. What's over is over.

Into her suitcase, along with the decent underwear, went blouses, sweaters, skirts (summer and winter), jeans, two summer dresses that she still liked, her one decent pair of pyjamas, her saddle shoes and her one and only pair of smart shoes (white, with little heels), bought for her high-school graduation and worn exactly once thereafter, six months ago, when Patrick took her out for dinner down in New Liskeard for a birthday treat. She'd be wearing her winter boots, which was just as well because they'd have taken up half the case.

Also into the suitcase went a miniature travel sewing kit (a twelfth birthday present from her mother that Megan had considered rather pointless at the time because she never went anywhere but that now, after nine years in the bottom of a drawer, might come in handy), a hot water bottle (she couldn't sleep without one) and a photo of the whole family, or as much of it as had existed at the time, taken by a travelling magician who had come boiling up the long and dusty road to Struan one summer's day in an ancient overheated Packard hearse. Megan had no idea where he had come from or where he went, but she remembered the evening he entertained the town. He'd put on a performance in the church hall and the entire population of Struan had attended, even her father, who never went to anything. She remembered the magician up on the stage, a tall thin figure, elegant in tails and top hat, producing streams of brightly coloured scarves out of nowhere, causing them to flow through the air like birds. He'd whirled hoops around, passing them through each other in impossible ways, and danced with a cane to the tune of "Yes! We Have No Bananas," played on an ancient gramophone borrowed from the school.

The next day the magician had set up a makeshift studio in one corner of the hall, pinning up as a backdrop a sheet with a Venetian canal painted on it, and took photographs of whoever wanted them, which was practically everyone, a great sprawling gaggle of farmers and miners and men from the lumber mill and teachers and shop owners and even a few loggers from the camp upriver, all in their Sunday best, all wanting a photo of themselves and their families, if any, something to record their existence, to anchor them to this place and this time: Struan, Northern Ontario, via Venice, circa (Megan studied the photo and decided she must have been about ten, which made it eleven years ago) 1954.

Again, Megan's father had come along and, astonishingly, had submitted to having his photograph taken with his family, so there they all were: Father and Mother standing at the back (Father looking impatient and Mother looking anxious, Megan thought, as though she were wondering if she'd left something on the stove). Mother was holding Henry, who was a few months old at the time. In front of them, arranged by height (which at that stage was also by age), were Tom, Megan and the twins, Donald and Gary.

Henry, the baby, had been born with a hole in his heart and died six months after the photo was taken. Peter, Corey and Adam hadn't been born yet. Before Adam made his appearance, Megan's mother had a stillbirth and two miscarriages, so he was the youngest by eight years.

In addition to filching the family photo, Megan sorted through a shoebox full of other old photographs, mostly taken by Tom with a Box Brownie, and found one of Peter and Corey playing on the beach and another of Adam when he was a couple of months old. At the bottom of the box there was one of her and Tom up in a tree, and she took that too. She couldn't recall ever climbing a tree and had no idea who had taken the photo (Tom was the only member of the family interested in photography), but she liked it, so she took it.

She felt no guilt about stealing the photos; no one else in the family ever looked at them and she was sure they wouldn't be missed. She put them in an envelope and slid it under everything else so that it would lie flat on the bottom of the suitcase. Then she tried to close the case and found she couldn't. She removed two sweaters, two skirts and the smart white shoes, leaned on the case, managed to close it and do up its shiny new latches and discovered she couldn't even lift it off the bed. So out came everything and she had another cull and then, at last, it was done.

She stepped back and surveyed her room. Nothing left. No dolls to linger over even if she'd been the lingering type; with all those babies in the family the last thing she'd needed was a doll. Likewise no dollhouses or miniature tea sets; "playing house" had very little appeal if you spent your days doing the real thing. Nothing on the window sills or on the walls, nothing on her narrow wooden desk. A clean sweep; it was immensely satisfying. Adam would have the room, she decided. Then he would no longer wake Peter and Corey or vice versa. When she came back for visits she would share with him.

The cardboard box full of rejects she stashed in the garage; she would sort through it later for serviceable clothes that could go to the Goodwill and take the rest to the dump. The contents of the suitcase went back, neatly folded, into cupboards and drawers to await departure day. The suitcase itself she put under the stairs.

What next? Megan thought, consulting her mental list. She'd already asked Mrs. Jarvis, who came in on Mondays to help with the laundry and the cleaning, to come on Thursdays as well, starting in two weeks' time. She'd made sure the house was stocked up with all the staples—tins of food, toilet paper, laundry soap. She would change all the sheets and do the laundry the Monday before she left.

That's it, she thought. All that remained was to tell her family and Patrick that finally—*finally*—after years of thwarted attempts, she was leaving home.

She started with her mother because that would be the hardest. The second hardest was going to be Patrick, but she wouldn't be seeing him until Saturday.

"Leaving?" her mother said, looking incredulous. You'd have thought no one had ever left home before, despite the fact that Tom had been gone for over two years. But of course, Megan thought grimly, Tom was a boy. No one batted an eye when a boy left home. If anything it was cause for celebration.

"I'm twenty-one, Mum." She dusted the kitchen counter with flour and began kneading a lump of pastry the size and heft of a cannonball. It was late afternoon and they were alone in the kitchen, preparing supper. "It's time I left."

"Why does being twenty-one mean it's time you left?"

Her mother was peeling potatoes, but she stopped, her arms in the sink, to stare at Megan.

Megan sliced the cannonball in half, briefly kneaded both halves, set one aside and began rolling out the other with brisk sweeps of the rolling pin. A small crease had appeared between her eyebrows. She'd known it would be like this. It's your own fault, she thought. You should have gone years ago.

"I told you I was going to go, Mum. When you were pregnant with Adam I said I'd wait until he'd arrived and settled in and then I'd be off. Remember?" She scanned her mother's face for any sign that she recalled the conversation. Not a trace. Lately Megan had started to wonder if her mother was going senile, but surely she couldn't be—she was only forty-five. More likely she'd simply erased it from her mind. She'd always been good at not hearing things she didn't want to hear; maybe forgetting was an extension of the same thing.

"That was a year and a half ago," Megan said, flipping the pastry over and rolling it out again. "I had to put it off because after Adam was born you weren't well. And then Adam got whooping cough, so I put it off again. Then Peter and Corey got flu. Then you got flu . . ."

Her mother's eyes had an unfocused, inward look as if she were searching through dusty files down in the basement of her brain.

"Now everybody is fine," Megan said firmly. "Tom's gone and the twins will be off soon and Adam's a very easy baby."

She could have added that she also happened to know that he would be the last baby, because in the aftermath of Adam's birth she'd overheard Dr. Christopherson telling her father so. She'd been coming downstairs with a pile of dirty laundry and heard the doctor, who was in the living room with her father, say, "This must be the last child, Edward."

Megan had paused on the stairs with her armful of dirty sheets. Her father mumbled something she couldn't catch, his voice strangled by embarrassment. The doctor said, "That may be so, Edward. It may be her wish. But you have a say in the matter too, and for the sake of your other children—for all your sakes—it must stop now. She is worn out."

At last! Megan thought. *At last*! The way her parents kept on having children was just plain ridiculous, in her opinion. It wasn't as if they were Catholics.

Now she looked at her mother to check that she was listening. "So now's the perfect time for me to go," she said. "It's time I started my own life."

She'd rehearsed that last line, but inside her head it hadn't sounded so corny. Her mother looked aggrieved.

"Megan, what nonsense! 'Starting your own life!' As if you didn't have a life here!" Suddenly she turned to fully face her daughter, the paring knife in one hand and a half-peeled potato in the other. Water trickled down her arms to her elbows and onto the floor. "Don't tell me you're marrying Patrick McArthur," she said. She looked appalled.

"MacDonald," Megan said. "No, Mother" (she called her mother "Mother" when she was annoyed with her), "I am not marrying Patrick MacDonald. I'm not marrying anybody. I'm going to Toronto. You're dripping all over the floor."

The kitchen door opened and Peter, age ten, prowled in, eyes scanning left and right, searching for something edible, anything at all.

"Out," Megan said, pointing a floured finger at the door.

Peter clutched his belly and made an anguished face.

"Out!" Megan said, louder, and he left.

"Mrs. Jarvis will be coming in on Thursdays as well as Mondays to help with the cleaning," she continued, "and I'll do a big shopping before I go."

"But you haven't told me why you're going! That's what I don't understand." There was a tremor in her mother's voice.

Megan hardened her heart. I don't care, she thought. I do not, will not, care. I'm going. And anyway, it will be good for her. She needs to take charge again. She's been depending on me too much.

"I'm not leaving for another two weeks," she said, striving for the right mix of firmness and reassurance. "And I'll come back and visit. I'm only going to Toronto, remember." Initially, at any rate, she added to herself.

"I don't understand you, Megan," her mother said. "All these years, and now suddenly out of nowhere you say you're leaving. Truly, honestly, I do not understand you."

"I know you don't," Megan said, her tone more gentle now that it was over. "You never have." She thought how pretty her mother was still—even now, when she was upset. Her face was as round and smooth as a child's.

Her father was next. He would be easier, Megan thought, if only because he wouldn't care so much. Nonetheless, an audience with her father always made her anxious. Whenever you knocked on the door of his study he gave the impression that you were interrupting him in the middle of something critically important.

"Leaving?" he said, gazing at her from behind his desk. Abutting the desk at one end there was a long table heaped with books and at the other end there was a small bookcase, so that he was surrounded on three sides. Like a fortress, Megan thought. A fortress of books. Protecting him from us.

"Leaving home? Or leaving Struan altogether?"

"Both," Megan said. "I'm going to Toronto to start with. And then when I've saved up enough money I'd like to go to England."

"England?" He looked startled, which Megan found gratifying. "Why England?"

"I have a friend there. Cora Manning. You remember Mr. Manning, the pharmacist? They moved to England a few years ago. Cora works in London now. She shares a house with friends. I could stay with her; she's invited me. And I'd like to see England."

"I see," her father said. He looked out of the window. Megan waited. She thought this was possibly the longest conversation she had ever had with him. Generally one sentence apiece would do it. The only one of his children he'd ever taken any notice of was Tom, and even then it hadn't been much.

"Do you have a job to go to in Toronto?" he asked finally.

"No," Megan said. "But I've saved enough money to last me for a couple of weeks. I'm sure I'll find something by then."

"I see," he said again. "You've been planning this for some time, then."

He made it sound like a bank raid, Megan thought, or maybe premeditated murder. But she would not allow him to make her feel guilty; she had done far more than her share. "Yes," she said briskly. "I'm twenty-one and I think it's time I started my own life." (It didn't sound so bad this time.) "I've arranged for Mrs. Jarvis to come in twice a week to help Mum."

Her father looked at her strangely for a moment as if he'd never noticed her before and was wondering who she was. Then he looked out of the window for such a long time that Megan began to wonder if the interview was over and she should simply leave the room. But finally he looked back.

"What sort of job do you expect to find in Toronto?"

"I don't know," Megan said. "Anything. Waitressing. I'll find something."

Her father nodded thoughtfully. "And how long do you expect it to take, working as a waitress, to save up enough money to go to England?"

It wasn't surprising that he sounded like a bank manager, Megan thought, given that he was one. What was surprising—amazing, in fact—was that he was interested enough in what she was doing to ask questions. It was most unlike him.

"I've no idea," she said truthfully. "Probably quite a while."

Her father picked up his pen, unscrewed the cap, screwed it back on again and put it down. "Quite a while is right," he said, still looking at his pen. "In fact, a very long while. You'll be paying rent for a start, and in Toronto the rents will be high. And you'll have many other living expenses. My guess is that you will be hard pressed to save anything at all for quite some time. Possibly years."

Megan opened her mouth to say that was okay, she didn't mind how long it took, that in fact going to England wasn't the important thing as far as she was concerned, it was leaving home, living her own life, that mattered. But her father looked up and something in his expression made her pause.

He said, "If you want to go to England and you have a friend there now, you should go now. These things—opportunities—have a habit of slipping away. I will stand you the money for a plane ticket and a little to tide you over until you find a job there. I believe there is an arrangement whereby Commonwealth citizens can work in the United Kingdom for a limited period. You'll need a passport, of course. I imagine you don't have one?"

Megan stared at him. She couldn't have been any more astonished if he'd suddenly climbed up onto his desk and danced a jig.

"Do you have a passport?" her father asked.

"Yes," Megan said faintly.

He looked surprised again but Megan was too confused to enjoy it.

"You seem to be well organized," her father said. "It's all settled then." He gave her what Megan thought of as his end-of-interview smile.

At the door she turned and said, "Thank you very much."

Her father was gazing out of the window again but he turned his head and looked at her. "I dare say you've earned it," he said, which was his most amazing comment yet, suggesting as it did that he'd actually noticed.

Megan went out and closed the study door and stood for a moment, not thinking of England or even of leaving home, but thinking instead how sad it was that she had never known the strange man who was her father and now she never would.

She phoned Tom to tell him. He was in a hall of residence down at the University of Toronto, so it was a long-distance call, but she decided it would be worth it to hear the astonishment in his voice. She timed the call for six o'clock at night, reasoning that he'd be home from his classes by then and not yet out for the evening with his friends, and she was right.

"*England*!" he said. "*England*—holy cow, when did all this happen?"

He'd been urging her to leave home and predicting that she never would for years. "You're gettin' old, Meg," he'd say, shaking his head over her. He was only a year older than Megan but he'd always acted as if she was his baby sister, and it drove her mad. "You keep saying you're going but you never do. How much do you want to bet you're still here when you're thirty?"

Now she said casually, "I've been planning it for a while. Dad seems to think it's a good idea. He's paying for the ticket."

"He's what?" Tom said. "He's *what*? You got *money* out of him?"

Then he said seriously, "That's really great, Meg. Congratulations—I never thought you had it in you."

Oh, but that last comment tasted sweet.

She told the rest of the boys at suppertime. She summoned them a few minutes early while her mother was still in the kitchen making the gravy. Their father ate separately in his study after the rest of them had finished. Megan had suggested the arrangement some years before and it had been a great relief all around.

The boys came promptly; there was a house rule—also of Megan's devising—whereby anyone who wasn't sitting at his place within five minutes of being called went hungry. No excuses. It had proved to be very effective. When she first instituted the rule Tom had accused her of being a dictator, and Megan had said, "Absolutely."

They shambled in two by two—like the animals in the Ark, Megan thought, apart from being all the same sex and considerably less appealing. Donald and Gary, age seventeen; Peter and Corey, age ten and nine. The latter two were bickering, as always.

"I never touched it," Peter said.

"You did too," Corey said. "I saw you."

"You couldn't have, *pig*, 'cause I never touched it."

"If you two don't shut up, I'm going to tear your heads off," Donald said. He sat down and heaved his chair closer to the table.

"Sit down, all of you," Megan said, stuffing Adam into his high chair. "I have something to tell you." She tied Adam's bib firmly around his neck and manoeuvred the high chair up to the table. Tom's empty chair was still there, taking up valuable space. Megan would have liked to shove it back against the wall, but her mother insisted on it staying where it was, like a ghost at the feast.

"Are you calling me a liar?" Peter said to Corey.

"Yeah, I am. Liar, liar, pants on fire!"

Donald half stood and reached across the table to cuff him, but Corey dodged out of the way.

Megan picked up a spoon and rapped the table warningly. They all looked at her. "I have something to tell you," she repeated.

Peter looked back at Corey. "Snot-head," he said.

Megan stepped around the table and rapped him on the head with the spoon.

"Ow!" Peter said, outraged, rubbing his head. "Megan! That really *hurt*!"

"Pay attention!"

Donald put his hand up.

"What?" Megan snapped.

"I'm really, really sorry to interrupt," Donald said languidly, "but I thought you'd like to know the baby is strangling."

"No, he's not," Gary said. "He's just having a crap."

"He doesn't go blue when he's having a crap, he goes red."

"Would you *please* not use words like that at the table," Megan said automatically. She glanced at Adam. He was making gasping noises and pulling at his bib and was indeed a little blue. She undid the strings of the bib, did them up again more loosely and patted him on the back. He took several deep breaths, yelled briefly and stuck his thumb in his mouth. Megan patted him again in approval; he was a stoical little soul. He was the only one of them she was going to miss.

"Now all of you, listen," she continued. "In two weeks' time I'm leaving home."

"Good!" Peter said.

"This is great, great news!" Gary said.

"Really?" Donald said. "You mean, for good?"

"Yes," Megan said. "For good. And it's going to affect all of you. You're going to have to do more to help around the house."

Corey said, "Can we eat now?"

"Did you hear what I said?" Megan demanded. "You're going to have to help Mum. She won't be able to manage without help. Did you all hear that?"

"Yes," Donald said. "Not being stone deaf, we all heard that."

"Good. I've made out a list of chores for each of you and I'm going to pin them to the wall next to the fridge. I'll go through them with you, individually, before I leave. You are to do them *without being asked*. Do you understand? *Without being asked*! I will be checking, *regularly*, with Mum." How she was going to do that from England she had no idea, but in any case she held out no hope that it would work. It just had to be said.

"Okay," Gary said. "Fine. Can we get on with supper? I've got homework."

"Corey?" Megan said. "Peter?"

"Okay! Okay! Okay! Can. We. Eat. Now?"

None of them had asked where she was going. I'm sick to death of the lot of you, she thought. I really am.

She told Patrick on Saturday night over coffee at Harper's. They always went to Harper's on Saturday night, along with everyone else in town under the age of thirty. The only other place to go was Ben's Bar, which on Saturdays was jammed with drunken loggers. In the summer there was the beach, but now it was February and minus twenty-six degrees outside and it hurt to draw a breath. In Harper's it was so hot everyone was stripped down to their shirt sleeves, but the snow tracked in on people's boots refused to melt. Mounds of parkas and hats and gloves were heaped onto hooks and stuffed into the corners of benches.

Patrick didn't say anything for a minute or two after Megan made her announcement. He studied the menu printed on the paper table mat in front of him as if he ever had anything but a cheeseburger and fries.

Finally he looked up and said, "Megan, will you marry me?"

Megan said, "Patrick, please."

He picked up a spoon and stirred his coffee. His head was tilted to one side, the way it always was when he was out of sorts. Not that he was often out of sorts, Megan conceded. He was a very even-tempered man.

"I've always said I was going to go," she said. She felt even worse than she'd thought she would. "Always."

"Not to England. Why England, for God's sake?"

"I've always wanted to see it," she said, which wasn't true, but going all that way just because her father would pay for the ticket and a friend was there didn't seem good enough reasons even to her.

Patrick went on stirring his coffee. "How long will you stay?"

"I don't know. A while, I think. I have an open ticket."

"How long is a while? Are we talking weeks? Months? Years?"

"I don't know."

There was a long pause.

Megan said, "Patrick, I've never been anywhere in my whole life. I've never been to a city. *Any* city. I want to *see* things. *Do* things. I've never done *anything*. I've never been *anywhere*."

Patrick shrugged. "Neither have I. Well, college in Sudbury."

"Don't you want to?" Megan asked. "Don't you want to see things? See other places?" Then she held her breath for fear he'd think she was asking him to come with her.

"Sure, someday," he said, and she let out her breath. "At the moment there are things I want more." He smiled at her wryly. "A lot more."

"Yes, well," Megan said.

There was another pause.

"England's a hell of a long way, Meg."

"Yes. I know."

So many things weren't being said but were nonetheless plain as day, chief amongst them that Patrick loved her and she did not love him, or at least not as much. The knowledge made her feel guilty, which in turn made her feel cross, because she had never led him on, never pretended to feel more than she felt. Maybe we're just at different stages, she thought. He's older, he's been to college. He's ready to settle down. I've been settled down my whole life. I've never been anything *but* settled down.

"When are you leaving?" Patrick said.

"The Thursday after next."

"*The Thursday after next!*"

"I booked it today. There was a seat on a cheap flight."

More silence.

"I'll drive you to the airport," Patrick said at last.

"That's very nice of you but it's way too far to drive. Really. It would be silly. I'll take the train to Toronto and get a bus or something to the airport. There must be all kinds of buses."

"I'm driving you to the airport," Patrick said. "I'll take the day off work." He put down the spoon and picked up his coffee.

And that was it. There was nothing left to do but go.

CHAPTER TWO

Edward

Struan, January 1969

I heard my father's voice today. Like the echo of a nightmare.

I was shouting at Peter and Corey—hardly an unusual event. I shout at them too much, I know that. When they are not around I think, From now on I will be different, I will be a better father, and ten minutes after they reappear I'm shouting at them again. But this is the first time I have recognized his voice, his rage, coming out of my own mouth.

Not that my anger wasn't justified. Their behaviour is intolerable; it is like a dentist drilling. The constant *noise*, the continual yelling and crashing about, make it impossible to concentrate on anything.

This afternoon was a prime example. I had been waiting all week for a chance to look at the books on Rome that Betty Parry got for me from the central library in Toronto. She has pulled strings on my behalf—I believe she said I was doing research, which is stretching things—and they have extended the borrowing period from three weeks to six, but today is Saturday, which means that already one whole week has passed without my being able to do more than flip through the pages. It is even more frustrating because all three of the books appear to be comprehensive and well written.

Rome is my subject for this winter. Over the past five winters I have done Paris, London, Cairo, Leningrad and Istanbul. I do one city or culture per year. You could call it a survival strategy, I suppose; the winters up here take some surviving. My life takes some surviving, come to that.

So this afternoon, as a birthday present to myself—as of today I have been on this earth for forty-seven years (no one has remembered, needless to say)—I decided to take advantage of the fact that Peter and Corey, beyond question the two most disruptive members of this family, seemed to have gone out, to ignore the pile of papers I'd brought home with me from the bank and spend the whole afternoon in Rome. If a miracle were to occur, if a genie popped out of the antique inkwell on my desk and said I could visit just one of the world's great cities, Rome is the one I'd choose. I nearly made it once but got several lumps of shrapnel in my legs instead.

From the photographs it looks as if two thousand years of history are just lying in the streets. There's a photograph of the Colosseum, for instance, with traffic roaring around it. The Colosseum—the actual Colosseum, the real thing, not a replica—is a traffic island. It's simply incredible. And then there's the Pantheon, built in 27 BC by Marcus Agrippa, son-in-law of Augustus. Apparently its dome is the largest masonry vault ever constructed. As near as I can figure it—all of the books seem to use the metric scale and I have to convert it in order to get a real idea of the size—it's 142 feet in both height and diameter. If you stand in the middle (you can still do this, it is virtually intact) light pours down on you through a thirty-foot-wide opening at the top. It must feel as if you are looking straight up to heaven. Think of the vision, the sheer genius required even to conceive of such a thing.

None of the books has a photograph of the dome itself, so I was sitting at my desk looking out at the driving snow—we have another full-scale blizzard on our hands—trying to visualize that vast and perfect space transfixed, as it must frequently be, by a great column of sunlight, when the boys announced their arrival home by slamming the front door.

It sounds a small thing, put like that: they slammed the door. Perhaps any single slam of a door is a small thing. But if it is not a single slam, if they slam it every time they go in or out, and if it is not one son who does it but every son, the effect is cumulative.

Nonetheless I did my best to ignore them. I told myself that it was my birthday and I wasn't going to let anything spoil it and attempted to think my way back to Rome. The boys fought their way across the living room and into the kitchen. I tried not to listen. The crashes continued in there for a minute or two and then there was a brief pause followed by Corey—I could hear him clearly, here in my study, with the door closed—saying, "There's *nothing* to *eat* in this place. There isn't even any *bread.*" His footsteps clumped out of the kitchen and across the living room to the foot of the stairs and then, rather than climb them, he yelled, "Mum! I can't find the bread! Is there any bread?"

By then I'd stopped pretending that I could ignore them. I sat here, struggling to contain the anger massing up inside me. I dimly heard Emily's voice making some reply from upstairs— she is the only member of the household whose voice has no carrying power—and Corey yelled, "What? I can't hear you!" And then Peter, still in the kitchen, shouted, "Stop shouting, stupid! You'll wake the baby!" and immediately the baby's wail drifted down the stairs. And suddenly I was beside myself with rage.

It's been a long time since I've been that angry. I'm not sure how to account for it. Perhaps it was a combination of turning forty-seven and having a week-old baby upstairs. I will be almost

seventy before this one is off my hands. I will have lived out—
used up—my three score years and ten. If someone had told me
thirty years ago that this was going to be the extent of my life, I
simply would not have believed him.

This new child—number nine, eight of whom survive—
wasn't even supposed to be. John Christopherson specifically
warned against Emily having more children after Adam was born.
But she insisted and it is the one thing I cannot deny her; she
knows it, and I know it. So maybe that was at the root of my fury.
I don't know.

Whatever it was, I heaved myself out of my chair and crossed
to the door and flung it open and roared at them, *bellowed* at them,
"*Will you be quiet! How many times do you have to be told!*"

And heard my father's voice. Exactly his voice. His rage. And
saw the rest of us, cowering.

It made me feel quite sick. The thought that I might be like
him in any way.

I am not like him. There is no comparison. He used to knock
us about—all of us, including my mother. I have never laid a
finger on any of them. Haven't even threatened it. Not once in
twenty-five years.

But I must not shout at them like that again.

There is no food in the house. The boys were right about that.
Presumably Emily has arranged for Marshall's to deliver the groceries this afternoon, though how they'll manage in this blizzard
I can't imagine. Fortunately I keep a packet of digestive biscuits
in my desk. I have one at the bank as well—I've become addicted
to digestives over the years. A harmless enough vice.

The kitchen is a disgrace. I went in to look for something to
eat when lunch failed to materialize and I've never seen such a
mess. I realize the arrival of a new baby means a certain amount

of disruption, but Emily has had nine months to prepare for it and God knows she is no novice. And she has help—I pay for a woman to come in twice a week. I assume she does come; I have no way of knowing as I'm always at work. There certainly isn't much to show for it at the moment.

It was never like this when Megan was home.

I ran into Tom in the kitchen last night. I've been having trouble sleeping lately; I get off to sleep easily enough but by three I'm awake again and that's it for the night. Either I lie there brooding on the pointlessness of life or I get up and go downstairs and get myself a bowl of cornflakes and do my brooding at the kitchen table. And as I say, last night I found Tom down there, no doubt doing some brooding of his own.

Neither of us knew what to say. No doubt from the outside it would have looked quite funny. Tom got up from the table and said, "I was just going," which was transparently untrue, and took his cornflakes up to his room.

I hesitate to go down there now. Probably he does too.

Tom was—used to be—the exception in this family in that even as a child you could imagine him amounting to something. He has a decent brain, which is more than can be said for the rest of them. Though I suppose you could say Megan has, in a different way. Megan was never a child, it seems to me. Always working alongside her mother, almost from the moment she could walk. It surprised me, three years ago, when she left. It demonstrated a spirit of adventure I had not credited her with.

But Tom I had real hopes for, which makes what has happened all the worse. Yesterday I asked him straight out what his plans were and he looked puzzled, as if he didn't understand the question, and then said, "None at the moment," as if that was a satisfactory answer. As if driving a snowplough was a suitable occupation for someone with an MSc in aeronautical engineering. He's wasting his life over this thing. Not that I deny it was a tragedy. But it has been a year and a half now and he shows no sign of pulling himself together. It has reached the point where it annoys me just to look at him.

You'd have thought he'd want to put as much distance as possible between himself and this place, with all its reminders.

The same applies to Reverend Thomas and his wife. They are still here too. It beats me why they stay. I saw Reverend Thomas last Saturday when I went to the library to collect the books on Rome, and he has changed so much I almost didn't recognize him. To begin with I didn't realize he was there. No one else was; it was snowing hard and people weren't venturing out for inessentials such as books. Our library isn't a good place to take refuge on a cold day; it's housed in the two rooms of Struan's one remaining genuine log cabin, which is a dark and draughty place even at the height of summer. Betty Parry had on her coat and hat and gloves and snow boots and was reluctant to take off her gloves even to check out my books. She's a smallish, roundish woman and her get-up made her look much the same shape as the pot-bellied stove behind the counter. The stove was roaring its head off but making no impression at all on the temperature of the room.

"I keep moving around it," Betty said, meaning the stove. "It burns one leg so I move to the other side and it burns the other leg, but the rest of me's still frozen stiff. I've been thinking of burning the place down so they'll have to build a new one."

I asked if she could give me a couple of days' notice so that I could come in and rescue a few of my favourite books, make sure they didn't go up in flames, and she said certainly, which ones did I want. I said the *Times Atlas* and the entire works of the historian and philosopher Will Durant. She said she'd put them aside for me. She said the handy thing was everyone would assume they'd been destroyed in the fire, so I could just keep them.

She's a nice woman. Rather plain, but very nice. I enjoy talking to her. I imagine I'm one of her best customers.

I'd turned to go when I saw a hunched figure sitting at the table in the other room. It took me a minute to work out that it was Reverend Thomas. He seemed to have shrunk. Even though he was sitting down, that big black coat of his hung on him as if on a skeleton. There was a newspaper on the table in front of him but it hadn't been opened.

It seemed a curious place for him to be. If he wanted to get out of the house, why not the church? It couldn't have been any colder than the library. But then I remembered; he has left the church. He's now just plain Mr. Thomas. James, his name is. Not Jim, of course.

My first instinct was to pretend I hadn't seen him but then I wondered if common decency demanded that I go over and say something. I hesitated, though. It would be awkward; apart from at his son's funeral, where I offered my condolences, we have not spoken for years. It crossed my mind that he might even think I took some satisfaction from his downfall, which is not so. It is hard to sympathize with someone you dislike, but no man could take pleasure in what has happened in that family.

"Dislike" is not the right word. I disliked James Thomas long before he made his slanderous accusations about me from the pulpit. In fact I disliked him from the moment we met. There is—was—an arrogant certainty about him that stuck in my craw. He is (only that should be "was" too, because even that appears to have changed) tall and straight—"upright" would be a good word—with pale hair combed back and a long thin nose, the better to look down on you. Almost patrician. I suspect he worked at it—at looking patrician. As if he sat at God's right hand and had a monopoly on the truth.

I remember he came to the house the day Henry died. Megan answered the door. Emily was in her bedroom and I was in my study. I heard Megan go upstairs, presumably to ask her mother if she wanted to see him, but she did not. She wanted to see no one, including me.

I am not a believer, as the Reverend knew very well. When he first arrived in Struan, fifteen years or so ago, and noticed that I was not a member of his congregation although Emily and the children were, he came to the house one evening to ask me why. I replied, quite courteously, I think, considering that it was none of his business, that I had no religious faith, whereupon he immediately set about trying to convert me, right there in my own living room. I had had a hard day at work and was not in the best of tempers, so it was a short discussion. Although polite on both sides.

So we both knew it was Emily he had come to comfort. I did not wish to speak to him or to any man—Henry had died in Emily's arms less than two hours previously—but I felt obliged to invite him in and he felt obliged to accept. I offered him a chair and he sat down, and the very first thing he said was, "Your child is at peace in the arms of the Lord, Edward."

I don't know why the words caused me such pain. Or perhaps it wasn't pain, perhaps it was rage. Henry was a squalling, fretful baby; I had felt almost nothing but irritation towards him while he was alive, which I knew was inexcusable with a child so ill. Now it was too late to make amends. Upstairs was my wife, utterly distraught, who had made it clear that she did not want me near her. And in walks a man who knows I am not a believer and tells me my child is at peace in the arms of the Lord.

I remember I had some trouble getting the words out and, when I managed, they came out through my teeth and with some force.

I said, "Have you any idea how *offensive* that sounds to some-one who does not share your faith?"

I remember the pleasure I felt as his face went first white and then deep red. I remember the silence that followed as he searched for and failed to find anything to say. I loathed him at that moment almost as much as I loathed myself.

Why am I writing about this? First my father and now the once-Reverend James Thomas! Why am I reliving events dead and gone and beyond redemption? It's my birthday. I should be thinking about something cheerful or at least interesting. I should be thinking about Rome.

The Pantheon. I will think about the Pantheon. That is worth dwelling on. Augustus dedicated it to the planetary gods—the dome represents the firmament. The opening at the top is called an *oculus*, from the Latin meaning "eye." Apparently there are holes in the floor beneath it to allow rainwater to drain away. I doubt that would work here. Not with a snowfall like we're hav-ing today. The whole building would simply fill up with snow. Lift up the dome and you'd find an igloo.

CHAPTER THREE

Tom

Struan, January 1969

He had turned the big winged armchair towards the window so that one of the wings shielded him from the rest of the room, which was why his father hadn't noticed him when he'd stuck his head out of the study to roar at the others. The roaring didn't bother Tom—in fact, it barely registered—but he'd automatically glanced up and as he was about to return to his paper a movement caught his eye: Adam, his youngest brother—no, second-youngest, as of a week ago—straightening up from a crouching position on the floor. He'd been playing with his Matchbox toys right outside the door of their father's study and must have curled himself into a ball, arms over his head, to protect himself from the blast. Now he was unfurling.

Their eyes met. It had been many months since Tom had noticed much of anything that took place either within his family or outside it, but he couldn't help noticing the anxiety in his younger brother's eyes and it struck him that a kid that age shouldn't be looking like that. Tom wondered vaguely how to reassure him. Make light of things, maybe. Turn their father's temper into a joke.

31

Keeping his voice down so that their father wouldn't hear, he said, "I reckon he was a little bit annoyed. Whaddya think?"

Adam nodded but didn't look particularly reassured. Maybe he was too young for humour.

"He wasn't mad at you, you know," Tom said. Probably their father hadn't even noticed him down there at his feet.

Another nod. Still not reassured.

Tom couldn't think of anything else to say so he returned to his paper. He read *The Globe and Mail* cover to cover, world news to racing results, every day; it was fascinating, every word of it, and it took up almost all of his free time. He had a lot of free time nowadays, more than he wanted, but the number of jobs you could find in a place the size of Struan involving no contact with people was limited, and that was his chief requirement. At the moment he drove the town's one and only snowplough, perched up high in the draughty, freezing cab, peering through the frosted windscreen, blinded by flying snow, terrified of mowing someone down. Once he'd pushed Paul Jackson's snow-covered Buick twenty feet before he realized it wasn't a snowdrift.

The job was shift work; he alternated with Marcel Bruchon, a farmer who augmented his income that way during the winter months. Marcel would be out there now, thundering down the main roads, snow flying off the blade of the plough like the wing of some gigantic bird, trying to get the roads cleared so people could get home from work. Marcel took the late shift and Tom took the early one, which suited him fine. He started at six in the morning, cleared the main roads—there weren't many, Struan was a small town—then worked his way out to the side roads. Some days the snow fell so fast there was no way to keep up with it and the farmers and other out-of-towners had to resort to snowshoes or skis or just stay home. The only drawback of the job was that if there was no snow there was no work, but from November onwards that was rare.

Summer had been more of a problem, job-wise. The previous summer he'd started off working at the gas station, but people kept talking to him while he filled up their tanks and cleaned their windshields so he quit. Then he got a job working as a ranger for the Forestry Commission. He'd spent the days perched in a fire tower on the top of Mount Allen, binoculars glued to his eyes, searching for telltale wisps of smoke above the endless rolling sea of trees. In theory it should have suited him even better than the snowplough—not a soul for miles in any direction—but in practice it had turned out to be a mistake. There was too little thinking involved and he couldn't read to distract himself, so his mind filled up with thoughts like lungs filling up with water till he could hardly breathe. At least with the snowplough you had to concentrate on the road. So he'd quit fire-watching too and got a job driving a logging truck, which had turned out to be just fine.

Something bumped into his shoe. Tom lowered his paper and saw that Adam was in the process of driving his battered fleet of Matchbox cars across the room and parking them at his feet. He must have felt Tom's gaze because he looked up guiltily.

"It's okay," Tom said. "You can play with them here. Just don't run into my feet."

Adam nodded and moved the cars carefully around the corner of the chair. But Tom felt a stirring of irritation in his guts; unlike his father he normally had no difficulty blocking out his family but now that Adam had intruded on his privacy other things were intruding too. He could hear the thudding of Peter's and Corey's feet upstairs in their bedroom; there'd be a scuffle followed by a loud thump as one or other of them collided with a wall and then more scuffling. In the study his father blew his nose with an angry blast. Down beside the chair there was a tinny crash as Adam staged a pileup. It had been a mistake to talk to the kid.

Tom tossed the paper onto the floor and stood up. Outside it was dark already, although it was only half past three. The wind was picking up, hurling gusts of snow against the windows. His stomach felt agitated. Maybe there wasn't enough in it, he thought. He'd had lunch at Harper's after his shift but that was a good while ago.

He wandered into the kitchen, opened the fridge and stared into it, then became aware that Adam had followed him and was standing by his left knee and staring into it too. Tom fought the urge to tell him to go away. Definitely it had been a mistake to talk to him. He had nothing against this particular brother—relative to the others he was a model of good behaviour—but he wanted to be left alone. His wish was to be invisible and he had the uneasy feeling Adam was starting to see him.

"Are you hungry?" he asked, trying half-heartedly to keep the irritation out of his voice.

Those anxious eyes again. A nod.

"What did Mum give you for lunch?" He never ate lunch at home himself. He had a bowl of cornflakes and a piece of toast first thing in the morning before setting out for the gas station where the snowplough was kept, and a hot beef sandwich with gravy and fries at Harper's restaurant when he finished, regardless of the time of day. There were two half-width booths at the back of the restaurant, one of which was usually empty. If not, he'd spread his newspaper over the table in one of the larger booths to deter company. He'd made a point of never getting into conversation with either of the waitresses; apart from giving his order, which he no longer had to do as they both knew what it was, he didn't have to say anything but thank you. The hot beef sandwiches were good, as were the fries, so in pretty much every way it beat eating with his family. In the evening he'd make himself a peanut butter sandwich and a cup of coffee. On Sundays Harper's was closed, so on Sundays he lived on coffee and sandwiches.

"She was busy with the baby," Adam whispered.

"You can talk normally," Tom said irritably. "He can't object to that. Didn't you have any lunch, then?"

"Cornflakes," Adam said, slightly louder. Then he added, "But the milk tasted funny."

Tom took the milk bottle out of the refrigerator, sniffed it, walked over to the sink and poured it down the drain. He went back to the fridge. Inside was a packet of lard, an egg box with two eggs in it, one shrivelled carrot and a plate with a bowl inverted over it, which turned out to contain a highly suspect lump of meat. Tom dumped the meat into the garbage bag under the sink. The meat smelled bad and the garbage bag smelled worse; he quickly closed the cupboard door again. He looked around the kitchen for any further traces of food. The counter was cluttered with unwashed dishes and saucepans and old papers and half-empty glasses and cups and somebody's shoes. The only food he could see was the box of cornflakes—empty, it turned out—and a jar of peanut butter so well scraped out there was nothing left but the smell. The bread bin was empty as Peter had so loudly observed.

Tom opened the food cupboard above the counter: one can of peas, two cans of Heinz baked beans, one of peaches, one of condensed milk, one of condensed mushroom soup, a carton of Minute Rice, a bag of flour, an open bag of sugar, a box of salt with a built-in spout, a jar of relish and a jar of dried-out mustard. He checked the cupboards under the counter: a box of Quaker Oats. That was it.

He opened the top cupboards again and took out the two cans of baked beans, then looked around for the can opener.

"It's in the sink," Adam said, whispering again.

Tom looked down at him. "You haven't been using it, have you?"

Adam shook his head but he looked guilty.

"Well don't," Tom said. "It's dangerous."

"Okay."

"How old are you, anyway?" Tom asked abruptly, because it somehow seemed relevant.

"Four and a half," Adam said. He hauled up his shirt and scratched his belly. He didn't smell too great, though not as bad as the garbage or the meat.

Tom thought suddenly, This place is going to hell.

He urgently wanted to get back to *The Globe and Mail*. He'd almost got to the obituaries, which were one of the best bits—all those people you'd never heard of and had now discovered just too late.

How long had it been since their mother had come downstairs and cooked a meal? Since before the baby arrived? He wasn't sure he'd seen her at all for a couple of days, not even drifting about with the baby in her arms. Maybe there was something wrong with her. It couldn't just be the new baby; she'd had babies before—eight of them, in fact—and he couldn't remember the place falling apart with the others.

Though of course, now that he thought about it, Megan had been here for the others. Maybe she was the one who'd kept things running. But Megan had been gone three years now. She'd flown the coop.

He went over to the sink. Adam was right: the can opener was in there, along with a tangle of dirty plates and utensils and saucepans, all of them now spattered with sour milk.

"Where's Mrs. . . . whatever her name is?" Tom said. "The lady who helps Mum clean the house. Has she been here this week?"

"I don't know. I don't think so."

Tom rinsed off the can opener, opened both cans of beans, looked for a clean saucepan, discovered there were none, rinsed off two spoons and gave one of them and a can of beans to Adam.

"Thank you," Adam said, very politely.

They ate where they stood, spooning in the beans. Tom had

to force them down. He was fighting a growing sense of dread, brought on by his small brother and the empty cupboards. There was something going wrong and he didn't want to know about it, far less deal with it. He pushed down the last of the beans, swallowing hard, dumped the can in the garbage, nodded briefly to Adam and went upstairs.

The door of his mother's room was closed. He hesitated for a moment and then tapped lightly.

"Come in," his mother's voice said.

He opened the door cautiously. She was sitting up in bed with the baby over her shoulder, gently rubbing its back.

"Donald," she said, and smiled at him. "Come in, dear. How are you?"

Tom decided against pointing out that Donald was on a ship on the other side of the world along with his twin brother, Gary, both of them having joined the navy two years ago. There was nothing particularly worrying about his mother mixing up her children's names though; she'd always done it.

"I'm fine, thanks," he said. "How are you?"

"I'm fine too," she said. "A little tired, but fine. Isn't your brother the sweetest thing you ever saw?"

Which one, Tom thought. I have many, none of them sweet. "Yeah, he's great," he said. "Um, I was wondering about food, Mum. There doesn't seem to be much in the house."

"Oh dear," she said. "Well don't worry, there'll be something."

Tom shifted his feet. "I've had a look and there's hardly anything. And I think Adam's been . . . hungry. Like, really hungry. He didn't have any lunch today. There isn't even any bread in the house."

"Oh," his mother said, and she did sound mildly concerned, which gave him hope. "Well, for the moment, could you just make him a sandwich? I'd do it but this little fellow is hungry too—he seems to be hungry all the time, day and night."

The hope drained away. Did she just not listen or was she going nuts? She was smiling down at the baby. Tom had a sudden fleeting memory of how it had felt to be on the receiving end of that smile. The warmth of it. The safety.

"Sure," he said. "Sure. I'll make him a sandwich."

He went back downstairs. The dread churning around in his stomach was mixed now with anger and frustration. He needed— not wanted, *needed*—to get back to his newspaper.

He crossed the living room and stood for a moment outside the door of his father's study. His father would be sitting at his desk surrounded by his bloody books; he'd look up and on his face would be an expression of barely contained impatience, as if this were the tenth time Tom had interrupted him in as many minutes instead of the first time in years. Once upon a time Tom wouldn't have been put off by that. Once upon a time he'd had privileged status with their father, though he'd never been quite sure why. But no longer.

He stood facing the door, head down, mouth a tight line. He had something important to say and he was going to say it. He would say, Dad, your wife is losing her mind, your four-year-old son is hungry and there's no food in the house. I thought you'd like to know. He wouldn't wait for a reply. He would turn around and go back to his obituaries.

On the other side of the door the silence was so deep that either his father was dead at his desk or else he knew Tom was there and was waiting for him.

Tom turned on his heel and crossed the living room again, into the entrance hall where the coats were piled on pegs and the floor was a mad scramble of boots. He found his own and savagely pulled them on. The twins might have been of some help had they still been home—they were both reasonably sensible—but the idea of either Corey or Peter doing anything was laughable and he wasn't going to waste his breath by asking them. It was easier to do it himself.

He checked his pockets for money, reckoned he had enough to buy the basics, looked up and saw Adam standing in the doorway, watching him, his hands clenched tightly under his chin.

"Don't stand in the doorway!" Tom said sharply. "You'll catch cold. I'm going to buy some food." He went out, slamming the door behind him.

It was so dark outside you'd think it was four in the morning rather than four in the afternoon. Marcel and the snowplough thundered by just as he got to Main Street, but even if it hadn't been snowing so hard there would have been no question of taking the car. The piles of snow thrown up by the plough blocked off all of the side roads; opening them up again was the second stage of the procedure and in weather like this the plough never got to the second stage. Anyway, it would have taken him at least an hour to shovel out the driveway. He walked along the road, following in the wake of the plough. From time to time muffled snatches of its roar were carried back to him on the wind.

It was viciously cold. He pulled his scarf up over his nose and his hat down to his eyes and bent his head into the wind. Snow was drifting back across the road—by the time the plough got to one end of town it would all need doing again. You could plough the same bit of road forever. Like Sisyphus, Tom thought, rolling his bloody rock up the hill.

There was a lull in the wind, and the roar of the plough was suddenly loud. He looked up and saw the tail lights winking in the distance, and all at once Robert was beside him and the two of them were staggering along this same stretch of road in a similar blizzard, howling with laughter and drunk as two skunks. Robert had filched a bottle of hooch from a logger who'd slipped on the ice outside Ben's Bar. Somehow he'd managed to hold the bottle aloft as he fell, and Robert had relieved him of it. They were fifteen or so and it was the first time they'd been drunk and it was wonderful. Rob found a hubcap half buried in a snowbank and insisted on taking it with them, clutching it close to his chest, crooning to it, and Tom had yelled, "Don't kiss it, don't kiss it!" afraid that his friend's lips would freeze to the metal, wondering how they'd explain that to the doctor.

Then the wind swung around and blasted him again, and Rob was gone.

It wasn't far to the centre of town—nowhere in Struan was far from anywhere else. Many of the stores had closed early to allow staff to get home while it was still possible. The post office, the drugstore, Harper's restaurant, all of them shut. Ben's Bar was still open, its windows lit by oily light. This being Saturday it would be full of loggers, most of them more than happy, storm or no storm, to spend the night on the floor.

Marshall's Grocery was still open, to Tom's relief. Better still there was no one in it apart from the girl behind the counter. What he feared more than anything was running into someone he knew, someone who might try to talk to him, or look at him with sympathetic eyes.

The wind caught the door when he opened it and he had to lean his full weight against it to get it closed again.

"Nice day, isn't it?" the girl behind the counter said.

Tom nodded, stamping his feet to get rid of the worst of the snow. He removed his gloves and hat and shook the snow off them, grabbed a shopping cart and headed straight down the first aisle before the girl had time to say anything else. He scanned the shelves, picking off likely-looking items as fast as he could and dropping them into the cart: two loaves of bread, a pound of butter, two quarts of milk, a box of cornflakes, four cans of Heinz baked beans. He slowed down, looking for something that could be called a meal, and finally selected four cans of stew.

Then he saw some cans of corned beef and got four of those too. He looked at the meat counter, but everything required cooking, so all he got was a dozen hot dogs in a plastic bag.

"If it keeps on I'll have to spend the night with Mr. and Mrs. Marshall," the girl said gloomily. She was still up at the counter, but the store was so small he could hear her easily. "My brother will never be able to get into town to pick me up. Which is a real drag, because this is supposed to be my last day. It's so boring here I can't stand it another *minute*! I've been counting the *seconds*, and now it looks like I'm going to be here all *night*!"

She had to be talking to him because there was no one else in the store, but she was hidden from view by a pile of toilet paper so Tom decided he could ignore her. He stopped alongside the canned fruit, wondering how much to get, then suddenly realized he was going to have to carry it all home. Damn it! he thought, *Damn it*! He retraced his steps, put back two of the four cans of beans, two of the stew, two of the corned beef. He'd only be able to carry enough to last himself and Adam for a couple of days. But that was okay, he decided; the others could look after themselves or starve, either would be fine by him.

Then he remembered his mother. She obviously couldn't fend for herself at the moment any more than Adam could. He retraced his steps again, picking up a third can of everything, then stood looking down at his cart. He'd need to make two trips, which would be impossible in weather like this. He couldn't come back tomorrow because tomorrow was Sunday and the store would be closed. In fact, from the look of the blizzard, it could stay closed for days.

"We have a sled you could borrow if you like," the girl said. Tom looked around but she still wasn't in sight. Was she a mind reader? But a sled was the answer, no doubt about it.

"Thanks," he said.

"You're welcome. Look at that snow. It's *disgusting*. I'm going to be stuck here *forever*. You know they say no two snowflakes look the same? Do you believe that?"

Tom gave a noncommittal grunt.

"Neither do I," the girl said. "And anyway, how would they know? I mean, there must be *billions* of them! So how would they know?"

Tom went back down the aisles picking up all the items he'd just discarded, then studied his load. Peanut butter. Honey. Cheese. Cookies. Coffee. Tea. More bread. That's it.

He pushed the cart to the checkout and began piling his purchases onto the counter, keeping his head down so she wouldn't talk to him. The girl began putting them in bags, punching numbers into the adding machine as she went.

"No vegetables," she said abruptly, one finger poised over the adding machine. "And don't say Heinz beans. Heinz beans don't count."

Tom looked at her properly for the first time. She was built like an Amazon, tall and blond, but she couldn't be more than sixteen—maybe eighteen at the outside. She was chewing gum and examining his purchases with narrow-eyed disapproval. He'd have said, How about getting your nose out of my business? but she was female and just a kid and he needed the sled.

"This is all I need," he said.

"I'll chuck in some carrots and cabbage for free if you like," the girl said. "They're getting kind of old. Mr. Marshall won't mind in the circumstances."

"I don't need them. Thanks."

"Tsk, tsk," she said. "Everyone needs vegetables. And fruit. How about some apples? We still have a few. They're old too, but they're still okay."

"No." He didn't bother with the thanks this time. He was starting to find it hard to get his breath. He needed to get out.

"Up to you," she said, chewing cheerfully. "Just don't blame me if you get scurvy."

She piled the remaining food into a final bag. "Back in a sec."

She disappeared in the direction of the back of the store and returned a minute later towing an old toboggan, its upturned nose battered and scarred by a thousand trips down the hillsides of Struan.

"Thanks," Tom said tightly. "I'll bring it back when the storm's over."

"Sure," she said, sticking a fresh stick of gum in her mouth to join the wad already there. "Hope you get home safe."

His relief at being out of the store was so great that he felt almost elated, but the mood soon wore off. The wind was stronger than ever. It was behind him now, pushing him along, which was fortunate because he didn't think he'd have been able to face into it. The cold sliced through his parka and he had to keep switching hands or his fingers would have frozen around the rope of the toboggan. There was no danger of getting lost—the snowbanks on either side of the road hemmed him in—but finding his own side road required concentration. It was important not to go past it. More than important—imperative. It was dangerously cold; he could feel it draining his energy. You're fine, he said to himself. You're doing okay. And you won't have to do this again. Not ever.

He started worrying about how to keep his purchases safe from his thieving brothers—they'd get through the lot in one night. He'd store everything under his bed, he decided. He'd show Adam where it all was, tell him he could help himself, but keep it secret from the others.

Then he remembered—Adam would need help opening the cans. The thought stopped him in his tracks. *Shit!* he thought. This was exactly what he'd been afraid of, the way one thing led to another, the way you got sucked into things, the way your painstakingly designed routine—job, meals, newspaper, sleep—all in solitude, solitude above all, could be shot to hell and you'd be in it up to your neck, you'd have no control over anything, there'd be no end to it, no peace, and he couldn't handle it, he just couldn't handle it.

He stood with his head down, breathing hard, talking to himself. Calm down. Just calm down, breathe slowly. And keep walking. It's okay. Adam can take the cans and the opener up to Mum. She's capable of opening a can, for God's sake. Or you can open the cans in the mornings before you go to work. Open them and stick them back under the bed. Tell Adam to take something up for Mum whenever he's hungry himself. He'll remember to do that; he's smart for his age. It'll be okay.

He switched the rope from one hand to the other and trudged on through the snow. It'll be okay, he thought. Everything's going to be okay.

CHAPTER FOUR

Megan

London, February 1966

Thinking about it afterwards Megan saw she'd made three very foolish mistakes. The first and most serious was not waiting until she'd heard from Cora before setting off for England. Megan had written to her immediately after the talk with her father, but there were only two weeks between her decision to go and her departure, scarcely time for her letters to reach England, far less for a reply to get back.

She'd have phoned but there was no phone—Cora had once described running out in her pyjamas to a payphone down the street.

There was no good reason why she couldn't have delayed her flight for a few weeks, but the truth was, having told everyone she was leaving, she was desperate to go before Fate stepped in and stopped her. Cora had been urging her to come for years, her last letter being only two months ago, so Megan was sure of her welcome. She had the address and decided that was all she needed. Which was rash, and most unlike her.

The second mistake was buying one big suitcase. She should have bought two smaller ones.

The third was not asking the taxi driver to wait while she rang the doorbell. That was just plain silly.

———

It was raining when they landed at Gatwick Airport, but she'd been expecting that. Everyone knew it rained all the time in England. She hadn't slept much on the plane (it was an overnight flight) but she felt fine. Inside the terminal there were trolleys for your luggage, which was handy because despite her ruthless packing she could hardly lift her suitcase, and it turned out there was a train directly from the airport to Victoria Station, in the centre of London. Megan bought a ticket and got on. She had some difficulty getting the suitcase up the steps into the carriage, but a guard saw her struggling and heaved it up behind her.

"What've you got in there, then?" he asked disapprovingly.

"Everything I own," Megan said cheerfully. As she said it the truth of the statement hit her; apart from this one suitcase she had no encumbrances whatsoever. No responsibilities. No fixed plans. For the first time in her life she didn't know what tomorrow might bring—it was the most amazing, wonderful, exhilarating thought she'd ever had.

She found a seat by the window and sat down, dragging her suitcase into the space beside her feet. The train moved off and she sat back and watched the countryside passing by. So this was England. "The old country" people at home called it. *I pledge allegiance to this flag and to my country, Canada*—they'd chanted it every morning at school when she was small, standing at attention, facing the flag in the corner of the classroom, the flag being the Union Jack. England: home of Shakespeare and Dickens and Henry the Eighth. The British Empire, pink on the map. Countless wars. What else? She searched her memory but came up with nothing. History had bored her at school—everything had bored her at school; she'd wanted to be at home in the kitchen helping her mother.

Well, you're making up for it now, she thought, wiping the steaming window with the side of her hand. You're seeing the real thing.

In terms of landscape the real thing was disappointing. She'd expected beauty—rolling hills, tranquil valleys—and instead, what little she could make out through the misted windows was flat and wet and a tedious shade of grey. She kept thinking it would get better around the next bend but there were no bends and it didn't; in fact, as they approached London it got dramatically worse. They passed mile upon mile of ugly blackened brick buildings, all jammed up against each other like rotten teeth and so close to the railway tracks she felt she could have reached out and touched them. At first she assumed they were warehouses but then she noticed strips of curtain hanging in some of the windows and in one she saw a woman holding a baby.

Megan was shocked. Slums, she thought. She hadn't known they still existed in civilized countries. Were there slums like this in Canada? Maybe there were, maybe all cities had slums; how would she know? She'd never been to a city before, not even Toronto. Patrick had driven her to Toronto Airport the previous day, but it was north of the city, so they hadn't had to drive through it.

Thinking about Patrick brought back the goodbyes. Saying goodbye to him had been difficult, but saying goodbye to her mother and Adam had been terrible. She'd seen that her mother hadn't really believed that she, Megan, would go until the moment Patrick loaded the suitcase into the car. Then Adam somehow sensed that she was abandoning him, and when Megan, who'd been giving him a final hug, tried to hand him back to her mother, he had screamed, which he almost never did, and clung to her so tightly she'd had to prise his fingers open. It had almost undone her at the time and it almost undid her again now.

Stop thinking about it, she told herself. He'll have forgotten all about it now. He'll be fine. She pushed the memory firmly out of her mind.

The train had been largely empty when they'd left Gatwick but every few minutes it would stop at a grimy station to collect more passengers and by the time they reached Victoria it was like a cattle car. People wedged themselves into seats or stood hard up against each other, shoulder to shoulder, holding on to the luggage racks strung like hammocks above the seats, rocking back and forth with the movement of the train. Megan's suitcase was monumentally in the way. The standing passengers contorted themselves around it, tight-lipped and grim. Nobody spoke. A fat man in a wet coat squeezed himself into the seat beside her, his legs sticking out sideways into the aisle. Megan didn't like the closeness of him; it made her tense. She wanted to tell him sharply to get up.

The train slowed to a crawl and people began to shift themselves and collect their belongings. The instant it stopped they all surged towards the doors. Megan stood up and began half lifting, half dragging her suitcase along the floor. A man behind her said crossly, "Here, let me take it." He pushed past her, grabbed the case and heaved it down onto the platform.

Megan stepped down beside it and turned to thank him but he was gone, swallowed instantly by a churning mass of people. She'd never seen so many people, never even imagined such numbers. It took her breath away. But worse—much worse—than the crowds was the noise; it was like an assault. She could feel it reverberating inside her chest, trains groaning to a stop as they rolled into the station, other trains rumbling out, carriage doors slamming, whistles shrieking, unintelligible announcements booming out of loudspeakers. Megan stood, stunned and breathless, people milling around her. Then someone bumped into her, hard, and gave her an exasperated look, and she pulled herself together.

What's the matter with you? she said to herself, ashamed of

the thumping of her heart. She shuffled the case and herself out of the way, stood beside one of the steel pillars supporting the roof and looked around.

The station was colossal. It was like a vast, echoing, underground cavern, except that it wasn't underground. Through an archway she could see daylight and cars passing by. She had planned to ask a porter how to get to Cora's but there were no porters to be seen. There were signs pointing to various exits—to the underground, to the buses—and there were people pouring in and out of all of them. She didn't know what was meant by "underground"—was it just another level of the station?—and through the archways she could see dozens of buses going by. How was she to know which one to get on? When she saw a sign saying TAXIS, her breath came out in a rush of relief. She would take a taxi to Cora's. It was a terrible extravagance but she would do it, just this once.

She dragged her suitcase down the length of the station, through the high archway. There was a lineup of people waiting but she didn't mind, it gave her time to collect herself. She stood beside her suitcase and watched the taxis, big black beetles with crowns on their heads, come and go at tremendous speed.

When her turn came she showed the driver the address on the back of Cora's last letter. He nodded wordlessly, waited while she heaved her suitcase and herself into the cab, and then drove off.

For a moment Megan sat with her eyes closed, savouring the luxury of it. The taxi driver would know where he was going; there was nothing more she needed to worry about. After a bit she opened her eyes. The slums had vanished. Imposing buildings now lined the streets. This was more like the London she had imagined. The traffic was astounding: swarms of taxis and big red buses, hundreds of cars, all of them competing for the same road space. The taxi driver sped amongst them, swerving, dodging, jamming on his brakes.

She leaned forward so that she could speak through the gap in the glass partition separating her from the driver. "Is it always like this?" she shouted.

He glanced at her in his rear-view mirror. She saw his eyes, fiercely blue under shaggy red brows. "Rush hour," he shouted back, and then added, "You from the United States?"

"Canada."

He shrugged and lost interest, swerved around a cyclist, rolled down his window and yelled abuse.

Megan looked at her watch; it said three a.m., which meant that here it was eight in the morning. She'd heard of rush hours, though it hadn't occurred to her that people literally rushed. Struan didn't have a rush hour. If all the cars within a hundred-mile radius of Struan descended on Main Street at once, Megan thought, they still couldn't produce a scene remotely like this one.

The same went for pedestrians. It was still raining and scores of umbrellas with legs sticking out beneath them were hurrying along the sidewalks, sidestepping each other, weaving around the puddles. The women weren't dressed for the weather—she'd noticed that on the train as well; their coats looked thin and they wore skirts so short they seemed scarcely worth bothering with. Megan saw a bottom, a sizeable one, clad in inadequate white panties, peeking out from under the shortest skirt she had ever seen. The bottom looked very cold, she thought. Then she saw a girl in a shiny green plastic mac, the rain running off it. Sensible! Megan thought. I'll get myself one of those with my first paycheque.

The taxi went over an elegant bridge with slender cables sweeping from one supporting column to another, crossing what must be the Thames. The large imposing buildings had been replaced by tall narrow houses all joined together like the ones she'd seen from the train, though less shabby. There were fewer cars or people about. As they went on, the streets became narrower, emptier, the houses smaller and shabby again. There were very few trees and only the odd patch of grass. But at least there's no snow, Megan thought. That's something.

She began to worry about the cost of the ride. She hadn't known the city would be so big, that the drive would take so long. And then suddenly, as if in response to that thought, the taxi swerved to the side of the road and pulled up.

Megan looked out of the windows. Mean, seedy little houses lined both sides of the road. She leaned forward again to speak to the driver.

"I don't think this can be it," she said.

"31 Lansdown Terrace," he said into the mirror. "SW2."

"Yes, but . . ." At home a terrace was like a veranda. She'd thought it sounded pretty, imagined it overlooking a park.

"This is it," the driver said.

"Oh," Megan said. "Okay."

There was a meter with numbers on it but she couldn't work out what it meant. She handed the driver a five-pound note and was relieved when he passed back some change. Her father had provided her with sterling and attempted to explain pounds, shillings and pence. She'd been in too big a hurry to listen properly but during the long hours on the plane she'd figured it out.

She opened the door and manhandled her suitcase onto the sidewalk. It was a ridiculous weight. Well, it doesn't matter now, she thought. I've made it. I'm here.

"Thank you," she said to the driver. He'd rolled down his window despite the cold and was looking expectant, fingers drumming on the outside of the door.

Megan paused. "Do people tip over here?" she asked.

"S'not a legal requirement," the driver said morosely. "But if you can afford a taxi you can afford a tip, my opinion."

Megan dug some change out of her purse and held it out in her hand.

"Take a reasonable tip," she said. He looked honest, she thought, and in any case she was suddenly too tired to care.

The driver picked through the change on her palm. "I'm takin' ten percent," he said, sounding markedly friendlier than before. "Fifteen percent's normal but you're foreign so we'll make it ten. You want me to wait till you're inside?"

"Oh no," Megan said. "I'll be fine, thanks."

The driver nodded and drove off.

Megan dragged her suitcase up the steps of number 31. There were three doorbells, which surprised her because the houses looked too small to be divided up, but she rang the top bell and waited, smiling in anticipation of seeing Cora. Would she have changed? It had been four years since they'd seen each other. Maybe she'd be wearing a tiny skirt—Megan almost laughed, imagining it. The two of them had been the "sensible ones" at school. Cora's mother was blind, so Cora had had responsibilities at home like Megan did. But her aunt lived in England and when the Mannings moved over here the aunt had taken on Cora's responsibilities, so Cora was finally free. Maybe freedom had changed her. Who knows? Megan thought, still smiling, maybe I'll change too.

There was no reply from the top bell, so she rang the next one, and then the third. No response. In the middle of the door there was a knocker in the shape of a lion's head. Megan tapped it firmly; it was possible the bells didn't work. Still no sound of movement inside the house. Tentatively, she tried the door handle but it was locked. She lifted the sodden doormat, wondering if Cora might have left her a key or a note, but there was nothing.

She turned and surveyed the street. It was scarcely wider than people's driveways at home, walled in with houses. There weren't many cars. Across the road a door opened and a large black woman came out. She wore a woollen coat and sandals with socks bulging out of them and she carried a shopping bag. She set off down the road with a rolling gait, holding aloft an umbrella with two prongs sticking out. When she turned the corner the road was deserted again.

Megan turned and rang the bells and hammered on the knocker once more. Silence. A small worm of anxiety stirred; she quelled it firmly. She sat down on her suitcase and thought. She removed her watch and set it to local time, which was now ten past nine. She wondered how she had failed to realize that this might happen—that Cora might not be home when she arrived. That in fact there might be no one home because it was a weekday and everyone would be at work.

It was still raining. She hadn't brought an umbrella on the grounds that it would take up too much room and she could get one when she arrived. Despite the fact that she was wearing a parka and snow boots capable of withstanding a Canadian winter she was becoming very cold. The cold was different here. It was wet. It was insidious in its wetness; she felt clammy inside her clothes. She stood up, pulled up the hood of her parka against the rain, went down the steps of number 31 and up the steps of number 29, rang all the doorbells (this time there were five) and hammered on the door. No reply. She went to number 27, then to 33 and 35. Then she went across the road and hammered on the doors of 26 to 36.

She walked out into the middle of the road and looked up and down it in the hopes that she would see somewhere she could take refuge—a café, for preference; she was hungry. There was nothing. There weren't even any cars going by. It was as if the entire street had died.

She came back and sat on her suitcase again. Her bones ached, from cold or tiredness or both. The problem, of course, was the suitcase. It was too heavy to carry any distance but if she left it on the doorstep it might be stolen. The porch of the house was nothing like big enough to hide it. Why hadn't she taken the taxi driver up on his offer to wait? She could have asked him to take her somewhere warm. This didn't look to be the sort of road where you'd often see a taxi.

Stop it, she said to herself. Just stop it. Concentrate.

She cast about in her mind for a solution. None presented itself. You can freeze to death or you can risk losing the suitcase, she told herself. Those are your options. She stood up and manoeuvred the case up against the front door. Maybe a potential thief would think she'd just let herself into the house and would be back for it in a second. Her valuables were in her purse—passport, money, ticket—with uncharacteristic generosity her father had bought her a return ticket. The thought of it was a comfort; if the worst came to the worst she could go home tomorrow. Provided you can find a taxi, she reminded herself. She tucked her purse under her arm and set off.

It was a quarter of an hour before she found what she was looking for: a row of shops, people in the streets. Squashed between a barbershop and a laundromat there was a bakery with tables and chairs along one wall.

Megan went in and the warmth and the rich sweet smell of bread engulfed her—a wonderful smell; it made her almost lightheaded. At the rear of the shop she saw a table with a cushioned bench seat against the wall; it reminded her of Harper's, so she made for it, pushing back her soaking hood and undoing her coat as she went.

The waitress—there was only one—came over to her, a tiny notebook in her hand. She was about fifty, Megan decided, with a fuzz of permed hair and a bright orange smear of lipstick. Her eyebrows had been plucked naked and then drawn in with thin black pencil lines half an inch higher than the originals. They gave her a startled look.

"Coffee?" she said.

"Yes. Thank you," Megan said. "And one of those." She pointed at a tray of pastries sitting on the counter.

"The Chelsea buns?" the waitress asked. She had a white apron wrapped around her middle making her look like a pig-in-a-blanket.

"I guess so," Megan said. "The ones that are all packed together."

"Chelsea buns," the waitress said. She scribbled on her tiny pad, tore off the sheet, set it on the table in front of Megan and smacked a salt shaker down on top of it.

"Which part of the States you from?" she asked, raising the already raised eyebrows.

"I'm Canadian."

The waitress frowned. "That the one with the snow?"

"Well . . . yes," Megan said. "In winter."

The waitress made her way back to the counter. She was wearing slippers with no backs to them and pale pink puffballs on the toes.

Two large women in woollen coats and head scarves were at the table next to Megan's. They were leaning over their coffee cups, whispering to each other. Their eyes flickered curiously over at Megan from time to time. At the front of the shop a younger woman and a little boy sat at a table in the window, staring out at the rain.

Megan stared out at it too. She wondered if her suitcase had been stolen yet. No one will steal it, she told herself. It's too heavy. She thought about Cora instead. Assuming she didn't get home until six, there were still more than eight hours to fill. A daunting thought, but once she'd warmed up she would ask the waitress where she could spend the day. There was bound to be somewhere.

The coffee, when it arrived, tasted nothing like coffee, but at least it was hot. And the Chelsea bun was fresh and warm and unexpectedly delicious. Not pastry, Megan thought. More of a bread; it'll have yeast. You'd roll it out in a rectangle and sprinkle on the raisins and the sugar and cinnamon and then roll it up like a carpet and cut thick slices and pack them side by side in a baking tin. Wouldn't take ten minutes.

She considered having another. She could feel warmth and comfort spreading out from her core to her extremities. Maybe she could stay here for the day, eating one Chelsea bun after another. But the café was too small for her to take up a table all day—three more women had just come in and were arranging themselves and their bundles. She closed her eyes for a moment, listening to the murmuring of the women at the next table, the shuffle of the waitress moving back and forth on pink-slippered feet. Into her mind's eye floated the doorstep of number 31 Lansdown Terrace. Empty. Devoid of suitcase. *Stop it*!

"More coffee?" the waitress asked and Megan jumped and opened her eyes.

"Um, yes, thank you," she said. "I wonder . . . do you know if there's anywhere that I could go and just . . . sit for the day? Anywhere warm and sort of . . . public?"

"Public?" the waitress asked, her eyebrows approaching her hairline.

"Yes," Megan said. "I've . . . I've been locked out of my house and I need to find someplace where I can wait until someone gets home. So I wondered if there was somewhere around here where they wouldn't mind if I waited."

The waitress pursed her lips in thought.

"There's the library," one of the women at the next table said, leaning towards them across the aisle. "That's where the vagrants go, this weather."

"Not *just* vagrants," her companion said. "People who read books go there too." She smiled brightly at Megan. "You could pretend to be reading a book, then they wouldn't mind if you sat there."

"It's just around the corner," the first woman said. "Out the door, turn left, turn left again, there it is."

The library had a vaulted ceiling and stained glass windows and a stone floor decorated with pictures made up of tiny tiles the like of which Megan had never seen. Better still, under one of the windows there were two comfortable-looking upholstered chairs with a small table between them.

There was a woman sitting behind a desk near the door. She glanced up as Megan came in and then went on stamping books. Megan looked around. Over to the left there was an area marked FICTION. She headed for it and began walking up and down the rows, searching for something that would help pass the time. She'd never been much of a reader. Tom was the one who always had his head in a book.

And there, suddenly, sitting right at eye level as if Fate had been listening in to her thoughts, was *The Catcher in the Rye*. Back when they were both still in high school Tom had raved about it. He'd said it was the one book she *had* to read if she never read anything else in her life. She remembered snapping at him, saying, "Fine, you get supper and do the dishes and that way I'll have time to sit and read books!"

But she would read it now. It would help to pass the time, and then in a day or two she would write to Tom and tell him how much she'd enjoyed it, thus demonstrating that it genuinely had been only lack of time that prevented her from reading it—or anything else—before.

She settled herself in one of the comfortable-looking chairs and began reading. Holden Caulfield, the hero's name was. She didn't like him very much. He went on and on about everyone being phony. He was a wallower, she decided. Like Gary, the younger twin; Gary harped on about things too. She had no patience with either of them.

But maybe she wasn't giving Holden Caulfield a fair chance because the truth was she wasn't concentrating. Despite her best efforts the image of her suitcase—or rather, the doorstep of number 31 without her suitcase—kept pushing its way to the front of her mind. She closed the book and put it on the small table beside the chair.

It's only clothes, she said to herself, studying the mosaic on the floor. But it wasn't only clothes. The photos of her family were in the suitcase.

After a while the librarian came over to her. Megan thought she was going to tell her to leave, but she didn't. She merely asked if Megan needed any help.

Megan said, "I've been locked out of my house. Is it okay if I sit here?"

The librarian looked her up and down and then said she didn't see why not and went back to her desk. Megan sat.

At one o'clock she braved the rain and went back to the bakery and ordered a cup of tea and something called a ham salad bap, which she ate without tasting it. She returned to the library and her comfortable chair, dizzy with fatigue, and tried to ward off the feeling of dread that seemed to have overtaken her. You're just tired, she told herself, but the dread remained. She must have fallen asleep then, sitting upright in the chair, because she seemed to be having a conversation with someone, and then she realized that the librarian was bending over her and saying gently that it was half past five and the library was closing.

It was pouring rain and dark as midnight outside, but when she was still some distance away she saw that there were lights on in number 31 Lansdown Terrace. Relief rushed through her. The doorstep was empty but surely that meant someone had taken the suitcase inside. Maybe it was Cora, Megan thought. Maybe she'd got home before the others and had seen the luggage label and given a shriek of laughter, knowing it was Megan's. She'd be in the kitchen now, preparing supper for the two of them.

As she got closer she heard music thudding out from the house, very loud. Maybe that was what caused the dread to seep back into her. She went up the steps to the front door and stood for a moment, her heart thumping the way it had earlier in the day. Then she knocked. For a minute there was no response, and then she heard footsteps and the clicking of a lock and the door was opened by a girl with white lipstick and huge feathery eyelashes. She was smoking a tiny cigarette and wearing one of those infinitesimally small skirts. She took the cigarette out of her mouth and said, "Yes?"

"Is Cora here?" Megan said, loudly, to be heard over the music.

There was no way she could have known what the girl was going to say but she did know, nonetheless.

"Who?" the girl said.

"Cora Manning," Megan said without hope. "She lives here." She was suddenly so tired she was afraid she might fall down.

"Are you from the United States?" the girl asked curiously.

From somewhere inside the house someone shouted over the music, "She moved."

Megan leaned around the girl and shouted, "Where did she go? Do you know?"

Another girl appeared. She was tall and skinny and wore glasses so big she looked like a bug, but she looked nice, Megan thought, and not as dim-witted as the first girl.

"She left a couple of weeks ago," the second girl said. She leaned against the wall beside the door. Behind her, two bicycles were leaning against the wall too, acting as coat racks. "You a friend of hers?"

The music thumped. The singer wanted satisfaction about something and apparently couldn't get it.

"Yes," Megan said. "She invited me to come over. From Canada. Have you seen a suitcase?"

The girl said, "What—you mean you've just arrived? From Canada? Just now?"

The first girl wandered off, twitching the tiny skirt in time with the music.

"This morning," Megan said. She felt sick. Surely no one would have stolen it. Surely they wouldn't. "I left my suitcase here. Right here, outside the door."

"Probably got nicked," the girl said. "Come in, we'll ask the others."

There were a surprising number of others, six or seven at least. They were in a spectacularly untidy room off the hall, squashed together on a battered sofa or sprawled on cushions on the floor, watching television through a haze of cigarette smoke. It was impossible to hear what the characters on the television were saying over the pounding of the music, but it didn't seem to worry anyone. They all looked half-asleep.

"Has anyone seen a suitcase?" the girl with the glasses shouted. Several heads turned towards them.

"Dark brown," Megan said desperately. "And very big. Has anyone seen it?"

"Hey!" one of the boys said, focusing on her with vague interest. "How's the war going?"

"What war?" Megan said.

He laughed. "Nice one! 'What war?' The little one you lot got going in Vietnam."

"Oh," Megan said. "I don't know. I'm not American."

"What are you then?" he said, sounding annoyed.

"Leave her alone, Zack," the girl in glasses said. "She's just arrived and she's lost her suitcase."

"I wondered if anyone brought it in," Megan said. "I left it on the doorstep." She couldn't remember ever feeling so close to despair.

All eyes were fixed on the television. They were watching a cartoon of a dog with a ribbon on its head. The music thudded on.

"Or does anyone know where Cora Manning is?" Megan said, with no hope whatsoever.

"France," somebody said. "She had a fight with Seb, didn't she, Seb? So she left. To be an au pair or something."

The girl in glasses gave Megan a little shrug and a smile of sympathy. "Sorry," she said.

Megan didn't know if the thumping inside her chest came from the music or her heart. She said to the girl, "Do you know a cheap hotel? Nearby? One I could walk to?"

"You can stay here if you like," the girl said cheerfully. "There are lots of mattresses."

"That would be . . . that would be . . . wonderful," Megan said. "Thank you. That would be . . . Just for tonight—I'll find somewhere else in the morning."

"No hurry," the girl said leading the way along the hall. "Stay as long as you like."

The mattress was one of four lying on the floor in a large cold room with a light bulb dangling from the ceiling and newspapers taped over the windows. There was a stained pillow with no pillowcase and a hard hairy blanket. No sheets. Megan took off her coat and boots and skirt, lay down and covered herself with the blanket and her coat. She was cold and her hot water bottle was in the suitcase. She was also exhausted beyond the hope of sleep, but such discomforts were nothing compared with the ache inside her. She thought it would help if she were able to cry, but she hadn't cried since she was a child and couldn't remember how to start.

The music continued to thump and wail. From time to time there was a shriek of laughter or a sharp argument from some other part of the house. After a long while, during which Megan lay unmoving, flat on her back, staring up at the dark, the door opened and two people came in, laughing. They turned on the light and one of them said, "Oops," and turned it off again and Megan heard them lie down on another of the mattresses and begin unmistakably to make love.

For some reason that released the tears. She cried soundlessly, the tears running down into her ears and out of them again and down onto the pillow. She cried as she hadn't cried since she was a small child and possibly not even then. She cried for the photographs. The other contents of her suitcase were nothing, but she didn't see how she could manage without the photographs. She needed them: they were all she had of home; they told her who she was.

She knew she was being ridiculous, that photographs were only bits of paper, but the tears rolled on. The more they rolled the more there seemed to be to cry for. She cried for her incomprehensible father behind his closed door and for her mother, who once had been the whole and sufficient centre of her life. She cried for Patrick, who loved her more than she loved him, and for Adam, whose small round weight she could still feel in her arms. She cried because everything had gone wrong and it was her own fault and she was alone in this sodden, wretched country where she didn't know one single soul. She cried because she had no clean underwear to put on in the morning and because the people here were so peculiar and wore such ridiculous clothes and because everyone thought she was American and blamed her for the war in Vietnam. She cried because six feet away two people were making love and she simply could not imagine anyone doing such a thing, knowingly, in front of someone else. And finally she cried because she wanted to go home to Canada, where she belonged, and knew that she would not.

She cried herself to sleep, like a child, and in the morning, when she judged by the silence that the others had either left or were intending to sleep all day, she got up and washed her face and went out to have a Chelsea bun for breakfast and buy a toothbrush and some underwear and find herself a job.

CHAPTER FIVE

Edward

Struan, January 1969

I appear to have unleashed a ghost. Since hearing my father's voice a week ago I cannot get rid of him. I keep seeing little snap-shots of him, always in a rage. Last night I woke in the small hours certain that he was standing over my bed. I switched on the bedside light and of course there was no one, but there was no question of going back to sleep so I got up and went down to the kitchen (checking under the door that the light was not on, meaning Tom was not there) and sat unable to read or even to think while the hands on the kitchen clock inched around. I kept seeing his face. He had a vertical vein in the middle of his fore-head that used to swell and go purple when he was angry. I was terrified of it when I was small; I thought it might burst. That was what I kept seeing last night. My father's face; that vein, engorged with blood.

After an hour or so the cold drove me back to bed but that was the end of sleep for the night. And today at the bank, every time there was a lull in my activities, back he came.

This evening, in the hope that it might help vanquish his image if I replaced it with my mother's, I got out what remains of her diaries—the ones that survived the fire. I keep them in two box files in the cupboard in my study. I read the ones from her childhood after her death but I've never been able to bring myself to read the rest for fear of what I might find.

Strictly speaking, only the ones from her childhood are proper diaries—notebooks in the conventional dated form. The writings from her adulthood, of which only enough to fill a slim brown folder survived, seem to be her thoughts and fears over the course of many years, scribbled on scraps of paper and tied together with coarse brown string. At times paper must have been hard to come by because many are written on pages torn from other things—the margins of the *Daily Nugget* or the *Temiskaming Speaker*, for instance—and the entries are in such a cramped, hurried hand that they speak of desperation. In some cases she has written lines on top of one another so that they are impossible to decipher. I can only think she must have written them in the dark.

That is a disturbing image: my mother in her nightgown creeping out to the kitchen in the dead of night, groping in the darkness for the newspaper and pencil she would have put aside for the purpose, spreading the paper on the kitchen table, feeling for the edge of it, blindly positioning her pencil and then writing, writing, the words pouring out.

There is no point thinking about it. Much better just to stick to the childhood diaries; they are anything but grim.

She began writing a diary on her sixth birthday, which, coincidentally, was the day her family set out for the North. Her mother gave her a hardback notebook as a birthday present and suggested she start by keeping a record of the trip. I know that because the first entry says so, in my mother's neat, childish hand. The spelling is suspiciously good, so I imagine she had some help with that.

5th June 1901

*My name is Elizabeth Anne Marie Stewart. All of that is
my own name. I am six and this is my birthday present and
two pencils. Mother says I may write about the journey. I
will be the <u>chronicler</u>, Mother says. But I may write whatever
I want. We are going to New Ontario because it is very nice
there and we will have a bigger farm and so will Uncle Alf
and Aunt Janet, theirs will be beside ours. All of us are
going from both families but not the rest of the family. There
will be four parents and eleven children and Tipper our dog
and four horses and Hercules, grandfather's ox, because he
doesn't need him anymore and six cows and twelve chickens.
The chickens will be in a box but they will be able to
breathe. I have to go now. Goodbye.*

Elizabeth Anne Marie Stewart

She told me a little about that trip. Told me in person, I mean.
I remember the occasion vividly because it was on my own sixth
birthday and she had just presented me with a diary of my own.
No doubt she hoped that I would find it a source of pleasure in
the good times and a solace in the bad as she had done, but our
family circumstances at the time and my feelings about them
were beyond my ability to put into words, so the diary stayed
blank. I suppose you could say I am keeping one now, though
that wasn't my intention when I started writing this. I was merely
hoping that the discipline of putting words down on paper would
help me sort out my thoughts. I'm using an old bank ledger. It
seems appropriate, somehow. "Balancing the books."

But back to my birthday. By some fluke, my siblings—I was
the third of five at that stage—were either asleep or elsewhere
and it was just the two of us, which was special in itself. Mother

was darning socks. I recall watching the swift, neat movements of her hands while she talked. Every now and then she would get up to check something on the stove and each time before sitting down again she would reach behind her and press both hands into the small of her back. I remember asking if her back was hurting and her smiling at me and saying, "It's just this baby," and in the morning I had another sister.

That day, though, it was just the two of us and she was telling me about her own sixth birthday. I remember trying to imagine her the same age as myself and finding it impossible.

As pioneer journeys go, theirs wasn't particularly arduous. They moved from Southern Ontario to the North, a matter of four hundred miles or so, taking days rather than weeks. But moving all your worldly goods was quite a procedure back then, especially if those goods included livestock. Transportation, where there was any, was primitive. From my mother's entries it appears that the journey involved three trains, a steamboat and several long hauls along bush roads by horse (or ox) and cart. The diary is low on fact—place names and the like—and I wish she had recorded more description of the route, but still it gives a picture. She seems to have been principally interested in the welfare of the livestock. The entry for the sixth of June 1901, for instance—day two of the trip, in the middle of which they evidently had to change trains—reads:

> *The trains are really noisy and steamy and sometimes they blow out soot and sparks and the cows don't like them and Hercules really, really hates them. Father and Uncle Alf and the engine driver and the fireman had to push all of them on and off both times and Hercules stepped on the engine driver and he was really cross and hit him with a stick. I think it was mean because Hercules was just scared.*

Her descriptions of the accommodation they had to endure en route are similarly low on fact—again not a single place name—and high on impressions. The first night was dominated by bedbugs; nothing else gets a mention. The second was spent in a barn with a leaky roof during what was clearly, from my mother's description, the worst thunderstorm since the dawn of time. On the third night they slept on the floor of a railway station.

> *But nobody could sleep*—my mother wrote—*because of the mosquitoes and because Tipper kept barking. He was outside with the cows and Father said he was imagining bears and Charlie said maybe he wasn't imagining them and what if it was a grizzly and Father said, well we have the rifles, and Uncle Alf said if it was a grizzly we should just give him the rifles and run and Father laughed. But I could hear the cows and horses and Hercules moving about and I think they were scared. But this morning they were all there, I counted them. But the mosquitoes are really big and there are <u>millions</u> of them, Charlie clapped his hands together and he killed <u>eleven</u> with <u>one</u> <u>clap</u> and when you have to go to the toilet behind a bush they get <u>all</u> <u>over</u> your bare bits so Mother came and stood behind me and brushed them off and I did the same for her and for Lily and Susan. I <u>really, really</u> <u>hate</u> mosquitoes.*

The final train they took must have been the lumber train to the southern end of Lake Temiskaming. It was literally the end of the line as far as either rail or road went back then. In winter, when the lake froze over, the ice acted as a road but in summer you could proceed farther north only by boat, so the two families and their long-suffering livestock would have had to unload themselves from the train yet again and then reload everything onto a steamer for the trip up the lake.

Mother's entry for that day is embellished with a drawing of herself and her family on the boat. Artistically it would win no prizes but she clearly took time over it and was at pains not to leave anyone or anything out. Animals and people are all mixed together: four adults, eleven children, one dog, six cows, four horses, an ox and a large box presumably containing the chickens. All but the chickens are standing at the rail and looking out over the lake. In reality I'm sure this couldn't have been the case—the livestock would have been down in the hold—but in my mother's mind they were all together. It reminds me of Noah's Ark.

That first diary of hers, chronicling the family's journey and most of their first year in the North, is one of only four from her childhood that survived the fire unscathed. The only reason any of them did is because Mother had hidden them under the floor-boards in the kitchen. I found them when I went back to the blackened ruins of our home a couple of weeks after the fire, to see if anything of value remained. The floorboards, which had been mostly burned away, had rested on rows of joists, which in turn rested directly on the rock and hard-packed earth beneath, and the gap between the joists was just large enough to contain her precious bundles. There must have been quite a few of them— there were four stacks and from the charred remains I reckon each stack was eight to ten inches high. The fire destroyed all but the bottom inch or so and some of those were badly singed at the edges. Her first diary was at the very bottom of a stack. It must have been particularly precious to her because it was wrapped in several layers of newspaper and then a piece of burlap sacking. When I unearthed it from the rubble my hands came out grey with ash. I remember thinking they looked like the hands of the dead.

As I said, I got out the diaries in the hope that they would exorcise my father's ghost, but in fact they had the opposite effect. They merely reminded me of how that brief, perfect interlude with my mother ended, my father slamming into the house unexpectedly early, purple-faced and stinking of drink, having no doubt been fired from or walked out of yet another job. When he saw my mother and me sitting there, he began shouting at her, calling her a whore, a slut, an ugly, lazy bitch, right there in front of me. Afterwards, when he had gone and it was safe to speak, she said quietly, looking down into her lap, "You mustn't think he means those things, Edward. It's just the liquor talking."

That wasn't so. I knew that even then. She was trying to protect me from the truth. It wasn't the liquor talking, it was my father's true self. The liquor merely loosened his tongue.

Anyway, I put the diaries away again, back in their box files. Since then I've been trying to concentrate on Rome, with mixed success.

———

A better night. But the here and now keeps demanding attention in the most irritating way. I had no clean shirts this morning. When I spoke to Emily about it she looked baffled, then said she would be doing laundry today. All very well, but I was reduced to wearing a dirty shirt to work.

And that is by no means the most serious thing she has forgotten lately. Last week, we ran out of food. Incredible but true. We live virtually in the centre of town. Not only is the grocery store nearby, but it will deliver groceries to your door; all you have to do is pick up the phone.

I didn't realize we were running low. It is not my job to oversee the day-to-day running of the house and in any case, for several years now—since Megan left, in fact—I have been having my meals at the bank during the week. Harper's restaurant is less than a hundred yards from the bank and Susan Harper is a significantly better cook than Emily, so I pick up coffee and a bran muffin on my way to work and then Jean, my secretary, gets me a sandwich at lunchtime and one of their hot beef (or pork or chicken) dinners, neatly double-wrapped in foil, at five o'clock. I eat in solitary splendour in my office when everyone else has gone. It means I get half an hour's peace at the end of the day, which is a bonus, but it also means that I don't know what the rest of the family is eating except on weekends.

Last Saturday—day one of our most recent blizzard—I noticed at lunchtime that amongst other things we had run out of bread, but I assumed Emily had arranged for Marshall's to deliver groceries that afternoon. It turned out she had not. She had no idea the fridge was empty. I didn't realize this until six in the evening, by which time it was too late to do anything about it.

I went up to her room—Emily and I do not share a room, Emily and the newest arrival share a room; I have my own room at the far end of the hall—and found her in bed, cradling the baby and looking as if she were posing for a painting of the Madonna and Child. Emily always becomes distinctly strange in the aftermath of childbirth. It's as if her universe shrinks right down until it contains nothing but herself and the baby. She makes a little nest in the bed and settles down in it as if she were hatching an egg and simply stays there. The rest of us might as well not exist. Formerly it didn't matter much because Megan was here to pick up the pieces, but it matters now. The other children, especially Adam, being so young, are not toys to be discarded on the arrival of a new model.

I asked if she was feeling all right—obviously if she was sick it was a different story—and she said yes. I confess I was relieved; I would not relish calling in John Christopherson, given what he said when Adam was born about Emily not being strong enough to have more children. I found it hard to meet his eye when he came to deliver this one.

I asked what she expected us to have for supper and she looked up at me with that blank expression of hers as if the question had never crossed her mind. I have wondered before now if Emily's vagueness is deliberate—an excuse for not taking her duties seriously. It's impossible to tell. I noticed there was an open packet of biscuits beside her bed, which helped explain why she wasn't hungry herself. (Curiously, they were the same as the ones I keep in my desk. I would have sworn Emily and I had absolutely nothing in common, but it turns out I would have been wrong: we both like digestives.)

I pointed out that it was half past six, that we were hungry and there was nothing in the fridge but two eggs and a carrot. I don't think my tone was particularly sharp, but she abruptly started to cry, silently, looking down at the baby, the tears running down her face and dripping onto his head.

I said tiredly, "Emily, for heaven's sake." I hadn't meant to upset her.

There was a box of Kleenex on the bedside table. I offered her one and she took it and wiped the baby's face and then her own. When she had pulled herself together I tried again. I asked as patiently as I could why she hadn't arranged for Mrs. Whatever-her-name-is to come in every day and help until she felt stronger. At that she seemed to gather her wits and said that Mrs. Whatever had phoned to say that she was sick but hoped to be back soon.

Clearly there was nothing to be done until after the weekend. I suggested carefully, gently, that on Monday morning she should make a few phone calls, first to arrange for Marshall's to deliver some food and second to find someone to come in each day and deal with the housework until Mrs. Whatever gets back. I asked if she thought she could manage to do those two things and she said yes.

I said, "As for the rest of the weekend, we will manage some-how, so don't worry about that." As if there were any question of her worrying about it.

Sometimes I cannot help comparing Emily with my mother, who had ten children, virtually no money and an abusive fool for a husband, but who nevertheless managed to have a proper meal on the table every day of our lives.

I suppose that isn't fair. My mother was a remarkable woman.

On my way downstairs I met Tom coming up, carrying a large cardboard box and closely followed by Adam. The stairs are narrow and we all stood aside for each other in that awkward way people do in doorways.

"Come on, then," I said. They came up past me—cautiously, it seemed to me, though there's an outside chance they were being polite. Tom had obviously been out—his face was mottled with cold and there was snow in his hair.

"Cold out, I guess," I said, trying to be pleasant. Following the business with Peter and Corey earlier in the afternoon I had resolved to be more pleasant with the boys. "What have you got there?"

"Nothing," Tom said. "Yeah, it's freezing." He carried on up, Adam almost literally clinging to his heels. It occurred to me that we don't know how to talk to each other in this family.

I went down to the kitchen and got out the eggs, the can of peas (I say "the" can because there was only one), the can of condensed mushroom soup (ditto) and the rice. There were no clean saucepans, so I used a dirty one. I read the instructions on the packet of rice and cooked it—it made a surprisingly large amount, but that was all to the good. I added everything else to the saucepan and cooked it a little more for the sake of the eggs. The result was rather glutinous—possibly I should have strained the water off the can of peas before adding them—but it didn't taste too bad.

I ate my share of it straight from the saucepan, there being no clean plates, and then went upstairs and knocked on the door of the room shared by Peter and Corey. Peter opened the door a crack and peered out as if I might be Jack the Ripper. I said, "If you're hungry, there's a saucepan of food on the stove. It needs to feed all of us for two days, so don't take more than your share." I turned to knock on Tom's door but he was already standing in the doorway. I said, "Did you hear that?" and he nodded. Adam was in there—I heard the whizzing noise his cars make—so at least I don't need to worry about him. I went back down to my study.

I had just settled into my chair when I realized that I had forgotten to tell Emily there was now something to eat. Fortunately Peter and Corey chose that moment to come thundering down the stairs, so I got up quickly and opened the study door. Both of them froze, mid-step, teetering on a stair apiece. I said, "Take some supper up to your mother," and they nodded mutely like some sort of comedy double act.

So that looked after Saturday's supper. On Sunday we ate the remains of the rice mixture and by the time I got home on Monday evening Emily was up and drifting around the house with the baby strapped to her front the way she always carries them when they're new. I assumed she had things back under control. Now, given the absence of clean shirts, it seems she has not.

Sometimes it is hard not to regret that Megan has left home. I didn't realize the extent to which she covered for her mother all those years.

———

The Giles's hay barn burned down last night. There were no livestock in it but they lost all the hay, which means that in addition to rebuilding the barn they will have to buy in winter feed for their cattle for at least the next three months—a significant cost in itself. And of course they had no insurance. If I had a nickel for every un- or under-insured business in this town, I'd be a wealthy man.

So this morning, in comes Archie Giles needing to borrow a significant sum. He says he cannot figure out how the fire started—he never leaves anything flammable about and there is no electricity in the barn. I could tell he was worrying away at the question while we were talking about the loan. He is a good farmer and the farm is surety, so I had no hesitation in advancing him the money, but taking him through the terms of the repayment took a long time and clearly made him anxious. Like many people up here Archie has very little formal education. "Formal" is the key word there—apart from the all-too-common stupidity of being uninsured he is by no means an unintelligent man. Still, it took a good while to reassure him that the repayments would be manageable. Normally his wife, Norah, comes in with him— she's more comfortable with figures—but she's in bed with flu.

The truth is, I don't have all that much formal education myself. I wanted very much to go to university but it was out of the question. I was lucky to be allowed to finish grade twelve—of the ten of us I'm the only one who did. People assume I'm better educated than I am. As with everything else, I have my mother to thank for that: she taught us all to speak properly and insisted that we do so. My father used to sneer about it. He overheard her correcting my grammar one day and I remember him saying, "That's right, bring 'em up to talk all fancy-dancy, see how much good it does 'em."

In fact it did me a great deal of good. I would never have made bank manager otherwise. You need a certain authority in a job like this and the fact is, people tend to respect you more if you speak properly. Maybe it shouldn't make a difference but it does.

My mother didn't get to finish high school herself. She told me once that she'd wanted to be a teacher but her father didn't believe in educating girls, which is a pity because she would have been a good teacher. She was very patient, very good at explaining things. She taught me fractions by cutting up an apple. She cut it into sixteenths, then showed me how two sixteenths were the same as one eighth, that sort of thing. At the end of the lesson I was allowed to eat all sixteen sixteenths, which seemed a fitting reward.

Megan could have had any education she wanted but she showed no interest in such things. None of them did except Tom. Though it's possible that Adam will turn out to have some academic ability. And the baby, I suppose. An unknown quantity at this stage. He could be another Einstein.

Dominic is his name. Dominic John Cartwright. So I'm told by his mother. She named all the children as they arrived in this world. I had no objection; they were all perfectly acceptable names. Dominic makes him sound like a monk but it won't do him any harm.

No doubt she will want him christened. I will go, of course— I've gone to all the children's christenings. It would offend half the town and humiliate Emily if I did not. God will not be offended by my hypocrisy as He does not exist. Reverend Thomas (although he's no longer reverend, I keep forgetting that) won't be there to take offence. He has been replaced temporarily by Reverend Gordon, who has come out of retirement to fill in until the church can persuade someone to come to this (I nearly wrote "godforsaken") place. Reverend Gordon was an army chaplain during the war and was with us in Italy. An intelligent man and a courageous one, he was with us every step of the way. He knows I'm not a believer but he won't be offended by my presence because he has too much sense.

Another bad night—a dreadful night, in fact. I dreamed about the fire. Our fire—the forest fire—not the Giles's, but no doubt that was the trigger. Though it could have been my mother's diaries, now that I think of it. For years I had recurring nightmares about it but I thought they were over. I have never known terror like it; the bombardments in Italy didn't come close.

In the dream my father was standing on the roof of the farmhouse, silhouetted against the approaching wall of flame, arms raised, shaking his fists at the sky. The grand, defiant gesture. Man against Fate. He was a big believer in Fate. In its malevolence where he was concerned.

He was up on the roof trying to soak the shingles in order to prevent the fire catching hold. I was at the pump, pumping as if our lives depended on it, whereas in fact they depended on us getting to the lake before our retreat was cut off. But my father, being my father, was determined to save the farmhouse. No little forest fire was going to get *his* house, no *sir*. My mother and those of my siblings who were big enough were passing the buckets of water up to him and he was flinging them over the shingles and passing them back down. As if a wet roof would have stopped that inferno. As if anything could have stopped it by that stage. It filled the whole horizon and the wind was blowing the flames straight towards us.

I woke up soaked with sweat. My pyjamas were wringing wet so I took them off. There were no clean ones in the drawer so I put on my long johns and my dressing gown and went down to the kitchen. By good fortune Tom wasn't there. I had a bowl of cornflakes and sat for a while, trying to read about Rome, until I was driven back to bed by the cold. No more sleep, though. In fact, I was afraid to go to sleep for fear I'd slide back into the dream. The look on my father's face, at the end.

I got up early and slogged through the snow to the bank—Tom and his snowplough had cleared the road less than an hour earlier but already it was filling in again—and started working through the pile of paperwork on my desk, glad to have something to occupy my mind. Then, at nine o'clock sharp, in lumbered Sergeant Gerry Moynihan, Struan's one and only officer of the law, shedding snow in all directions and eating a doughnut.

"Good morning, Sergeant," I said. "How are you?"

He mumbled something and waved the doughnut apologetically.

"Don't worry," I said. "Take your time. Have a seat." If he'd wanted to talk about his finances, such as they are, he'd have made an appointment, so I was curious to know the reason for his visit.

He sat down heavily in the chair opposite my desk, swallowed a couple of times, licked the sugar off his fingers and said, "Archie Giles."

"Oh yes?"

"You know 'bout his barn burnin' down?"

"Yes, he came in to see me yesterday."

"Know of anyone who might have a grudge against him?"

I was taken aback. "You think it was arson?" I said. I recalled that Archie had seemed uneasy when I asked about the cause of the fire.

"Footprints 'round the barn," Gerry said. "Two sets. They don't match nobody in the house. It was snowin' Tuesday night, so maybe they thought that would cover their tracks, but it quit 'round about midnight so they were just dusted over. Filled in now, of course. Just wondered if you'd heard any rumours about . . . anythin'. Anyone actin' strange. Makin' threats, maybe . . ."

"No," I said slowly. "I haven't heard anything of that kind."

There were, of course, two obvious candidates and Gerry Moynihan knew it as well as I did. The previous fall Archie had taken on two of Joel Pickett's boys to help with the harvest, which was good of him considering the Picketts' reputation as ne'er-do-wells, but after a week or so of the lads failing to turn up until noon Archie ran out of patience, paid them what they were due and told them not to come back. Apparently the boys were furious. They started shouting threats and Archie told them to get off his land. Hardly a rational excuse for burning down the barn, but then "rational" isn't a word you'd associate with Joel Pickett, and his boys appear to take after him.

That's the problem, of course—if something of a criminal nature takes place in this town, Joel or his sons are always the prime suspects. I could see that Gerry didn't want to be too quick to point the finger for that very reason. Gerry's a redneck and has some backward views but he takes his duties seriously and he's not a fool.

"Archie's a nice guy," I said at last. "Hard to imagine anyone—" I nearly said "anyone *else*" but caught myself in time—"having it in for him."

"Archie didn't say anythin' 'bout having suspicions?"

"No. I didn't know he was thinking along those lines."

Gerry nodded. We looked at each other in silence for a minute or two and then he sighed and got to his feet.

"I'll let you know if anything comes to mind," I said. I stood up and opened the door for him and he made a sort of salute and left.

After he'd gone I sat for some time thinking about Joel Pickett. He and I have a history, you might say. That's why Gerry Moynihan came to see me, of course. He's guessing that the affairs of the Pickett family are still of some interest to me and that I will have my ear to the ground where they are concerned.

In fact Joel's and my history isn't particularly long or complicated, although the repercussions were. A few years ago he applied to the bank for a loan and I turned him down. That was all there was to it. In the course of my work I make such decisions all the time and no doubt I sometimes get it wrong, but in Joel Pickett's case I was unquestionably right. He had a well-earned reputation as a drinker, a gambler and a fool. Even if his proposal had been a good one, no bank manager in the country would have felt confident about giving him a loan.

I'd had no direct dealings with Joel before that day but when he walked into my office I confess I disliked him on sight. There was something about him, a glibness, an oiliness in his smile. Nonetheless, it is in the bank's interest as well as the town's to encourage new business and investment in the area, so I invited Joel to take a chair and listened to what he had to say. Put simply, he wanted the bank to cover the cost of converting the old mill down at Beller's Creek into a hunting lodge. Struan could do with another hotel, he said, something "swanky," something with a little "class."

As a matter of fact, he was right about that; our only hotel, Fitzpatrick's, was, to put it kindly, a little rough, and we did need something to cater to the top end of the tourist market. That was why the building firm Waller and Sons was, even as Joel Pickett sat in my office smiling his oily smile, engaged in negotiations to buy a plot of land with lake frontage a mile or so north of the town. (Their bid was successful. The new lodge is scheduled to open this summer. It looks very nice and will provide a good deal of employment for the town.)

I mentioned this other proposal to Joel and although it was common knowledge it was clearly news to him. It didn't faze him though. "Plenty of room for both," he said, crossing his legs and leaning back in his chair. Something about his manner bothered me and I couldn't figure out what it was.

I agreed that there might be room for both but said that in my opinion his plan had a serious weakness, namely that the Beller's Creek site wasn't on, or even near, the lake.

I should say here that the lake is our biggest asset—in fact, the lakes in general are the North's biggest asset. They are beautiful and tranquil and clear as glass and full of fish; every year thousands of people come hundreds of miles to enjoy them. To build a hotel or hunting lodge up here and site it anywhere but on a lake is utter foolishness.

But Joel brushed that point aside too. The mill was a pretty spot, he said. There were some nice birches on the lot. People would love it. He'd talked about it with Reverend Thomas and Reverend Thomas thought it was a wonderful idea, so much so that he'd told Joel he'd vouch for him if I asked for a reference.

That took me aback, I have to say. If Reverend Thomas had wanted to ensure that I turned Joel Pickett down, he could hardly have thought of a better way. Still, I reminded myself that personal feelings have no place in professional decisions, and I carried on. I asked Joel why he was so set on the Beller's Creek site and whether he would consider a lakeside property instead. At that he uncrossed his legs and sat forward in his chair. He'd won the property in a poker game, he said, and the moment he'd set eyes on it he'd known it was perfect for a lodge. He said it aggressively, as if challenging me to make something of it, and all of a sudden I realized what it was about him that made me uneasy: he reminded me of my father. My father had the same totally unjustified confidence in himself—not the confidence of a man well versed in his subject but the confidence of a man who has no idea how little he knows—and the same instant aggression towards anyone who challenged him.

Needless to say, the similarity wasn't in Joel's favour, but I am clear in my own mind that neither it nor the endorsement of Reverend Thomas influenced my decision. I told Joel, courteously, that I didn't think his plan was viable in its present form and I brought the interview to a close. As far as I was concerned that was that.

It didn't surprise me when I later learned that after he'd left the bank Joel Pickett got blind drunk and began spreading his version of the story around town. Everyone in Struan knew his word meant nothing. It didn't even concern me unduly when a couple of nights later a rock was thrown through the bank's window. Joel was seen by two people, one of whom happened to be Sergeant Moynihan.

None of that surprised me. What did surprise me—what rendered me speechless with astonishment and still does whenever I think of it—was that, a few days after our interview, who should come into the bank requesting a few minutes of my time but the Reverend James Thomas. We had not spoken since the day of Henry's death but of course I offered him a chair and asked what I could do for him.

He began by saying he had not come on his own behalf but on the behalf of a "deeply troubled man."

"A few days ago," he said, "a member of my congregation applied to you for a loan to help him start up in the hotel business."

I held up my hand. He stopped, but I was so incredulous that for a moment I couldn't think what to say. Finally I said, "Mr. Thomas—"

"Reverend Thomas, please." (Said with that smile of his.)

"Reverend Thomas. The bank does not discuss the affairs of its customers with other people under any circumstances."

"It isn't the bank I've come to talk to, Mr. Cartwright. It is you."

"In my capacity as manager of the bank."

"No, in your capacity as a human being."

"As a human being I have no authority to grant loans."

He smiled, as if at a particularly stubborn and foolish child. "All right," he said. "I concede the point, as it troubles you so much. Let me just put a hypothetical case to you."

He put the tips of his fingers together so that they formed a little steeple and touched them to his lips. I wondered if in the course of his day he ever made a single gesture that was not contrived.

"Let us imagine a man who has made some serious mistakes in his life," he said. "Some bad decisions, which have affected not only him but also his wife and his five young children. Let us suppose that by God's grace and through the unceasing prayers and support of those in the church community who have refused to give up on him, he has put all that behind him. He has changed. I truly believe that. I deal with human weakness every day, Mr. Cartwright" (a sorrowful smile this time—oh, the pain of dealing with human weakness every day!) "and I believe this man sincerely wants to make a fresh start.

"He has always wanted to set up in the hotel business. He tells me it has been his dream ever since he was a boy. Although I am no expert in such matters, it seems to me that it is a good dream, not just from his own perspective but because it would also benefit the whole community, bringing more tourists into the area.

"However—and here's where you, in your capacity as a bank manager, come in—he needs some financial help to get started.

"Now then." (The steeple of his fingers touched his lips, once, twice, a third time. If that's what a university education does for you, I don't regret not having one.) "A hypothetical question to go with a hypothetical case: if you were in a position to help such a man, knowing that you would also be helping his family and the wider community, wouldn't you want to do so?"

I pushed back my chair and stood up. I said, "Excuse me, Reverend Thomas, but this conversation is ridiculous and I have a lot to do today."

He stayed seated. He said, "Mr. Cartwright, this is a good man we're speaking of. He has weaknesses, as do we all—only God is perfect—but he is at heart a good man, and I believe he deserves a second chance. Don't forget he won't be on his own this time—he will have the grace of God and the support of the church community behind him. And I, personally, will vouch for him."

By this stage I was having great difficulty controlling myself. "Will you, personally, guarantee the loan?" I said tightly.

"I beg your pardon?"

"Will you, personally, guarantee the loan?"

To my pleasure he flushed. "If I had the resources I certainly would, but I'm afraid I don't." He paused, then tipped his head to one side. "Mr. Cartwright, I'm beginning to wonder if you have a personal grudge against this man. You are in a position to help him and yet you won't even consider it. Why is that? I find it very strange."

"I am not in a position to help him," I said. "The money in this bank is not mine. It is money entrusted to the bank by its customers and I have an absolute duty to safeguard it and not expose it to undue risk. On the other hand, if you would guarantee the loan by, say, taking out a second mortgage on your home, the risk to the bank would be greatly reduced and I'd be happy to arrange it. As you have such faith in him, presumably you'll be happy to do that."

His face went a pleasing ripe-tomato red, apart from his lips and the end of his nose, both of which were pinched white. He stood up.

He said, "I came here this morning because I thought, despite our differences, that you were a reasonable man, Mr. Cartwright. All I was asking was that you reconsider your decision in this case. I don't think that's too much to ask when a man's future is at stake. But apparently you do."

I walked over to the door and opened it and he walked out. As he passed me he said, "I am disappointed in you, Edward Cartwright. Profoundly disappointed. I expected better, even from you."

I still can't help wishing I had knocked him down.

That was not the end of the affair, not by a long way. The following Sunday Reverend Thomas stood in his pulpit and preached a sermon on the evils of those who set themselves up in judgment over others. I wasn't there, of course, but I heard about it afterwards. It was a very powerful sermon, apparently, and somehow he managed to make it clear whom he was talking about. It was all around Struan within a matter of hours. As a result a number of our customers—not many but even one would be too many—withdrew their money and took it to other banks in other towns.

Until that day I believe the people of this town, virtually without exception, trusted and respected me. That meant a great deal to me. I'd go as far as to say I valued it above almost anything else.

Now there are exceptions. I cannot begin to say how painful that is and how bitterly I still resent it.

Why do I keep thinking about things like this? It's almost as if my brain actively seeks them out. It's absurd. I will stop.

One more thing, though. One final thing I want to say before closing the book on the subject once and for all: in the years since that incident Joel Pickett has gone from bad to worse and taken his family with him. He has never held a job for more than a couple of weeks, he has spent many nights in the jail cell after drunken and aggressive behaviour, his boys have been constantly in trouble practically from the moment they could walk, and now, it would appear, they have become arsonists.

Reverend Thomas no doubt maintains that this is my doing—that by not giving Joel Pickett a loan at a critical point in his life I condemned his family to a downward slide into poverty and disgrace. The truth is, if I had approved that loan, when his absurd hotel scheme failed, and it would have failed, Joel would have owed so much money that he would have lost his home along with everything else and his family would now be on the street.

They would be destitute. That is the truth of the matter. I am not the cause of Joel Pickett's ruin; Joel Pickett is.

There. I am not going to think about it ever again.

⸻

Saturday. I shouted at the boys again. They broke the lamp in the living room. They were fighting. It wasn't even eight o'clock in the morning and they were fighting. I cannot understand why they don't just keep out of each other's way if they hate each other so much. It seems such a simple, obvious solution. Instead it's as if they are glued together; you never see one without the other.

I heard the crash and opened the door of my study to see what the commotion was, and there was the lamp in pieces on the floor, the boys staring down at it in wonderment as if it had fallen from the sky. I was . . . incandescent. The room echoed afterwards.

But the worst thing was that as I turned to go back into my study, I saw Adam, crouching down beside the old armchair Tom has adopted as his own. (Tom was out on his snowplough.) I hadn't realized he was there. He had curled himself into a ball with his arms covering his head as if to protect himself.

I knew I must speak to him, reassure him somehow, but before I could say anything Emily appeared at the top of the stairs, clutching the baby. She stared at me with those huge eyes of hers and said in a whisper, "Edward? What is happening? Are you all right?"

I crossed to the entrance hall and hauled on my coat and boots and left the house. It was murderously cold. I pulled my scarf up over my nose and mouth but still the air seared my lungs. When I reached the road I stopped; I didn't know what to do, where to go. It was too cold to stay outside for any length of time but I didn't want to see anyone. Not even Betty. Particularly not

Betty. In any case the library doesn't open until nine. Nowhere does except Harper's, so in the end that was where I went. Thankfully the cold had kept everyone else at home.

The frightening thing is that it felt as if I had no control over it—over the shouting. As if it wasn't me.

That is a ridiculous statement. If Joel Pickett is responsible for his own actions, then I am responsible for mine. If you don't accept that, then your life is not your own. You are nothing more than a puppet, with your ancestors pulling your strings.

CHAPTER SIX

Tom

Struan, January 1969

His goal was to construct each day like the hull of a ship, every action a plank fitting exactly up to the next, no gaps or holes where thoughts might seep in, no changes to throw him off course, no surprises. Work, eat, read the paper, go to bed; stick to the routine and you'll make it through the day.

At 5:15 a.m. the alarm went off and he hit the stop button and swung his legs out of bed. Off with pyjamas, on with long johns, jeans, two pairs of thick woollen socks, down the hall to the bathroom for a wash (at least at this hour he didn't have to stand in line with sundry sleep-sodden, bad-tempered brothers), back to his bedroom, on with undershirt, flannel shirt, sweater, grab a Hershey bar from the secret stash behind the bookcase by his bed, downstairs for cornflakes and toast, eaten standing up at the kitchen sink, fill the Thermos with coffee, out to the entrance hall to search, cursing, through the jumble of outdoor gear for his own boots, scarf, hat, parka, gloves, grab the Thermos, tuck it under his arm, pull open the inner door, push open the outer door, slam both behind him and off into the frozen dark.

Sometime during the night the snow had stopped and the

clouds had cleared and now the piercing, brittle stars moved with him as he walked. At the end of the road he had to climb over the bank of snow thrown up by the snowplough over the previous days, hard and steep and pitted with footprints, each footprint a dark soft shadow in the starlight.

There was only an inch or so of new snow on the main roads, so today, finally, he would be able to make a start on the smaller side roads, which had been clogged up like frozen rivers for days. Then the citizens of Struan would be able to shovel out their driveways and get their cars back on the road and the town would be back in business.

The snowplough lived around the back of the gas station, crouched amidst the snowdrifts like the prehistoric heap of junk that it was, a Sicard, 1940s model, headache yellow, a basic truck with a plough on its nose. Tom climbed up on the step, slammed his shoulder hard against the door of the cab three times while simultaneously heaving violently on the handle—the door was always frozen shut and it took brute force to break it free—climbed into the cab and stuck the key in the ignition. After a couple of goes the engine caught and roared into life and he raised and lowered the shovel to get everything moving, then ploughed his way around to the front of the gas station. In exchange for parking, the deal was that he and Marcel Bruchon, on the late shift, would keep the garage forecourt free of snow, so he did that first and then set off down the road.

The main roads were still empty of traffic and he rumbled down them as fast as he dared, the new snow flying off the blade of the plough in a great soft arc. The roads were cleared in order of priority: access to the fire station, the police, the doctor's office, the school, then Main Street and the major crossroads within the town, then the main road out as far as the New Liskeard turnoff, where the Department of Highways snowploughs took over, then the major roads on the school bus route and finally the minor side roads, some of which might be snowed in for a week if there was a heavy and prolonged snowfall.

By the time he reached the side roads it was light enough to turn off the headlights but still he moved cautiously. Marcel hurtled down even the smallest roads at terrifying speed but he'd had twenty years to learn the difference between a snow-covered road and a snow-filled ditch and could tell at a hundred yards whether a snowdrift was really a snowdrift or a car in disguise. Though even Marcel made the occasional mistake. The previous week he'd ploughed up a dead moose out along the Harper Side Road.

"Made me feel not too good, I tell you," he'd said to Tom afterwards. "Engine, she give a liddle grunt like she does, cab, she shake a liddle bit, den all at once d'ole damn snowdrif' she shif' 'bout tree feet an' up come dese four legs, stickin' straight up like candles on a cake. I tink, Whoa, Marcel, dem's legs! What you doin' ploughin' up legs? But den I tink, well, leas' dey don't have boots on, dat would be worse."

There had been worse. A couple of years back Marcel had unearthed a car containing a family of four, all dead. They'd pulled over to the side of the road to wait out a blizzard but it lasted two days and buried the car and they ran out of air.

The thought of it—coming across a car full of dead bodies—made Tom sweat. He'd wanted to ask Marcel what it had felt like when he cleared the snow away and saw the people inside. That moment of realization when they didn't respond to his banging on the side window—what had that been like? He would have shouted encouragement to them and no heads would have turned. No one would have moved.

But probably he'd known they were dead earlier than that. There would have been something about the silence inside the car. Not an empty silence; something more final.

When he'd seen what appeared to be a heap of clothes at the foot of the cliff Tom had known instantly that it was not a heap of clothes. It had nothing to do with recognizing what Robert had been wearing, he never noticed what anyone wore. It was something else. He and Simon had reached the bottom of the ravine and come around the corner of the rock face, picking their way over the rubble of glistening boulders at the river's edge, and he'd glanced up and seen the bundle lying there at the foot of the cliff, directly below where they'd been standing half an hour earlier, and he'd known at once.

The unforgivable thing was that, along with the icy wave of sick, cold horror, he had felt absolute outrage. His first thought had been, What kind of friend would do that to you? Would kill himself virtually in front of you, and with a stranger present?

The real question was, what kind of sick bastard would have that as his first thought on seeing the dead body of his closest friend. It was monstrous; he could hardly believe it of himself, but that was what he'd thought, what he'd felt. He'd felt as if the act were aimed at him, as if Robert had stepped off the cliff (and he had stepped, he hadn't jumped or hurled himself, because if he had his body would be a few feet out from the cliff instead of right at the foot, almost touching the sheer rock face)—as if he had stepped off the cliff purely and simply to punish Tom, as if he were speaking directly to him, saying, You don't seem to care what I've been going through, you and this new friend you're having such a good time with, so I'm going to show you. Take a look at this.

He never thought about anything but death anymore. It was with him every waking moment and stalked his dreams at night. When he read the papers death leapt up at him. One single death or mass extinction, murder or genocide, war, famine, plague, disease: it called to him, drew him in. There had been four columns of death notices in *The Globe and Mail* the previous morning and he'd been unable to stop himself from reading every one. It was as though his brain were scrabbling around like a rat in a cage trying to find a way to rationalize what had happened. Look at all these deaths, it was saying. Everybody dies, so what's the big deal? Everybody dies; people are dying all the time, literally all the time, every second of the day or night. Some die old, some die young, but they all die and in the great scheme of things the fact that someone dies earlier than he otherwise might have doesn't matter a bit. It doesn't matter because nothing matters, in the great scheme of things.

In any case—this was another thing his brain constantly told itself with no effect at all—there was nothing he could have done.

The church was on the corner of Main and Cleveland Street. Turn down Cleveland and Reverend Thomas's house was the first on the left. The car was a whale-shaped hump under three feet of snow; it hadn't moved all winter. Kindly souls kept shovelling out the drive but some sense of delicacy seemed to prevent them from clearing the snow from the car itself. A narrow path from the road to the front door testified to the endless stream of ladies from the church bearing casseroles and pies.

Tom looked resolutely straight ahead as he drove past the house, just in case Reverend Thomas should happen to step outside onto his porch. According to gossip Tom had overheard in Harper's, Mrs. Thomas had left him, which meant that Reverend Thomas had now lost not only his son and his faith, but his wife as well. Lost everything, in effect.

What do you say to someone who has lost everything? How do you meet his eye? If you were the last person to have seen his son alive, if you were with him for virtually the whole morning before he died but you were so busy having a good time you didn't even notice the state he was in. Or worse, you did sort of notice, but it merely irritated you because it was such a great day and you didn't want anything to spoil it.

What do you say?

By the time he'd finished ploughing the side streets, people were up and about, shovelling out their drives or trudging along the edge of the road, hats pulled down, hoods up, shoulders hunched against the cold. They'd raise a hand to Tom as he went by and he'd raise his in return, grateful for the isolation of the small, freezing cab. One of the advantages of the job was that no one expected him to stop for a chat.

He knew most of them—had known most of them all his life, though none of his friends from school was still here. There had been five of them who hung around together, Miles Cooper, Wayne Patterson, Elliot Park, Robert and himself, though Robert was the only one he'd been really close to. After high school Miles and Wayne had both gone to the mining school in Haileybury, Elliot had joined Ontario Hydro and Tom and Robert had gone to U of T, Tom to study aeronautical engineering and Robert to study history. They'd roomed together in their undergraduate years and it had been a blast, but then on their first day back at the start of their postgraduate terms—Robert was doing an MA and Tom an MSc—Robert had announced casually that he'd decided to change courses and study theology. Tom thought he was joking and laughed, and then realized he was serious and was dumbfounded. *Robert*? Study *theology*?

It was true they'd never specifically talked about religion—in your teens there were things you didn't talk about even with close friends (your parents, for example, whose very existence was too embarrassing for words), and religion was one of them. Maybe by the time they reached university they could have discussed it the way they discussed the various new ideas they were coming into contact with—everything from philosophy to free love—if it hadn't been that the subject of religion was inextricably bound up with the subject of Robert's father, who in Tom's opinion was an arrogant jerk. Not only that, but Robert had once said something that strongly suggested he thought so too. Which must be tricky for him, Tom thought. His own father was pretty much a dead loss as far as parenting went, but at least you could respect him. At least he didn't humiliate you in public by standing up in front of the entire town and preaching at everyone with a patronizing smile on his face. He didn't know how Robert stood the shame.

The thing Robert had said—the revelation of his feelings about his father—had come out when he was drunk, years back, when they were still in high school. It was a summer evening and they were down at the beach polishing off the remains of a bottle of Jack Daniel's that Robert had swiped from the back seat of a tourist's car.

That was the summer Robert started drinking seriously. Legally you couldn't drink until you were twenty-one and illicit booze was hard to come by, but that summer Robert devoted himself to the task of procuring it by any means possible, up to and including theft. He'd slip into people's houses when they were watching television, raid tourists' cabins, saunter into Fitzpatrick's Hotel and lift something from behind the bar. It made Tom's hair stand on end; the consequences if Robert were caught didn't bear thinking about.

But he didn't get caught. He was a very good thief. He'd spot an opportunity, seize it and be walking down the street with a bottle under his jacket before Tom even realized what was happening.

Tom didn't know what was behind it. Robert had never been the hellraiser type. He was a quiet, reserved sort of guy, so it was way out of character. But the "over twenty-one" law was ridiculous and deserved to be broken and anyway, the unspoken rules of friendship demanded unconditional support, no questions asked, so Tom said nothing. He didn't take part in the stealing, though, and was glad Robert didn't seem to expect him to. He'd have been a lousy thief. He'd have had guilt written all over him.

And though Tom shared in the spoils he didn't overdo it; he was too wary of his father's reaction to risk staggering into the house drunk. Whereas Rob seemed positively to relish the idea of his father finding out.

"My father advises me to lay off the hooch."

That was what Robert had said that night on the beach—his opening statement. He'd said it as if they'd been talking about either his father or booze, which they hadn't. They hadn't been talking about anything much, they'd been having a stone-skipping contest, passing the Jack Daniel's back and forth between them, thinking their own thoughts. It had been hot and humid all day but now there were storm clouds building up over to the east and the lake was so still it seemed to be holding its breath.

"He doesn't forbid it," Robert went on. "Nothing is ever forbidden. Everything is up to me. My decision entirely." He'd had quite a skinful already, but no matter how drunk he got Rob never slurred his words. It was his coordination that went—that and control over his extremities.

Tom didn't say anything. You couldn't agree with someone that his father was a jerk. He continued turning over stones with his foot, looking for the perfect skipper.

"He's very patient, very holy, when he explains things," Robert said, in a patient, holy voice unnervingly like his father's. "Explains them over and over again. Reasons why I shouldn't drink. The pain it causes my mother, the bad example I'm setting to those less fortunate than me."

He bent down to pick up a stone, swaying slightly. He was holding the bottle but it remained magically upright as if his hand were a natural gyroscope.

"That's the main one, actually," he said straightening up and examining the stone. "They look up to me, apparently. Those less fortunate. They follow my example because of who I am. So if I drink they will too. So if they become drunken bums it will be my fault. Very logical. He's very logical, my father."

He threw his stone. It went more or less straight up in the air and landed with a plunk about three feet out from the shore.

"Tragic," Tom said. "Minus five."

His foot uncovered the stone to end all stones, flat as a pancake and almost perfectly round. He picked it up, weighed it in his hand for a minute to find the balance of it, leaned over, took aim and threw. The stone skittered off across the water in a long smooth curve, circled all the way back on itself and disappeared neatly into its own ripples.

"Now *that* is a ten!" he said. "No way is that not a ten."

Robert nodded and took a swig. "Whaddya think he means by that?" he said.

"By what?"

"The bit about those less fortunate looking up to me because of *who I am*. Who am I?"

"Good question," Tom said. "Always wondered that myself." He took a mere taste from the bottle and passed it back. He was about as drunk as he allowed himself to get.

Robert found a stone and gave a mighty sling but missed the lake altogether and sat down hard. He didn't bother trying to get up after that, just sat, cradling the bottle in both hands, looking out over the lake. Every now and then a streak of lightning flashed beneath the dark belly of the clouds.

"Guess it doesn't matter," Robert said. "Because what he really means is who *he* is. People look up to me because I am his son—that's what he means. Not because I'm me, why would anybody look up to me because I'm me, for Christ's sake? But if I get drunk, he looks bad. Embarrasses him. That's the only reason he gives a shit, nothing to do with other people becoming drunks. He's such a fucking hypocrite. If he'd just be honest for once, if he'd just say it embarrasses him, I'd quit. Swear to God. I'd respect him for it, and I'd quit."

They watched the storm approaching, lightning forking down, thunder rumbling away like doomsday. Tom thought about his own father, wondered why he was so mad all the time.

"He says he has great faith in me," Robert said after a while. "Great faith. Knows I'm a fine person at heart." He took a long swig from the bottle. "Makes me want to puke."

That was the only time he'd been so forthcoming about his father but Tom had the distinct impression that his opinions hadn't changed in the intervening years. The drinking certainly didn't change; Rob spent most of his undergraduate years in an alcoholic haze, though at least the booze was easier to come by on campus and he didn't have to steal it.

He was a good-natured drunk and everyone liked him. And he was very smart, with a near-photographic memory, so his grades didn't suffer. Tom's course was heavier and he didn't fool around as much, so he was generally working in their room when Rob was delivered back to the residence at the end of an evening out. A couple of friends would haul him up the stairs, dump him on the bed, nod blearily at Tom and weave their way out again. Before going to bed himself, Tom would station the plastic wastepaper basket beside the bed in case Rob decided to throw up in the middle of the night, and sling a blanket over him. It was all part of the normal routine of student life and neither of them gave it a thought.

When they were doing their master's degrees they had single rooms and saw less of each other than before, but they still got together a couple of times a week and Rob was always his same old irreverent self. Which was why it came as such a surprise when they met for a drink one night and Rob, holding a bottle of Coke, of all things, announced that he'd had a long talk with his father over the summer, as a consequence of which he'd decided to go into the ministry. And then added that as a first step he'd given up booze.

"So that you don't influence those less fortunate?" Tom had said in the seconds before he realized Rob was serious.

Rob looked slightly taken aback but then smiled and said, "That's right. 'I am my brother's keeper' and all that."

Tom had been so embarrassed for him he didn't know what to say.

He needn't have worried, though. Partway through the year Robert started backsliding on a regular basis and by the following summer, although in theory he was still studying theology, he was pretty much himself again. Both of them had summer jobs at the lumber mill that year but in the evenings they'd get together, generally down on the beach, and everything proceeded more or less as it had always done until the day of the car accident, when everything changed.

———

Out along Crow River Road Tom stopped the snowplough, switched off the engine and got out and stamped about a bit to restore the circulation to his feet. He dug out the Hershey bar from the pocket of his parka, unscrewed the top of the Thermos and stood looking out across the snow-covered landscape. Everything monochrome, shades of white and grey. Snake fences tacking their way down the edges of the fields, every rung neatly capped with snow. Dark, snow-laden trees beyond the fields. Sky a flat and endless grey. All around him snow stretched pure and clean and untouched apart from the path of the snowplough, a scar across a perfect face. Now and then a couple of crows lifted from the trees like scraps of charred paper, floated for a moment in the still air, cawing harshly to each other, then dropped back into the woods. No other sound.

He finished his coffee, relieved himself at the side of the road, the urine drilling a strangely obscene hole in the snowbank, then climbed back into the cab and set off once more, working his way down the side roads. The final section of his route was along Whitewater Road. It was pure bad luck that it came last; he would have done it first if he could, to get it over with, but that would have involved retracing his route, which would make no sense. When he started the job he'd imagined that in time he would cease to dread or even to notice the turnoff to the ravine. It was so narrow, no more than a track, really. You'd never spot it if you weren't aware of its existence.

But he was acutely aware of its existence. Always, as he got close, he could feel the tension building inside him and no matter how hard he tried to focus on the road ahead he couldn't help seeing it at the periphery of his vision, a narrow ribbon of white leading off into the woods. It had become overgrown again, but only with small stuff. A car would still be able to get down there if the snow weren't too deep. With the snow-plough he'd be able to get through now. Sometimes he wanted to. Sometimes the pull of that narrow track was so strong it scared him.

But then it would be behind him and ahead there were simply more roads to plough, the home stretch and then a hot beef sandwich and fries at Harper's, reading the paper, which he would continue to read when he got home. That would take him up to bedtime and he'd have made it through another day.

He bought his paper at the drugstore and took it into Harper's with him. It was past lunchtime and the place was empty apart from a couple of men wearing Ontario Hydro jackets in a booth by the window. Tom went straight to his favourite half-booth at the back, removed his coat, hat, gloves and scarf, settled himself into his seat, spread out the paper and scanned the front page. No major disasters. No plagues, no new wars. Prime Minister Trudeau had danced until 2:30 in the morning at the Quebec Winter Carnival, a dozen Mounties dogging his steps. Had the Mounties danced? It didn't say.

There was an interview with Frank Borman. Apparently the men on the Apollo 8 moon mission had given themselves an eighty percent chance of surviving the trip. NASA scientists had said ninety percent, but the astronauts themselves thought it was more like eighty. Frank Borman had laughed when asked if they'd been provided with poison capsules to take if the spacecraft were lost in space, and said no. No, they hadn't.

Tom thought about it. Wondered how much the risk had worried them. Probably not much. In any case they wouldn't allow themselves to dwell on such things. There would be a rigorous selection procedure for astronauts and anyone given to lying awake at night imagining his own death—anyone like himself, for instance—would be screened out at an early stage.

But how could you help it? Given the disaster of Apollo 1 they must have thought about it. They must surely have imagined possible scenarios: if not another explosion on takeoff, then a malfunction, a miscalculation by someone at mission control, a faulty connection. An explosion at least would be quick. But the other possibilities . . . unless you ran out of air first, it could take weeks. Weeks, drifting in utter darkness, simply waiting for the end.

He wondered about "the end." After it there was nothing, presumably, in the same way that there was nothing before you were conceived. And that was fine, there was nothing to fear from nothing. But the moment of death itself—the time between being and not being—that was the bit that was beyond comprehension. What was it like? Was it a fading away, a soft rope slipping through your fingers, your grasp on it so light, so gentle, that in "the end" you couldn't tell if you were still holding it or not? Or was it like the flick of a switch? Alive—dead. Like that. Alive—dead. Nothing.

In the case of a violent death—Robert's, for instance, because all deaths came back to Robert's now—it must have been the latter. Instantaneous. "Mercifully quick." Which was good, of course, except that the thing he couldn't get around in Robert's case, the thing he couldn't bear to think about but thought about all the time, was the falling. The horror of those final seconds. When you dreamed you were falling the sensation was so terrifying it woke you up. How long had that lasted, for Rob? It would be simple to work out the actual time, the height of the drop, the speed of the fall accelerating at thirty-two feet per second per second, but how about the *perceived* time, because time was relative, and quite conceivably a split second could seem to last an eternity. An eternity of terror.

Abruptly, a glass of iced water appeared in front of him. Tom stared at it, disoriented. For a minute he didn't know where he was. A knife and fork appeared. Jesus, he thought. Pull yourself together.

There were two waitresses, Jenny Bates and Carol Stubbs, who worked alternate shifts. This was Jenny. He knew by her hands, which were thin and long-fingered, the nails short and neatly filed. Carol's hands were fat and white, with perpetually chipped nail polish. Both women were in their thirties so hadn't been in school with him, but he knew them because he'd always known them—they'd been at Harper's forever.

Jenny vanished. She didn't have to ask what he wanted. His heart was banging about in his chest. He took a deep breath, then let it out slowly. Jenny reappeared and set the hot beef sandwich and fries down in front of him, the whole lot swimming in gravy. "Plate's hot," she warned, as she always did.

Tom cleared his throat. "Thanks," he said, still without looking up. To his relief his voice sounded normal.

But she didn't leave. She stood beside his table, which she never did. Reluctantly, he looked at her.

"I just wanted to say goodbye," Jenny said. Her tone was apologetic, as if she knew he wasn't to be spoken to. "This is my last day. There'll be a new girl starting tomorrow. We're moving to Calgary."

"Oh," Tom said. Something more seemed to be called for, so he tacked on, "Well, good luck."

"Thanks," she said. "And you." She hesitated and then added, "I hope things work out for you, Tom."

He felt himself flush and looked down. She knew the story, then. Of course she did. This was Struan: everybody knew everything. No doubt they talked about him behind his back. Used words like "breakdown." Phrases like "life must go on."

He was afraid Jenny might say something more, but she didn't. She just rested her fingers on the table for a minute and then went back to the till.

It was quiet after that. He spent an hour over his paper, Jenny refilling his cup from time to time without being asked. When he finished he left a good tip by way of thanks and to show that he held no grudge against her for speaking to him, tucked the paper under his arm and made his way home through the snow.

———

Sherry Rutledge was in the kitchen when he got in. She wasn't supposed to be; she was supposed to come in the mornings and to be finished by lunchtime. Mrs. Whatever was still sick and no one seemed to know when she'd be back, so Sherry was filling in, helping with the housework. Tom knew her slightly from school. They were the same age but she had been several grades below him due to having a brain the size of a baked bean. She was also, in his opinion, a slut of the first order and kept flirting with him. Tom erected a wall of ice around himself to freeze her out— never looked at her, never spoke, never acknowledged her presence in any way—but Sherry was so dumb she didn't notice.

"Hi there, Tom," she'd say, teasingly, cutely, nauseatingly, every time she saw him. "I saw you out'n the snowplough this morning. I waved but you din't even see me."

Or, "What's so interestin' in that old paper, Tom? Every time I see you you're readin' that old paper! *Every single time*!"

Did she know it wasn't the same paper *every single time*? Quite possibly not.

Now he stood in the entrance hall hanging up his coat and prising off his boots as quietly as he could. He could tell it was Sherry rather than his mother in the kitchen by the sounds she made. His mother sounded as she looked, vague and forgetful. Her footsteps paused a lot. Retraced themselves. Paused again. Sherry crashed about in a way that reminded Tom of Megan in a bad mood, but at least in Megan's case there had been something to show for it at the end of the day. Sherry did nothing, as far as he could see. The noise was just for show. He would have fired her after one day.

He stood in the entrance hall in his socks, undecided and annoyed. He could go up to his room, but it was freezing up there. She must be nearly finished—maybe if he moved the armchair around so that it was out of the direct line of sight from the kitchen door she would leave without noticing that he was home.

He crept into the living room and started to move the chair, then saw that Adam was crouched around the side of it, looking up at him with startled eyes. Since the day of their father's outburst, Adam had claimed the two square feet of floor between Tom's chair and the wall as his refuge whenever their father was home, but until now Tom hadn't seen him there at any other time. Did it mean he was afraid of Sherry? The thought came to him in a violent rush that if he ever had reason to think Sherry was being unkind to Adam *in any way*, he would grab her by the hair and throw her out the door. The savagery of the thought took his breath away. It was as if it had been lying in wait in some dark cave inside him and had suddenly burst out.

"What are you doing?" he whispered to Adam.

Adam looked at him, eyes wide. "Nothing," he whispered back.

"Has she been mean to you?" Tom jerked his head in the direction of the kitchen.

Adam shook his head.

"Why are you hiding in there, then?"

"I don't like her," Adam said. Then looked anxious, as if such an answer might not be allowed.

Tom suppressed a snort of laughter. "Neither do I. Why don't you go up to Mum's room?"

She would be in bed—she always lay down in the afternoon even if there wasn't a new baby—but probably not asleep.

"She's with the baby."

"That doesn't matter. You can be in there too. Mum won't mind."

Adam looked down. He rolled a blue and yellow dump truck back and forth along the edge of the rug. Tom felt frustration rising. Did his mother simply not *see* Adam? Could she not see that he was feeling displaced? Wouldn't any normal mother be aware of that possibility, with the coming of a new baby?

He thought back over the arrival of his various brothers, trying to remember how his mother had behaved, but it had all been different because Megan was there. He had a memory—many memories—of his mother drifting around with a baby curled between her breasts in a sling contraption she had devised in order to have her hands free. Probably she had been just as preoccupied then as she was now, but no one was aware of it because Megan, in her fearsomely efficient way, provided for all their needs. It came to Tom suddenly that his mother didn't actually care for her children very much once they passed the baby stage. It was just babies she liked. Maybe that was why she kept having more.

Now he looked at his youngest-brother-but-one and reluctantly took pity on him.

"You can come up to my room with me until she goes," he said, deciding not to risk staying downstairs. If Sherry spotted him she'd start talking to him, and the thought of it made his stomach turn. "Just this once. Understand?"

Adam nodded. He stood up quickly and gathered a few cars from his Matchbox fleet in his arms and the two of them crept up the stairs.

They sat on the bed. Adam ran his cars up and over the mountain ranges of the bedclothes. Tom stared at the wall, loathing Sherry Rutledge. He'd left his paper downstairs and didn't have anything to read. The safe, smooth pattern of his day had been reduced to rubble. This is ridiculous, he thought. In his mind's eye he saw himself and Adam, sitting side by side on a bed in a freezing cold room. Hiding from the hired help. How absurd could you get? He should go downstairs, tell her to get out and from now on to come in the mornings like she was supposed to. But that would mean talking to her.

Something was gnawing at the edges of his mind, demanding attention. It was a smell. A bad smell. He looked around the room trying to trace the source and found it right beside him. Adam.

Tom looked at him properly, saw that his hair was matted, glued down with something or other, possibly snot. There was food encrusted around his mouth, his ears were disgusting, and he was wearing pyjamas with a sweater on top, socks that didn't match and no shoes. Plus he stank. There was no other word for it.

"How long is it since you had a bath?" Tom demanded, still keeping his voice low.

Adam looked up at him guiltily.

"You haven't done anything wrong," Tom said impatiently. "I just want to know when you last had a bath. Have you had one since the baby was born?"

Adam thought about it. Shook his head.

How long ago was that? Three weeks, more or less. Apprehension joined the frustration washing around in his guts.

"Has Mum been up today? Did she come downstairs this morning?"

Adam nodded.

"Did she get you lunch?"

"Yes."

"What was it?"

"Soup."

Well, that was something, Tom thought. And at breakfast there had been cornflakes and milk and bread. So the basics were under control, which meant he didn't have to worry about it. He wouldn't worry about it. He refused to. So what if Adam smelled like a cesspit; he had his own bedroom—Megan's old room—so no one had to sleep with him. No one ever died of needing a bath.

There was a sound from downstairs—the kitchen door opening. Tom found himself holding his breath. What if she came upstairs and saw the two of them sitting there? Who gives a shit? he told himself furiously. Who gives a shit what Sherry Rutledge sees or doesn't see?

He could hear her walking about in the living room. Her footsteps crossed to the foot of the stairs. Adam was holding his breath too.

Abruptly, a door slammed—the outside door, and then the inner door—and Corey's voice said, "—blood all over the snow! Go look if you don't believe me!"

The boys, coming home from school.

"Blood doesn't prove anything, *moron*." (Peter's voice, curdled with contempt.) "Someone could have had a nosebleed, or run over a dog or something, and anyway if she broke his *jaw* it wouldn't *bleed*, jaws don't *bleed*."

Sherry's voice, shrill and angry: "What're you two doin' comin' in here in your boots? Now you've tracked snow and muck all over the floor!"

There was a brief pause during which Tom imagined Peter and Corey giving Sherry their dead-fish stares and then Peter said, "And anyway she wouldn't be strong enough to break anybody's jaw. She's a *girl*, in case you didn't know. She's got *tits*."

And Corey said, "I know she's got *tits*, *stupid*, that's why she hit him—he tried to grab her tits, right there in the *street*! And it *bled* 'cause she knocked out some of his *teeth*. Teeth *bleed*, in case you didn't know. She didn't just slap him, she hauled off and *punched* him. She punched him right in the *face* and knocked him down and somebody had to go get Dr. Christopherson and everything. And she just *stood* there, looking down at him, and then her brother came and she got into his car and drove off. It was *fantastic*!"

A crow of delight from Peter: "You're in *love* with her! I'm going to tell *everybody*, I'm going to tell the whole *world*!"

There was a crash and a yell and a violent thump and then Sherry's voice shrieked, "You are the stupidest kids I ever seen in my *life*. I'm *goin'*, and if this house isn't clean it's you two's fault!"

And there was the sound of her stomping across the room and into the entrance hall and a minute later the inner door slammed and then the outer door and she was gone.

Tom looked down at Adam, who was looking up at him, hope in his eyes.

"Saved!" Tom said, and Adam grinned at him and the two of them got up and went downstairs.

CHAPTER SEVEN

Megan

London, February 1966

Megan's first job was selling cosmetics at Dickins & Jones on Regent Street but she only lasted a week. It wasn't the makeup that got her down—she'd had a lipstick herself until it got stolen along with her suitcase—it was the day creams and night creams and the promises of eternal youth. She went back to Mrs. Jamison in Personnel and asked if there might be a job in some other department.

"What's wrong with cosmetics, Megan?" Mrs. Jamison asked. "It is Megan, isn't it?" She was in her late thirties, Megan guessed, and very smart in both senses of the word. She wore a crisp black trouser suit just like a man's but it looked better on her.

"It's the face creams," Megan said. "They're just . . ." She was on the point of saying "ridiculous"—why not call a spade a spade—when it occurred to her that Mrs. Jamison might use them herself. ". . . So expensive," she finished lamely.

Mrs. Jamison nodded gravely. "Some of them are," she agreed. "But you don't need to buy them, Megan, you just need to sell them. If women want to spend their money on such things, it's their choice, isn't it?"

"Yes, but . . . ," Megan said. She liked Mrs. Jamison and didn't want to appear difficult. ". . . Sometimes they ask if the creams actually work, if they really keep you looking young. It doesn't feel . . . it just seems . . ."

Mrs. Jamison looked as if she was trying to hide a smile. "You don't have to say they work," she said. "If you like, you can say you haven't tried them yourself so you can't say for certain. You don't know they *don't* work, now do you? Not everybody is lucky enough to have lovely skin like yours, Megan. Some women feel they need a little help with their appearance, especially as they get older. And if it makes them feel better, what's wrong with that?"

It seemed to Megan there *was* something wrong with that, but she couldn't put her finger on exactly what. "I think I'd rather sell something people actually need," she said decidedly.

Mrs. Jamison studied her for a moment, the smile still lurking at the corners of her mouth. "How about clothes?" she said. "There's a vacancy in women's fashions. You'd agree that people need clothes?"

"Absolutely," Megan said gratefully. "Especially in this weather." It was still raining—it hadn't stopped since she arrived—and it felt colder outside than she remembered ever being in Struan, despite the fact that the puddles she negotiated on her way to and from work weren't even close to freezing.

Mrs. Jamison laughed, though Megan hadn't meant to be funny. "Go and see Mrs. Timms," she said. "First floor. Tell her I sent you."

Women's fashions got Megan down too, but she stuck it out for Mrs. Jamison's sake and because she knew there wouldn't be anything better. She had no objection to the clothes—not all of them were absurd and some of them, mostly the sweaters ("jumpers" or "jerseys" they called them), she liked very much and wished she could afford. It was because a lot of the time there was nothing to do and doing nothing nearly killed her. On Saturdays and on Thursday evenings (Thursday was late-night shopping) the store was frantic but during the week there were sometimes more sales assistants than customers.

The other assistants, most of them her own age or younger, seemed quite happy chatting with each other for hours on end. They talked exclusively about clothes and boys and wore miniskirts and skimpy dresses with bright circles or squares all over them. When one of them bought something new the others got so excited they screamed.

Megan, conscious of her sensible skirt and plain white blouse, both bought for the interview, did her best to join in, though not with the screaming. She'd smile at some new purchase and say, "That looks nice," but the girls would look at her with puzzled smiles as if she were talking a foreign language.

Tracy, who was small and pretty with hair cut in a neat dark cap, was getting married as soon as she and her boyfriend had saved enough money to buy a house because she "*refused full stop!*" to live with his parents. She was on "The Pill" (when she first mentioned it, Megan had no idea what pill she was talking about) but kept forgetting to take it and was constantly having scares. Julie's mum was divorced and going with a man who drove a Bentley and had a son who looked like Mick Jagger but without the lips. (*Ooooh!* the other girls said, and shrieked with laughter.) Viv, who was tall and thin with elegant legs and long blond hair, wanted to be a model. She practised walking as if her hips were dislocated, up and down the aisle between the dresses, when Mrs. Timms, the floor manager, was on her lunch break.

All these things and more Megan had learned about her fellow shop assistants, and yet the girls remained as unknown and unknowable to her as a flock of flamingoes. It wasn't that they deliberately tried to exclude her—she could see that—it was that they seemed to exist in a different world. Like aliens, she thought. Except that she was the alien. They were so strange that sometimes she wondered if she were making them up—maybe the whole thing was a dream and when she woke she'd be back in her own bed in Struan and it would be time to get up and turf the boys out of bed and get breakfast on the table. Many times she wished that were so, and that wish dismayed her. Who'd have thought she could be so unadventurous, so timid?

You need to pull yourself together, she said to herself. This is what you wanted—something new, something different. You should be enjoying it! She gave herself an ultimatum: enjoy it or go home. But it was an empty threat. She knew she couldn't go home, not yet anyway; she'd only been here six weeks. And no matter how hard she tried she didn't seem to have the strength, or the will, to enjoy it.

She searched the papers for other jobs but apart from being a waitress or a cleaner—and she'd spent her whole life so far being both—everything required qualifications she didn't have.

During her lunch hour she grimly put up her new umbrella (she'd have happily sold umbrellas all day long) and explored the streets around Dickins & Jones: Regent Street, Oxford Street, Bond Street, Carnaby Street—famous names, she knew that now. With the sole exception of those living in the Canadian North, everybody on the planet knew about Carnaby Street. She tried to immerse herself in this new world—the chaotically colourful stores, the constant background beat of music leaking out of doorways, the clothes and shoes and jewellery spilling out onto the streets—but there was too much of everything. She found herself longing for the drab ordinariness of the Hudson's Bay store in Struan with its wide, dark aisles and piles of shirts and socks and underwear that didn't change from one year to the next.

She couldn't seem to focus on anything here, far less become a part of it. Sometimes when she got back to Dickins & Jones she couldn't remember a thing she'd seen.

There was an ache inside her, centred more or less mid-chest. It was with her all the time; sometimes she was conscious of it even in her sleep. It exhausted her, she who normally had enough energy for ten people. She wondered if she could be ill. Maybe she had some low-grade infection that was pulling her down. Perhaps that was what prevented her from enjoying things.

Morning and night she had to gird herself for the ordeal of travelling to work and back. She went by "underground," which turned out to be a long tubular version of hell, especially at the end of the day. At the evening rush hour people poured down the steps at Oxford Circus in a flood, great waves of them surging down the escalators, along the echoing corridors and out onto the platforms, where they waited, heaving and swelling, for the trains. There would be a thundering in the tunnel, growing with tremendous speed, and a train would roar out of the darkness and come to a stop. The doors would roll open and people would pour out and then the waiting throngs would lunge forward, forcing their way onto the train, more and more of them, until they were crammed together so tightly Megan could hardly breathe. She was always dizzy with relief when she reached her station and could push her way out at last into the cold night air and walk home alone with her umbrella through the dark wet streets.

She thought of the space, back home in Canada. The vast and glorious emptiness of the North. So much land, so few people. She hadn't appreciated it, hadn't realized how beautiful it was, until now.

———

The journey into work and out again was not the hardest part of her day. The hardest part was the moment she opened the door of number 31 Lansdown Terrace. Although she had stopped expecting to find her suitcase waiting for her in the hall, she could not rid herself of the hope that the photographs would be there. Whoever stole the suitcase could have no earthly use for them and surely he or she would realize their importance to her. It would be so easy to put them in an envelope and slip them through the let-terbox—or not bother with the envelope, just shove the photos loose through the door. Every evening she searched through the pile of bills and papers that no one else bothered to pick up off the floor. The first time she did it she found her last letter to Cora, unopened and mottled with footprints, but the photos were never there. Every evening she had to fight down the disappointment. You're being ridiculous! she thought, heaping her coat on top of one of the bicycles in the hall and making her way through to the kitchen at the back of the house. Just ridiculous! Grow up!

When she'd first seen the kitchen Megan's immediate impulse had been to buy herself a pair of rubber gloves and an economy-size container of household bleach and scour it top to bottom, but she'd stopped herself in time. She hadn't flown three thousand miles to fall into that trap again. Besides, none of the others would notice, or if they did, they wouldn't like it. They were like her brothers, the girls included: they seemed to like squalor; they cre-ated it wherever they went. So each evening she cleared just enough space on the kitchen counter to prepare and cook her supper and just enough space at the kitchen table to sit down and eat it to the accompaniment of music pounding through the walls. She knew the names of some of the bands now—Beatles, Monkeys, Animals. Like a zoo. She sometimes thought that if she'd had control of the volume she might even have liked some of them.

From time to time one of her flat-mates would wander into the kitchen. Megan would say hi and sometimes they'd say hi back, depending on how stoned they were. She'd figured out what the strange smell in the flat was.

She never saw any of her flat-mates prepare a meal. Sometimes there would be a loaf of sliced bread sitting amidst the chaos on the counter, the slices gradually disappearing as the evening wore on, but that aside, they all seemed to exist on fish and chips that they brought home wrapped in newspaper and stinking of vinegar. The oily, reeking papers littered the flat.

She was powerfully aware of not belonging. As with the girls at Dickins & Jones, there seemed to be no common ground. Sarah, the girl with the bug-like glasses who had been kind to her on the night of her arrival, Megan liked, but even she was exceedingly strange. It turned out she owned the flat—in fact, owned the whole house. Her parents, it seemed, were rich. Megan tried to pay rent, but Sarah wouldn't take the money. When Megan protested, saying she couldn't simply stay without paying, Sarah had smiled her gentle, unfocused smile and said, "Why not? Everybody else does."

Megan would have liked to get to know her better but somehow it wasn't possible.

"Do you have a job?" she asked tentatively one evening.

"Oh, sort of," Sarah replied, lighting a misshapen little roll-up. "I work in an art gallery. Just a commercial one."

"Oh," Megan said. "That sounds interesting. What do you do?"

"Nothing, really. Just smile at people. Have you seen my handbag? I put it down somewhere." And she wandered out.

Maybe it was the pot. They all lived in their own little clouds. It surprised Megan that any of them managed to get up and go to work in the mornings. Not all of them did; some appeared to spend twenty-four hours a day slumped in front of the television. Sponging off Sarah, who didn't care.

The only one who seemed even to notice Megan was Zack, the hairy, bearded one who had blamed her for the Vietnam War the night she arrived. He'd hang around in the kitchen in the evenings when she was making supper (a chop or a piece of chicken or sometimes a stew), getting in the way and trying to persuade her to smoke a joint. Megan had no intention of being persuaded to do anything by anybody, least of all Zack.

"What is it with you American-sorry-sorry-Canadians?" he would say petulantly. (He reminded her of the twins—they used that same tone when they didn't get their own way.) "You don't drink, you don't smoke, you don't do drugs—what do you do?"

"We work," Megan said. It made Canadians sound prissy, but she didn't care what Zack thought of Canadians.

Zack snorted—he wouldn't have touched work with a barge pole. "You want to try living a little." He'd hold his damp little weed in front of her nose. "One puff. Jesus, what's the matter with you, just take one little puff."

"Do you mind getting out of the way? I need to get to the sink."

"How about sex? Do Canadian women ever have sex?"

"Do English men ever grow up?" Megan said, straining rice. "Or do they stay twelve years old all their lives?"

"Jesus, you're one uptight female, you know that?"

She'd found a tiny box room, hardly bigger than a cupboard, to sleep in so that she wouldn't have to listen to people having sex two feet away. It was full of cardboard boxes, which she dragged out and deposited in the centre of the living room floor to see if anyone would notice and throw them away, which nobody did. The boxes stayed as she'd left them for three days, after which they were gradually trampled flat and became part of the carpet.

The box room was exactly the width of the mattress and about four feet longer, long enough that she could close the door at the foot of it and stash her few belongings at the head. Along with a new hot water bottle, she'd bought herself two pairs of sheets and pillowcases and two blankets. With her coat on top of them she was warm enough to sleep. There was no light in the room but she bought herself a flashlight—a "torch" they called it here. One night Zack stumbled in and lay down on top of her. She hit him in the face with the torch and he retreated, bellowing. After that she shoved the mattress down to block the door before getting into bed.

She felt safe in her cupboard. Safe from what she didn't know, because there was no real threat in the house—the likes of Zack didn't worry her. It was just that the tough, resilient core of herself, on which she'd always assumed she could rely no matter what, seemed to have developed cracks, and she didn't want to strain it any further. Maybe it had never been as tough as she'd thought.

She found it impossible to imagine Cora in this house. Cora wouldn't have fitted in any better than she did. Supposedly she'd left after having a fight with Seb, which suggested she'd had a relationship with him, but Seb spent his life in a virtual coma on the sofa in the living room. When Megan asked him if Cora had left an address or been in touch, it took her question so long to penetrate the fog she wondered if he was asleep with his eyes open. Then he slowly turned his head, focused on her face and said, "What?"

The Cora whom Megan remembered was far too sensible to get involved with someone like that. Could she have changed that much? Could people become *less* adult and sensible over time rather than more? Or had Megan not known her as well as she thought? Maybe Cora had decided to "live a little" as Zack put it. Maybe the fact that Megan didn't fit in here was nothing to do with being foreign; maybe she, Megan, was simply stuck in a rut and determined to stay there, afraid to try new things.

So I'm a coward, she thought, curling herself around her hot water bottle, safe in her cupboard. I'm a coward.

After supper each evening she searched the Rooms to Rent section in the *Evening Standard* but there was nothing she could afford that she wouldn't have to share. She longed for a place of her own. She thought she wouldn't be so lonely in a place of her own.

———

10th February 1966

Dear Megan,

We haven't heard a word from you since you left home and I haven't been able to sleep, I'm so worried. Please write to us.

Love, Mum

She hadn't written home because she hadn't known what to say that wouldn't reveal her unhappiness. But when she saw her mother's writing on the envelope, she saw her mother's face, the strained look she had when any of her children were later home than expected or in any way unaccounted for. It wasn't fair to make her so anxious.

26th February 1966

Dear Mum and Dad,

I'm sorry I haven't written sooner but I've been really busy. London is amazing. I've got a job—I work in a big store on Regent Street, which is one of the main shopping streets in London. The buildings are huge and really grand. The store I work in is called Dickins & Jones and it's about as big as Struan all on its own. It sells clothes and stuff, all really expensive. There are thousands and thousands of people everywhere you go. The streets are crowded all the time and the roads are so busy you wouldn't believe it. There is never a single minute when it is totally quiet, even at night.

How are you all? How is Adam? I'd really like a picture of him if you can find the camera. Tom might have taken it with him to Toronto. Will he be coming home for Easter? He could take some pictures then. I'd really like pictures of all of you.

Well, that's all the news for now. I'll write again soon. I'd love a letter from you if you have time to write.

Love, Megan

She was pleased with the letter. It made her sound like the person she used to be.

13th March 1966

Dear Megan, (her mother's somewhat flowery hand)

Thank you for your letter. I was afraid something terrible had happened to you!

There is no news here except the twins say they're going to join the navy. They don't realize that they could be sent anywhere, especially if there's a war.

Peter and Corey were both sent home from school for fighting. They weren't fighting each other, they were fighting other boys. The school says they can't go back for a week.

*Your holiday sounds very interesting. When do you
expect to get home?*

Love, Mum

15th March 1966

Dear Megan, (her father's precise, business-like script)

*Thank you for your letter. I'm glad you've settled in all
right.*

*It's interesting that you are working on Regent Street.
It will have been named after the Prince Regent. His father,
George III, was insane, so George (IV) ruled as "Regent"
in his place from 1811 until 1820, when his father died and he
ascended the throne himself.*

*I believe Regent Street was designed by John Nash as
part of a grand development of the centre of London during
the Regency period.*

*That's about all the news from this end. Everyone is
well. Tired of the snow, of course.*

All the best,

*PS I assume from your letter that you are managing all
right financially, but it would be a shame if, due to travel
costs or entry charges, you were not able to visit some of the
great sights of the capital (the Tower of London, St. Paul's
Cathedral, the National Gallery, etc.) while you are there.
If that is the case you should let me know.*

The problem was that, having relearned how to cry, she now
had difficulty not crying at the drop of a hat. When she read her
parents' letters (sent in the same envelope to save postage) she

cried even though she was in the kitchen and anyone could have walked in on her. Her mother's letter made her cry because it reminded her of why she couldn't go home; her father's because in the whole of the English language there weren't words to describe how little she cared about the Tower of London, St. Paul's Cathedral and the National Gallery.

Her father hadn't signed his letter for the simple reason (this she knew) that he hadn't known whether to put "Father" or "Dad," and for some inexplicable reason that made her miss him. Neither letter had so much as mentioned Adam, and Megan knew as well as she knew her own name that no one would ever send her a picture of him.

———

From time to time Mrs. Jamison walked through Women's Wear on her way to somewhere else. Whenever Megan saw her coming she tried to look busy and efficient, but on a Monday morning in April she didn't see her coming. There were no customers. Tracy and Julie were giggling over by the till and Megan was standing alone by the window in the coat department, watching the silver trickles of rain running down the glass. Suddenly there was Mrs. Jamison, two feet away and smiling at her. The other two girls began refolding sweaters, trying to look busy.

"Well, Megan," Mrs. Jamison said. "How are you getting along?"

"Very well, thank you, Mrs. Jamison."

"Are you enjoying fashion more than cosmetics?"

"Yes. Yes, I am. Thank you very much."

"Good," Mrs. Jamison said. "I'm glad to hear that." But she looked at Megan with a searching expression for a moment more before going on her way. The searching expression worried Megan. It worried her still more the following day when Mrs. Timms came and told her Mrs. Jamison wanted to see her in her office. She wondered if Mrs. Jamison had seen through her and knew that she didn't like the job and was no good at it. Or if maybe Mrs. Timms had complained about her lack of enthusiasm. She thought Mrs. Jamison was going to give her the sack.

"Sit down, Megan," Mrs. Jamison said. "I thought it was time we had a chat."

She had a large desk in a small, cramped office. There was nothing on the desk except a green blotter, a pen and a sheet of paper Megan recognized as her own application form.

Megan sat down, her heart thumping. It occurred to her that the reason she was afraid of being fired was not because she didn't want to leave Dickins & Jones but because she didn't want to leave Mrs. Jamison. For some reason Mrs. Jamison seemed to like her and to be interested in her, which made her unique in the world outside Struan.

Mrs. Jamison's hands, which were slim and elegant like the rest of her, were folded neatly on the blotter in front of her. "Now then," she said. "Tell me how you're getting on. Not just here at work, but generally. Have you found somewhere nice to live? Do you have friends over here? Or relatives?"

To her horror Megan felt a lump rise up in her throat. She looked sharply away, appalled at herself.

Mrs. Jamison waited for a moment and then carried on smoothly as if she hadn't noticed anything. "I know it can be quite difficult when you're starting out," she said. "Particularly if you're a long way from home and don't know anyone. And if you're having problems of any sort I hope you would tell me about them. But we can discuss that later, if you like. Or another time. For now let's just talk about your job."

She paused, and Megan managed to look at her and make a stab at a smile.

"My guess is that you're a very capable young woman," Mrs. Jamison went on, "and I imagine you don't see yourself being a shop assistant forever."

Megan swallowed. The lump seemed to have subsided, more or less. "Oh, it's fine," she said, and her voice sounded all right. "I mean, maybe not forever, but for now it's fine. Really."

Mrs. Jamison nodded. She seemed to be waiting for Megan to go on.

"It's not always very busy, that's all," Megan said. "Sometimes there's not much to do. I'm used to being busy all the time, so it's a bit . . . slow. Just sometimes. Mostly it's fine."

Mrs. Jamison picked up Megan's application form and studied it.

"You're twenty-one?"

"Yes."

"And you have no formal qualifications. That's right, is it?"

Megan nodded.

"Why is that, Megan? A clever girl like you. We didn't really go into that at your interview, did we?"

"I was needed at home," Megan said. "There are nine of us—well, there were—and the others are all boys and my mother wasn't very . . . my mother needed help."

She had a sudden vivid memory of her mother smiling down at her, saying, "What would I do without you, Megan?" She couldn't have been more than seven or eight at the time. She'd adored her mother. The other little girls in her class had gone to each other's houses after school to play at dressing up or some other silly game and Megan had felt sorry for them. She'd gloried in being needed and, as time went on, she was needed more and more.

When Henry, brother number four, was born with a hole in his heart, her mother's attention was entirely taken up with him. After he died, she'd seemed to lose interest in everything for a while. Then she became pregnant again. By the time Peter arrived, closely followed by Corey, the roles were set: Megan's mother looked after the babies and Megan looked after the rest.

She didn't mind. She was proud of how much her mother relied on her. In any case it had seemed perfectly natural; she was better at running the house than her mother. As the boys got older she'd been better at running them too. Boys needed a firm hand and her mother's hands weren't firm. Megan's were.

When she was in grade eleven Mr. Hardy, her history/guidance teacher in high school, had called her into his office one day for a "little chat" about her future. He'd suggested secretarial school or maybe a course in home economics. Megan had replied that her mother couldn't spare her and Mr. Hardy had smiled and said she had her own future to think of and he was sure her mother wouldn't want to stand in her way.

Megan had been insulted by his easy dismissal of how indispensable she was. She'd wanted to say, My mother has just had a miscarriage and is probably crying in her bedroom right this minute and you think I should go off and be a secretary. Who's going to get supper?

He asked her to talk to her parents and come back and see him in a week, and she'd said she would and then didn't.

Now, sitting in Mrs. Jamison's office three thousand miles from home, it occurred to Megan that her mother might have been better off if she'd had to get supper. If she'd had more to do and to think about, maybe she wouldn't have gone on to try for yet another baby, and had another miscarriage and then a stillbirth.

Perhaps Mr. Hardy had been right after all. She should have detached herself from her family much earlier. Why hadn't she seen that? Maybe it wasn't that her mother genuinely couldn't manage without her; maybe it was the other way around: she—Megan—had made herself indispensable because she was afraid of leaving home. Of leaving her mother.

It was Tom, home from university the summer Megan was nineteen, who had finally forced her to confront the question of her own future. "There's a world out there, Meg," he'd said seriously, not teasing for once, "and you're going to miss it. If you don't get out of here soon, you won't get out at all."

She'd been angry with him at the time, but it made her think. She'd looked around and seen that those of her classmates with anything about them had gone. The others had married young and were raising families of their own. She was the only one still at home. She saw that Tom was right, but even then she'd almost left it too late. She was nineteen when she decided to leave and twenty-one before she finally managed to go.

The radiator against the far wall in Mrs. Jamison's office was blasting out so much heat that she'd opened the window, and Megan could hear traffic far below. London, going about its business.

Mrs. Jamison was waiting patiently.

"It was my own fault," Megan said. "Not getting any qualifications. I just didn't . . . I guess I didn't want to think about it back then."

Mrs. Jamison nodded. "Well, it's not the end of the world," she said. "There are still lots of jobs where you can work your way up. The problem is, we don't have anything of that kind here at the moment. So I'm afraid that for now, if you stay with us, it's the shop floor."

"That's all right," Megan said, so relieved that she wasn't being dismissed that for the moment she positively loved the shop floor. "It's fine. I like it. Really."

"Well, that's good," Mrs. Jamison said, though she didn't sound convinced. "But you need to give things some thought, Megan. You need to work out what you really like doing, what you're particularly good at, and then you need to find yourself a job that makes proper use of you."

"Oh, I know what I like doing," Megan said, straightening up and squaring her shoulders. "I like organizing things. I like being busy, really busy, all the time. Getting things done. I'm good at getting things done."

Mrs. Jamison smiled. "That I can believe," she said, and she stood up and the interview was over.

Megan went back to her job ridiculously buoyed up, considering that, really, nothing had changed. And somehow it didn't surprise her when, a week later, a disapproving Mrs. Timms told her that Mrs. Jamison wanted to see her again.

Mrs. Jamison said it was funny how these things sometimes happened, like two pieces of a jigsaw suddenly coming together. Friends of friends of hers had bought a small hotel, a new venture for them, and were looking for someone to help with . . . "Well, with everything," Mrs. Jamison said. "Apparently it's very run down and there's a great deal to do in order to get it up and running. And once it is, of course, there will be even more to do: hiring staff, managing the front desk—all the things that go into running a hotel."

She smiled at Megan. "I shouldn't really be doing this, Dickins & Jones isn't an employment agency, but we're not making proper use of you here, Megan. I think you should go and talk to them. I've given them your name. I'm making no promises, you understand. It will be up to them. And to you, of course."

And like two pieces of a jigsaw suddenly coming together, that was that.

CHAPTER EIGHT

Edward

Struan, February 1969

The thermometer read thirty degrees below zero this morning. It was so still out there, so silent, it was as if the air itself was frozen. You felt it might crack at any moment and shower down around you in infinitesimal slivers of ice.

In the summers we get a lot of tourists up here and there's no denying it is very beautiful then, what with the lakes and the forest and the long hot days. You hear people—Canadians, Americans, even some from overseas—say they'd love to buy a place in this area when they retire, and live here all year round. I'd suggest they come and spend a winter first. Cold is one of those things it's very hard to imagine in the abstract; you have to experience it for yourself.

And it isn't just the cold that makes the winters hard; the snow means communities like ours are effectively cut off from the rest of the world for significant stretches of time. Now that there are Ski-Doos and decent snowploughs it's better than it used to be, but we're still frequently snowed in and the sense of isolation can be profound. A few weeks ago—on Christmas Eve, in fact—American astronauts orbited the moon, arguably the most significant achievement in the history of the human race, and I read afterwards that "The whole world" had watched it on television. Not us. For a start we don't have a television—we do not need another source of noise and irritation in this house—but even those in Struan who do saw nothing. The first blizzard of the winter hit us that week; all the power lines were down and the roads and the railway were blocked for three days. By the time we read about it, saw that staggeringly beautiful photograph of our Earth suspended in the infinity of space, the event itself was already history.

The photograph made me feel lonely. Not just for myself but for all of us, living out our insignificant lives on this small planet. For the first time I understood why people the world over feel the need to believe that we are part of some great purpose, that somebody "up there" cares what happens to us. Unfortunately, wanting something to be so does not make it so. My feeling is that we are very much on our own.

Personally I think there is dignity in accepting that. Whatever the once-Reverend Thomas might say.

At lunchtime today I braved the cold and went to the library to order Gibbon's *The History of the Decline and Fall of the Roman Empire*. He wrote it between 1776 and 1788 and I thought it might be interesting to read it alongside more modern texts.

Betty was wearing a sleeping bag, one of the old army issue ones that go right up over your head and cover everything but your face. She looked like the caterpillar in *Alice in Wonderland*. I had been feeling out of sorts—this business of shouting at the boys has been on my mind—and it lifted my spirits in the most remarkable way. She'd made slits at elbow level so that she could get her arms out to stamp the books and so forth. I asked if she'd be able to get out of the bag quickly if there were a fire and she said she wouldn't bother, she'd just stay where she was and get properly warm for the first time in six months. That reminded me of Robert Service's *The Cremation of Sam McGee*. I asked Betty if she'd read it and of course she had. That in turn reopened our discussion about books I would want to rescue before she burns down the library. I told her I would like the *Encyclopaedia Britannica* and all of the Year Books to date. I asked if she were intending to take anything herself and she thought for a minute and then said everything ever written by Margaret Laurence plus *Gone with the Wind* and *Little Women*. When I confessed that the only one of those I'd heard of was *Gone with the Wind*, she looked shocked and said, "Mr. Cartwright, you're not seriously telling me you haven't read *Little Women*!"

I don't think there's anyone else in Struan I enjoy talking to as much.

After Reverend Thomas gave his sermon on the iniquity of those who set themselves up in judgment over their fellow men (about which I was not going to think ever again), she was one of the few members of the community who seemed to have no trouble meeting my eye. I know she would have heard the sermon—she's a regular churchgoer. But Betty thinks for herself.

She says his wife has left him. Apparently she's gone to stay with a brother in Ottawa, whether as a permanent thing or not nobody knows. So he's alone in that house. Betty says she has knocked on his door several times and various other members of the congregation have done so as well, bearing food. (Women seem to think the answer to everything is food.) He answers the door and thanks them for the food but he doesn't invite anyone in.

I still cannot find it in myself to pity him.

This afternoon, not an hour after my talk with Betty about burning down the library, Sergeant Moynihan came to see me for the second time in two weeks.

"You got a minute, Mr. Cartwright?" he said, standing in the doorway of my office. He pretty much fills it, excluding the corners. The doughnuts have something to do with that, but he's a big man anyway.

"Of course," I said. "Come in. Take a seat."

He shook his head. "Somethin' to show you outside."

So I pulled on my coat and followed him out of the bank, through the parking lot at the side and around to the back. There's no reason for anyone to go around there, so it doesn't get ploughed and the snow was more than two feet deep. There were three sets of footprints—except they were more like "leg" prints—marching across the snow, leading to a trampled area under my office window. Right up against the wall there was a bundle of charred sticks.

I stopped dead when I saw them.

"Three people this time," I said after a minute. There was an odd, hollow feeling in the pit of my stomach.

"Nope," Gerry said. "One set of tracks is mine."

"Oh, of course. When did you find it?"

"Just now. I was walkin' through your car park—shortcut to Harper's, haven't had lunch yet. Saw tracks leadin' nowhere so I followed them."

"When do you think they were made?"

"Last night. Gotta be. It snowed yesterday afternoon, stopped about six, so sometime after that."

"At least you've got good footprints to work with," I said.

"Nope. They stepped in their own prints on the way out, did a good job of messin' them up. Anyway, wouldn't help much. We all wear the same damned boots in this town. Even mine are the same."

"Yours are significantly bigger." Gerry's prints wouldn't have shamed a polar bear.

"Mine are bigger'n everyone's," Gerry said. "That's why I'm not a criminal, I'd be caught'n ten minutes flat."

I laughed but the truth was I didn't feel any too happy. "It looks kind of personal," I said. "That's my office window."

"If they'd wanted to hurt you they'd have set fire to your house during the night, not the bank when it's shut. They just want to scare people. That's a pretty amateur fire, not like the one at the Giles's farm. That one went up like a torch. This one they haven't used no gasoline, nothin'—I reckon it was out before they got 'round the corner of the building. Kinda strange. But I wanna catch them before they make a mistake and somebody does get hurt."

"So what's the next step?" I said.

"You made any enemies recently?"

"Not that I'm aware of."

"You know anyone else who's had a run-in with the Picketts? Not sayin' it's them, just wonderin'."

"I haven't heard anything of that nature."

He nodded. "Okay. So. Next step is I go to Harper's and have lunch. Can't think on an empty stomach."

He's right, I know: if Joel Pickett and/or his sons intended me actual bodily harm they wouldn't target the bank knowing I wasn't in it. But still. Fire is my particular terror.

It is Sunday night already. I'd intended to spend the whole week-end in classical Rome, in a manner of speaking, instead of which I have spent it in Northern Ontario circa 1920. All to do with my father, of course. This business of his anger, which he seems to have bequeathed to me.

Anger was his defining emotion, you might say. I'm not sure what lay behind it. In fact, considering his influence on me it's remarkable how little I know about him. I suspect even my mother didn't know much. I think he arrived in the North sometime in

1919 claiming to be a war hero, though there is no reason to believe the latter is true. (There is no reason to believe anything my father said was true; he lied as naturally as breathing.) My mother told me that he was from Hamilton and that while he was off winning the First World War his brothers had cheated him out of the family business, but that would merely have been what he told her.

She didn't say what brought him north, but I can hazard a guess. Silver was discovered up here in 1903 when they were building the railway. According to local folklore a blacksmith who was working on the railway came out of his tent one morning and saw a fox prowling around the camp. He picked up a hammer and threw it at the fox, missed, hit a rock, chipped off a chunk of it and exposed a vein of pure silver lying underneath.

Whether or not that tale was true, the find triggered a spec-tacular silver rush. If my father hadn't heard about it before he went off to war he certainly would have when he got home. By that time everyone in North America had heard about it. The largest chunk of solid silver ever discovered—the so-called "sil-ver sidewalk"—was found less than thirty miles from where I'm sitting now. The ore lay close to the surface—in some places you could literally pick it up off the ground—so in theory at least, even men who knew nothing about mining had a chance of strik-ing it rich.

Easy money. The kind my father liked best. I can just see him, newly arrived from the civilized south, stumbling around in the bush in his cheap city shoes, feverishly chipping away at bits of rock without the first idea of what raw silver even looked like. He wouldn't have asked anyone because, firstly, that would have meant admitting that there was something he didn't know, and secondly, he would have assumed whoever he asked would lie to him. My father had the lowest view of human nature of anyone I have ever known. In later years, when he made one of his many soon-to-be-proved-worthless discoveries and had to leave his

claim in order to go to the recording office down in Jupe to record it, my brothers and I would be recruited to stand guard until
he returned. He used to arm us with sticks of dynamite to chase
off claim-jumpers. I'd have been about seven the first time. He
made us practise lighting the fuse and throwing the stick at a tree.
If he hadn't been so deadly serious—"Aim for the head," he'd
roar, having notched the tree at head height—we might have
considered it fun. As it was, I was so terrified I didn't sleep for
nights afterwards.

As it happened, he and the others who joined the rush at the
end of the war were too late. Men had been crawling over the area
like ants for well over a decade by then and the time of picking up
raw silver on the surface was long gone. Fortunes were still being
made, but only by the cigar-smoking "Silver Barons" from the
south—Toronto, Chicago, New York—who came up to visit the
area now and then in private railway carriages decked out with
dining cars and libraries. They could afford to sink shafts and follow the seams of silver down into the ground. For the solitary
prospector , though, it was over.

But nobody told my father that and he wouldn't have believed
them if they had. He believed—because he wanted to believe and
because, as time went on and the days became weeks and then
months and then eventually years, he *had* to believe—that beneath
the next rock he turned over would lie a seam so rich, so pure,
he'd be spooning out the silver like honey from a pot.

I don't know how he met my mother but my guess is he went
looking for her, or someone like her, soon after arriving in the
North, not for the normal reasons but because prospecting costs
money. You need to eat, your boots wear out, you run out of
dynamite; maybe you want to buy a stake in a promising claim.
You don't want a job because that would mean time away from
prospecting, so what better than a wife from a well-to-do family?
By that time my mother's family, canny hard-working Scots that

they were, had a prosperous farm and shares in several profitable mines. So no mystery there.

The mystery is what attracted my mother to him and what possessed her parents to allow the marriage. Possibly they were starting to fear that time was running out for her. She had a strawberry mark on her cheek, not a very large one but maybe it counted against her in the marriage stakes. By the time she and my father married she was twenty-four, which was old to be unmarried back then. And of course my father was a stranger to the North so they would have no way of checking whatever story he told. He could be very charming, very convincing.

He was handsome in a rough kind of way. From what I've read (I've finally started going through her adult diaries) it's clear that my mother thought he was the man of her dreams.

=====

Emily thought I was the man of her dreams. I know that because she told me so after I got home from the war. Tears streaming down her face. She said I had deceived her, which was not the case. In fact, it was the other way around; she deceived me. She made me think we shared the same dreams when in fact her dreams were limited to a ring on her finger and a baby at her breast. She had—still has—no more curiosity about the outside world than an oyster.

But that is by the way.

=====

I spent the whole of yesterday in a welter of frustration, trying to do justice to the books about Rome and instead reliving things from the past that would have been better left forgotten, and as a consequence, of course, I couldn't get to sleep last night. I kept seeing the image of my father I dreamed about a few weeks ago—him standing on the roof of the farmhouse, outlined against a wall of flame so vast that it seemed to fill the whole horizon.

Anyway, after lying awake for what felt like half the night I came downstairs and got out the box file containing the diaries from my mother's adult years. It wasn't that I expected to learn anything from them, just that I decided it was better to know what was in them than to keep wondering.

As I believe I said earlier, very little of what my mother wrote in adulthood survived the fire, and many of the scraps that did survive were so frail and brittle they began to disintegrate as soon as I touched them. It took me several hours last night and most of today to get them into any sort of order, and it would have taken longer had my mother's handwriting not provided a clue. I was able to see straight away that the writings related to two separate periods in her life, one at the beginning of her marriage and the other about fifteen years later. In the early ones her writing is firm, rounded and flowing—the writing of a confident young woman. In the later ones it is tight and cramped, as if scribbled in great haste; there is a kind of fearful urgency about it, as if she was afraid of being discovered, of being "caught in the act."

I haven't got as far as reading those later portions yet and I don't think I'm up to it this evening. But in the earlier ones I did find the answer to a question I have wondered about for years, namely why, given that they lived less than thirty miles away and must have known at least something of the situation, my mother's parents didn't help the young couple out in the desperate early years of their marriage.

It turns out that they did; in fact, they were extremely generous. As a wedding present they gave my parents a considerable sum of money, enough not only to build themselves a house but also to start up an outfitters in the nearest mining town, supplying necessities to prospectors and townspeople.

There is no other outfitter within two days' travel along
bush roads—my mother wrote—*so there is genuine need*
of such an establishment. Father and Mother feel that it will
provide a more reliable income than investing in a mine,
and Stanley agrees.

So the four of them had discussed the plan and my father let them think he went along with it. But then, shortly after they had moved to the new mining town and before work on the new house had begun, came this:

Stanley says there has been a great discovery in Quebec,
which he believes we must inspect before others learn
of it. He says there is no proper town there yet, but that
will be to our advantage as we will have our choice of
sites for our camp.

I wish that it were not so far away from Mother and
Father but I told Stanley, truthfully, that I did not mind
where we lived so long as I was with him.

There is no suggestion that she was concerned about abandoning the plan they had agreed on. Perhaps my father told her it was just a temporary detour. In any case, at that stage she probably trusted his judgment; she hadn't had time yet to find out that he had none. What he had instead was a lethal combination of pride and stupidity that was going to take them straight to the bottom, but she clearly had no inkling of that.

Conditions in the mining camps back then were very primitive but that didn't seem to worry my mother either; in fact, she seems to have enjoyed the challenge.

. . . no streets, just tents and shacks amidst a great swamp
of mud and tree stumps. Water must be fetched from the

lake and I cook our meals over the campfire in front of our
tent. Last night I procured a dining table—a dynamite box
(empty!), turned on its side. It serves very well and I am
proud of it!

All day the woods ring with the chinking of picks
and hammers on rock, with now and then the deep boom
of blasting. The men talk of nothing but silver. They
say this is the richest discovery that has ever been made!
Stanley has bought a fifty percent share in a mine. He is
tremendously excited . . .

I find it painful even to read those last two sentences. The
writing is all fast, looping, free-flowing curves, the hand of a young
woman carefree and optimistic almost to the point of foolishness.
And still not the faintest hint of concern about my father's use of
their money.

Unsurprisingly, her parents weren't as happy with the turn
things had taken. My mother wrote to them regularly (she men-
tions receiving their responses) and I imagine her tone was much
the same as in her diaries. They must have been appalled. The
letters would have taken months to go back and forth but eventually, having learned amongst other things that my mother was
pregnant, they decided enough was enough, and my grandfather
set off to track them down. The result was a furious confronta-
tion between him and his son-in-law. My mother's distress was so
great that when she recorded it later the nib of the pen scored
through the paper.

. . . shouting at each other right there in front of our tent
and I could see that Stanley was beside himself with the
shame of it, his wife's father shouting at him like that for
everyone to hear . . . never seen him so angry, I feared that
he would strike my father.

*. . . when Stanley had still not returned I went down to
the lake and walked along the shore, sobbing with anger and
grief. At first I did not know what, exactly, I was grieving
for, but then I realized it was for my parents, my closeness
to them, which today has come to an end. My loyalty is to
Stanley. Just days ago he said to me that I was the first
person in his life ever to have faith in him, which is both
terrible and wonderful. I will never let him down. What
my father said to him was unforgivable. I have told
Stanley that I will never speak to him, or indeed to any
of my family, again.*

In the end she broke that promise for our sakes and I will be forever grateful to her for that. But she stuck to it for eight long years, refusing to see her family or to accept help of any kind from them, and those years must have been punishing even by the standards of the day. Her pregnancy turned out to be twins, my elder brothers, Alan and Harry. They were born in a tent. Less than a year later, so was I, though by that stage the tent was pitched in a different mining camp.

We moved many times in those early years, in pursuit of one rumour after another, and later, when the money ran out altogether, in pursuit of jobs, and each time we moved there were more of us. Mostly we lived in shacks thrown together out of whatever timber was lying around. There was never running water, far less electric light. My mother's days would have been spent in a constant struggle to feed and clothe us. She was the most resourceful person I have ever known, but it must have called for every ounce of her strength and ingenuity.

I don't know how long it took for her optimism and her faith in my father to be worn down. Quite some time, I imagine; a commitment as strong as hers would have been hard to break. Pride probably came into it too—she wouldn't have wanted to admit, even to herself, that her father's assessment of her husband had been right. Nonetheless, the time did come. I found proof of that on a long thin strip of newsprint torn from the margin of the *Temiskaming Speaker*.

> *When Stanley came in he was so excited, he seized me and*
> *began dancing around, laughing and saying that this was*
> *all we had dreamed of and more, a deep, rich seam, and*
> *this time there was no doubt, any fool could see it was*
> *the real thing. I rejoiced with him, of course, I genuinely*
> *rejoiced, but . . .*

The "but" says it all.

I remember him doing that—picking her up and whirling her about the room, whooping with joy. God knows how many times she had to endure that over the years, each time trying so hard to believe in him, hoping and praying, for all our sakes, that this time he would be proved right. I remember watching her as she laughed and danced, seeing the tension at the corners of her mouth.

The next day he'd take a sample of the ore to the assay office and it would turn out to be worthless. He'd be dumbfounded. Absolutely dumbfounded. And then incredulity would give way to rage. The assayers were out to swindle him, to get him to abandon his claim so that they could take it over themselves. Or they were in cahoots with some mining consortium from the USA. Anything but accept that he'd been wrong again. In fact, the more often it happened the less he could accept that possibility, because as time went on the only conclusion you could draw about someone who was so consistently and repeatedly wrong was that he was a fool.

Then the drinking would start, fuelling his fury.

"*I fear that Stanley does not take disappointment well,*" my mother wrote.

That was for sure.

The carefree loops and swirls of the early days have gone from her writing but it is still fairly firm, fairly confident. I'm guessing that means he hadn't yet started to take out his "disappointment" on her physically. She wasn't frightened of him yet, in other words. Knowing her, knowing her inner strength, I imagine she didn't become truly frightened until he started taking it out on the rest of us. Specifically, on me.

If I start thinking about all that I will never get to sleep. I will stop this now.

A very strange thing has happened. I had just put the papers back in the file and was closing this ledger when there was a knock at the front door. I waited for someone to answer it but of course no one did, so eventually I went to answer it myself, glancing at my watch as I did so. It was one o'clock in the morning. In this town everyone's in bed by nine, so I wondered what catastrophe had taken place. When I opened the door there was no one there.

I stuck my head out, letting in an icy blast of air, and saw Reverend Thomas climbing over the snowbank at the end of our drive. There is a streetlight beside the road and it was unmistakably him. As I watched he clambered down the other side and began walking down the road towards his own house.

I considered calling to him but he couldn't have heard me. I'd have had to put on my coat and boots and go chasing after him, which, given that I have nothing to say to him and no wish to hear anything he has to say to me, seemed unwarranted. In any case, I hadn't taken all that long to answer the door, so he must have decided against saying whatever he had come to say.

I had just closed the door when Tom appeared, bleary-eyed, evidently wakened by the knock.

"Who was it?" he said.

"Reverend Thomas."

He looked startled. "What did he want?"

"I don't know. He'd gone before I got to the door."

Tom pushed past me and opened the door, letting in another flood of air. I said sharply, "Close the door—we'll freeze to death. He'll be practically home by now."

He closed the door and turned around and leaned against it. He looked very strained. Very anxious. He closed his eyes for a minute and then opened them again and looked at me and said, "Dad, do you think he's all right?"

He hasn't called me "Dad" in years. It surprised me and also, I confess, gave me an unexpected surge of pleasure, suggesting as it did that he was appealing specifically to me rather than merely to whoever happened to be standing there.

The answer to his question was clearly "no," but instead I said, "Tom, nothing of what happened in that family was your fault. You know that, don't you?"

He closed his eyes again. I said, "Let's go into the kitchen. It's warm in there."

For a moment I thought he would, but then he shook his head. "I have to get back to bed. I'm up at five."

And he turned and went upstairs.

I should have called him back. I should have insisted that we talk about whatever it is that is worrying him so much. I think he would have, if I'd insisted, and it might have helped.

CHAPTER NINE

Tom

Struan, February 1969

A mouse drowned in the honey. Someone had left the lid off overnight. It had gone in head first and its tail was sticking out like the wick of a candle.

"He went to the bathroom in it," Adam said. He was kneeling on a chair, peering into the jar.

"You're right," Tom said. There were ant-sized pellets in the vicinity of the tail.

"Was he hungry?" Adam said.

"Probably to start with," Tom said, "but probably not by the end."

"What will happen to him now?"

Tom thought about it. Would the honey preserve it? Candied mouse? Unlikely. There'd be enough air trapped in its fur for decomposition to take place.

"He'll rot." Death again. It followed him around like a dog.

Adam looked troubled; two short vertical lines appeared between his eyebrows. Tom wondered suddenly if this was his first acquaintance with the concept—the fact—of mortality. He didn't want to traumatize him.

"It won't hurt him," he said. "He can't feel anything anymore."

The vertical lines were still in situ. "But can we still eat the honey?" Adam said. "From around the edges?"

———

Another blizzard. Out by the Dunns' farm the snowplough slid into the ditch—the ultimate humiliation. Tom was rescued by Arthur Dunn, a case of the present being rescued by the past because Arthur Dunn still worked his land with horses. Huge animals, big as buses, they'd looked like something from a Greek myth when they loomed up out of the snow. Arthur tied a rope around the rear axle of the snowplough and the horses hauled it out as if it were one of Adam's Matchbox toys.

"Thanks very much," Tom said.

Arthur nodded. "Wanna come in an' get warm?" He was a shy man and looked at his feet when he spoke.

"I'd better get on with it," Tom said, "but thanks again."

Arthur and his team dematerialized and there was nothing left but the snow.

By morning the storm had passed and the sky was a clear and innocent blue. Tom and Marcel worked overtime and managed to get the roads clear just as the first flakes from the next storm started drifting down.

"Dis is one stupid job," Marcel said disgustedly. "Ever' year I say to myself, Marcel, nex' year you jus' pack up de wife an' go to Florida till Easter, an' ever' year I forget."

The roads were now mere corridors between snowbanks four feet high. In the centre of town the sidewalks had been abandoned weeks ago; everyone walked on the road. There were gaps in the snowbanks outside the entrances to the stores and businesses, shovelled out afresh each morning, filled in again each time the snowplough passed. People who needed their cars to get to work had to shovel out their driveways both morning and night. Leave a car parked at the side of the road and you wouldn't see it again till spring.

At six fifteen in the morning, rumbling down Cleveland Road on the snowplough, Tom saw Reverend Thomas standing outside on the porch of his house in his bare feet. The porch light was on, otherwise Tom wouldn't have noticed him. He appeared to be looking at his car—or rather at the three feet of snow that covered his car—down in the driveway. He was wearing pyjamas and no shoes or socks. Tom saw it clearly: there were three or four inches of new snow on the steps but there was less than an inch on the porch itself, and Reverend Thomas's bare feet were unmistakably planted in it.

Tom's heart began beating painfully hard. He kept on ploughing, unsure what to do. He should go back. But how could he go back? The last thing Reverend Thomas would want would be for the snowplough to stop at his front door and Tom, of all people, to get out and ask him why he was standing there in his bare feet.

But what if he'd had some sort of breakdown, had suddenly lost his mind? In the circumstances that had to be a possibility. And if you'd stand in the snow on your porch in your bare feet, what was to stop you from walking down the steps and keeping on walking until you froze to death in the street? At this temperature it wouldn't take long.

At the end of the road he turned left, then left, then left again and rumbled slowly back down Cleveland, past the house. The porch light was off and a light was now on inside the house, which he was pretty sure it hadn't been before. Which was good news. But though he couldn't see the porch clearly, there now being no light, Tom saw something that had not been there five minutes ago, namely footprints in the snow leading down the steps and across to the car. Two sets of footprints, one going there and one going back. The Reverend had waded barefoot through the snowdrifts to look at his car. There was no way he could have actually seen it without digging it out from under the snow, but he'd gone out and stood beside it nevertheless.

He couldn't sell the car; Tom understood that perfectly. There was nothing wrong with it apart from the small dent in the front fender on the passenger side. It was in good running order, a solid, reliable Ford, black and sedate as befitted a clergyman, but Reverend Thomas wouldn't be able to bring himself to sell it because the idea of somebody driving around with that dent in it would be unthinkable. Likewise he couldn't get it repaired—get the dent hammered out—because it was impossible even to contemplate repairing a dent of that sort. A dent of the sort that would be made if a car going at considerable speed hit a small, light object such as a child on a bike.

———

Depending on your point of view it had happened either very fast or very slowly. From the point of view of the rider of the bike and her mother, who was running along beside her cheering her on (because as it turned out it was the first time the small rider had managed to ride her bike unsupported and, although she was a bit wobbly, she was quickly getting the hang of it)— from their point of view, because the car was coming up behind them around a bend in the road and they would have neither seen nor heard it, it must have seemed to happen in an instant. From the driver's point of view it had probably seemed like an instant too. He was going very fast and, due to the large amount of alcohol in his bloodstream, his reaction time was slower than normal. When he rounded the bend and saw the child on her bike he would have been on top of her before his brain had fully registered that she was there.

Whereas from Tom's point of view, watching from the beach, with a clear view of the section of Lower Beach Road the little girl was on, it had seemed to happen very slowly, because he was able to see not only the child on her bike with her mother running beside her but also the cloud of dust churned up by the car as it approached the bend. Tall reeds obscured his view of the car itself, but from the dust he could see how fast it was going, and he also knew, though he wasn't consciously thinking about it at the time, that although it was nine o'clock in the morning Rob was still drunk from the night before—all of them were still drunk because they'd been partying on the beach all night. So he'd been watching the car's approach with a faint, almost subconscious shimmer of anxiety, and when the moment came, it seemed to him that he'd known it was coming for quite a long time.

The plan had been that the twelve of them would get together for a class reunion down on the beach at Low Down Bay, just as they'd done in previous summers. They'd make a gigantic bonfire and watch the sun go down, eat a bit, drink a bit, swim a bit, then watch the sun come up again. The guys would bring stuff for supper (hot dogs, hot dog buns, potato chips, booze); the girls would look after breakfast (powdered orange juice, instant coffee, French toast). They'd cook everything over the fire—the girls brought three big frying pans for the French toast—and generally make it a night to remember. And everything worked out perfectly: the night was warm for June and the bonfire kept the bugs away and, though the lake was still ridiculously cold, quite a few of them did go in. There was a stupendous amount of hooch, thanks mostly to Rob, who had contact with a couple of guys from the sawmill who'd set up a highly illegal distillery in a shack off in the woods. They mixed it with Coke to hide the vile taste and sat around the fire and passed it around and talked and sang silly campfire songs that somehow didn't seem silly at the time but kind of nice and nostalgic, reminiscent of their youth, which with hindsight had been special. Some of them rolled themselves in picnic blankets and got a little sleep and some of them rolled themselves in picnic blankets and got a little sex, though probably less than they let on. By morning they were all ravenous, so the girls brought out the ingredients for French toast, which was when they realized they'd forgotten to bring margarine or butter to cook it in.

If only. The two most pointless words in the English language. If only it hadn't been Rob, who'd had more to drink than any of them, who volunteered to go home and get some margarine. If only he hadn't then decided to drive back in his father's car to speed things up. If only Tom had gone with him. He might not have been able to persuade Rob to walk back, because when he was drunk Rob wasn't good at listening to reason, but at least he'd have been able to say, Hey man, slow down. We're coming to the bend. Slow down.

The worst thing had not been the child's body, which was almost unmarked, or Rob's face, which was so shocked, so white, that he'd looked as if at any moment he would pass out. It had been the way the child's mother, sitting in the dust at the side of the road, cradling the little girl in her arms, kept rocking her, kissing her, telling her everything was all right, it had just been a little bump—"Don't cry, sweetheart, don't cry"—when the child was not crying and it was absolutely, unmistakably clear from the way her head lolled whenever her mother moved her that she was dead.

Because of the blizzard no newspapers had made it as far north as Struan for the past three days but Tom kept a copy of *The Grapes of Wrath* in the cab of the snowplough in case of just such an eventuality and he took it with him into Harper's to read over lunch. It wasn't that he particularly wanted to read it again—when they'd studied it in high school Rob had summed it up as the longest sermon ever written and Tom had pretty much agreed—but he needed something dark to match his mood and the only alternatives in his bookcase apart from books about airplanes were *Moby-Dick*, which just plain had too many words in it, and *Jude the Obscure*, which was so depressing it had made him feel suicidal even when he was sixteen.

There were half a dozen people in Harper's, including a big blond guy sitting at the back in the half-booth across from the one Tom considered his own, but he was reading last week's copy of the *Temiskaming Speaker* and didn't look the gabby type, so that was okay. Tom had read the *Speaker* twice already. It was full of the upcoming winter carnival: dog-sled races on the lake, speed skating competitions, hockey games, ice sculptures—fun and games for all. The whole idea made Tom so tired he could hardly hold his head up. Photos of the seven girls competing for the title of Carnival Queen adorned the front page ("Seven Pretty Young Ladies Competing," the headline said) and they made him tired too—his interest in girls seemed to have vanished along with everything else. So now I'm a eunuch, he thought. The idea didn't bother him much.

He took off his coat and hat and gloves and tossed them into the corner, settled himself into his place and opened *The Grapes of Wrath*.

"To the red and part of the gray country of Oklahoma, the last rains came gently, and they did not cut the scarred earth. The plows . . ."

A hand Tom didn't recognize set a glass of water down in front of him.

"Hi," the owner of the hand said. "What can I get you?"

He didn't recognize the voice either. What was a stranger doing waiting on tables in Harper's? Then he remembered: Jenny Bates had left, gone to Calgary. This would be the new waitress.

"A hot beef sandwich, fries and coffee," he said, not looking at her. It wasn't polite, but she needed to know from the outset that he didn't welcome chit-chat.

"Oh, hi, it's you!" she said. "Did you get home all right that night with all that food on the sled?"

Tom's head jerked up. It was her—the Amazon—the nightmare from the grocery store who'd tried to force carrots on him.

"I had to spend the *night* there!" she said, happily rattling on. "It was my last day and I was so bored in that job I was counting the *seconds* and then that stupid storm came along and my brother couldn't come to get me and I had to spend the *night*! Anyway"— she grinned at him—"it's great here. I love it! I'll get your lunch, hot beef, fries and coffee coming up!" She bounced off in the direction of the kitchen.

Tom stared at the table, incredulous. It was unbelievable! Not only was Harper's the only place to eat for thirty miles, it was his one remaining refuge. He couldn't go home because Sherry the Slut would be there, he couldn't go to the library because Reverend Thomas might be there, and there was nowhere, literally nowhere, else to go.

Calm down, he told himself. You're overreacting. Just ignore her. She cannot make you talk to her. Read your book.

He pulled *The Grapes of Wrath* closer and leaned over it, elbows on either side, head in hands, like he was studying for some critical exam and must on no account be disturbed.

"To the red and part of the gray country of Oklahoma, the last rains came gently, and they did not cut the scarred earth. The plows . . ."

A bowl of coleslaw landed on the table in front of him.

"Our extra-special Coleslaw Deluxe!" the Amazon announced proudly.

Tom stared at it: bits of raw vegetables sticking out of a thick white goo.

"It's on the house!" the Amazon said. "It's our new campaign to help everybody in Struan keep healthy over the winter. For the next two weeks everybody who orders a meal gets free coleslaw thrown in!" She was beaming at him. He wasn't looking at her but he could feel the beam.

His mouth had gone dry. He licked his lips. He hated all vegetables without exception and he hated goo even more. "I don't want it," he said, his voice scraping out.

"You haven't tried it yet! You'll love it! It's got apple and cabbage and carrots and onion and chopped walnuts and homemade mayo. I made it myself and Mrs. Harper thinks it's fabulous!"

"I don't want it. I hate coleslaw."

"This is absolutely nothing like normal coleslaw! I promise! You'll *love* it! And it's really, really good for you!"

He could leave, or he could throw it at her and then leave; those were the only options.

"Excuse me," a voice said.

The big blond guy in the booth across the aisle was leaning sideways, trying to catch the waitress's attention. Tom could see him in the periphery of his vision.

"Could you come here for a minute, please?"

"What?" the waitress demanded. The cheerful tone disappeared as if she'd chopped it off with an axe.

"Could you come here, please?"

Out of the corner of his eye Tom saw her go. She stood in front of the man, hands on hips. The man said something to her in an undertone.

"I wasn't!" the waitress said hotly.

The man said something else.

"Well, he doesn't have to eat it! I'm just offering it! Mrs. Harper said I could!"

The man's voice became fractionally louder—he sounded as if he was holding onto his temper by a rapidly fraying thread. "She didn't say you could ram it down people's throats! Take it *away*! Bring him what he *asked* for!"

The waitress spun on her heel, marched over, whipped the coleslaw from under Tom's nose and marched out. The kitchen door swung shut.

Tom glanced at the man and inadvertently met his eyes. The man looked embarrassed. He gave a slight shrug and said, "Just ignore her. She'll probably get the sack in a day or two." He went back to his newspaper.

Tom felt dazed. He wasn't sure what had happened. It seemed as if he'd been rescued by a total stranger. Was that right? If so, had he looked as if he needed rescuing? Did he look that bad, that near the brink? Because obviously, if that were the case—if a complete stranger felt he had to intervene on his behalf when a waitress brought him an unasked-for salad—then he mustn't come here anymore. It wasn't fair on other customers. He'd have to go straight home when he finished his shift.

The thought appalled him. He realized suddenly how much he depended on Harper's. It provided human contact without making any demands on him. Going to a café and having something to eat—that was a normal thing to do, it made him feel normal. And the irony was he'd thought he was doing better over the past few weeks. The feeling of balancing on a knife edge had eased; things didn't get to him as much as they had.

The waitress set his hot beef sandwich down in front of him, went across to the counter, brought back the coffee pot, poured his coffee, set down the cream.

"Say if you want more coffee," she said. Her tone was sulky, like a kid who's been told off.

The hot beef sandwich looked just as usual but he was no longer hungry. He sat motionless, listening to the background chatter around him. More people were coming in, taking advantage of the clear roads, seeking company after a week of enforced isolation. The waitress sped back and forth to the kitchen. She moved so fast he could feel the air stir in her wake.

The stranger in the booth opposite stood up—again Tom saw him in the periphery of his vision—and started pulling on his coat. When the Amazon passed on her way to the kitchen he caught her arm.

"Six o'clock?" he asked.

"Half past." She sounded sullen. "I have to tidy up and help wash the dishes."

"Okay. I'll be back then."

She started to turn away but he caught her again and said in an undertone, "And don't *bully* people. They don't like it."

She shrugged him off.

It wasn't until the outer door of the café swung shut behind the stranger that the words and the tone in which they were spoken sank in and Tom realized their meaning. Then it was like breaking the surface after a long dive, relief like oxygen flooding through his veins.

The way the man spoke to the waitress—that was not a tone you used with a stranger, it was a tone you used with someone you knew very well who irritated the shit out of you on a regular basis. He was coming to collect her at the end of her shift. "My brother couldn't come and get me," she'd said, referring to the night at Marshall's Grocery. He was her *brother*! The way they responded to each other—instantly annoyed—obviously they were siblings; he of all people should have recognized that. They even looked alike, both of them big-boned and blond. The guy was quite a lot older, mid-thirties, whereas the girl was in her late teens, but there were bigger gaps than that in Tom's own family.

"Don't bully people," the man had said. "They don't like it." "*They* don't like it," not "*He* doesn't like it." Which meant—this was the critical bit, and Tom examined it from all angles to be sure he wasn't kidding himself—that the reason he had intervened when she was going on about the coleslaw was not that Tom looked as if he was about to fly apart but because she was always going on about bloody vegetables and it drove him, her brother, insane. Tom was so relieved he felt like laughing. God help the poor guy: she was even worse than Meg.

He started eating his hot beef sandwich. It was no longer hot, but he didn't care; it was excellent anyway. He watched the girl surreptitiously as he ate. Her bounce had come back now that her brother had gone. She was chatting to everybody as she steamed by. Most of them were obediently eating the coleslaw, laughing about it. "Now you eat that up!" he heard her say. The door opened and a woman came in with a little kid bundled up in a snowsuit. The waitress squatted down in front of him and said, "Well, hi, handsome, how are you today? You're all snowy—is it snowing out there?" and the kid's face lit up. You could see he thought she was the best thing since sliced bread.

She wasn't really that bad, Tom decided. He recalled that she'd offered him the sled at the grocery store without him asking for it, which was a point in her favour. Yes, she was irritating, but it wasn't the end of the world. He could put up with that.

"More coffee?" she asked a minute later as she whizzed past his table.

"Yeah," Tom said. "Thanks."

There is a law of nature—or at any rate of human nature—that says you should never, ever, allow yourself to think for a single minute that things are finally getting better because Fate just won't be able to resist cutting you off at the knees.

At five o'clock that afternoon his mother appeared in the doorway of the living room looking wild, her hair all over the place, her face white as chalk. "He's gone!" she said.

Tom lowered last week's paper. "Who is?"

"The baby! Dominic!" Her eyes were wild too, ringed with dark circles.

"Where did you see him last?" Tom said.

"I don't know! I don't know! I had him but now he's gone!"

"He won't have gone far, Mum. He can't even crawl."

"But he's gone! He's gone!"

Adam emerged from his lair beside Tom's chair. A waft of stale urine came with him. "He's there," he said, pointing at a pile of blankets on the sofa. As he spoke the blankets twitched and a very small foot appeared.

"Oh my darling!" their mother said. "Oh my darling. My darling." She picked up the pile of blankets and buried her face in it.

Tom watched her uneasily. Maybe she'd been like this after the rest of them were born, but it definitely seemed to be getting a bit extreme.

Adam was standing watching her, his fists tucked up under his chin.

"Mum," Tom said, "Adam needs a bath." But she didn't seem to hear him. That at least was normal.

After she'd gone Adam said, "I can do a bath."

"Can you? Can you soap yourself?"

"Yes."

"Okay. Go do it, then."

He went back to the paper. It was distinctly old news but it was either that or start *The Grapes of Wrath* for the third time.

The waft of urine returned. Tom looked up from the paper. Adam was standing in front of him with nothing on, shivering.

"What's the matter?" Tom said.

"I can't do the taps."

"Oh. Okay." Reluctantly he put down the paper and went upstairs, Adam at his heels. The bathtub looked disgusting. In fact, the bathroom looked disgusting. Tom refused to notice it but was suddenly hot with fury that his father obviously refused to notice it too. He put the plug in and turned both taps on full. Adam was standing on the outside edges of his feet, toes curled in to limit contact with the freezing linoleum. His dirty clothes were in a heap on the floor.

"Do you have something clean to put on?"

"I don't know," Adam said. His teeth were chattering. Tom felt the bathwater. "Get in," he said, turning off the taps. "It's warmer in there." Adam climbed into the bath. His ribs looked fragile as a bird's nest. Were all four year olds that thin? How should *he* know? *Why* should he know?

In an expanding rage Tom went down the hall to what used to be Meg's room and was now Adam's. The smell assaulted him as he walked in. The bed had been roughly made but apart from that the place was a dump. His anger billowed out to include Sherry the Slut. She had to go; someone had to tell her to go and it wasn't going to be him. And since his mother wasn't in a state to do anything about anything, it was his father's job. Why the hell hadn't he done it already? Why the fuck haven't you fired her and got in somebody good? he said to his father inside his head. Why the *fuck* aren't you *doing* anything about this *fucking family*!

He jerked open the drawers and rummaged about until he found a reasonably complete set of clothes and took them back to the bathroom. Adam was curled over, soaping his feet. His vertebrae stood up like tiny mountain peaks. His hair stuck out all over the place. It had snot in it; there was nothing else it could be.

"How about your hair?" Tom said. He must have sounded angry because Adam looked at him quickly, his eyes wide.

"Can you wash your hair yourself?"

A shake of the head.

"Lie back, then. Get it wet."

He washed Adam's hair, tipped him back and sloshed water around to rinse it, sat him up again and washed his back and around his neck and under his arms. It was all he could do not to scrub him savagely—he felt savage; he was so angry he could taste it in his mouth like bile. When Adam was clean he hoisted him out of the bath and wrapped a dirty towel around him.

"Okay," he said. "Dry yourself and put these on."

He went downstairs and knocked on the door of his father's study. His heart was pounding so hard it shook his chest. When there was no reply he opened the door and went in. His father wasn't there. Tom checked his watch—it wasn't yet six o'clock. He swore. He wanted to confront his father *now*, this minute, while he was still angry enough not to chicken out. But then, as he was leaving the study, he heard the front door open. He swiftly crossed the floor to the entrance hall. His father was hanging up his coat.

"I need to talk to you," Tom said.

"Oh?" His father looked at him in surprise. Then he said, "Well, good, I've been wanting to talk to you too. Let's go into my study."

They went into the study and his father sat down at his desk. "Take a seat," he said, nodding at the chair in the corner. His tone was formal but pleasant. Tom guessed it was the way he spoke at work. He hadn't switched into family mode yet.

"No thanks. It'll only take a sec. I just wanted to say—"

"Take a seat, Tom."

Tom dragged the chair out of the corner and sat down. He could feel the anger giving way to dread or despair or whatever it was his father inspired in him nowadays. He was bitterly aware of his father's disapproval of him, of the fact that he still hadn't "pulled himself together." He was aware of it every minute of the day. But he needed to put it out of his mind because it didn't matter now. What mattered now was that he said what had to be said, which was, This family is going to hell and you have to do something about it.

He looked down, focused on the floor, trying to summon up the force that was needed to get the message through.

"Now then," his father said. "You go first. What was it you wanted to say?"

Tom drew a breath. "There's something wrong with Mum," he said, still looking at the floor. "She's not—"

The outer front door slammed and then the inner door. Peter yelled, "You fucking moron!" and the boys charged through the living room and into the kitchen.

"I don't know what it is," Tom continued, "but there's definitely something wrong with her. And Adam—"

Corey yelled, "Bastard! You stupid, bleeding, bloody . . . *bastard*, I'm going to tell—" A crash, followed by a cry of rage or pain, followed by the familiar sound of a body bouncing off a wall.

Tom looked up and saw the anger rising in his father's face, saw that he wasn't listening. This is useless, Tom thought. He's useless. This whole fucking family—the whole fucking world— is useless.

He stood up and walked out and went up to his room and shut the door.

CHAPTER TEN

Megan

London, February 1967

Megan lost her virginity—or more correctly, gave it away—on a wet Wednesday night a year and a bit after arriving in England. She was glad to be rid of it. It was a leftover from childhood, a barrier, mental as well as physical, to seeing herself as fully in charge of her life.

She'd always disapproved of "sleeping around" on principle and had no intention of doing so, particularly as men kept trying to talk her into it, but over the course of many long nights alone in her box room and then many more long nights alone on the top floor of the hotel, she'd had time to think about such things and had failed to find a single reason why people shouldn't sleep together if they wanted to. If you weren't being pressured, if you were old enough to know what you were doing, if you took care not to beget an unwanted child, why exactly shouldn't you? This business of saving yourself for your husband—if ever there was an idea indisputably thought up by a man, that was it. And anyway, she wasn't going to get married. Marriage led to children and she'd done children. So the only question was, might she want to have sex, if not now then at some not-too-distant date, and the answer was yes, if she happened to feel like it and the time/place/person were right. Judging by the amount of time other people spent doing it and talking about it, it was something you didn't want to miss out on altogether.

Having made her decision, she went to a GP and asked to go on the Pill so as to be ready when the right person happened along. The GP didn't want to give it to her (he was a man) and tried to talk her out of it, but Megan said very firmly that she was nearly twenty-three and it was her body they were talking about, not his, and in the end he gave in.

She was picky and it was a while before the right person turned up but eventually he did, in the form of a Scot named Douglas whose employers had sent him down to London from Edinburgh for a six-week senior management training course. Megan selected him because he had nice eyes and didn't remind her of any of her brothers and had expressed an interest in having sex with her in a polite and non-pushy way and, most importantly, because he would be going back to Edinburgh when his course came to an end, so there wouldn't be any question of things developing further. It was only her virginity she wanted to lose, not her freedom.

She'd wanted to know what sex was like and now she did. It was messy, but that aside she'd enjoyed it. She suspected it ruined your judgment though, because after Douglas left she rather wished he'd come back, but that wore off quite quickly.

All this took place some months after the Montrose Hotel was up and running. Before that all of Megan's time and energy had been focused on the great and glorious task of bringing the hotel back to life. Megan loved the Montrose with a passion and ran it like Captain Bligh.

"This is a clean bathroom," she'd say, gesturing at a gleaming bathtub/basin/toilet, to the various girls who replied to her advertisement for cleaners. "I expect it to be this clean all the time. I check every room every day and I look in every corner; if it's not clean, you'll get two warnings and then you're out. The same if you're late for work. Do you still want the job?"

Sometimes they didn't and sometimes they did.

The renovation of the Montrose had taken six months and was the most fun Megan had ever had in her life. She and Annabelle and Peter Montrose did most of it themselves. They hired an electrician to do the wiring and a plumber to put basins with hot and cold water in every room and redo the bathrooms (one on each floor, plus a cloakroom, which was what the British called a washroom, off reception), but the three of them did all the tiling and the painting and the papering and the selecting of fabrics and the choosing of furniture and lamps and pictures to hang on the walls. It was Annabelle and Peter who did the selecting; Megan just went along for the fun of it. If it had been up to her, she'd have painted everything white and covered all the furniture in hard-wearing, stain-resistant, dark-coloured cord. But Annabelle and Peter had taste, she could see that. She hadn't known what taste was (people in Struan didn't think along those lines—if they wanted a lamp they bought a lamp) and she wasn't sure she approved of the concept (how could one person's opinion of what looked nice be "better than" another's?), but if there was such a thing as good taste, then Annabelle and Peter undoubtedly had it. They went to antique stores and house clearances and auction houses and came home with junk Megan wouldn't have paid two cents for, which turned out to look great when stuck in a particular corner of a particular room.

All three of them worked twelve-hour days and seven-day weeks and to Megan it felt like one long party.

"Megan, you *must* take a day off," Annabelle would say from time to time, a frown drawing a single fine furrow across her brow. "You haven't had a day off in weeks! You're not making the most of your time here—you should be seeing the sights."

"I will when we're finished," Megan would say. "When it's up and running, I'll have Tuesdays off every week."

She still hadn't seen the Tower of London, St. Paul's Cathedral or the National Gallery, or indeed anything else. The idea of trudging around a bunch of old buildings bored her, or at least that was the explanation she had been giving herself. But the truth was more complicated, and she knew it. The truth was that none of those old buildings would mean a thing to her because she didn't know anything about them. She didn't know anything about anything: history, art, other countries, world religions, the Vietnam War—all the things that everyone around her was talking about. The breadth and depth of her ignorance had become apparent to her over the months she'd spent in England and it astonished and embarrassed her. How could you put it right, ignorance on that scale? Where did you start? It was like someone presenting you with a book, saying, "This is fantastic, you'll love it," and when you opened it you found it was written in a foreign language and you couldn't read a word.

Whose fault was it? She couldn't blame her education and she couldn't blame Struan—Tom knew things and so did her father. In fact, her father knew a lot; Megan hadn't been aware of how much until she left home. She'd learned more about him through his letters over the past year than in the twenty-one years she'd lived at home. He hadn't been to university like Tom—he hadn't been anywhere apart from during the war—so he must have learned it all from books, which in Megan's view was hard work.

Well, it doesn't matter, she told herself, expertly pasting a length of wallpaper for the downstairs cloakroom. Nobody cares whether or not you know things. It's not going to make any difference to the world. It turns out you're good at papering walls, so get on with it. She carefully turned up the bottom of the paper and passed the sheet up to Annabelle, who was standing on top of the stepladder.

The paper was creamy with a fine pink stripe. Separately both it and the room had looked bland and uninteresting; together they were wonderful. When the papering was finished Annabelle stood in the doorway for a few minutes looking at it thoughtfully and then went off to a junk shop and came back with a hideously ornate gold-painted mirror. Now *that* is a mistake, Megan said to herself, but it wasn't. When the mirror was hung above the oval wash basin so that it reflected the two candle lights on the opposite wall, the whole room took on a rich, golden glow.

"What are we trying for here, Versailles?" Peter asked when he saw it—he'd been off talking to the bank manager.

"Exactly," Annabelle said. "Versailles is what cloakrooms should be. Are you converted, Megan?" (Which meant she'd noticed Megan thinking it was a mistake.)

"Yes," Megan admitted, running a finger around a curly bit of the frame and checking for dust, of which there was an abundance—Annabelle had been too impatient to get it up on the wall to let her clean it first—"but it's going to be murder to keep clean."

In the evenings—or more likely late at night—when they had finished whatever task they had set themselves for the day, the three of them would sit on beanbags amidst the paint pots on the floor and survey their handiwork, eating exotic (and frequently disgusting) cheeses from Harrods Food Hall with chunks of

French bread and wine Peter had stolen from his father's wine cellar. Most of the time they were modestly admiring of what they'd achieved, though not always.

"Everyone else is doing Habitat," Annabelle said anxiously one evening. "Stripped pine. Clean lines." Despite being absolutely confident in her own taste she was prone to last-minute doubts— later than last minute in this case: they'd completed all the bedrooms and were well advanced with the ground floor.

"Here we go again," Peter said.

"You don't think we're out of step with the times?"

"I *know* we're out of step with the times. We're *deliberately* out of step with the times! Stop thinking about it, for God's sake."

"What do you think, Megan?"

It surprised and flattered Megan when they asked her opinion but she was perfectly happy to give it. "I think foreigners will love it," she said.

"Do you?" Annabelle said hopefully.

"Yes. It's old-looking and England's supposed to be old."

"Spot on," Peter said. "Have some more wine. What do you think of this wine, Meg?"

"Not much."

"No palate, this girl," Peter said sadly, which pleased Megan. Most people would have said, "No palate, these Canadians," as if her lack of palate were to do with her being Canadian instead of with her being her. Wine was another thing she didn't know anything about and she was happy to leave it that way. Peter's one fault, from what she'd seen so far, was that he drank too much of it, and when he did, he was impatient with Annabelle. Annabelle's one fault was that she didn't slap him down on the spot. She was too nice, that was the problem. In Megan's view, if you're too nice to a man he'll take advantage of you every time.

But mostly, they were good to each other. And always, they were good to her.

———

It was only at night that she felt alone nowadays. Of course, she *was* alone at night—during the renovations and for the first few months after the hotel opened she slept in one of the single rooms on the top floor. Annabelle and Peter had a flat a few streets away, so when they left each evening she had the hotel to herself. Annabelle had worried about this. "Are you sure you won't be nervous, Megan? You're very welcome to sleep on our couch. These old houses tend to creak."

"I'll be fine," Megan replied. "Creaks don't bother me."

Which they didn't. It was the distance between herself and home that bothered her. For some reason, now that she was doing a job she loved and that looked set to evolve into one she could imagine doing for many years—she was to be responsible for the day-to-day running of the hotel—she ached more for home than she had when she was shut in a cupboard in Lansdown Terrace. There it had felt like a holiday gone wrong, which, being a holiday, would soon be over. Now she could see herself here in five years' time. In ten. Her family going on its way without her. Thinking of her less and less, as she would probably think of them less and less. Her mother growing old without anyone to make sure she was all right. Adam, whose small warm shape in her arms she still missed, growing up a stranger. The emptiness inside her gradually filling with other things, other people. The word "home" taking on a different meaning, so that when she went back to visit she would no longer belong there. She would no longer be the person she would have been if she'd stayed.

She'd fall asleep with a kind of grief lying in her, a kind of bereavement. But then in the morning she'd wake to the thought that today they were starting on the second-floor landing, which was to be papered in a soft, deep plum overlaid with a tracery of mellow gold, which sounded absolutely disgusting but would turn out to be exactly right.

The Montrose was in a terrace (nothing like Lansdown Terrace, though—these houses were tall and clean and proud) near Gloucester Road, convenient for the airport buses to and from Heathrow and walking distance from the Victoria and Albert, the Science Museum and the Natural History Museum. It had fifteen bedrooms spread over three floors, a large, welcoming lounge and a small but elegant lobby. The ceilings were high with elaborate cornices and ceiling roses three feet across. Annabelle had already designed the brochures. (*"Fifteen beautiful bedrooms, twelve doubles, three singles, full central heating, hot and cold water in every room, sprung interior mattresses, bedside lights, shaving points, comfortable lounge with colour television."*) They would provide a turndown service (the hotel would have a higher AA rating if they did) and a bar that would operate on an honesty basis.

Their target clientele was businessmen during the week and discerning Europeans and out-of-towners on the weekends, plus North Americans who didn't quite fall into the "wealthy" category in the high seasons.

"People who are prepared to pay a little extra for something nice," Annabelle explained.

"And we want them to come back," Peter added. "We're not out to milk them for every drop and then never see them again, we want them to return year after year and recommend us to all their friends. We want the Montrose to be so good that even if they could afford to stay at the Ritz and have their own private bathrooms, they'd come here instead."

Up until now Megan had never knowingly met anyone who fitted Annabelle and Peter's description but she realized she had two examples right in front of her. The Montroses were exactly the sort of people who would stay in the sort of hotel they intended the Montrose to be. They weren't exactly wealthy but they flew to Paris or Rome or Florence a couple of times a year and always stayed somewhere "nice." They were taking on the hotel not because they desperately needed the money but because they somewhat needed the money and thought running a small hotel would be rather fun.

Annabelle was tall and pale with luxuriant chestnut hair that she piled up on her head when she and Peter were going out for the evening and tied back with a scarf when they were tiling the bathrooms. Peter was handsome and clever and, apart from when he'd had too much to drink, clearly besotted with Annabelle even though they'd been married for five years. Megan had never seen a good marriage at close quarters before. This looked like one and she strongly approved.

Annabelle was to be "front of house," taking bookings, welcoming guests, advising them on what to see and where to eat while they were in London. Peter would look after the business end—keeping the books, arranging advertising, dealing with problems as they arose.

Megan was to be the housekeeper. It would be her job to make sure the whole thing worked. There were to be two girls to do the cleaning—three if it turned out to be necessary—a handyman and a part-time, all-purpose receptionist/dogsbody to look after things in the evenings and on Megan's day off. All of them were to be under Megan's personal supervision. "I'd like to hire them myself if that's all right," she'd said to Annabelle when they were discussing all this. It was this business of Annabelle being too nice. She'd hire girls she felt sorry for and be unable to fire them when they turned out to be useless.

"Of course," Annabelle replied meekly. "All that side of things is up to you."

In the month prior to the opening, when the carpets were

being laid and the chandeliers hung and doorknobs put on the doors, Megan spent a night in each of the bedrooms in turn to ensure there were no dripping taps, no faulty electrical connections, no leaky radiators. That was when the Montrose really became hers. She loved every room more than the last.

Each morning she went through a list of problems with the handyman. He was the first person she hired. His name was Jonah and he had just one tooth, top row (though there was no row), dead centre. Megan didn't see the point of one tooth—surely you needed at least two so that they'd have something to gnash against—but she liked the fact that Jonah automatically took off his shoes when he came in the door and the way he looked around him, head slightly forward, searching out loose hinges or missing screws like a tracker dog.

"We need someone who can do everything," she'd said. "Painting and carpentry and blocked drains and radiators. Can you do everything?"

"Yup," Jonah said. "That window sash's loose, s'gonna rattle in the wind."

20th November 1966

Dear Mum and Dad,

I'm sorry to have been so long in writing, but we've been really busy getting the hotel ready for opening before Christmas. We've pretty much finished now—today we put up a Christmas tree in the reception and that was our last job. Everything looks really beautiful, and our first guests are arriving next week. Last night Annabelle and Peter took me out for dinner to celebrate. We went to a posh restaurant called the Gay Hussar—it serves Hungarian

*food, which was delicious. We had Champagne to celebrate
and they gave me a really beautiful watch.*

*How are you both? Have the twins gone to sea yet?
Is Tom coming home for Christmas? What stage is he
at in his degree? I forget. Are Peter and Corey behaving
themselves? How is Adam? I'd really love a picture of
him. Would you ask Tom to take one while he's home
and send it to me?*

*Has anything interesting happened in Struan
lately? I'd love to hear all the news when you have
time to write.*

Love, Megan

*PS I am enclosing a brochure of the hotel so you can
see what it looks like.*

8th December 1966

Dear Megan,
—Megan could hear her father's voice in his
handwriting, but strangely it was the voice she
imagined him using at the bank rather than at
home: measured and rather formal, as opposed
to irritated and impatient—

*Thank you for your letter. It is good to know that your
hotel is up and running. Your employers sound like nice people.
Regarding your celebratory dinner out, the Gay Hussar is
a curious name. The Hussars were light horsemen in the
Hungarian army, dating back to the 15th century. They
were an elite regiment and no doubt had more to be happy
about than the average foot soldier (hence "gay").*

Thank you for sending the brochure of the hotel. It looks a stylish place. I was interested to see that it is near the V&A Museum, which is world-famous for its art and design. Its founding principle was that works of art should be available to all—quite an advanced idea in its time (the early 1850s). If it is as close to your hotel as it appears to be in your brochure, you could easily walk there in your lunch hour.

We are all well. Your mother is writing to you also and will no doubt pass on such news as there is.

All the best.

Tuesday

Dear Megan,
—Her mother she saw, rather than heard: her smooth, pale face and large, always anxious eyes, her soft fair hair, so fine that it drifted about her, defying all efforts to pin it down—

It was very nice to hear from you. Your hotel looks expensive. Could you afford to stay there yourself?

Yes, the twins have gone. Their ship is the HMCS St. Laurent and they are on NATO patrol. I don't know where and I don't know if they're enjoying it because they haven't written a single letter. I expected the house to seem very quiet when they left but Peter and Corey make so much noise it hasn't changed much.

There isn't much news. You remember I told you Tom's friend, Robert Thomas, accidentally killed a child on a bike in the summer? It turned out that he was drunk at the time. After the inquest he had some sort of breakdown and didn't go back to university. It was a terrible thing.

Tom is coming on Friday but going back to Toronto straight after Christmas. He has exams quite soon. He's doing a second degree on top of the first one. He always was crazy about planes.

Adam is growing very fast. You will hardly know him when you get home. You still haven't said when that will be. Soon, I hope!

Love, Mum

Did they simply not see her request for a photo of Adam? Or did they see it but couldn't be bothered even to comment, far less to act? She had written to Tom twice herself but of course he hadn't replied. Though maybe he was preoccupied with worry about Robert. That at least would be understandable. She couldn't imagine how you went about comforting someone who had killed a child.

Her parents, though, had no excuse. Why do you keep trying? she asked herself angrily. You're just setting yourself up for more disappointment.

But it was astonishing how much she still missed Adam. It felt wrong, fundamentally wrong, not to know what he looked like.

She was about to throw the envelope away when she saw that her mother had written something on the back. "*A letter has come for you from Cora Manning. I will put it in this envelope. But why has she written to you? Aren't you living with her?*"

You're getting worse, Megan said to her mother inside her head. She checked the envelope: there was nothing in it. Par for the course.

She'd almost forgotten Cora; it was as if she belonged to another place and time. She wondered whether they would ever meet again. It was strange to think someone could have such a huge effect on your life and at the same time vanish from it completely.

On the way to John Lewis on Oxford Street to look at bed linen (they needed a considerable amount and were hoping to do a deal) Megan's eye was caught by a display of tiny cars in the window of a newsagent. She stopped and peered in. The cars were very cute and there were lots of them, including—best of all—a bright red London bus and a shiny black London taxi. Megan turned and went in.

"I'll have those two," she said to the newsagent, not bothering to ask the price. She didn't care about the price, she who was always so careful about money. Each car had its own neat little box with its picture and the word "Matchbox" on it. They were smaller than the Dinky Toys the other boys had had, which in any case had been lost or smashed to bits years ago. She'd never seen the point of giving toys to very small children—they were just as happy playing with a spoon—but this was different; this was for her as much as for Adam.

She imagined her mother unwrapping the cars for him one at a time and exclaiming over them. "These are from Megan, Adam! From your sister Megan, way over in England! Aren't they cute?" She imagined Adam's grin as he seized them. He would try to eat them—he was nearly two and a half now—but they were too big to swallow and looked sturdy enough to survive, and he would enjoy them more and more as he got older. She would send the bus and taxi now, by airmail, expensive though it would be. All the Christmas presents had gone by surface mail weeks ago but this would be a little something extra. From now on she would send him another every couple of months until he had the whole set. It would be her way of keeping in touch with him.

———

The night before the Montrose opened for business they had a hotel-warming party and invited people from the press and the AA and the RAC and anyone else they thought might be interesting or useful. There were nibbles from Harrods and Champagne in tall glasses. Megan's job was to circulate and keep people's glasses topped up.

She wore a slim black trouser suit of impeccable cut, a surprise gift from Annabelle and Peter. (She'd been planning to wear a perfectly acceptable black skirt and white blouse.)

"But you gave me the watch!" she'd protested when Annabelle lifted the suit from its layers of tissue paper.

"That was a thank you," Annabelle said. "This is your uniform for when you're front of house, and you shouldn't have to pay for your uniform. And these go with it." She lifted a pair of shiny black stilettos out of a shopping bag, then laughed at Megan's expression. "You don't have to wear them ever again, they're just in honour of the occasion. Try them on, and if they kill you I'll take them back."

When she came downstairs in all her finery just before the first guests arrived Peter did a double-take and said, "Good God, Meg, you're a stunner!"

"She is, isn't she?" Annabelle said. She studied Megan as if she were a newly decorated room still in need of a little something. "I like your hair tied back like that, it's very chic, but I wonder if you should loosen it a bit. Like this." She carefully eased the knot in the fat black ribbon tying Megan's hair back. They were standing in front of the huge mirror in the lounge (another junkshop find). "There. What do you think?"

Megan considered the effect. It softened her face, gentled her firm chin. "It's nice," she admitted, "but it will be all over the place in a few hours."

"The party will be over in a few hours," Annabelle said. Her own hair fell in ravishing curls from a pile on top of her head. She wore a very short, very red dress with shoes to match and would have stopped the traffic in the streets. "How are the shoes?"

"Bearable for a bit, I guess," Megan said, she who had always sworn she would suffer the pain of silly shoes for no one.

So during the evening, when Megan—circulating with the Champagne bottle and smiling politely and explaining that no, she wasn't American she was Canadian, and yes, she was enjoying her stay in England—caught sight of herself in the mirror in the lounge she should have been pleased, but in fact her appearance startled her and made her uneasy. It wasn't her, that elegant girl. Not that she wanted to look like a country hick but she did want to look like herself. Anyone looking at her would think she was one of them, but the minute she opened her mouth they would know that she wasn't and would think she'd been pretending. For the first time since meeting Annabelle and Peter, she felt unsure of herself.

But then, halfway through the evening, she was rescued quite unintentionally by a photographer from the *Evening Standard* who asked her to pose by the fireplace in the lounge and then tried to chat her up. He wore a black leather jacket and had hair like the Beatles, and Megan suspected he spent a lot of time in front of a mirror, like the twins. (They'd spent hours and hours in the bathroom, heads together, slicking back their hair and admiring themselves while various desperate brothers pounded on the bathroom door. Megan had tried confiscating the key so that they could be barged in upon but there was a general riot so she'd had to put it back. Finally, much against her better judgment, because in her view the only thing more pathetic than a vain female was a vain male, she'd put a mirror in their room.)

"What are you doing afterwards?" the photographer asked, taking a shot, moving six inches to the right, crouching down and taking another. "When everyone's gone."

"Going to bed," Megan said.

"Alone?" he said, with blinding predictability, leering at her over his camera.

And all at once Megan felt just fine. The photographer looked exceedingly sophisticated and maybe he was, but at heart he was an idiot, and with the exception of Annabelle and Peter, that probably applied to everyone in the room. Megan knew where she was with idiots; she'd been dealing with them all her life.

———

In later years, when she looked back on her time at the Montrose, Megan had trouble remembering the order of things. The events of the first few months were easy to place—the hotel-warming party, for instance, was immediately followed by her first Christmas in England (spent with Annabelle and Peter and won- derful apart from a phone call home, during which her mother wept and her father almost audibly counted the cost of each second). That was followed by a quiet patch—so quiet that they wondered if the hotel was going to go bust before it had a chance to show the world how good it was—during which Megan made use of her free time to lose her virginity to the Scot named Douglas.

Then came her second English spring, which was remark- able because it was such a contrast to the first. It was still wet, of course, but when the sun did come out London was trans- formed. Buildings that mere days ago had looked old and grimy suddenly became majestic. Trees burst into flower, cov- ering themselves in great billows of pink blossoms and lolling about in the breeze. After a few weeks the petals loosened their grip and began blowing around like snow and that was more beautiful still; they flowed across the pavements in gentle drifts, then picked themselves up and whirled off again. Small parks ("squares," they were called, though many of them weren't square) sprouted up everywhere, with trees and flower beds and carefully tended grass. They must have been there all along, but somehow she had failed to notice them before. During lunch hours the parks erupted with office workers eating sandwiches and reading books. As soon as it was warm enough—in fact, before it was warm enough—they stripped themselves of every permitted layer of clothing and sprawled on the grass, presenting their bodies and faces to the sun as if they'd turned into plants themselves.

Megan couldn't recall seeing any of this the previous spring. She must have been blinded by homesickness.

In April business picked up. There were several favourable reviews of the Montrose in the right publications and they were now often full to capacity, which meant that the room Megan had been using was needed for guests, so she moved into a tiny room on the top floor that they ultimately intended to use as a linen cupboard. Annabelle in particular was distressed about this— "Megan, it's disgraceful! What if someone were to find out that we keep our housekeeper in a linen cupboard! It would be a scandal!" ("Great publicity, though," Peter said. "Maybe I'll leak it to the press.")

But Megan had been adamant. In due course she would have a place of her own but it was early days in her career as housekeeper and she was still doing things for the first time—the first Easter, with its flood of tourists all arriving at the same time and the lobby overflowing with luggage, the first complaint by a guest (noise from the room next door—a tricky one), the first overflowing toilet (Jonah muttering about "wimmin's things" under his breath). She wanted to be on hand to deal with such problems herself.

In any case, as linen cupboards went it was a sizeable one, Buckingham Palace compared to the box room in Lansdown Terrace. It even had a light and a rail to hang her clothes on and shelves where she could put a kettle and a hotplate.

How long had she slept in there? It felt like just a couple of months but it must have been more like a year. She was there when letters from her parents arrived telling her of the suicide of Robert Thomas—she knew that because she remembered holding the thin airmail sheets up to the ceiling light and reading her mother's letter through several times, trying to take it in. She couldn't make it seem real. She'd known Robert quite well, but reading the letter, his death seemed so distant—that part of her life seemed so distant—it was as if he'd existed only in her memory: an idea, not a person. She couldn't feel the horror she should, and that worried her, because it emphasized how far away from home she was, in every sense.

There'd been something else troubling in the letter as well, quite apart from its content. Her mother had always been very good at spelling but she'd written, "*he jumped of the clif down at the gorge.*" She'd also failed to sign the letter or even send her love, which was unlike her too. Maybe it was because she was upset by Robert's death—the accompanying letter from Megan's father had suggested that. He'd said, "*The entire community has been very shocked, as you can imagine. Your mother has been in rather a state over it.*" So perhaps that was the explanation—her mother was merely more distracted than usual.

From then on, though, her mother's spelling was unreliable even when there wasn't any obvious excuse. But over time the unreliability became normal and Megan stopped noticing.

She was still in the linen cupboard in the autumn when she went out with a policeman who came to investigate the theft of their colour television from the lounge. That relationship lasted a couple of weeks. Then there was the businessman who took Megan to a party and introduced her as "my little colonial" as if she were a pet chimpanzee and then tried to make love to her in a taxi on the way back to the hotel. That one lasted about five hours. After that there was a very nice but rather dim dentist who took her home to meet his mother on the first date. After that, astonishingly, it was the hotel's first birthday (free Champagne in the lounge for the guests and a nostalgic dinner at the Gay Hussar for Megan, Annabelle and Peter), followed immediately by Christmas and New Year's. And then, incredibly, it was 1968 and Megan had been in England for two years.

Sometimes it felt like a couple of months. Mostly it seemed like a lifetime.

In March 1968 Megan decided it was time she had a place of her own. She'd resigned herself to a bedsit; a bedroom-cum-living room with either its own kitchen or its own bathroom but not both. Annabelle and Peter paid her well but even so there was no way she could afford a flat of her own anywhere near the hotel; it was either a bedsit or sharing a flat with a group of others, as in Lansdown Terrace, and she wasn't going to do that again.

She wasn't in a rush and she was very picky, so it took a while—three months, in fact. In the end she saw it in the window of the newsagent's where she bought Adam's Matchbox cars, printed neatly on a postcard, stuck up alongside notices about lost cats and cleaning ladies: a bedsit with its own kitchen and a bathroom shared with just one other person. And the address was a ten-minute walk from the hotel.

The room was on the top floor of an old house, up under the eaves, so it was full of odd corners and sloping ceilings and there were a good many places where you couldn't stand upright, but that merely added to its charm in Megan's view. It was painted a drab green but she would change that—the landlady seemed to have no objection. The kitchen, stretched along one wall and closed off from the rest of the room by means of a sliding door, contained all the essentials, including the smallest refrigerator Megan had ever seen. Its interior measured one cubic foot. Megan mentally measured it for milk, butter, orange juice, meat and cheese, and decided it would be fine. Perfect, in fact; no wasted space. She was delighted with it; she was delighted with everything. Even the shared bathroom was fine: it was clean, which was all she asked.

"I'll take it," she said to the landlady, a tired-looking woman with a small girl clinging to her knee.

"But Mummy, you *said,*" the child said. She had a well-practised whine that made the hairs on the back of Megan's neck stand on end.

"All right, darling, in a minute," her mother said. To Megan she said, "Oh good, I'm so glad."

"But Mummy!"

"Who do I share the bathroom with?" Megan asked.

"Mummy, you *said!*" The little girl was hauling on her mother's skirt.

Give me five minutes alone with that child, Megan thought. To the mother she said politely, "Do you live here too?" because much as she loved the room, if she had to listen to that whine it would be a deal-breaker.

"Yes, on the ground floor. The first floor is a flat and then the second and third each have two bedsits."

Excellent, Megan thought. Two full floors of insulation should do it. "And who do I share the bathroom with?"

"*Mummy, you said!*"

Megan's mouth went tight. Maybe not, she thought. Maybe I couldn't even stand hearing it occasionally on the stairs.

Across the hall a door opened and a man came out. He gave the child a look of intense disapproval, then looked at Megan and smiled.

"Hello," he said. "Are you taking the room next door?"

Megan looked at him. Looked again. "Yes," she said decidedly. "Yes. I am."

CHAPTER ELEVEN

Edward

Struan, March 1969

Sometimes I am tempted to move into the bank. Take up residence there rather than coming home to a fresh set of problems every night. An added bonus would be that the bank doesn't smell; there's a very unpleasant smell in this house. Initially it was just upstairs but now you can smell it in the living room too. Emily isn't keeping up with the laundry—the towels in the bathroom haven't been changed for a long time—but I don't think that's enough to account for it.

And then there are the everlasting problems with the boys. Yesterday evening when I got in there was a letter waiting from Ralph Robertson, the principal of the high school, asking Emily and me to come in and talk to him about Peter and Corey. I took it up to Emily to ask if she knew what it was about, but of course she didn't, so I went down the hall and knocked on Peter and Corey's door. They opened it a crack, looking furtive.

"I have here," I said, pushing the door farther open, "a letter from your principal asking your mother and me to come in and talk to him about the two of you. What's it about, do you suppose?"

They glanced quickly at each other and then at the floor, looking guilty of virtually any crime you'd care to suggest.

"Well?" I said when the silence showed no sign of coming to an end. I don't know what it is about the two of them that makes my blood pressure rise so fast and so high. They are indescribably annoying. They give the impression that as far as they're concerned you don't exist, you're just a hazard to be avoided, like a hole in the road.

"Dunno," Peter said, studying his feet. Corey did likewise.

"Everything's been going all right at school, then?" I said. "Neither of you is in any kind of trouble?"

Peter gave a minimal shrug. Corey did likewise.

I managed to simply turn and leave, which was an achievement. My father would have knocked them both across the room.

Just for the record, I did not want any of this. A home and a family, a job in a bank. It was the very last thing I wanted. I am not blaming Emily. I did blame her for a long time but I see now that she lost as much as I did. She proposed to me rather than the other way around, but she is not to blame for the fact that I said yes.

That phrase they use in a court of law—"The balance of his mind was disturbed"—sums it up very well. I married Emily while the balance of my mind was disturbed.

Back downstairs I noticed Tom, sitting in that damn chair. He has it partially turned towards the wall so as to block off the rest of the room. Either he doesn't want to see us or he doesn't want us to see him. Or both. I know the feeling. I considered suggesting that he come into my study so that we could try yet again to have a talk, but I was feeling too annoyed about the boys.

There was a time when I found it possible to talk to Tom. Him alone, of all the children. I remember having quite a long conversation when he was in his early teens about the building of the Canadian Pacific Railway. The cost in lives, whether the end justified the means, that sort of thing. It was the first time we'd had a proper discussion and I remember being impressed by the seriousness with which he considered all sides of the matter.

We had other discussions over the years. Not many, but one or two. In his final undergraduate year we had a talk about whether or not he should go on and do his master's in aeronautical engineering. He was at the Institute for Aerospace Studies at the University of Toronto and wanted to do his MSc there. It was going to cost a fair bit of money and he asked rather tentatively if I would fund him. There was never the slightest risk of my saying no but I asked him a good many questions purely for the pleasure of hearing him talk about this great interest of his.

I wish I'd talked to him more. Not just then but earlier. The fact is, I didn't know how to go about it and still don't. You can't just decide to have a conversation with someone, or at least I can't. It's easy at work because there's always a point to the discussion, a reason for it. I have no trouble with that. Or with talking to Betty. Books provide the starting point there.

He did extremely well in his MSc—Tom, that is. Just over eighteen months ago, when he finished the course, which coincided more or less with the suicide of his friend, both Boeing and de Havilland contacted him via the university inviting him for interviews. Boeing is based in Seattle. Imagine being paid to go and work in Seattle.

He didn't even reply to their letters. It made me almost sick with frustration. Still does.

I've taken to visiting the library in my lunch hour. I'm not in love with Betty, nothing so foolish. I like her and admire her and I enjoy our conversations very much and generally feel better for them, although today, in fact, I did not.

We've never talked about our families before but today she asked how Tom was. The difficulty was that I couldn't think what to reply. Finally I said that he seemed to be having a hard time getting over the death of his friend and that I suspected he felt responsible in some way. I said he didn't seem to want to talk about it and that I didn't know what to do for the best. I told her I was considering kicking him out, purely for his own good.

Betty nodded, then asked what Emily thought about it. Another straightforward question but again I was stuck for an answer. I couldn't very well say, "I haven't asked her" without explaining why I hadn't asked her, which would involve discussing Emily herself and her inability to focus on anything more than six inches from the end of her nose. Finally I said she was rather preoccupied with the new baby and Betty smiled in that particular way all women do at the mere mention of babies and asked how he was and what we were going to call him and so on and so forth, and we sailed safely into the calm waters of new babyhood.

Betty hasn't had an easy life herself. She has just one child, who was born with some form of brain problem. I don't know the details. Dr. Christopherson sent the boy down to the Hospital for Sick Children in Toronto but nothing could be done. He's in his teens now and as far as I know isn't a particular problem aside from the fact that he'll never be able to fend for himself. So Betty is serving a life sentence, you might say. Though possibly she doesn't see it that way. Her husband clearly did—he took off a long time ago.

As she'd brought up the subject of children, when we'd finished with babyhood I asked how her son was making out (by some miracle I managed to remember that his name is Owen).

She said he never varied much. There was a short pause while I tried to think what to say to that. Finally I said something about it not being easy.

"Oh well," Betty said, with a smile. "Whoever said it would be? Never mind. Ever onward."

Ever onward. I imagine that sums up her attitude to life. I find it admirable and rather shaming.

When I got home I went up to Emily's room. She was talking to the baby while changing his diaper—I heard her as I opened the door, though she stopped when I came in. The baby was waving his arms and legs about like they do, his eyes fixed avidly on Emily's face. He was naked and looked alarmingly small and vulnerable but at the same time entirely content. Emily glanced up when I came in and said hello as if she wasn't entirely sure who I was.

"How are you both?" I said with an attempt at a smile, inclining my head at the baby.

"We're fine," she said cautiously. "We're both very well. How are you?"

"I'm fine too," I said. "I'd like to talk to you. Do you have a minute?"

"Talk?" she said, looking alarmed. I tried not to let it irritate me.

"About Tom."

"Oh."

For some reason that seemed to relieve her. She pulled a tiny woollen undershirt over the baby's—I must stop calling him that; his name is Dominic—over Dominic's head and deftly eased him into a many-buttoned sack-type thing that contained his feet. I was reminded of Betty and her sleeping bag.

"You'll have noticed Tom's still here," I said, though there was no guarantee of that. "It's been more than eighteen months since his friend died but he seems unable to get over it. At least I assume that's at the root of the problem. I was wondering what we should do about it. He can't just sit in the living room for the rest of his life."

"Can't he?" Emily asked vaguely, doing up buttons.

"No, he cannot," I said, unable to keep the annoyance out of my voice. She'd switched off—it was perfectly evident—and I can't believe it isn't deliberate; she simply prefers not to think about anything difficult or unpleasant. "He's wasting his life and it's time he pulled himself together. I've been trying to think what we could do or say to help him and I wondered if you had any thoughts on the subject."

"Me?"

"You are his mother, Emily. What do you think we ought to do?"

She looked at me and just for a moment it was as if a fog had lifted and she'd actually heard me and taken in what I'd said. Then it was gone. She turned back to the baby and gathered him up, cupping his small bald head in her hand. "I don't know what to do about anything," she said to him. "Except you. I always know what to do about you."

———

This morning I phoned Ralph Robertson at the high school. I explained that Emily was fully occupied with a new baby and I was very busy and asked if we could have our chat about Peter and Corey over the phone instead of my going to see him. He said he'd rather I came in, which is irritating. We've fixed a date for next week.

On the plus side, a letter has arrived from Megan. She wrote and posted it more than three months ago, so it predates several we've had since then. God knows where it's been in the interim. Anyway, it seems that a mere three years after arriving in England

Megan has finally paid a visit to the National Gallery. If I were a drinking man I'd have a drink in celebration. She describes it as "really amazing." High praise. She enclosed a postcard of *The Execution of Lady Jane Grey* by Paul Delaroche, of whom I'd never heard. A strange choice of picture on Megan's part, I would have thought, but Delaroche is clearly very good, I will have to look him up. Lady Jane Grey I have heard of. I believe she was a pawn in the games of powerful men around the time of Henry VIII and ended up having her head cut off. I'll look her up too.

I took the letter up to Emily and found her drifting around the room in her nightgown with the baby over her shoulder—it made me wonder if she's been dressed at all today. When I said there was a letter from Megan she gave me an angelic smile and continued drifting. I put the letter on the bed for her to read when she comes back to earth. I didn't give her the card. I thought the subject might disturb her.

She was looking quite beautiful. That is the one thing about Emily that has not declined over the years; if anything, I'd say she is more beautiful now than she was when I first met her. Not that beauty matters, but for some reason when you're young you think it does. Though possibly when you're young you just don't think.

Emily's father became the principal at our high school during my final year—the family moved up from Hamilton in order for him to take the job. From my point of view the timing was good because by then things had become very bad between me and my father, and Emily was a welcome diversion, you might say.

In addition to being the best-looking girl I'd ever seen, I thought she was the cleverest, though it turned out I was wrong about that. Coming from an educated family she spoke well, and I mistook that for intelligence. I'm not saying Emily is stupid, just that she isn't as smart as she sounds.

Even so she was the only one of my classmates I was ever

able to talk to. I don't recall now what we talked about but travel and art certainly came into it. She let on she shared my dreams of seeing the world and I was innocent enough to believe her.

That isn't fair. It suggests she was like a spider, spinning a trap, and I don't suppose she consciously did that. No doubt she imagined herself in love with me and was trying to be interested in my interests. I imagined myself in love with her too. It has always struck me as a mistake on Mother Nature's part that we make the most important decisions of our lives when we're too young to have any idea of the consequences.

———

I've returned to Mother's diaries—the final section. I've been putting it off, but having started this venture I feel I owe it to her to finish it. Then I will know her story, as much as it can be known.

I would have been in my teens when she wrote the last of the entries that survived the fire, and by then we had been on the farm for some years. Our lives were incomparably easier there than they had been in the early days, so it is ironic that this was when the deterioration in her writing began.

The farm was a gift from my mother's parents. I didn't realize that until today and it explains a lot, but it puzzled me considerably when I read it. For eight years she had refused to see or accept help of any kind from her family and then all of a sudden she capitulated and accepted a farm. That was quite a climb-down. There was nothing in the diaries to account for it and it wasn't until I was working out how old we children were when we moved to the farm that it suddenly made sense.

I was seven and Alan and Harry were eight. School age. Out of loyalty to my father my mother had been prepared to sacrifice almost anything, but she couldn't bring herself to sacrifice our schooling. She'd been teaching us herself for several years but she would have been aware of her own limitations. The only solution was for us to stop traipsing around the North and settle down near a town with a school, and her parents offered her the only means of making that happen.

She must have agonized over that decision. She would have known how my father would take it, the message it would send to him. But she'd also have known there was no other choice. He'd been prospecting for the better part of a decade by then, promising the earth and delivering nothing, and had walked out of or been fired from every job he'd ever had.

"*Stanley says he will not work for fools,*" she has scribbled on a scrap of newsprint not much bigger than my thumb, "*and that they are all fools.*"

Quite.

The farm was certainly a generous gift but probably not as extravagant as it sounds. It was 1929 when we moved there. The price of silver was falling and the mines were closing. Towns that had grown up around them were dwindling away until in some places nothing was left of them but the giant corrugated iron head frames that towered over the landscape. Some of the head frames are still there. They are magnificent in their way. Like giant rusted dinosaurs.

With the miners gone, the surrounding farms had no one to sell their produce to. Eventually many of the farmers just upped and left—walked out of their farmhouses with nothing but what they could carry on their backs and headed south, looking for work. Their loss was our gain; my mother's father would have picked up the farm for a fraction of what it was worth. It was thirty miles from his own farm. I'm sure he and my grandmother would have preferred it to be closer, but my mother would have drawn the line at that.

To anyone accustomed to a halfway normal existence the farm would have looked alarmingly primitive but from my mother's point of view it must have been luxury. It was just three miles from the lumber town of Jonesville, which is a ghost town now, but back then it boasted a church, a post office and a general store as well as the all-important school. After the isolation of the mining camps it must have seemed like a metropolis.

The farmhouse itself was only a log cabin but it was large and well-built, with three good bedrooms and a big living room/ kitchen with a fireplace at one end and a range at the other. We children thought it was a palace and after so long in the bush I imagine my mother did too. I remember her standing in the centre of the living room on the day we arrived, very slowly turning full circle to take it all in—the rounded, well-chinked logs, the solid floor and neat, tightly fitted windows—her expression a curious mixture of disapproval and delight: disapproval because an easier life for herself had not been her goal; delight because she was a woman, after all, and a home meant a great deal to her. She was probably trying not to love it. Trying but failing. I remember when she'd completed her circle she walked over to the range and bent down and kissed one of the stove lids, then straightened up and turned to face us, laughing, her mouth and nose all black from the stove, her face luminous with relief and joy.

It is hard to overstate the difference it must have made to her life. Up until then we had moved so often there had never been time to get a vegetable garden established or enough land cleared to raise a single cow. It was a hand-to-mouth existence in those early mining camps, and that is desperate enough if you have only yourself to feed. The farm, by contrast, although small— just fifty acres—came complete with four cows, half a dozen chickens and a large kitchen garden. It was far enough from town that there was game around and from the first snowfall each year we would put out a couple of handfuls of hay every day to attract the deer and whenever we needed meat we'd shoot one. There were ducks and geese in season, there were eggs from the chickens and milk, cheese and butter from the cows. In the summer there were wild blueberries and strawberries, which Mother bottled and sold in the town along with any surplus from the garden.

I'm making it sound idyllic. It was subsistence farming and grindingly hard work, but now at least there was always something to put on the table at suppertime. You had to grow it or catch it or shoot it and you had to know where to look for it and you had to know how to preserve it, but having come from a pioneering background my mother knew all of those things.

My father did not.

Stanley says farming is work for a peasant, not for a man with anything about him. I asked was it not satisfying to watch things grow, to provide food for your family through the work of your own hands. It was foolish of me to say such a thing. Stanley became furious, thinking that I was saying he could not provide for us, which is not what I meant at all. He upset the table and everything crashed to the floor.

She was right, it was a foolish thing to say.

I wonder if he knew, deep down, that he was not very smart and had no talents and no skills and nothing special to offer the world. I've always assumed the opposite—that he had a ludicrously high opinion of himself—but maybe that wasn't so. Maybe in the darkest hours of the night a cold chill of self-knowledge stole in and he saw that by his own definition he was a nobody. A failure. Maybe that was at the heart of his anger.

In which case when my mother, breaking her promise to him, accepted the farm from her parents, he would have seen it as proof that she saw him for what he really was.

Is that enough to explain the change in my mother's writing and the bruises we hid under our clothes? I think it could be. Back then a man who couldn't support his family was not a man. The farm would have reminded him of that every day.

Why didn't he leave us? God knows I for one fervently wished that he would. But he wasn't one to let anything go, my father. My mother was his and so the farm was his, no matter that he despised it. It gave him free bed and board, and if my mother managed to sell some of the produce from the kitchen garden, well, the money was his too. It kept him in drink.

I have found something—it caught my eye because of the name on it. My mother wrote it on the back of a brown paper bag, the sort that flour and sugar used to come in.

> *Yesterday I spoke to Mr. Sabatini and he said that he was certain Edward had a great future if only he could stay on at school. I dare not mention it to Stanley—he is taking against Edward more and more—but I wish there were someone with whom I could share my happiness. I thanked Mr. Sabatini from the bottom of my heart.*

Mr. Sabatini was my geography teacher. A remarkable man; Italian, as his name suggests. He had a flair for languages and had been everywhere, not as a tourist but living and working in each country for a year or more, generally as a teacher. I don't know how he ended up so far north. Perhaps he was running from something, or perhaps someone told him that the essence of this country is not to be found in its cities but in its wilderness. Either way, I was fortunate that he did.

For the two years he taught us, our geography classes included history, art, philosophy, politics, religion—just about everything, an education in the fullest sense of the word. He started off by introducing us to the countries of the Mediterranean and by way of illustration brought in a selection of his own photographs for us to see. I was stunned by them. The photographs themselves were extraordinary, but more than that, I'd never imagined such astonishing places existed. When we were dismissed at the end of the day I went back to his classroom and asked if I could look at the photographs again while he was tidying up. The next day he brought in several of his own books on art and architecture and said I could borrow them.

I hid them under my bed. I wasn't afraid my younger sisters would get hold of them, I was afraid my father would.

I'm sure Mr. Sabatini guessed that things were not good at home. I remember him telling me that he'd been flung into jail once in some foreign port and to keep himself from despair he would call up in his mind the wonderful places he had still not seen, and plan the order in which he would visit them when he got out. It can't have been mere chance that he told me that.

It would be an exaggeration to say that he changed my life but he certainly made the one I had more bearable. He gave me something to dream about, something to strive for. I'll never achieve it now but just having the dream was valuable. It has broadened what has otherwise been a very narrow life.

Here's an ironic thing: after all my dreams of travelling the world I am the only one of my siblings still in the North. Alan and Harry live on adjoining farms in Manitoba. They married sisters and have at least a dozen children between them. Margaret married a Toronto man and seems quite happy down there. They have four children. My other sisters are dotted across the country. Margaret's the only good letter-writer in the family. She keeps the rest of us up to date.

One way or another this has been quite a night. I was sitting here at my desk, thinking about Mr. Sabatini, when the door of my study opened and there stood Emily in the doorway.

She was looking . . . I'm not sure how to describe it. She was looking unlike herself. For a start she wasn't holding the baby, and Emily looks incomplete without a baby, but more than that she looked wide awake and much more focused than usual, rather as she did for a moment a few days ago when I went up to speak to her about Tom.

Before I could speak she said, "Edward, what did I do wrong?"

Her voice was unsteady but she asked the question with such directness that I was taken aback.

"What do you mean?" I asked.

She said, "I must have done something wrong but I don't know what it was. I've never known. You never said."

I said, "Emily, what are you talking about? I don't know what you're referring to."

"You and me," she said. "You used to love me and then you didn't, and I don't know what I did wrong."

She wasn't crying but her lips were trembling. I felt the most crushing sense of shame. I stood up quickly and went around the desk and stood for a moment, uncertain, and then put my arms around her. I don't tend to do that sort of thing but I couldn't think what else to do.

She gave a little start but she didn't pull back, just stood with her head bowed, her forehead not quite touching my shoulder.

I said, "You didn't do anything wrong, Emily. I'm sorry. It wasn't your fault. None of it was your fault. It was mine."

We stood for a minute like that. I didn't know what else to say, so I said again that I was sorry.

"It's all right," she whispered. "It doesn't matter."

That made me feel even worse—her saying it didn't matter. As if her life didn't matter. Or as if she assumed I would think that.

I said, "Yes, it does. It does matter. I'm sorry," knowing that repeating those trite words couldn't make anything right.

After a moment she stepped back and looked up at me and said, "I want to go back to bed."

"All right," I said. "I'll come up with you."

I followed her upstairs. The baby—Dominic—was asleep in a tangle of bedding, his mouth making those involuntary sucking motions Mother Nature has programmed into them.

Emily looked up at me anxiously.

"What is it?" I said.

"I only want to go to sleep. By myself."

"That's fine," I said, somewhat stiffly. "That's what I thought you meant." I have never insisted on "relations." I've left it to her to make the advances.

I went back downstairs, still with this terrible weight of shame. I didn't know what to do with myself. I didn't want to read; I didn't want to think. I went into the entrance hall and pulled on my out-door clothing and went out into the dark. I walked fast into town.

Walking from one end of Struan to the other takes less than ten minutes. If you kept walking south and east eventually you would hit civilization; if you kept walking north and west you would hit Crow Lake, where the road comes to an end. In either case you'd freeze to death long before you got there. When I reached the gas station at the far northern end of town I turned around and walked home.

I knew there was no point in going to bed, so I went into the kitchen and got myself a bowl of cornflakes, more for something to do than because I was hungry. I took it into my study thinking that I'd look through one of the books on Rome while I ate, but I found I didn't want to think about Rome. I ate the cornflakes staring at my desk. When I'd finished I decided to go through the few remaining scraps of Mother's diaries. I felt so terrible already that I thought nothing I found there could make me feel worse.

In the end, only one of the entries was complete enough to make any sense, and Mother's writing was so shaky that in some places I couldn't make it out at all, but it reported an incident I remember only too clearly. I can date it exactly because Mother wrote it in the margins of a page torn from the *Temiskaming Speaker* and the date is still legible—18th September 1934. I would have been twelve.

> . . . the children were screaming and all three of the boys tried to shield me but that made him angrier still, and he turned on them savagely, knocking them away, first one and then another, and all the while I was pleading with him to stop but that only made him worse, and it wasn't until he had worn himself out that he finally stopped and left the house. All of us were crying, myself as well. I have never cried in front of them before and it terrified them. It was more than an hour before I had calmed them all down and got them into bed. I believe my arm is broken, and my eye is very bad, but worse than that, worse by far, is that the children witnessed it.
>
> After about an hour Edward came out from his bedroom. His face was red and swollen, partly from Stanley's blows and partly from tears. He stood in front of me and said, "Mother, if he does that again I will kill him."
>
> I was so horrified I almost cried out. I said he must never, ever, allow himself even to think such a thing again. I tried to make him promise, but he wouldn't promise . . .

The next bit is indecipherable but at the bottom of the page there are several more lines.

> Edward has been my joy, my consolation. To see his intelligence develop, to watch his face as he reads and see him so transported, has given me hope that he will escape all this

and that some good will have come of my life. But now I am
fearful for him. Very fearful. I believed he had the strength
of character to rise above hatred and bitterness against his
father, but now I am not sure. But I must have faith in him.
Those were words spoken in anger and he is still very young.
I must have faith. He is a kind and loving person; he will
put this behind him. I know he will.

I sat until after midnight, reading and rereading those lines.
I don't know how to deal with them. I don't even know what
to feel.

CHAPTER TWELVE

Tom

Struan, March 1969

Eleven inches of snow in one dump. Marcel took it personally; in a fit of fury he drove the snowplough just that little bit too fast and the heavy snow shooting off the end of the plough created a vortex, a mini tornado, and demolished six road signs in the blink of an eye.

"Rip' 'em right off der posts," Marcel raged. "Now I gotta go an' put 'em up agin, gonna take me a week. I piss on it! I piss on dis goddam' snow!" and he unzipped his pants and did so.

On Crow Lake Road there was an exposed stretch where the wind played tricks, scooping snow into fantastical shapes on one side, scouring it down to bare ice on the other. Tom was heading home at the end of his shift when a truck in a hurry overtook the plough, hit a patch of ice, went into a spin and shot off into the bush. Tom stopped the plough so fast it was a miracle he didn't leave the road himself. He leapt out and ran down the track left by the truck, cursing as he went. The truck's driver was cursing too—Tom could hear him as he came up, so at least that meant he was okay. He was trying to get out, but the truck had embedded itself in deep snow and he couldn't get the door open. Tom shovelled the snow away with his hands. It was heavy work and he was panting by the time he was done.

"Thanks," the driver said as he climbed out, but he sounded madder than hell. "Thanks very much, but God damn it!"

"You okay?" Tom asked, still breathless.

"Yeah, but I'm gonna be late! I have to meet this guy . . ." The man stopped, recognizing Tom at the same moment Tom recognized him—the man who'd rescued him from the coleslaw at Harper's restaurant. "Hi," the man said, calming down a little. "Didn't realize you drove the plough. Thanks for stopping."

"That's okay," Tom said. To anyone else he would have said, "What do you think you're doing going that fast on a road like this?" but he owed the guy. "Want a tow out?"

The man looked at his watch and shook his head. "Thanks, but it'd take too long. Could I hitch a lift? I'll get it towed out later."

"Sure."

"Just gotta get some stuff from the truck."

The sign on the truck said, "Luke's Rustic Furniture." The man—Luke, presumably—disappeared inside the cab and reappeared with a large cardboard box. "Samples," he said. "And they're not broken, so that's something. This is great of you. I appreciate it."

The hurry, it turned out, was because he had an appointment with the boss of the hotel/hunting lodge that was being built out along the lakeshore. He was hoping to get the contract to make the furniture for the lodge.

"The boss-guy phoned from Toronto first thing this morning," the man said when they were under way. He was cradling the box of samples on his lap. "Said he was going to take advantage of the weather and fly up for the day. He's got some people to talk to, said would I like to meet him for lunch and discuss things. I heard the plane fly over about an hour ago, so he's here."

He looked across at Tom. "I'm Luke Morrison, by the way. And thanks again."

"Tom Cartwright," Tom said. "No problem."

That was it for a couple of miles. Luke sat in silence, seemingly mesmerized by the plume of snow streaming off the blade of the plough. It was hypnotic, Tom knew: he'd had to train himself not to look at it.

Eventually Luke stirred himself. "Cartwright, did you say?"

"That's right."

"Your dad manager of the bank?"

"Yeah."

"He helped me a lot when I was starting up my furniture business," Luke said. "Ten, fifteen years ago. I was just a kid, really, knew nothin' about nothin'. I went to him for a loan. He showed me how to draw up a business plan, work out what I needed to borrow—all that sort of stuff. He took a lot of time over it. Really helpful."

"No kidding," Tom said, trying not to sound as sour as he felt.

Luke nodded. "Nice guy."

Dr. Jekyll and Mr. Hyde, Tom thought bitterly. Maybe he should make an appointment to see his father at the bank. That way, he might get ten minutes of his time.

More miles went by. A couple of inches of new snow covered the road, easy for the plough to deal with. What it couldn't deal with was the treacherous layer of compressed snow underneath, hard as ice and just as lethal. Chains were the only answer to that and most cars had them, but even so people ended up in the ditch on a regular basis.

"Speaking of families," Luke said. "The . . . ah . . . waitress at Harper's the other day? Sorry about her, she's a pain in the ass. Best thing is to ignore her."

"You're related?" It seemed polite to pretend he hadn't worked that out.

"She's my sister."

Tom tried to think of an appropriate response. "Sorry to hear that," might be a little impolite. "She seems to have a thing about vegetables," he said at last.

"Been going on about them for years."

"That must be kind of . . ." he searched for a word . . . "wearing."

"You cannot imagine," Luke said.

Tom laughed. He hadn't laughed for a long time and it felt good, felt as if it loosened things that had been clenched up inside him.

"What do your parents think?" he asked.

"They're dead, so they don't have to deal with it."

"Oh. Sorry."

Luke lifted a hand dismissively. "Years ago."

Ahead of them a moose stepped out of the bush, ambled into the middle of the road and stopped. Tom touched the brakes carefully, then stepped on them harder, and the snowplough slewed sideways, straightened up again and came to a stop. The moose paid no attention. He was gazing into the woods on the far side of the road, lost in thought.

"Sometimes they don't seem any too swift," Luke said.

"That's for sure." Tom honked the horn. The moose swung his head around, gave them a baleful look and sauntered on.

After that they sat and watched the snow-laden trees go by until they got to Struan, where Tom realized he'd not only managed to carry on a whole conversation without breaking into a sweat but had passed the turnoff to the ravine without even noticing.

Luke Morrison was meeting the boss-guy at Harper's, so Tom dropped him off there and went and parked the snowplough.

When he got to Harper's himself, Luke and a bald guy in a suit were ensconced in one of the bigger booths. Along with their lunches there was furniture—dollhouse size—all over the table. The bald guy was forking fries into his mouth with one hand and picking up pieces of furniture with the other, turning them this way and that. ". . . As many as you need," Luke was saying as Tom walked by. "The numbers wouldn't be a problem."

Tom stole a quick look at the models as he went past. They looked good. There were three or four different designs, some of them fancy, some of them plain, all of them sturdy and graceful-looking. He'd have liked a closer look at them himself.

He'd picked up a copy of *The Globe and Mail* on his way to Harper's but before he could spread it out the Amazon sped by carrying two plates of hamburgers and fries. She delivered them to a table near the front, then headed back towards the kitchen, pausing, as if purely in the pursuit of duty, at Luke's table.

"How's your dinner, sir?" she asked the bald man solicitously, inclining her head to show her genuine interest and concern. "Are you enjoying the hot turkey sandwich? How about the coleslaw—isn't it just the best?"

From where he sat Tom could see the man's face and Luke's back. Luke was running his fingers through his hair—a gesture of stress, Tom guessed. You could bet this wouldn't have been his choice of meeting place. But the bald guy smiled widely. "It's real good," he said. "All of it, coleslaw included. What's your name, miss, if you don't mind my asking?"

"Bo," the Amazon said. "Good, that's what I like to hear, a rave review. And you, sir," she turned graciously to Luke, tipping her head to the other side. "Are you enjoying your meal?"

Tom looked away—it seemed cruel to watch. Luke must have forbidden her to let on they so much as knew each other and she was having so much fun with the situation she hardly knew what to do with herself.

"Well, there we go!" Tom heard her say. "Two rave reviews. The chef will be so pleased. Now how about dessert? There's blueberry pie apple pie, lemon meringue pie, black cherry pie, pecan pie and Mrs. Harper's world-famous brownies, all with cream or ice cream. My own personal recommendation would be the blueberry pie because our blueberries up here are the best in the country, but they're all delicious."

"Well, I for one am going to have exactly what you recommend," the bald man said. "And some more of your excellent coffee."

Luke's hair was starting to resemble a well-ploughed field. He muttered something and the Amazon said, "Excellent choice, sir! Coming right up!" and bounced off to the kitchen. The bald man followed her with his eyes.

"Now she is something else," he said admiringly. "Didn't know you grew them like that up here!" He was all but licking his lips.

You dirty bastard, Tom thought, with disgust. You've got to be pushing fifty!

On the way home he took a detour down to the lake to have a look at the plane. It was sitting on its skis out on the ice, a Beaver, as Tom had guessed it would be, a single-engine, propeller-driven little workhorse designed by de Havilland Canada and purpose-built for the rigours of the Canadian bush. Back when he was four or five he'd been playing on the beach one day when an unimaginably wonderful machine had swooped down out of the sky, skidded along the top of the water, settled down on its floats and taxied right up to the shore. The door opened and a man leapt out and splashed barefoot to the beach, pausing just long enough to tousle Tom's hair as he went by. Tom had been so astonished he couldn't speak.

He'd been hooked then and there. The miracle of flight—the

glamour of it, the romance, the nonchalant ease with which man defied the law of gravity—everything about it enthralled him. Two decades later, still enthralled and studying aerodynamics in Toronto, he'd come to realize that the truly astonishing thing was that it *wasn't* a miracle: man had worked out that it could be done and therefore he had done it; it was as simple as that. Now man had taken on space itself; he had broken free of Earth's gravity and orbited the moon. Soon he would land on it. No miracles required, just a little imagination and a lot of math.

Tom's own particular passion wasn't outer space, it was supersonic flight, and it seemed to him that if there were a miracle involved it was that he happened to be born when he was, because in the whole history of flight there had never been a better time to be an aeronautical engineer. Over in Europe, Concorde was under development; out in Seattle, Boeing was working on the supersonic transport program; down at the Institute for Aerospace Studies in Toronto, having completed his final exams, Tom was called into his professor's office and told that his name had been put forward to both Boeing and de Havilland and he would probably be receiving letters inviting him for interviews shortly. If that wasn't a miracle for a boy from the bush, what was?

Three weeks later, back at home for the summer, he had rounded the corner of a sheer rock face and seen the crumpled heap of his friend's body at the foot of it, and twenty years of passion had vanished in a heartbeat.

Now Tom walked around the little plane trying to work out what he was feeling. Nothing much. But he didn't think he'd have been able to come and look at it a couple of months ago, so maybe that was progress.

He walked along the shore, keeping close to the edge, where the wind had left enough snow to provide some traction. The sun had gone and a few large soft flakes were drifting down—the plane would have to leave soon or not at all. Once he rounded the point that sheltered Low Down Bay from the wind, the snow was thigh deep and within yards he was breathless and sweating. As soon as Lower Beach Road came into view he stopped. No need to go farther.

The bay looked entirely different in winter, barren and hostile, the point where land and water met erased by ice and snow, the curve of the rocks obscured by drifts. The trees were so burdened with snow they looked like figures hunched against the wind.

The cottages were deserted—they had no insulation, so were only for summer use. The one the little girl and her parents had been staying in was at the far end of the road, with the beach on its doorstep and its back to the woods. It was the one they always stayed in. They came for a month every summer to enjoy the beach and the lake and the wide curving beauty of the bay. They loved the peace and quiet, the child's mother had said that day in court, her mouth so distorted with grief and rage that the words had to be squeezed out one by one. The peace and the quiet and, in particular, the lack of traffic.

Robert was convicted of manslaughter, which surprised no one. What surprised them all was the sentence passed down by the Crown attorney: three months of service in the community. Robert had looked stunned by it. He'd expected a prison sentence.

Tom had been standing beside Robert when the child's mother came up after the trial—Robert's parents were on the other side—so he heard what she said. She was shaking so hard with anger that the words came out in fractured syllables, but they were still comprehensible. She said that justice had not been done and that Robert knew it. She said she hoped that the image of her child's dead body would be at the forefront of Robert's mind every minute of every day from now until the day he died.

She said that Robert had destroyed her child's past for her as well as her present and her future; she could no longer see her daughter in her mind's eye as a baby or a toddler or a little girl learning to ride a bike—her memory no longer held those pictures. The only picture it held, the only thing left to her, was the image of her child's dead body, head lolling back, mouth gaping open, as they had lifted her into the doctor's car. And therefore her prayer now, her constant prayer, was that it would be all Robert would ever see either, now and forever.

Tom had known he should stop her; he'd known he should step between her and Robert and say, "Ma'am, excuse me, but you don't want to say those things, you really mustn't say those things, please come away now." He should have put an arm around her and steered her away, forcibly if necessary, given her into the safekeeping of someone, anyone, so that she could not let loose into the world words that should never, ever, have been spoken. He knew he should do that but he was unable to move. He felt rather than saw Robert stagger back, though the woman hadn't struck him with anything but words. Later he saw that Robert's mother had collapsed and that people were gathered around her. He also saw Robert's father, Reverend Thomas, standing as if carved from stone, one hand partially raised as though to stop the appalling words before they reached his son, his mouth half open as if he'd tried to say something but at this, the most critical moment of his life, had lost the power of speech.

By a stroke of luck Shelley the Slut wasn't there when he got home. Adam was in the living room playing with his cars. Tom sat down in his chair, leaned his head back and closed his eyes. Apart from the sound of Adam's cars there was silence, a rare and beautiful thing in this house. He thought he might even fall asleep, and then thought he was asleep, and then he woke up because the sound of cars had stopped and he smelled an odorous presence. He opened his eyes a slit. Adam was standing by his knee looking at him with serious eyes.

"Hello," Tom said, not bothering to lift his head.

"Are you sad?" Adam asked.

"I guess a bit," Tom said.

"Why?"

Tom sighed and straightened up. "A friend of mine died. It was a while ago, but it's still sad."

The by now familiar crease appeared between Adam's eyebrows. "What *is* died?" he said.

Tom opened his mouth to say, "Like that mouse we found" but stopped himself. The concept was difficult enough without the kid thinking that everybody ended their days upside down in a jar of honey.

"It's like . . . you just aren't there anymore. It's kind of hard to explain."

"Where do you go?"

"Nobody knows. Nowhere bad, though."

Adam thought about it long and hard. Finally he held out a car he'd been clutching. "This is my new car," he said.

"That's called a change of subject," Tom said, taking the car. "This is new, is it? It's very shiny. Do you know what kind it is?"

A shake of the head.

"It's a Mercedes sports car. They can go really fast."

A vigorous nod. "Is that colour called silver?"

"It is. Where did you get it?"

"It was on the table."

"What do you mean, on the table? In a box or something?"

Adam shot off and returned with a little Matchbox box and handed it over.

"I see," Tom said, examining the box. It had been considerably squashed. "That's very neat. Where did it come from?"

"It came with the letters."

"Someone sent it to you? That's nice of them. Do you know who it was?"

A shake of the head.

"Do you have the paper it was wrapped in?"

Adam shot off again and returned with a jumble of brown paper.

"Right," Tom said, smoothing out the paper on his knee and fitting pieces together. "Somewhere here there should be a return address . . . look at the stamps, they're different—well hey! Whaddya know—it's from Meg. Do you remember Meg? I guess you wouldn't; she left a long time ago. She's your big sister. She lives in England."

Adam hauled up his T-shirt, releasing a fresh puff of stink, then hauled it down again. "Why doesn't she live here with us?"

"That's a good question," Tom said. "I wish she did, then you wouldn't smell like you do and we wouldn't be in this mess. Have all your cars come like this?"

"Yes."

"So Meg sent you all those cars. Wow! That's really nice of her, isn't it? I think she must like you. She's never sent me anything."

Adam looked thoughtful. For a moment he seemed to debate something with himself, then abruptly he disappeared behind the chair, rattled cars briefly and reappeared with a red and yellow dump truck that had seen better days.

"You can have this," he said.

"You mean to keep?"

"Yes."

"Thank you," Tom said. "That's very generous of you. I'm touched."

CHAPTER THIRTEEN

Megan

London, July 1968

His name was Andrew Bannerman and, apart from having an attractive smile, there was nothing remarkable about him. He had brown hair in need of a cut and a pleasant enough face and dirty jeans and a sweater that was unravelling at the collar. His bedsit room, across the landing from her own, was a shambles—at least the bit she caught a glimpse of through the open doorway was. Clothes and books and papers everywhere.

A standard male, in other words. He was on his way out when she met him on the landing and said he'd be away for a couple of weeks but would knock and introduce himself properly when he got back, so she only had that one brief look at him and he was nothing special. That was what she decided.

He seems nice enough, she told herself as she painted the window frame. It'll be good to have someone nice across the landing. Did I just paint that bit or not?

Annabelle and Peter came over to view the room the evening after Megan signed the lease, bearing a bottle of wine and a set of wineglasses with delicate twisted stems.

"To your new home!" Peter said, raising a glass. "This is a real find, Meg. And that's quite a view." He went over to the big sash window. (Megan had washed it, inside and out, at no little risk to life and limb, as soon as she took possession of the room.)

"You've got your own private nature sanctuary," Peter said. Birds were flitting about, squirrels were flowing up and down the trees. It was like a miniature forest, and from the road you'd never have guessed it was there. Just before Annabelle and Peter arrived there'd been a short but vigorous downpour and now the evening sun was glancing off the rooftops as if the whole thing had been stage-managed for the specific purpose of impressing Megan's visitors.

Annabelle turned back from the window and contemplated the room with a decorator's eye. They had offered to help Megan do up the flat before she moved in. "Have you decided on the colour?"

"Pale yellow-gold." (Two years ago she would have painted everything white and never given it another thought.)

"Perfect," Annabelle said. "I think you need another armchair for when someone comes around. Would you like the Windsor chair in the office? We never use it."

Megan imagined Andrew Bannerman sitting in it, glass of wine in hand.

She took a week off to paint and decorate the room. Janet, her assistant housekeeper at the hotel, was quite capable of filling in for her now, and in any case Megan was still sleeping at the hotel, so she could keep an eye on things. Annabelle and Peter came around on a couple of evenings to help out and it was just like old times, though in fact it was the days on her own that Megan enjoyed most. She'd never had a holiday before, at least not since she was too young to remember. In between coats of emulsion she sat at the table by the window, looking down into people's back gardens and thinking about the strangeness of the past two and a half years: the desperate homesickness of the early days, how close she had come to giving up and going home, how much she would have missed if she'd done so. Here she was in a place of her own, paid for with her own money, earned by doing a job she loved. And who knew what tomorrow would bring?

When the decorating was finished she went shopping. Around the corner there was a hardware store that sold all kinds of things for the kitchen. She bought a set of crockery (plain white, four of everything), cutlery, saucepans, a bread board, a chopping board, kitchen utensils and a fat brown tea pot. Then she went to John Lewis ("Never knowingly undersold") and bought an electric kettle, a toaster, a coffee percolator and a casserole dish nice enough to put on the table should she happen to invite someone for dinner. She had to take a taxi to get everything home.

On Sunday, the final day of her week off, Megan moved in. It didn't take long; apart from her recent purchases she still had very few possessions. She'd invited Annabelle and Peter for dinner that evening to celebrate, so after sorting out where everything went she started cooking. She made a chicken pie for the main course, just to check that she hadn't lost the knack of making pastry, and fresh poached plums for dessert. Then, because she'd been wanting to make them for two and a half years and now she finally could, she made Chelsea buns to serve with the plums. They weren't considered a dessert, but so what? She served them warm with custard and they were a triumph.

———

Megan was so happy that day she almost burst with it, so it was strange that she had a disturbing dream that night. In the dream she went back to see her family and they weren't there anymore. Nothing was there: not the people, not the house, not even Struan itself. It and they no longer existed. The dream didn't provide any explanation. Megan awoke to a feeling of loss and grief she hadn't felt since her days at Lansdown Terrace. Why would you have a dream like that at a time like this?

On Monday morning she got a letter from her father—just her father, which was unusual; normally her parents wrote at the same time so as to economize on stamps. Megan opened it with a vague sense of apprehension (the dream was still lingering in the back of her mind) but by the time she finished reading the letter it was no longer apprehension she felt but outrage.

6th August 1968

Dear Megan,

Thank you for your letter dated 15th July. I am glad you have found an apartment close to your place of work. That will be a considerable advantage, saving time as well as travel fares. Provided the roof is sound, being on the top floor will be an advantage too, as there will be no noise from above.

Things here are much as usual. Your brother Tom is driving a lumber truck for the summer and appears to have no plans to return to his chosen career. We've had no word from the twins for a good while, so we don't know where they are, but there is nothing new in that. Your mother is expecting another baby after Christmas.

That's about all the news, apart from the fact that
we have had a spell of dry weather so the mosquitoes
are not as bad as they were earlier, which is a consider-
able relief.
    Everyone is well. I hope you are too.

The way he slipped it in: "*Your mother is expecting another baby after Christmas.*" As if it was of no particular consequence. As if he hadn't been told, straight out, by Dr. Christopherson—Megan had heard it with her own ears—that there were to be no more babies. Her mother wouldn't be able to cope, the place would be utter chaos. But more important than that, much more important, was Adam: who would look after him while his mother fell in love with the new arrival? Megan was so furious she wanted to phone her father and shout, "You're a disgrace!" down the phone line.

Fortunately, things were busy at the hotel. Mondays were Annabelle's day off, so in addition to her other duties, Megan was front of house. An elderly lady guest had been taken by surprise by a spider in the bath and had to be soothed and brought tea and the spider disposed of. Someone had stolen a bottle of Harveys Bristol Cream, a bottle of Courvoisier and the contents of the honesty box from the bar. (A guest? A member of staff? Someone off the street? There was no way of knowing.) Megan grimly made a note of it and sent Janet out to buy more. Doing the rounds with Jonah (he of the single tooth), she happened to catch sight of his hand, which he had stabbed with a screwdriver the previous week. Megan didn't like the look of it. "That's infected," she told him. "Go to the doctor. Go this minute." Jonah said he didn't have a doctor, he'd never had a doctor, he didn't believe in doctors. Megan phoned the nearest surgery, made an appointment for him and threatened to escort him if he didn't go at once. An American couple arrived with no luggage: they'd flown overnight from New York to Heathrow while their luggage had flown from New York to Singapore. Megan was very sympathetic—she didn't have to pretend. She gave them complimentary toothpaste and toothbrushes and promised to make the airline's life hell until the luggage was returned.

Whenever her father's letter entered her mind she reminded herself that her mother had coped without her for two and a half years now and Mrs. Jarvis came in twice a week and would doubt-less come more often if necessary. And Adam was nearly four and, unless he had changed his personality since she'd left (and he wouldn't have—in Megan's experience they were who they were from the moment they drew breath), was a steady little soul. He'll be fine, she told herself, just fine.

She did a reasonable job of convincing herself, but back at her bedsit that evening she reread her father's letter and saw some-thing she had failed to take in earlier—that Tom was still at home—and that made her mad all over again. Neither of her parents had mentioned him for a while and she'd assumed he'd managed to pull himself together and get on with his life. She should have known better. Tom had always been a brooder. As a child, when any little thing had gone wrong—someone stepping on his Lancaster bomber, his prize penknife vanishing—he'd withdrawn into himself and brooded for days.

She decided to write to him. Somebody had to do something or he'd sit there for the rest of his life. She got a pen and an air-mail form from the kitchen drawer she'd dedicated to such things and sat down at the table by the window. "*Dear Tom*," she wrote, and paused. What she wanted to say was, "*Dear Tom, I know Robert's death was terrible, but I hear from Dad that you are still at home sitting on your backside brooding about it and I was wondering exactly what you thought you were achieving by that and when you were going to get on with your life,*" but she suspected that would be a mistake. She was still puzzling over it when there was a tap at the door. She answered it absent-mindedly, pen in hand.

"Hi," Andrew Bannerman said. "I've come to say welcome to the top floor. Oh . . . ," he broke off, noticing the pen. "Sorry. You're in the middle of something. I'll come back another time. But welcome anyway." He gave her his very nice smile and started to turn away.

"No," Megan said hastily. "It doesn't matter. I was just writing a letter. I can do it later. Please come in."

"Just for a sec," he said. "I can't stay—I was just going to say hello. Wow!" He looked around the room. "What a difference! It looks amazing. It's a great colour."

"It was easy because it was empty," Megan said, ridiculously pleased. "I did it before I moved in."

He looked at her uncertainly. "I'm useless at accents but I think I detect one. Where are you from?" (How could you fail to like someone who phrased it like that?)

"Canada."

"Canada," he said, looking thoughtful. He seemed to be mulling Canada over.

"It's above the United States," Megan said dryly. (She was used to this now but nonetheless a little disappointed—she'd expected better of him.) She pointed upwards. "North."

He looked down at his feet and grinned. "I did know that much, believe it or not. I was just wondering if I knew anything else. I know it's big and there's a lot of snow. Let's see: there's the Northwest Passage and the Franklin Expedition—they all died. Polar bears. Mounties, of course, always getting their man. Lumberjacks—there are lots of lumberjacks, right?"

"Some," Megan said. He was joking but she didn't mind. He was older than she'd thought, maybe close to thirty, and much better-looking. How could she have thought his face merely pleasant?

"I think that's about it," he said. "Sorry."

"That's okay," Megan said. "That's more than I knew about England when I came. Would you like some coffee?"

He had the nicest eyes she'd ever seen. Honest eyes. They were blue (unusual with such dark brown hair) and direct, and you didn't get the feeling that behind them he was wondering how soon he could get you into bed.

"I'd love to," he said. "But I can't just now. I have a deadline. But definitely another time. Or you come over to my place, except I'll have to clean it first."

He only stayed a minute after that, just long enough to say that he sometimes had the radio on when he was writing up his "stuff" (he was a journalist) and if it disturbed her she should knock and he'd turn it down. So he couldn't have been there longer than five minutes in total, but still, by the time he left, Megan felt as though she were running a temperature. She went over to the window, opened it fully and stood looking out over the quiet gardens. Don't you get carried away, her rational self said. He's nice—I'll grant you that. He's very nice. You like him and he likes you—because he did—she had felt that immediately—but that's all there is to it, so don't pretend there's more.

But another self, a self that despite the absurdity of pop song lyrics did indeed seem to be located somewhere down near the heart, safely beyond the reach of common sense or reason, said, This is it. He's the one.

When she finally turned from the window and saw the air-mail form lying on the table, for a moment she couldn't remember who she'd been writing to. Then she picked it up, refolded it and put it back in the kitchen drawer. Not tonight, she said to Tom in her head. Sorry. I can't think about you tonight.

———

Three weeks after he first knocked on her door Megan decided to invite Andrew Bannerman to dinner. She'd thought about it long

and hard beforehand. The man was supposed to do the asking—
it was silly but that was how it was, which was why she'd spent
three weeks waiting for him to invite her over for coffee. The fact
that he hadn't was disappointing, but she reasoned that it didn't
necessarily mean he wasn't interested. It was possible, of course,
that he already had a girlfriend, though if so he never brought her
back to his room in the evenings. It was also possible that he
hadn't had the time—certainly she heard his typewriter rattling
away at all hours of the day and night. But the most likely reason,
from what Megan knew of the male sex, was that he was chron-
ically disorganized and simply hadn't got around to it yet.

It seemed to Megan that inviting him for dinner would do no
harm. If she made it a casual, spur-of-the-moment, "I just happened to make too much of this stew" sort of invitation, it would
look like a neighbourly gesture rather than anything more. Where
was the harm in that?

She considered the menu carefully. It needed to be something tempting, something really good, but it also needed to be
the sort of thing she'd cook for herself or he'd smell a rat. Men
loved pies, but no one made pies for themselves. They loved
steak, but you couldn't "accidentally" buy twice as much steak as
you could eat. She went to a bookstore on her lunch hour and
browsed through cookbooks, looking for inspiration, and found
it in the form of something called coq au vin. It sounded delicious. It also sounded posh, but she could call it a chicken casserole and he'd never know.

She left work early and bought the ingredients on the way
home: a chicken, streaky bacon, butter, olive oil (she'd never heard
of it), garlic (ditto), button onions (ditto), button mushrooms
(ditto), herbs (mostly ditto), a quarter bottle of brandy (you only
needed two tablespoons but you couldn't buy two tablespoons)
and a bottle of Burgundy (you only needed half a bottle but they'd
drink the rest). It cost a fortune but she didn't care. She carted it all

home, the plastic bags cutting into her fingers. It was an oppres-
sively hot day but she didn't care about that either. It took her the
better part of an hour to bone the chicken and peel the onions and
make the stock and cream the butter and flour for the roux, and
she loved every minute of it. It wasn't until she'd put the dish in the
oven and was standing back, hands on hips, smiling at the wreck-
age of her tiny kitchen, that she suddenly caught sight of herself in
her mind's eye and realized she was behaving *exactly* like the sort of
female she most despised, the sort she'd seen in ads on the television in the bar at the hotel, the sort who longed for nothing more
than to spend her life chopping onions in order to please a man.

Worse still, she was deceiving herself. If he'd been interested
in her, he would have shown it by now. And he wasn't stupid; if
she knocked on his door with some story about having made too
much stew, he would know precisely what she was doing and why.

Megan, already hot from slaving over the stove, went hotter
still with shame. I will *not*, she said, silently but furiously, not just
with her rational self but with every molecule, every atom of her
being, I will *not* make myself ridiculous for any man. I will eat it
myself. It will keep a couple of days in the fridge. And I'll drink
the wine too.

She had a cool bath to lower her temperature and put on
jeans and a none-too-clean shirt and her Scholl sandals and was
on her way back to her room when Andrew's door opened and
he came out, stopped dead in his tracks and said, "My God,
Megan, what are you cooking? It smells fantastic out here!"

He was originally from Leicester, where his parents still lived, but
when he was young the family had spent a couple of years in
Edinburgh and in the summers they'd gone to the Isle of Skye
for their holidays and stayed in a small town called, of all things,
Struan. He was twenty-nine and had an older brother and a

younger sister. He'd always wanted to be a journalist. (The problem was, he said, so did everyone else, so it was a crowded field, which was why he was permanently broke.)

He had a habit of looking down at his feet when he was joking or expressing an opinion, as if he thought he shouldn't force it on you, but then when he looked up he met your eyes so directly that it made you feel he was looking straight into your soul.

He seemed fascinated by Megan's description of life in Struan. His interest made her feel interesting, though afterwards she worried that she'd talked about herself too much. She told him about never having been to a city before she came to London, and he shook his head in amazement. She told him about her arrival at 31 Lansdown Terrace and losing her suitcase. She laughed as she told the story, remembering how naive she'd been, but he didn't laugh. He said, "That isn't funny, it's terrible. What an introduction to England!" so she hastily told him about Mrs. Jamison at Dickins & Jones and Annabelle and Peter and how she loved working at the Montrose.

When they'd finished their dinner (she'd explained the coq au vin away as part of her plan to teach herself some fancy European cooking), he insisted on helping with the washing up—the first time she'd ever known a man to do that. As he was leaving he said, "That was a really great meal, Meg—thank you. Next time you have to come to me if you're brave enough. I'm not up to your standards but I do a mean spaghetti bolognese."

———

Three weeks. Four. They ran into each other frequently on the landing and he always seemed pleased to see her and never seemed in the least embarrassed or apologetic about the passage of time since the spaghetti invitation. Maybe he hadn't meant it. Or maybe he was the sort of person who took relationships seriously and didn't rush into them. Which, of course, was good.

Once she came up the stairs just as he was on his way back to his room from the bathroom, wrapped only in a very small towel. His hair was wet and he looked so astonishingly beautiful that Megan felt the blood rush to her face. Fortunately, he misinterpreted it. "Sorry, Meg," he said. "Timed it wrong." He didn't try to make anything of it, as she suspected most men would have done.

His door didn't latch properly unless he leaned against it, so generally it was open a few inches and if Megan left her door open too, she could see his right elbow as he sat at his desk. Now and again he'd tap at her door and say, "Coffee?" and her heart would give an enormous lurch and warmth would flood through her like a tide.

On and off he was away for a few days. The top floor felt wrong then. The silence echoed, and sometimes Megan heard the whining brat downstairs.

———

"We've been thinking," Peter said.

They were in the office, behind the reception desk. It was three in the afternoon, a quiet time of day.

"We think we're going to sell the Montrose."

Megan stared. The front door opened and the young couple from Paris came in. Megan got up automatically, went out to the desk, smiled, gave them their room key and returned to the office.

"That was not a good way to break it to her, Peter," Annabelle said. "Megan, you've gone pale. You're not going to be out of a job. We want to buy another old hotel and do the same as we did with this, and of course we want you to be part of it. We wouldn't dream of doing it without you."

"We'll get a good price for the Montrose," Peter said. "It's the right time to sell. And we'll buy something a bit bigger, twenty to thirty rooms."

"It'll be a challenge," Annabelle said, smiling at her. "And we know you like a challenge."

Sell the Montrose? They wanted to sell the Montrose? She couldn't believe it. The Montrose was theirs—they had made it, the three of them. They had poured their hearts into it. They *were* the Montrose. How could they sell it?

Annabelle and Peter were watching her.

"It's not going to happen straight away," Peter said. "Probably not until next year, unless we stumble on the perfect place before then. Come on, Meg, you look as if someone had died. Think what fun it was last time."

Megan collected herself. "Yes," she said. "Yes, of course. Of course."

At home that evening she sat at her small table watching the swaying of the trees against the darkening sky. Cold rain splattered against the window. It was October and the nights were closing in. When Peter had made his announcement it was as if the world had tilted—everything that had seemed fixed was suddenly shown to be precarious.

With hindsight, Megan thought, there had been signs recently that Peter was restless; he'd taken to standing on the porch of the hotel, hands in his pockets, looking out at the road as if he was waiting for something to happen. It had crossed her mind that he didn't have enough to do, but she'd thought no further about it. Now she saw that Peter having too little to do was the source of the problem. The Montrose was running smoothly, they were frequently fully booked and their accounts were in good order. All of those things were a source of satisfaction to the three of them, but for Peter they also meant that the hotel was no longer a challenge. He was the one who liked a challenge. And what Peter wanted, Annabelle would persuade herself she wanted too.

At least, Megan thought, they're looking for another property in London. They could have decided to start up a hotel in

France, or Italy, or Spain. They could still decide that. They both spoke several languages and loved going abroad. But if that happened, she would not want to go with them. She had no gift for languages and in any case it would be one step too far. She wasn't an adventurous person. She knew that now.

So what would she do? If Peter and Annabelle left London or tired of the hotel business, or if there was some other unforeseen eventuality, what would she do? She'd have to start over and she didn't want to start over—it was too hard. She saw that it wasn't England or even London she'd been living in for the past almost-three years, it was the Montrose Hotel. Outside its walls she was still a stranger here. It was her own fault: she should have pushed herself, met more people, tried new things. But it had been easier not to.

There was a tap at the door. Megan went over and opened it. Andrew Bannerman, wearing an apron and holding a glass of red wine in each hand, said, "Spaghetti?"

She'd never known anyone who listened as intently as he did. She told him about Peter's announcement, making light of her reaction to it, but he saw through that. "New things are scary, but nothing stays the same, Meg. You have to go with it, grab opportunities when they come along."

"I know," she said. "I know."

He smiled. "Sorry. Unasked-for advice. Have some more spaghetti."

She liked the fact that he gave unasked-for advice. It was a sign that he was interested. But she didn't want to talk about herself again, she wanted to know more about him. She asked about journalism and he described his early days in London, trying to sell his work. It had been a struggle, he said, and she guessed it had got him down sometimes; he wasn't as laid-back as he looked. He was the only member of his family who wasn't a doctor—two grandfathers, father, mother, brother and sister. "They don't think journalism is a real job," he said ruefully. "They're all infuriatingly patronizing, even my little sister. *Especially* my little sister."

Megan nodded. "My older brother used to patronize me. He did it all the time. I got so fed up I banned it, in the end."

"Banned it?" Andrew said with a grin. "How do you ban being patronizing?"

"Well, there were certain phrases he used that made me mad because they didn't sound rude but you knew they were. You know, things like 'If you think about it,' which means you're not thinking about it, and 'With respect,' which basically means without respect. 'I think you'll find' is another one. I fined him twenty-five cents every time he said something like that."

Andrew let out a whoop of laughter. "Brilliant!" he said. "Did he pay up?"

"I was in charge of the pocket money, so I just deducted it. Some weeks he didn't get any at all."

Which Andrew thought was funnier still.

Megan wasn't sure what he found so amusing. Though now, looking back, she suddenly wondered if Tom had found it funny too, funny enough, in fact, to be worth sacrificing his pocket money for—that possibility hadn't occurred to her at the time. But regardless of the reason, she was glad she could make Andrew laugh. There was no reserve in his laughter and she was becoming aware of a shadow of reserve in him the rest of the time. Not exactly guardedness. "Carefulness" would be a better word. Maybe he'd been hurt in a previous relationship. But then, the English were famous for their reserve, weren't they? So maybe it was just that.

She asked what he was working on at the moment and he said he was doing a piece on a painting at the National Gallery.

"Have you been to the National Gallery?" he asked.

"No," Megan said. "I haven't been anywhere." She'd been dreading that question—it was bound to come up sooner or later.

But if he was horrified he didn't show it. "Buckingham Palace? Hampton Court?"

"No," she said. "Nothing like that. I don't know anything about history or art or anything, so I'm afraid I wouldn't get a lot out of it. To be honest."

"You don't need to know anything. I don't know much myself. It doesn't matter. Look, I'm going to see the painting again on Thursday—I need another look at it. Do you want to come? Can you get time off? Say, Thursday afternoon?"

"Yes," Megan said. "Yes, I can get time off. Yes, I'd like to come."

Who'd have believed she would ever accept an invitation to the National Gallery with such a leap of the heart?

Though when it came to it, the gallery was just as she'd thought it would be, only bigger. Room after enormous room filled with paintings of absurdly dressed men and women looking down their noses at you or unreal landscapes or ships being tossed about in storms or pictures of angels and saints with golden halos. They left Megan cold.

Andrew pretended not to be watching her. Every now and then he'd tell her who someone was or the story behind a painting.

"You recognize this guy?"

A skinny-looking guy wearing armour and sitting on a horse with a head too small for the rest of it.

"No, but I can read. It's Charles I—it's on the plaque." Much as she loved him, she wasn't going to let him patronize her.

"Ah, so it is." She could hear his grin.

They entered yet another room, filled with yet more paintings. Andrew steered her over to a large picture with several figures in it, all of them in dark clothing, the room behind them dark, everything dark apart from the central figure of a pale girl in a pearl white dress with a blindfold over her eyes.

"This is the one I'm doing a piece on," Andrew said. "*The Execution of Lady Jane Grey.* The National Gallery's just acquired it."

"Who was she?"

"She was queen of England back in 1553. She reigned for nine days and then she was sent to the Tower. And after a bit they chopped her head off."

The blindfold covered almost half of the girl's face, but nonetheless you could see that she was very young, and you could also see that she was absolutely terrified. Her lips, which looked very soft, like a child's, were slightly parted and she was reaching out her arms as you would if you couldn't see what was in front of you. What was in front of her was a chopping block. Beside it was a man dressed in dark red tights, leaning casually on an axe. An old man in a fur-lined coat was guiding the girl down towards the block, helping her to kneel. In one corner, two women were swooning against the wall.

"How old was she?"

"Sixteen."

"Sixteen!"

If you reached out and touched her hand it would be like ice.

"Who are the other women—the ones against the wall?"

"Her ladies in waiting, I imagine. Overcome with horror and grief."

Megan studied them, her lips tight. Get up, she thought. Go over to her, kneel down beside her and talk to her. Stay there until she's dead. Then you can be overcome with horror and grief.

"It wouldn't have happened quite like he's painted it," Andrew said. "For a start they wouldn't have executed her indoors; they'd have taken her outside and done it on Tower Green. And her dress is wrong for the time."

Who cares where it happened or what she was wearing,

Megan thought. She was astonished by the intensity of emotion
the painting conveyed. Who'd have thought you could paint terror and dread?

"It's powerful, isn't it?" Andrew said. "I've always been interested in her because she lived very close to where I grew up. Her
home was in Bradgate Park, up near Leicester. The day her head
was cut off, her household lopped off the tops of all the oak
trees. Decapitated them as a gesture of respect for her. A few of
them are still there."

Megan tore her eyes from the girl's face. "The actual trees?
Didn't you say it was 15-something?"

"That's right." He studied her, smiling at her interest. "Would
you like to see them? I'm going up there next week—I want to
mention them in the piece I'm writing, and I need a photo. I'm
borrowing a car, so if you want to, you could come and see them
for yourself."

They arranged to go on Tuesday, Megan's day off. She spent the
intervening days storming around the Montrose with an energy
born of joy. She reorganized the linen cupboard, harried Jonah
to check and bleed the radiators in preparation for winter, took
down and cleaned the chandeliers on the landings, rehung the
curtains in room 8. In the evenings she spring-cleaned her flat as
well. It didn't need it but she had energy to burn. She wanted it
perfect to come home to, in honour of the fact that, although
ostensibly everything would be the same as when they set off, in
reality everything was going to be different.

It was a three-hour drive to Bradgate Park, and they were going
up and back in a day, so they set off early. The sky was overcast
and the landscape en route flat and uninteresting but when they

finally arrived, the park made up for it. It was bigger than Megan had expected and wilder and far more beautiful. Hills covered with bracken, their surfaces broken here and there by granite outcrops, areas of woodland, a wide clear stream. The leaves were turning. They didn't have the drama of Fall at home—the colours were softer and more muted—but with every gust of wind the leaves went swirling through the air in clouds of russet and gold.

They came across several of the ancient oaks straight away: huge trunks abruptly sliced off about ten feet from the ground, topped by a mass of smaller branches sticking up like fingers on a hand. One of the trees was dead, its mutilated body stark against the sky. Megan thought of the girl with the childish lips and icy hands; thought of her seeing that tree when both she and it were young. She might have sought out its shade on a hot day, sat under it peacefully. Not knowing its Fate. Not knowing her own.

It had never struck her before that the people you read about in history books had actually lived. Theoretically you knew they had, but in practice they'd been no more than words on a page. The tree was proof. It made Megan wonder who had killed the girl and why, but she didn't ask Andrew because if she had he would have told her, and that would have turned it into a history lesson and destroyed her feeling of connection with the girl. She would ask him another day.

They wandered, Andrew stopping now and then to take photographs. One tree in particular seemed to please him. They passed it early on and after exploring elsewhere they returned to it and he spent a long time photographing it from different angles. At some stage in its history it had been struck by lightning—one side had been partially burned away, leaving a great black cave at its heart. Incredibly, several branches were still reaching up, topped with small crowns of crisp brown leaves. As Megan watched, a gust of wind made the leaves shiver; several of them lost their grip and whirled away.

"A true survivor," Andrew said. "Still soldiering on."

A few yards away there was a log. Megan sat down and wrapped her arms around herself. The wind was cold. While they'd been walking the sky had clouded over, and her feeling of closeness with the place and its history had drained away. She was just herself now; herself, sitting on a log, trying not to think about the fact that time was passing and the day was more than half gone. In a few minutes Andrew was going to say he had enough photos. They'd go back to the car and drive somewhere for lunch, and then they'd head home and the trip would be over.

Which would have been fine if the trip had been truly and solely about Lady Jane Grey, but it was not. Megan had imagined herself and Andrew walking through this park hand in hand; she'd seen him leaning back against one of the ancient trees, wrapping his arms around her. Kissing her. Holding her to him. Ridiculous women's magazine images, but it turned out there was a core of truth in them because—she knew this now—when you were in love with someone you wanted to be as close to them as it was possible to get, you wanted to weld yourself to them, become part of them, make them part of you. You needed to touch them, you needed them to touch you. And he hadn't touched her. He'd never touched her and had shown no sign of wanting to. Never kissed her. She'd been certain that today, finally, would mark a turning point in their relationship, but once again, nothing had changed.

Andrew had climbed up as far as he could get into the ancient trunk and was taking a photo down into its hollowed-out innards. "I have fond memories of this particular tree," he said. "My brother and I used to pretend it was a castle—we had to defend it against all comers. Our parents, in other words. Our parents and our little sister. She was a ravening wolf. She didn't want to be a ravening wolf, she wanted to be inside the castle with us, but we needed a ravening wolf and she was it. Very mean."

A response was required. Megan said, "So this is really close to where you lived, then?"

"About ten miles. We came here a lot at weekends."

She tried to imagine him young, scrambling over the rocks with his brother, but she could only see him now.

"I'm nearly done," he said from inside the trunk. "Are you cold?"

"No, I'm fine." She wasn't fine. She was wretched.

"Good. I'll . . . Bugger, that's the end of the roll. I guess it'll have to do." He climbed out of the tree and came and sat down beside her. "There's a pub in the village," he said, opening the back of his camera. "We'll get some lunch there and warm up before heading back." He took out the roll of film and put it in his pocket. Then he looked at her and smiled. "So what did you think of the trees? I hope it hasn't been a waste of a day off."

"No," Megan said. "They're amazing."

She wanted him so badly she didn't dare look at him; he would see it in her eyes.

A minute passed. Andrew said, "You okay, Meg?"

"Yes, of course. I'm fine," she said, not looking at him. "Do you want to stop and see your parents on the way back?"

"No, not this time."

She could feel him watching her and tried to pull herself together. "Are you sure? Because I'm not in a hurry, if you want to." She had assumed he would—she'd wondered if they would like her.

"It wouldn't be smart," he said.

Which was such an odd thing to say that she looked at him. He was watching her. There was something in his eyes she couldn't read.

He said, "Meg, there's something I think you should know."

He hesitated, and looked away for a minute, then looked back and smiled. She couldn't read the smile either. "You've probably guessed, but I need to be sure, because I like you a lot—really a lot—and I don't want you to get the wrong idea. I'm getting the feeling—maybe I'm wrong, in which case everything's fine— but I'm getting the feeling that maybe you'd like there to be more to our friendship than just . . . friendship."

She looked down at her feet. She was cold right through to her bones. If he was telling her he already had a girlfriend hidden away somewhere, she wished he would say so.

Andrew said, "Basically, what it boils down to is I'm not good boyfriend material."

What did he mean by that? She was getting angry with him. Was he saying he was married?

"Are you married?" she said, looking at him fiercely.

He smiled, but his smile was tired, as if he'd had this conversation before and would rather not be having it again. "No. No, I'm not married. And I don't have a girlfriend. I've never had a girlfriend. I'm homosexual."

Megan felt a jolt go through her, felt colour flood her face. She turned sharply away. On the hillside to the right of them there was another of the ancient oaks, dead but still standing, black against the sky.

He said, "You didn't realize. Sorry. I should have told you sooner."

She couldn't look at him. She kept her eyes on the ancient oak.

He said gently, "Megan, say something. You've heard of homosexuality, right? Even in Northern Ontario they've heard of homosexuality?"

She had heard of homosexuality but only as a term, as a concept. She'd never met anyone—or at least never knowingly met anyone—who was homosexual. Mostly it just seemed to be a term of abuse used against boys by other boys. "*Homo*."

In the trees behind them some rooks were squabbling. Apart from that there was no sound.

Andrew said quietly, "You are making this hard for me, Meg."

She had to say something. She cleared her throat. "I've never understood it," she said.

"Okay, good. You're talking." Relief in his voice. "What don't you understand?"

"I don't understand why it would happen. Why would such a thing . . . ?"

"Yes, well, the problem with these 'why?' questions is there's no one to ask. It just happens. Always has, always will, unless they find some way of wiping us all out, which no doubt they're working on."

It just didn't make sense. Surely, Megan thought, surely if he were homosexual then her love for him—this incessant, desperate longing—would not have come about; her body would have known that his body didn't want hers and that would have been the end of it. Instead of which she had loved and wanted him more every time she saw him. Surely that meant it couldn't be true.

"But, Andrew, how can you be sure? I mean—"

He stood up quickly, cutting her off, and walked away and stood with his back to her, hands in his pockets, looking out over the park.

She saw that his back was taut with strain, that there was strain in every line of his body. She saw that telling her had not been easy for him. That nothing about it was easy for him. That he would not have said it unless it was true.

She wanted to go home. Not home to London, home to Struan. She wanted to go home to her own bed in her own room and stay there because life was too much for her. Too complicated, too painful.

Finally he came and sat down beside her again.

"Sorry," he said. "Difficult subject." He reached out and rubbed her back. "Let's go and have lunch."

It was the first time he'd ever touched her.

How are you supposed to stop loving someone you love?

CHAPTER FOURTEEN

Edward

Struan, March 1969

I need some time off. I don't mean from work. I'm entitled to two weeks' annual vacation, which I never take because being at work is so much less stressful than being at home. I mean time off from the escalating chaos in this family. There are things I need to think about and they're important, because it seems to me that if I could get a sense of perspective on the past I'd be able to deal better with the present, but there's no time; the present goes from one crisis to the next so fast that there's scarcely time to draw breath, far less think.

This afternoon I had the interview with Ralph Robertson, the principal at the high school. It was very inconvenient to have to go—there were a great many papers waiting on my desk at the bank—but I went. Robertson is a grey man. He wears grey and he looks grey. He greeted me rather anxiously, I thought, and spent an unnecessarily long time on the pleasantries, but eventually I managed to steer the conversation around to the purpose of our meeting.

"You wanted to see me about Peter and Corey," I said when we were both sitting down.

"Yes," he said, frowning at his pen. "Yes, I thought perhaps we should have a word . . ."

I nodded encouragingly. I was recalling that he has a wife and three teenage daughters, all of whom disappear off to Sudbury with his chequebook from time to time and manage to spend more in an afternoon than he earns in a month. I wondered if they'd done it again and seeing me reminded him of his bank account and that was why he was looking anxious.

"Nice boys," he was saying. "Though at a difficult age, of course."

"I take it they've been misbehaving," I said, trying to speed things along.

"Not seriously," he said. "Well, by and large not seriously. By and large just the usual things, fighting in the schoolyard, smoking in the toilets, failing to do homework, that sort—"

"Smoking?" I said. It's the most ridiculous habit known to man; quite apart from its effect on your health, you might as well roll up a dollar bill and set fire to it.

"They all do it," he said, taking off his glasses and rubbing his eyes. "It's because it's forbidden. And now there's all this new stuff, marijuana, LSD, who knows what else. LSD hasn't reached us up here yet—or at least I don't think it has. Makes them go out of their minds, apparently, but with some of ours it can be hard to tell. In my view we should make it compulsory, all of it, then they'd stop." He put his glasses back on. "But with Peter and Corey the greatest concern at the moment is the absentee-ism and the—"

"Absenteeism?"

"Yes, lately they've been regularly missing a day or two a week, sometimes more. They weren't in at all last week and only on Tuesday the week before. Our secretary, Mrs. Turner, phoned your wife several times to see if they had colds, but there was no reply. So I thought it would be a good idea to speak to you."

It didn't surprise me that Emily hadn't answered the phone—she probably can't even hear it, up in her room with the door closed—but the boys playing truant was something else. It wasn't only the fact of them missing lessons that concerned me, it was also the thought of what they might be up to instead.

"Also," Ralph Robertson said. He was hunched over his desk with his shoulders up around his ears and his hands clasped in front of him, and I suddenly noticed that he was twiddling his thumbs. Literally twiddling them—they were spinning around each other like little turbines. I've never seen anyone actually do that before. I thought it was a figure of speech. If I were Robertson, that is a habit I would break. His pupils must love it.

"Also—and this I can't verify, it is merely hearsay, but I thought I should tell you just in case—one afternoon last week they, or two boys looking very like them, were seen down at the sawmill apparently trying to set fire to one of the old shacks. Well, partially succeeding—it was the smoke that drew attention to them. Though I believe it soon went out. The wood, of course, was very wet."

I was frozen to my chair.

"As I say, the boys weren't identified for certain, but I thought I should pass it on to you. Because your two weren't in school at the time."

All sorts of images were scrolling through my head. Archie Giles's hay barn. The charred sticks behind the bank. Joel Pickett and his sons. Sergeant Moynihan filling the doorway to my office.

"I see," I said.

I stood up. Ralph Robertson stood up as well.

I said, "Thank you for telling me. Are they here now? At school?"

"Er, no. I don't think they've been in today."

I didn't go home to see if they were there. I didn't dare. I was so angry I didn't trust myself anywhere near them. I drove directly to the police station. Fortunately Gerry Moynihan was there. He offered me a chair and I sat down but I was so agitated it was all I could do to stay seated.

"It was my sons," I said to Gerry without preamble. "Peter and Corey. They burned down Archie Giles's hay barn. You don't need to look any further. It goes without saying that I will—"

Gerry raised his hand and I stopped. He said, very calmly, "Sorry, Mr. Cartwright, can we start again? What's happened? Take your time, sir. We've got plenty of time."

I took a breath. My lungs didn't seem to be expanding properly. It was as if they were in a cage that had become too small, too tight. It took a huge effort to speak normally—in fact, it took a huge effort not to shout—but I managed to relate the details of my interview with Ralph Robertson. Gerry listened quietly, looking attentive but unperturbed.

"So it was them," I said when I'd given him the facts. "It goes without saying that I will repay Archie every cent he lost, the barn, animal feed, any expenses, anything. The question is—"

Gerry raised his hand again. "Hold on, Mr. Cartwright," he said. "Hold on. I appreciate you comin' to tell me this—not everybody would—but I'm pretty sure your kids didn't burn down that barn."

I was concentrating so hard on trying to keep a lid on my fury that I didn't hear him properly at first, but after a minute the words sank in, and even though I was sure he was wrong I'd never heard sweeter words in my life.

"I've thought all along the jobs were different," Gerry said. "Whoever did Giles's barn meant business. They used gasoline, gave it a real soaking. Whereas with the fire behind the bank, your boys, if it was your boys—"

"It was," I said. "Thank you, but I know it was."

"Well, no, you don't, sir," Gerry said mildly. "There's no evidence it was them, nobody saw them, and from what you tell me there wasn't a positive identification down at the sawmill either, so you don't know, you're just suspicious."

"All right," I said. "I'm suspicious. I'm very, very suspicious."

"Okay. So what I was sayin' is, whoever set that little fire at your bank was an amateur. Didn't know the first thing about it. Struck me the minute I saw it. I reckoned it was kids and they were copy-catting. They'd heard about the Giles's fire and thought it'd be kinda fun to try it. Same applies down at the sawmill. I'll go take a look at it but from what you say they didn't even manage to get the fire properly started."

He paused, watching me. After a minute he went on.

"So the question is, what're we gonna do about it. Seein' that there's no proof it was them and no damage has been done."

"What would you normally do in such circumstances?" I said tightly. "I don't want them treated any differently from anyone else. No differently at all."

Gerry cleared his throat. "Well, I'll tell you, the theory is all kids are the same so all kids get treated the same, but the fact is they aren't and what I do depends on what I think of their parents. In cases such as yourself, a good family, I would normally just report my suspicions to the parents, let them handle it. If I thought the parents wouldn't care too much or had no control over their children, I'd haul the kids in to the station here, ask 'em a few questions, maybe show 'em what a prison cell looks like. Give 'em a little bit of a scare, you might say.

"This case is a bit unusual in that you've come to tell me rather than the other way 'round, which I appreciate. And because of that and because I know you, I'm not inclined to do anythin' more." He paused, studying my face, and then added, "Unless you want me to, of course."

I sat for a minute. It wasn't only a matter of how much control

I had over the boys, it was also a matter of how much control I had over myself. I was still so angry I didn't want to be within ten miles of them. Added to that, I strongly suspected they would pay no attention to anything I said.

"If it's all right with you, I'd like you to talk to them," I said at last.

"Do you want me to bring 'em here? Into the jail?"

"Maybe at home—at our house. If you would do that."

He nodded. "Sure," he said. "Fine by me. I'll come knockin' on your door tonight."

"What if they're not in?" I realized I had no idea how the boys spent their evenings.

"I'll find 'em."

He would too. The relief of handing the whole business over to someone who knew what he was doing was indescribable.

"Thank you," I said. "Thank you very much."

I started to get up but Gerry said, "One more thing I should say, Mr. Cartwright. Arson's a serious crime and you were right to come in and tell me about it, but your boys, if it was them, aren't the first to do somethin' like this. They're young and they're male and that means they're stupid, it doesn't mean they're criminals. I'm just telling you that in case you're feeling a little . . . upset."

He came at eight, in uniform, looking as if he meant business. The boys were in. I hadn't seen them—I took care not to see them—but the usual thumps and yells were reverberating through the house. I called them downstairs and when they saw Gerry their faces went almost green. Frankly, I felt a bit sick myself. I showed the three of them into my study—Tom and Adam were in the living room—and retreated to the kitchen. I couldn't sit down. I paced back and forth, back and forth. I kept thinking about what Gerry had said: if it was a good family, he told the parents and let them handle it. He classed ours as a good family and no doubt anyone from outside would say the same. But what people actually mean by that phrase, when you take it apart and look at it, is a family that lives in a nice house with a father who earns a decent wage. I was thinking as I paced that if you knew what went on inside our family, by no sensible criteria could you call it "good." Right now, in my study, a policeman—who as it happens isn't married and has no children of his own—was talking to my sons because I, their father, was afraid that I might do them actual bodily harm if I tried to do it myself, and also because I was afraid that they would pay no attention to me regardless of what I said. Meanwhile, upstairs, my wife had just produced another son, on whom she would dote for a year and whose upbringing thereafter she would totally neglect. A son who might well turn out to be a disgrace to us and a menace to society. I thought about this community we live in and how hard I have tried over the years to be a useful and respected member of it. I thought about my good name. It is hard to say whether rage or shame was uppermost in my mind.

After a while I heard the boys come out of the study. I waited until I heard them go upstairs and then went in to see Gerry.

"Well, we had a little talk," he said easily, leaning back in my chair. "It was like I thought: they did the fires at the bank and the sawmill, but not the barn. I doubt they'll do anythin' of that sort again. They're not bad kids, Mr. Cartwright."

"Thank you," I said. I wanted to ask him what I should do now. How I should go about managing them from here on, because I had absolutely no idea. I wanted to explain to Gerry that I had never wanted to be a father and lacked the qualities necessary to do the job. I wanted to ask if he'd do it for me, if he'd just take them off my hands.

I offered him coffee but he declined. I showed him to the door and thanked him again and he gave that salute of his and set off into the snow.

I went back in. As I passed his chair Tom looked up from his newspaper.

"Trouble?" he said.

It was the first time in a year and a half that I'd heard Tom initiate a conversation but I was in no state to be encouraged by it.

"Arson," I said, bitterly.

He raised his eyebrows. "Anything major?"

"Not yet. But only because they're incompetent."

"They were probably just messing around," he said. "You know them." He watched me for a minute and then added, "Anyway, he read them the riot act. They looked pretty scared when they came out."

He went back to his paper. I went into my study and closed the door.

I sat at my desk, remembering the first time I heard the police knock on the door. I'd have been about ten. There were two of them and sagging between them was my father, mumbling drivel and stinking of vomit. It happened many times after that but I remember that first occasion vividly. The shame of it. I'd wanted to deny all knowledge of him, all connection. I'd wanted them to lock him up and throw away the key.

Now, sitting in my study, I thought, Here we are again. From the police knocking on the door back to the police knocking on the door in two generations. Never mind that I'd asked Gerry to come; in essence it was the same.

After a while I heard Tom and Adam go up to bed. I stayed where I was, in a kind of daze of confusion and incomprehension, trying to figure out how my life had become what it was. I thought about the five sons I had sleeping upstairs. Two more on the far side of the world. One in the cemetery beside the church. One daughter, three thousand miles away.

I wondered how I had come to father all those beings, having wanted none. I wondered, for the hundredth time, how I had come to marry Emily, given that I didn't love her. I decided there were many reasons, none of them good. I married her because she was in love with me and I was amazed and flattered by that. I married her because I mistakenly thought we wanted the same things out of life. Because she was beautiful. Because I was grateful to her parents for accepting me as a suitable partner for their daughter despite my father being a drunkard and a fool. Because I was about to go off to war and would be killed and wanted to have sex before I died. I married her because she asked me to and it would have been impolite to say no. I married her because the stench of the fire was still in my nostrils and the balance of my mind was disturbed.

———

We seem to be programmed to seek answers. Something happens and we need to know why. We chase around inside our heads, trying on this theory and that theory, searching for one that fits. But often there are no answers, or too many. You could say, for instance, that what happened during the fire was a consequence of my doing well at school. You could say it was a consequence of my brothers Alan and Harry going off to war. They may seem like tenuous links but they're real and they're important. Without them, what happened wouldn't have happened.

That bit in her diary where my mother wrote that she didn't dare tell my father how well I was doing at school because he was "taking against" me more and more: that was true. The others came in for their share of abuse but I was the one he hated and it was at least in part because I was a whole lot smarter than he was and he knew it and knew that I knew it. Worse still, I was smart in the way he despised and envied most: I was book-learning smart.

My mother was book-learning smart too but she took care not to let it show. I'd have had an easier time of it if I'd done the same and I knew that; I just couldn't put it into practice. My hatred of my father for the way he treated us—my mother in particular—was so great that when he came into the room I would start to shake. It was loathing, not fear, but I knew it looked like fear and for my own self-respect I had to find a way of standing up to him. Physically I stood no chance—he was a big man and his fists were hard as stone—so I fought him with my intelligence. I fought him with irony.

In the evenings I'd do my homework at the kitchen table and he'd come in after a hard day drinking or chipping away at rocks—the last man in Canada to realize there was no longer a market for silver—and find me with my head in a book and instantly he'd be furious. It was like flicking a switch. He'd say, his voice low and dangerous, "What you sittin' there for, doin' nothin' like you own the place?" and I'd quickly get to my feet and stand almost, but not quite, to attention, hands at my sides, willing my body to be still, and say something like, "I'm sorry, Father, I need to work out these equations for school. But I can do them later if there's something you want me to do." Very earnestly, very respectfully, with not the faintest hint of sarcasm in my voice—or only the faintest hint. He'd look at me with eyes like slits. Not sure.

I loved that look. The suspicion, the uncertainty in his eyes. I paid a high price, but it was worth it. I never did it when my mother was in the room, though. Which I suppose is another way of saying I knew it was wrong.

The twins saw what I was doing and they thought I was crazy. I remember one night in our bedroom when I was studying my bruises, Harry said, "Just stay out of his way, for Christ's sake, Ed! Do your bloody homework in here where he can't see you."

I said I had a right to do my homework wherever I liked. Harry shook his head in disgust and said, "Thought you were supposed to be smart."

With hindsight the twins were remarkably good to me. We had nothing in common but it didn't seem to matter. Both of them left school at sixteen to help with the farm, whereas I stayed on. It meant I didn't do my share of the farm work but they didn't hold it against me. School was my refuge and I guess they knew that. I had my eye on university and had decided that when I had my degree I would do what Mr. Sabatini had done: teach my way around the world. When Emily arrived on the scene I confessed my dream to her and thereafter she dreamed it too, or let on she did. The two of us were going to travel the world together.

The dreams of the young. They're particularly tragic, it seems to me, because they are based on the assumption that you control your own destiny. On the third of September 1939 a lot of dreams came to an end, including ours. I was seventeen, too young to sign up, but the twins were eighteen. I remember the evening they told me they were going. "It's your turn now, kid," Alan said, meaning my turn to quit school and look after the farm.

I felt as if I'd been kicked in the stomach, and it must have shown, because he punched me lightly on the shoulder and said it wouldn't be for long; the war would be over by Christmas and if it wasn't, then as soon as I turned eighteen I could join them.

I knew that wasn't so. There was no way all three of us could go, leaving our mother with only the girls to help with the heavy farm work and, more than that, leaving her at the mercy of our father. It felt like the end of everything, the end of the world.

I hadn't realized the extent to which the twins had acted as a buffer, shielding me from my father. Once they left, things became very bad between us. I was big enough by then that he hesitated to attack me when he was sober but he was sober less and less of the time, and when he was drunk he was savage. I couldn't stay out of his way because I didn't dare leave my mother alone when he was around.

My schooling was over, and with it my contact with the outside world. Emily and I saw each other only at church on Sunday and for an hour or two in the evenings if I was sure my father was off on one of his prolonged binges. Those few hours aside, I was a prisoner on the farm.

I prayed every night for the war to end so that Alan and Harry would come home and rescue me. I don't know why it took me so long to work out that they never would. It finally dawned on me one night when I was sitting in the doctor's office in town. My father had arrived home raging drunk and when I tried to bar the door he smashed his way in and came at me with a broken bottle. I raised my arm to shield my face and the glass sliced through my arm from wrist to elbow. With my other hand I grabbed a kitchen chair and hit him so hard I knocked him cold. I believe I would have gone on to kill him then, had my mother and Margaret not stopped me.

Margaret drove me to the doctor's and it was while he was stitching me up that it suddenly came to me that, even if they survived the war, Alan and Harry would not be coming home. Why would they? The farm wasn't worth much, certainly not enough to compensate for life with our father. They'd made their escape and I couldn't blame them; they'd have been crazy to come back. That was when I realized that while my father was alive I was never going to be able to leave. So that was when I started lying awake at night planning how to kill him.

The phrase "every cloud has a silver lining"—I'd like to know who thought that up. One morning late in the summer of 1942, almost three years after Alan and Harry went off to war, I stepped out onto the porch and saw a strange cloud on the horizon. At first I thought it was a storm cloud and I was glad to see it—there had been no rain for six weeks and the fields were parched. During the morning the cloud continued to build and when I came out after lunch the underbelly had taken on a lurid light. I called out my mother and Margaret to have a look and the three of us watched it uneasily. We live in a tinderbox up here. We're surrounded on all sides by thousands upon thousands of square miles of grade-A firewood.

At length Mother said, "I think it's a fire."

It was a long way west of us and I remember thinking we'd be okay unless the wind changed. By three o'clock you could see flames beneath the cloud of smoke. I propped a ladder against the house and climbed up onto the roof to get a better look and saw a vast curtain of fire at least twenty miles wide. I still thought it would miss us but I decided to take the cattle down to the lake, half a mile away through the woods, just in case.

By four o'clock great billows of smoke were beginning to block out the sun. Fires create a ferocious updraft, sucking up air as the heat rises, and from the roof I could see flaming treetops being tossed miles ahead of the fire itself. It was still a long way off but the danger lay in a stray gust blowing smaller branches or twigs in our direction, so I decided to soak the roof of the house as a precaution. My mother and Margaret took turns at the pump and those of my sisters who were big enough formed a chain and passed the buckets up to me.

We were in the midst of this when my father showed up. We hadn't seen him for several days, which generally meant he'd been off on a bender, but either he hadn't had all that much to drink or the sight of the fire sobered him because he seemed to grasp what was needed. I left him on the roof slinging water on the shingles and went down to take my turn at the pump.

The next time I went up the ladder, the sky to the north and west of us was dark with smoke and beneath it the flames seemed to fill the whole horizon.

"It's getting too close," I said. "Time we left."

My father said, "We ain't leavin' this house to burn, so you can put that idea out of your head. Get back to the pump."

As he spoke I felt a breath of hot air on my face. Just a breath, very slight. Then a moment later, another one.

I didn't bother replying to my father. I turned and went down the ladder fast. My mother and the girls had left the pump and were clustered together at the foot of the ladder, looking up at us. Amy, the smallest, was clutching Margaret's legs and crying with fear.

I said quietly to my mother, "I think the wind's changing. You need to take the girls to the lake before it gets too dark to see the path."

She was nearly wringing her hands with distress. She said, "Edward, we cannot leave the house to burn. We cannot."

From the top of the ladder my father roared, "Bring up the buckets! What're you waitin' for?"

My mother started to run back to the pump but I grabbed her arm. "Mother! You have to take the girls! It might still miss us, but we can't take the chance."

My mother turned to Margaret and said, "Margaret, you take them. Edward and I will stay and help your father."

"I will not!" Margaret said, furious and terrified. "We will all go together!"

My mother didn't reply. She was looking past me, over my shoulder. She said, "Edward . . ." her voice scarcely above a whisper.

I turned and saw that the wind had swung around and was blowing the fire straight towards us. Above it, darkness was rolling out across the sky.

The worst thing, the most terrifying thing, the thing that has stayed with me over all these years, was not the sight of the fire's approach, though it seemed to be coming at the speed of an express train, but the *sound*. It was like nothing I had ever heard. It bore no relation whatsoever to the spit and crackle of branches when you throw wood on a campfire; it was a deep, cavernous *howl,* like some gigantic creature gone insane. Trees were exploding at its approach—they weren't "catching fire," they weren't "bursting into flames," they were literally exploding—huge fireballs belching 150 feet into the air, clouds of smoke and sparks roaring upwards. The *sound* of it. I'll never forget it. If hell has a sound, that is it.

For a moment I couldn't even draw breath. Then I turned. Margaret was holding Amy. I picked up Jane and tried to press her into my mother's arms.

"Take her!" I said. "Go! Now!"

But my mother wouldn't take her. She backed away from me. "You have to go with them, Edward. I'm not leaving your father."

"I'll bring him!" I shouted. "We can run faster than you!"

"He won't come with you, you know that! He won't listen to you!"

"I'll make him!" I shouted, or started to shout, because at that moment there was the most desperate, terrifying shriek and we turned and saw that my sister Becky's hair was alight. It was flaming out around her and she was spinning in terror, shrieking above the roar of the flames. I ran, tearing off my jacket, and flung it over her head and Mother joined me and we put out the flames. The other girls were screaming hysterically. I lifted Becky and gave her to my mother and put my mouth to my mother's ear and said, "Take them now, Mother, or they will die. We will catch up with you."

She was shaking violently but she nodded, and kissed me, and she and Margaret gathered the girls together and they ran.

When I turned back to the house my father was standing on the roof, silhouetted against a sky that seemed itself to be exploding with flame. The urgency of the situation had driven everything else, even the state of war between us, from my mind, and until that moment I hadn't given him a thought. Now, as I watched, he raised his fists to the flames and roared his defiance

and I suddenly realized that after all those sleepless nights planning his death, all I had to do was turn around and walk away.
Just leave him, because left to himself you could guarantee that
he would leave it too late. Just walk away, and all our problems
would be solved.

I would like to be able to say that I couldn't do it, that in the
name of humanity I could not leave without at least trying to
make him come down. Or that in the horror of that moment I
had some sort of revelation and saw in my father, this man who
had battled the Fates and lost time and time again, a nobility that
I hadn't recognized before. But it's the truth I'm trying to write
here and the truth is, I could have walked away without a qualm.
The sole reason I didn't was because I couldn't have faced my
mother if I had.

I ran to the foot of the ladder and shouted up to him, but he
couldn't hear me above the roar of the fire. Cursing, my guts
cramping with terror and frustration, I climbed the ladder and
scrambled across the roof to him. He was standing with his back
to me, facing the approaching flames. I grabbed his arm and he
turned and looked at me. I yelled, "Come on! If you don't come
now it'll be too late!"

I don't think he even knew me. He was covered in soot and
ash and his hair was wild and his eyes, bloodshot and streaming
from the smoke, were completely mad. He batted me off as if I
were an insect, a mere distraction, and turned back to the fire,
and I realized that God himself could not have made him leave.
I turned to go, but a flaming branch landed on the roof beside
us and instantly the roof shingles caught alight. Before I'd managed to stamp them out another firebrand landed, and then a
third. I yelled a warning but my father didn't even turn to look.
That was it for me. My courage broke and I scrambled back to
the ladder and climbed down, coughing and choking from the
smoke, and ran.

When I reached the path I looked back and saw him, almost obscured by smoke and flame but still facing that towering wall of fire, arms raised, fists clenched. And that is my last memory of my father: shaking his fists at the sky. *Shaking his fists*, for the love of God! Shaking his fists at a holocaust.

By the time I reached the lake it was so dark and the air so full of smoke that you couldn't see two feet in front of your face, so it wasn't until the fire burnt itself out early the following morning that I found the others. They were sitting on a small crescent of beach, soaking wet from having spent most of the night in the lake, huddled together like refugees from some bloody but nameless war.

My mother stood up when she saw me and came to meet me. There was no question in her face—there could only be one reason why I was alone. I told her that I had tried. I am glad I was able to say that.

I have comforted myself over the years with the thought that the fact that I tried means that, strong though my father's influence on me was, my mother's was stronger still. I don't know if that is true.

We made our way back along the shore until we reached the edge of the fire's destruction and then worked inland back to Jonesville. I was afraid there would be nothing left of the town, but though the stench of burning was thick in the air and a layer of ash covered everything, it had largely escaped the fire. Emily's parents took us in. After a few days with them, we went by truck and train to my mother's family, thirty miles away. When everyone had settled in I told my mother I had decided to enlist. She didn't try to stop me. I imagine she knew that I had to get away.

Emily did try to stop me. I returned to Jonesville to tell her and she wept and pleaded with me not to go. Finally, when she saw that I was adamant, she asked me to marry her, saying she'd be able to bear it better if we were married. I said yes. I could see no reason not to, given that I was sure I'd be killed.

The following day we were married. I was still so dazed from the fire that I have no recollection of the wedding. We had one night together before I was shipped off to training camp and six more nights before I was sent overseas. During one of those nights we created Tom.

CHAPTER FIFTEEN

Tom

Struan, March 1969

Overnight the wind swung around to the south and when he left the house in the morning he could feel the difference in the air and hear it in the snow under his feet—a wet crunch rather than a dry squeak. He knew better than to think spring had arrived—another blizzard was on its way—but it gave you hope.

When he passed Reverend Thomas's house the porch light was on again. Tom slowed down and anxiously scanned the house and front yard but there was no sign of the old man, barefoot or otherwise. He was so busy looking for him he almost failed to notice that the car had been partially cleared of snow. The top, and the sides down as far as the bottom of the windows, were exposed; it no longer looked like a hump but instead like an island or the back of a whale. The driveway hadn't been cleared, so Reverend Thomas couldn't have gone anywhere even if he'd been able to open the doors, but maybe that would come next.

Tom searched around in his mind for conclusions to be drawn and decided it was a good sign. If you lived in the centre of town like Reverend Thomas did, you didn't really need the car on a day-to-day basis, so it suggested he wanted to go somewhere, and that

in itself could be considered a positive thing. Maybe he was thinking of driving down to wherever it was his wife had gone. Maybe
eventually they'd be okay. Not happy, of course, but okay.

Luke Morrison was in Harper's reading the paper, the box of
models beside him on the bench seat. He glanced up when Tom
came in and nodded a greeting. Tom paused at his table.

"How'd the interview go?"

"Okay," Luke said. "Nothing definite but I think he liked the
stuff."

"That's great."

"He's bringing his wife up today. Wants her to see the models, help decide which ones they want to go for."

"They're here," Tom said. "I saw the plane coming in just now."

"Thanks. Better get things out, I guess." He opened the box
and started unpacking various pieces of furniture.

Tom slid into his half-booth, across from Luke and one row
down, and spread out his paper. Nobody dead on the front page.
Prime Minister Trudeau was shaking hands with a sleazy-looking
guy with dark glasses. They were smiling at each other like sharks.

A glass of water landed on the table.

"Same old thing?" the Amazon asked.

"Yes. Thanks."

"Boring, boring." She sped away.

The door opened and the boss-guy came in accompanied by
a woman wearing dark glasses and more dead animals than Tom
had ever seen all together in one place before. Fur from head to
toe. The hat on its own had to be a whole silver fox, the coat . . .
Tom did a quick count and reckoned it had to be at least fifty
mink, maybe double that. Her feet and legs up to mid-calf were
each inside a baby seal. Conversation in Harper's ceased altogether for a count of ten, then resumed in an awed murmur.

The woman seemed at ease with that. She stood in the doorway, smiling faintly behind her dark glasses, and waited to be shown to her seat.

The boss-guy spotted Luke, waved to him, then guided his wife down the aisle. Luke got up and stepped out of the booth. His back was to Tom, which was a pity, Tom thought, because he would have liked to see his face, but on the other hand he got to see the woman and that was an experience you didn't get every day.

"This here is Luke Morrison, furniture-maker extraordinaire," the boss-guy said with a wide smile. "Luke, I'd like you to meet my dear wife, Cherie. She's the brains of the business. As well as being the beauty, of course."

"Nice to meet you, ma'am," Luke said.

The woman took off her dark glasses and smiled at him. Her face was a work of art.

"Isn't this a cute place you have here," she said. She allowed her husband to help her out of her coat and slid into the booth opposite Luke. Without the coat she was a bundle of twigs.

"And this is the furniture," she said. "And isn't it cute too."

The men sat down and watched her. The whole of Harper's watched her. She picked up a miniature circular table, turned it around, turned it over, put it down, picked up a chair.

A hot beef sandwich and fries appeared in front of Tom. Perched on top of the sandwich was a solitary pea. Tom's retinas registered the pea but the optic nerves were busy with the woman and failed to pass the message on to his brain. Despite five years in Toronto he'd never seen anyone who looked quite as unreal as the boss-guy's wife. Every eyelash looked as if it had been meticulously crafted and glued in place that very morning.

Bo was setting down iced water in front of the newcomers. Seeing her beside the woman, Tom suddenly realized that Bo was a knockout. He wondered how he'd failed to notice it before;

maybe he'd never really looked at her, in case she started talking to him. In addition to being tall and blond, she was clear-eyed and long-legged and looked fit as hell. If the boss-guy's wife worked at it for a million years she'd never come close to looking as good as Bo did without lifting a finger, which when you thought about it was kind of unfair.

"Very nice to see you again, sir," Bo was saying. "How are you today, ma'am? Isn't it a lovely day?"

"Lovely," said the woman.

"Are you ready to order yet?"

"Um, no," said Luke quickly. "Give us a minute."

"Absolutely, sir," Bo said. "No problem. The menu's on the table mat in front of you when you're ready, ma'am."

"I know what I'm having," the woman said, making a little rocking chair rock with the tip of her finger. "This is delightful," she said, smiling at Luke. "May I have this?"

"Sure," Luke said. "Sure, of course."

"I'll have an omelette," the woman said. She balanced the rocking chair on the palm of her hand and raised it to eye level. Everyone watched.

"That's a good choice, ma'am," Bo said, taking out her notebook.

"Please tell the chef to use two eggs, fill it with fresh spinach and grate a little Parmesan on top."

"Fresh spinach?" Bo said, her pencil pausing.

The woman looked at her for the first time. "You don't have fresh spinach?"

"Not at the moment," Bo said, looking out of the window at several million square miles of snow.

"I wasn't assuming you grew it in your garden," the woman said, her mouth going thin. "I was assuming you would have it flown in."

"I'm afraid not, ma'am," Bo said. "I'm pretty sure we have tinned spinach, though. Would that do?"

"It's not that kind of town, Cherie," the boss-guy said jovially. "This is the *North*."

"Have you *frozen* spinach?"

"I'm afraid we don't have that either. How about peas? We have frozen peas."

"A *pea* omelette?" the woman asked glacially.

"Or how about potatoes?" Bo said, warming to the subject. "They're fresh. Potatoes are great in an omelette. And onions—how about a potato and onion omelette with cheddar cheese? That would be delicious! We could add some peas as well for colour if you like. It would be healthy too."

"Are you saying you have no fresh vegetables apart from potatoes and onions?"

"Oh no, we have carrots, cabbage, squash, turnips . . . a turnip omelette would be different. How about that?" There was a dangerous light in Bo's eyes.

Luke was squirming in his seat. Tom knew it would have been a kindness to look away, but it was too good to miss.

The boss-guy said, "Why don't you have one of their hot beef sandwiches, Cher? They're damned good and it wouldn't hurt you for once. I eat them all the time and look at me."

"I have looked at you," his wife said, not looking at him. "I'd like to speak to the chef."

"Sure," Bo said. "I'll just get her." She sailed away.

"Do you think people who have enough money to be flown all the way up here by seaplane will be happy to stay in a place where there are no fresh vegetables?" the woman asked her husband. Her tone was enough to freeze your balls off, Tom thought. Which might explain why the guy looked as if he didn't have any. It was funny, when you thought about it, how many rich guys looked like eunuchs.

"We can get them flown in if they really want them," the man was saying. "But this isn't Toronto, Cher. That's the whole point!

People will be coming up here for a new and absolutely authentic experience." He stretched his arms out to encompass the magnificence of the Canadian North. "That's what we're offering them—that's why it's so special. They'll experience the North as it really is, up to and including the food of the region."

"I think you should be very worried about this," his wife said, scanning the menu.

"Not everybody likes raw spinach, dear. Some people prefer normal—"

"I think you should be losing sleep."

Luke was scrabbling frantically around in his box of models. He brought out something wrapped in newspaper and began unwrapping it with great care.

"I, um, brought this in to show you," he said. "Just in case you were interested. It isn't something I could do in quantity; each piece takes a long time to make. But I thought . . . you know . . . you might be interested in having one or two."

He set a small chair down on the table in front of the woman. The seat was a smooth silver-grey disc of driftwood resting on slender legs. The back was formed from a delicate branch, or maybe several branches, each twig arching up or curving around to lend itself to the whole.

Wife and husband looked at it.

"I want twelve," the woman said.

"Twelve?" her husband said. "I mean it's gorgeous, I agree, but do you think it's right for what we—"

"Not for the hotel," the woman said impatiently. "People up here wouldn't appreciate how unique they are. I want them for us. For the dining room."

She turned to Luke. "Can you do me twelve? And I want a table to match. I'll leave the design to you."

"I couldn't do it in the time frame we're talking about, ma'am. I'm sorry, but they're handmade and each one depends on me finding just the right-shaped branches. Takes a really long time, so they'd be kind of expensive. Actually, very expensive."

Mrs. Harper appeared, Bo at her elbow. "I'm the chef," Mrs. Harper said. "Bo here says you wanted to see me."

"Just bring me a plain omelette," the woman said. "I'm sure it will be fine." To Luke she said, "You can discuss the price with my husband. It doesn't matter how long it takes, send me each one as you finish it. As for furniture for the hotel, I think this style here would be most suitable for the lounge . . ."

Tom found he was sitting with both elbows on the table, his knife and fork sticking straight up in the air. Bo, passing by, said, "That's what I like to see. An empty plate. How are you feeling?"

"What?" Tom said.

"How do you feel? Sometimes when your body's not used to a certain food it can upset your stomach a little bit to begin with. That's why it's a good idea to build up gradually."

"What?" Tom said.

"Never mind," she said kindly. "If you feel a little strange this evening just lie down for ten minutes. You'll be fine."

"I'm going to need more guys," Luke said. "Want a job?"

"Making furniture? I've never done anything like that." Tom was examining the models—he'd taken a seat in Luke's booth. "This is really nice stuff. I'm not surprised they want it."

"These are all machine-made," Luke said. "Not hard to learn."

Tom would have liked to have a close look at the branching handmade chair, but the woman had taken it with her.

"You have work lined up for after the snow goes?" Luke said.

"Not sure. Last summer I drove a lumber truck. Is your work-shop out at Crow Lake?"

"Yeah. It's in the garage. I'm going to need to extend it, get more machines. I've got to go see your dad, talk to him about money."

Tom put down a chair and picked up the circular table with its central leg and three elegant feet.

"I did aeronautical engineering," he said. He hadn't realized he was going to say it until it was out. "I was working on supersonic flight."

Luke raised his eyebrows. "Wow! Sounds really interesting."

"Yeah. It was. But things got a bit . . . messy, a year or two back. Personal things."

Luke nodded.

Bo appeared with more coffee. "Make him treat you to a brownie," she said. "He's going to be rich."

"Want a brownie?" Luke said.

"I'm okay, thanks."

Bo smiled at him and vanished.

Luke started wrapping up the models and putting them back in the box. "Well, like I said, I need to talk to your dad again, arrange some financial stuff before I know how much I can offer money-wise, but I definitely need more guys, so the job's there if you want it."

"Thanks. I'll bear it in mind. And congratulations, by the way. Glad you got the contract."

While he'd been in Harper's the wind had changed again and tiny stinging flakes were driving into his face as he walked home. He wondered what it would be like to work with a bunch of other guys. Six months ago—even six weeks ago—he couldn't have considered it, but he liked Luke. He was a straightforward sort of guy and working with him might be okay. As for the others, if there were machines going, they probably didn't talk much anyway. He could just keep himself to himself. It would be a completely different life from the one he'd imagined for himself, but that in itself might be good.

The downside would be that, to start with at least, he'd have to live at home and he'd been thinking it was time he got out. Things seemed to be falling apart there and it was definitely no longer a refuge. He needed to give the whole thing some serious thought.

As he was walking up the drive he noticed the sled he'd borrowed from Marshall's Grocery leaning against the side of the house. He'd meant to return it weeks ago. He looked at his watch, then studied the sky. If he took it back right now he'd have time to get home before the weather got serious.

He flipped the sled over and towed it around to the front of the house. As he passed the living room window something made him look up. Adam was standing right up against the glass, hands clenched under his chin.

"Shit!" Tom said to his feet. "Shit, shit, *shit!*" He dropped the tow rope and went in. Sherry was bashing about in the kitchen. Adam was watching him, his whole body taut with longing.

"I'm taking the sled back to the grocery store," Tom said sharply. "You can ride there but you'll have to walk home. Can you walk that far?"

Adam didn't waste time replying. He shot into the entrance hall and started pulling things from the rubble. "Is this your coat?" Tom asked, taking a coat off the hooks.

"Yes." Adam's face was shining like a candle; it made Tom want to smash the wall with his fist.

"Boots," he said. "Scarf, hat, mitts. That hat isn't warm enough—put this one on top of it. Okay, we're off."

The wind had dropped, which was something. He walked fast, listening to the swish of the sled's runners on the hard-packed snow. Each time he looked back Adam grinned up at him like a jack-o'-lantern. You'd have thought he'd never been on a sled before. The thought made him wonder if Adam *had* ever been on a sled before. It's not your bloody fault, he said to himself. It's not up to you, it's nothing to do with you, it's not as if he's starving or living in a doghouse, just fuck off and leave me alone.

Marshall's was on the same side of the road as Harper's and three stores farther along. The worst thing that could possibly have happened, the thing so bad that even he with his genius for imagining disaster hadn't thought of it, was that as they passed Harper's Bo would be serving someone in one of the window booths and would happen to look out and see them.

She was out the door in a split second.

"And who is this?" she demanded, hands on hips, looking down at Adam with astonishment. "Who is this and why haven't I met him before? Hello, gorgeous, what's your name?"

"Adam," said Adam.

"Adam is a wonderful name," said Bo, "and you have the biggest eyes I've ever seen in my *life*. Is this your daddy?"

She gestured at Tom without looking at him.

"No," said Adam.

"We have to go," Tom said. "Sorry, but we're in a hurry."

"So, if he's not your daddy, who is he?"

"Tom," Adam said. "My brother."

"Okay, good. I know all about brothers. Is he nice to you?"

"Yes," Adam said. He'd tipped his head back as far as it would go in order to take in all of her, which made his mouth hang open and his parka hood come down over his eyes.

"That's good," Bo said, "because otherwise I was going to have to kill him. Would you like to come in and have some ice cream?"

"We can't," Tom said, very fast. "We have to get this sled back and get home before the storm sets in."

"What storm?" Bo said, still looking at Adam. "How would it be if you came in while your brother takes the sled back, which will take him quite a long time because he'll have to apologize *profusely* to Mr. Marshall for keeping it so long. Does that sound like a good idea to you?"

Adam looked anxiously at Tom. Tom couldn't look at him.

"We don't have time," he said. "I'm sorry. I'll bring him back another day but we don't have time now."

"You do if I get Luke to drive you home," Bo said. She looked him in the eye. "Small boys need ice cream," she said. "This is a fact."

His fear was that when Adam took his coat off Bo would recoil with shock at the stench. In the event, maybe due to all the other odours in the place, it didn't seem too bad, but Tom was still in a sweat of anxiety the whole time. He declined Luke's offer of a lift home because the cab of the truck was so small Luke would be bound to notice the smell and anyway, there was a whole lot of stuff jostling around in his mind and he needed to think and walking was good for thinking. Things couldn't go on as they were, that was the gist of it. It just couldn't go on.

He walked faster than he should have, but Adam trotted beside him, uncomplaining. His uncomplainingness was one of the things that bothered Tom most. If he'd whined and sulked and been a pain in the ass like other kids, it would have been easier to ignore him; it was the fact that he was so good and had such low expectations of everyone around him that got you in the guts.

When they got in, when he was helping Adam take off his boots, Adam said, "I liked it."

Tom looked at him. His eyes were still shining.

"What did you like?" Tom said.

"The lady and the ice cream and the room with all the people. Mostly the lady and the ice cream."

Tom forced a smile, but it was hard. He hauled off his own coat and boots and went into the living room and then paused.

Sherry was still in the kitchen. He'd thought she'd have gone but maybe it was good that she hadn't. He crossed the room and went upstairs.

Pushed out of his mind these past weeks, because to acknowledge it would mean dealing with it, was the knowledge that only one thing could be causing his four-year-old brother to smell like he did. When he opened the door of Adam's room the stench almost made him retch. In the week or two since he'd last been in, it had become far worse. He crossed over to the bed. It had been made, but badly, the bedspread hauled up over crumpled blankets and sheets. He pulled it away and stepped back, covering his nose and mouth with one hand, his eyes stinging from the ammonia. Sheets, blankets, everything sodden. He grabbed the bedding, tore it off, flung it on the floor, took the mattress by one corner and heaved it up. It was saturated—it sagged under the weight. How did the kid climb into that bed every night? How did he even stay in the room?

He went out into the hall, closing the door behind him, and stood for a few minutes, head down, taking deep breaths. Adam was standing at the top of the stairs, looking at him.

"Go into Mum's room," Tom said. "And stay there."

He felt amazingly calm; a flat calm, quiet and still. He waited until Adam had disappeared and then went downstairs. Sherry turned around as he came into the kitchen and her face lit up.

"Well hiya, Tom," she said. "It's a long time since I seen you. How you bin?"

"Come upstairs," he said. "There's something I want you to see."

"Well now, that's a nice invitation," she said, tipping her head down and looking up at him under her eyelashes.

"Upstairs," he said.

She rolled her hips up the stairs ahead of him. When they reached the top she headed for his bedroom but he put a hand on her back and steered her along to Adam's room. "In here," he said.

"We ain't goin' in there," she said, stopping abruptly. "I don't like that room."

"Why is that, Sherry?" Tom asked. "This is a nice room. Why don't you like it?" He gripped her arm with one hand and opened the door with the other.

"I ain't goin' in there!" Sherry said, louder, pushing against him, but he shoved her in and stepped in behind her and closed the door.

"Okay," he said. "You wanted a bed. Here's a bed."

"You leave me alone, Tom Cartwright!" Her voice was shrill. "You don't—"

"Don't you want to lie down, Sherry? You were so keen a minute ago."

She tried to get to the door but he blocked her.

"Lie down, Sherry."

"You let me outta here, Tom Cartwright, or I'm gonna say you raped me!"

"Now why do I think you'd have trouble getting anyone to believe that, Sherry? A girl with a nice clean reputation like yours. I just want to know why you won't lie down on this bed but are happy for a four-year-old kid to sleep in it every night for weeks on end."

"It ain't my job to clean up after some filthy, stinkin' kid who wets his bed!"

"Yes, it is. It is exactly your job. You are paid to clean this house. Would you call this a clean room? At the very least, at the very *least*, you should have told my mother he was wetting the bed."

"Your mum ain't right in the head! I could'a told her ten times and she'd never do nothin'. And if you din't know about it yourself, that's 'cause you din't want to know, 'cause anyone could smell that stink a mile off."

"Get out," he said, sick with disgust, because there was no answer to her accusations. She was right in every respect. "Just get out."

"I ain't goin' without my money!"

"Oh, but you are." He opened the door and propelled her out. "You are going now. You haven't earned a goddamned cent since you came into this house. I could sue you for taking money under false pretences. In fact, maybe I will. Down the stairs. Down." He grabbed her arm, forced her down the stairs.

"You let go of me!" Sherry screamed. "You let go of me, you bastard!"

"And out we go," he said, propelling her across the living room and into the entrance hall, opening the two doors and heaving her out into the snow, which was coming down fast now, spearing through the dark.

"One coat!" he yelled, throwing it out after her. "One pair of boots!"

He closed the doors, leaned against them, then pushed himself off and back up the stairs. Adam and his mother, holding the baby, were at the top, looking down.

"Go back to bed, Mum," Tom said. "Adam, go with her. I told you to stay in her room."

He went into the bedroom, gathered up the sodden sheets and blankets, took them down the stairs and into the kitchen, opened the back door and threw them out. He went back upstairs.

Adam was there again. He was crying. "I'm sorry," he said. "I'm sorry."

In the past year and a half Tom had never seen him cry. Not once. He pointed a shaking finger at him. "Stop crying," he said. "And stop saying you're sorry. It isn't your fault. It. Is. Not. Your. Fault. Do you get that? Do you understand? So stop crying."

He went back to the bedroom, heaved the mattress off the bed and out the door and down the stairs and through the kitchen and out the back door to join the blankets. He washed his hands at the kitchen sink and went back upstairs to his mother's room. Adam wasn't there but his mother was in bed, holding the baby to her. She looked at him with wide eyes.

"Mum, Adam's started wetting his bed," Tom said. "He needs to have a diaper at night."

"Oh," his mother whispered. "All right."

She wasn't taking it in. Tom went back downstairs. Adam was standing in the living room. Tears were still rolling down his face but maybe he couldn't stop them.

"I need the paper your new car was wrapped in," Tom said. "Do you know where it went?"

Adam ducked into the space beside Tom's chair and came back with the paper. Tom smoothed it out on the table, then took it over to the telephone. He phoned International Inquiries and asked for the number of the Montrose Hotel. He glanced at his watch, then dialled the number. There was a pause, then a couple of clicks, and a phone rang twice.

"The Montrose Hotel," Megan's voice said crisply. "May I help you?"

"Hi, Meg," Tom said. "It's Tom."

CHAPTER SIXTEEN

Megan

London, December 1968

Most of the time things were very good. In the evenings, if Megan wasn't on duty at the hotel and Andrew wasn't out researching, they would sometimes eat together. She would cook or he would cook and they would share a bottle of Mateus Rosé or Chianti and talk about their days and then Andrew would go back to his desk and carry on with his work. Often they left their doors open and then really it was like having one large flat instead of two small ones. It was like being married, Megan decided, thinking of her father shut in his study. But hers and Andrew's was a much better marriage than her parents', more like Annabelle and Peter's. Though, of course, without the sex.

If you didn't want children, which she didn't, sex was no big deal, was it? You can't have everything. Most of the time she was able to convince herself of that.

A couple of times, when her day off coincided with Andrew having some free time, he took her to see something famous, something he thought she really shouldn't miss, such as the Tower of London (amazing) or Buckingham Palace (disappointing) or

Hampton Court (wonderful curling chimneys). Megan sent postcards home to please her father.

So most of the time things were very good. It was when her body refused to listen to her head that it became difficult. She had worked very hard at making Andrew think that what he'd told her in Bradgate Park was of no particular importance to her—that she considered him just a friend—with the consequence that the guardedness she'd noticed previously had left him. Not that he walked around naked or was given to displays of affection, but sometimes he'd put an arm around her in a brotherly fashion, rather as Tom used to do. (Though Tom only did it when he was teasing or trying to get something out of her.)

That was what she found difficult. Being so close to him. Touching, but not properly touching. Sometimes that hurt so much she wanted to cry.

Occasionally he was out very late. She couldn't sleep until she heard him come in and then she couldn't sleep for wondering where he had been and with whom.

Once he seemed low and when she asked, cautiously, if he was all right he said he'd met someone he liked but it hadn't worked out. Then he'd smiled at her and shrugged and said, "Never mind. It'll happen."

That was very, very hard. To know that he wanted someone, but not her.

Most of the time, though, she was able to not think about it and things were good.

One night Andrew said, "When am I going to see this hotel of yours?" so she took him there on one of her evenings off. Annabelle and Peter were supposed to be out for dinner with friends but as it happened the friends had cancelled and they were still at the hotel. Megan had carefully never spoken about

Andrew, so they were a little surprised when she showed up with a strange man, but they were friendly and gracious, as she'd known they would be.

"This is Andrew Bannerman," Megan said casually. "He lives across the hall from me." (She'd worked out how she'd introduce him just in case something like this happened.)

"We'll give you a guided tour," Peter said expansively. "This is the bar, which is the perfect place to start. You'll need to fortify yourself for the tour; it's very strenuous. What'll you have?"

It turned out that Peter hadn't yet unbooked the table they'd booked, so after the tour the four of them went out for dinner. Megan sat in a haze of happiness, watching these three people she loved so much. Peter and Andrew got onto the subject of old cars: if it didn't have a solid chassis it didn't rate as old, they agreed.

"How about the Jowett Jupiter?" Peter said. "Now that was a great, great car."

"It was," Andrew agreed, "but it was ugly."

"Ugly!"

"All right, not ugly. But put it alongside the Morgan Plus 4, for instance. Poetry in motion."

"If you two don't stop," Annabelle said, "Megan and I will go elsewhere. Won't we?"

"Yes," Megan said. But she would have gladly stayed there forever, watching them, basking in the wonderfulness of them getting on so instantly and so well. They could talk about whatever they liked.

"Megan, he's one of the nicest men I ever met," Annabelle said afterwards, "but promise me you won't fall in love with him. You do know he's homosexual, don't you?"

Fortunately Megan was hanging up her coat, so Annabelle couldn't see her face.

You're too late, she wanted to say. Just as Andrew himself had been too late that day in Bradgate Park, when he'd said he didn't want her to get "the wrong idea." Love was not an idea; you couldn't choose to get it or not get it any more than you could choose to catch or not catch flu.

———

She'd hoped they could spend Christmas together but Andrew said he'd be going home. His parents had a big house and always hosted a family Christmas. His brother and his brother's wife and three kids and his sister and her husband and a one-year old and another on the way—they all stayed over and it was four days of bedlam.

"Do you enjoy it?" Megan asked.

"Mostly. It's great seeing them all. Though the past few years it's been a little . . . awkward at times. You know parents. They keep wondering when I'm going to bring home a girl."

"Don't they know?" Megan asked cautiously. It was the first time they'd mentioned the subject since Bradgate Park.

"My brother and sister do. Not my parents."

"Aren't you going to tell them?"

He smiled at her, the same strained smile he'd had that day. "No. I love them and it would hurt them. They wouldn't understand. Their generation grew up thinking it was something you chose to be." He changed the subject. "How about you? Do you miss your family at Christmas—your parents and all those brothers of yours?"

Megan thought about it. Christmases had always gone by in a haze. From the moment she got out of bed on Christmas morning, she'd been either in the kitchen or whirling around tidying up. With hindsight she could see that it had been her own fault. She remembered coming into the living room—it was her last Christmas at home and Tom had arrived back from university the night before—to find it once again strewn with paper and discarded presents and dirty plates and half-empty cups of coffee, standing with her hands on her hips and saying, "I don't know why I bother." Tom, who was sitting on the sofa fiddling with a 3-D puzzle the twins had given him, looked up and said, "I don't know why you bother either, Meg. Nobody else cares if it's a mess. Sit down, why don't you?" He'd patted the empty seat beside him. "Tell me what you've been doing lately. How's life treating you?"

She'd snapped at him, saying he'd be the first to complain if the turkey didn't get cooked, and he'd said cheerfully, "No, I wouldn't. I'd have another piece of Christmas cake."

But of course she'd gone back to the turkey.

If she could do it again, she thought, she'd sit down and talk to him. She'd always admired Tom, although he'd driven her at least as mad as the others, but she'd never really got to know him and she regretted that.

The only thing she'd actively enjoyed that Christmas was Adam, whose first real Christmas it had been. He'd loved the noise and the fuss and had chewed his way through quantities of wrapping paper and grinned like a maniac the whole day long. She'd carried him about with her, quite unnecessarily—he was perfectly happy on the floor—because she'd known by then that she'd be leaving home soon and wanted to store up the feel of him. She had no idea what it was about Adam that tugged at her so hard; at that age the others had left her cold.

"I do miss them," she admitted now to Andrew. "Some of them more than others."

"Have you thought of going home for Christmas?"

"I've thought of it, but I can't go now because my mother's expecting another baby and if I went home I know I'd get sucked into it all again."

As usual she spent Christmas Day with Annabelle and Peter. They had Christmas lunch out (a different restaurant every year) and opened their presents over coffee, and it was easy and uncomplicated. After lunch the three of them returned to the hotel to pass around mince pies and Champagne to the guests, and that was fine too. At four p.m. Megan phoned home—the one bit of Christmas she dreaded. She could have gone back to her flat to make the call—there was a pay phone in the hall on the ground floor of the house—but it felt too public for such a conversation and it was simpler to use the phone in the office. On her father's instructions she reversed the charges but then spent the call counting the seconds because she knew he'd be counting them too.

Her mother answered the phone. She sounded serene rather than flustered, which meant the baby was going to arrive any day—Megan knew the signs. She was so calm she didn't even ask when Megan was coming home. Everyone was well, she said. Yes, yes, she had everything ready for the birth.

Megan asked how Adam was; her mother said he was fine, just fine.

"Has he opened my present to him yet?" She'd been hoping to hear the sound of Matchbox-sized collisions in the background but there was only the distant sound of Peter and Corey fighting.

"I don't think so," her mother said vaguely.

"What do you mean you don't think so, Mum? Have the rest of you opened my presents?"

"I'm not sure who's opened what . . ." Her mother's voice trailed off.

This was what she was like before a baby and wasn't in itself a cause for concern, but that didn't make it any less frustrating.

Next Megan spoke to her father, who wasn't sure her mother had got around to the presents yet. Megan wanted to yell, What do you mean you're not sure? Either you've opened your presents or you haven't opened your presents. You live there, you're not unconscious, you must know! She controlled herself and thanked

him for the cheque he'd sent—the only Christmas present she'd
received from her family, but at least it was a generous one.

Next she asked to speak to Adam, who turned out to be
asleep although it was eleven in the morning their time. So Megan
asked to speak to Tom, who was out on the snowplough—there'd
been another blizzard, and Christmas or not, the main roads
had to be kept open. Then she spoke to Peter, who said Merry
Christmas and vanished before she could reply, and finally the
phone was passed to Corey, who was eating toffee and couldn't
disengage his teeth. Nobody mentioned her presents, which was
absolutely par for the course.

When she'd put down the phone Megan went up to the linen
cupboard, shut the door behind her and cried, another thing she
did every year now. Then she washed her face and redid her hair
and went down to make coffee and be pleasant to the guests.

For 364 days of the year, her family seemed so far away and long
ago they might have been characters in a book she'd once read,
and yet the minute she heard their voices they became so painfully, infuriatingly, achingly close she might as well not have left
home at all.

———

Early in the New Year Annabelle and Peter found a hotel they
liked the look of and, rather to her surprise, Megan liked it too. It
was very different from the Montrose—art nouveau rather than
Victorian, according to Peter. It had tall stained glass windows and
sculpted cornices and a curling wrought iron staircase spiralling up
the four flights of stairs. It also had collapsed ceilings in half the
rooms and wallpaper hanging off the walls in great damp sheets.

"That's the only reason we can afford it," Peter said. "There
was a leak—more like a flood, in fact—in the water tank in the

loft. It's too big a job to do ourselves, we'd need help, so the first step is a structural survey and then we'll get some quotes from builders. Then we'll decide if it makes sense to take it on."

Megan found herself hoping that it would make sense. For her the Montrose would always be special, but the idea of a new challenge was growing on her too. Conveniently, the new hotel was only a mile away from her bedsit; she wouldn't even have to move to be near it.

She talked about it with Andrew—in fact, they all did—they went out as a foursome from time to time. He demanded another grand tour, so they took him to see it.

"Whoa," he said, looking at the sagging ceiling in the main reception room. "Looks as if an elephant sat on it. You're sure about this, are you?"

"Well no," Peter said. "Not sure. We're waiting for the results of the survey."

"Will you sell the Montrose to finance it?"

"We thought we'd have to but now we're wondering if maybe we could keep it—get another mortgage on the strength of it."

They adjourned to the pub on the corner and spent the evening talking about bankruptcy. Peter seemed to find the subject funny, which made Megan anxious. Sometimes it seemed to her that Peter treated the whole business of money as a joke.

Andrew didn't. At heart Andrew was quite a serious person. It was another thing she loved about him.

Later Annabelle said, "Megan, I know it's none of my business but I'm worried about you. Because it looks to me as if you're in love with Andrew."

Megan felt herself flushing but she said calmly, "He's just a good friend. A very good friend."

"Good," Annabelle said, still sounding doubtful. "Because it wouldn't work, you know."

It was the first time Megan had ever been cross with her.

Who was she to say what would or would not work, as if there were rules?

———

On a Wednesday morning towards the end of January a letter arrived from Megan's father telling her that she had another brother. His name was Dominic John. He and his mother were both doing well.

Megan phoned and spoke to her mother, who said everything was fine, just fine.

"Brother number eight," Megan said, tight-lipped, to Andrew that evening. "Though Henry died when he was a baby, so there are only seven."

Weeks ago she'd bought a tiny Babygro—yellow to allow for either sex—and wrapped it and stuck it in an envelope. Now she was wrapping two Matchbox cars for Adam, to enclose in the package—or at least she would be if Andrew would stop playing with them.

"Are they Catholic?" Andrew asked, opening and closing a car door.

"No. They have no excuse whatsoever. Our doctor told them after Adam was born that there were to be no more babies— I heard him, I was there. But here we are. It's irresponsible and it's disgraceful."

Andrew grinned.

"It's not funny," Megan said.

Andrew blew his nose and hid the grin in his handkerchief. "Sorry. It's just that you do disapproval so well. Why does it make you angry?"

"Because they're not capable of looking after the ones they have and I know what's going to happen. The house is going to fall apart and my mother is going to write and ask me to come home and sort it out, and I'm not going."

"Well, why be angry about it? Just tell her no."

"You don't understand," Megan said.

"The graveyards are full of indispensable people, Meg. You've been away three years and they've managed without you all that time. Things change in three years—people change."

"Not my parents," Megan said.

"I bet they have. In fact, I literally bet they have. I'll bet you five pounds your mother doesn't write that letter."

"Done," Megan said.

In a sense he won the bet. The weeks ticked by and no letter arrived, and Megan was getting ready to pay up when the phone in the office rang one evening towards the end of March and Tom's voice said, "Hi, Meg. It's Tom."

"Tom," Megan said, instantly gripped by an icy dread. Tom had never phoned her, never so much as written to her. Nothing but a catastrophe would drive him to this.

"How are you?" Tom said. "How're things?"

"Is it Mum?" Megan said, seeing her mother dead, herself not there with her at the end.

"What?" Tom said. "Oh. No, Mum's fine. At least, not exactly fine, but she's not sick."

"What's the matter with her?"

"I don't really know. Maybe nothing . . ."

Megan's hands were shaking. "Tom, what is this phone call about?"

"Well, I guess it's mainly about Adam."

Her heart seemed to stop beating altogether. "Is he sick?"

"No, but things haven't been great here lately, Meg. Mum's kind of . . . lost it. Nothing's getting done."

"She's always like that after a baby. Tell me about Adam. List every single thing that is wrong with Adam, starting now."

"Okay. Well, for a start, sometimes there isn't any food in the house and I think a couple of times he's actually gone hungry. And also, he's started wetting his bed and nobody's done anything about it, so he's been sleeping in a wet bed for weeks and he really stinks. And Mum's completely wrapped up in the new baby and Dad's at work and even when he's home he's not at home—you know how he is. And I'm at work, so Adam's on his own a lot and he's . . . unhappy, I think. He seems kind of . . . lost. So basically that's the state of things. I thought you'd want to know."

Megan was so angry her jaws were locked. The phone line hummed back and forth across the Atlantic.

"Meg? You there?"

She drew a breath. "You thought I'd want to know that Adam's been hungry because there isn't any food in the house and he's been sleeping in a wet bed for weeks?"

"Megan—"

"There are three adults in that house, Tom! *Three adults*! And you've phoned to tell me that none of them can be bothered to see to the *basic needs* of one four-year-old boy!"

"Stop yelling at me, Meg. I've been doing my best, but I'm going to be leaving in a few weeks' time. I just called to tell you that things really aren't good here. Mum's genuinely kind of nuts, and Dad doesn't want to know. We even had the cops here the other night—well, Sergeant Moynihan—because it turns out Peter and Corey have been setting fire to things. The cleaning lady hasn't been in months and Mum got someone else to come who was completely crap and I've just thrown her out. Like, literally thrown her out. I've also had to throw out the mattress on Adam's bed because it was saturated with piss—all the sheets and blankets, everything's soaked. So I'm sorry if I've disturbed you, but I thought you'd want to know. In fact, I thought you'd be extremely upset if nobody told you. That's why I phoned."

The phone line hummed.

"Megan?"

"Where's Dad in all this?" Her hands were still shaking.

"In his study. Where else?"

"It's his responsibility."

"Maybe you could phone and tell him that. I've tried."

"You want me to come home—three thousand miles—and sort it out. That's why you phoned, isn't it?"

"No, it isn't, I—"

"Yes, it is."

"Look, obviously it would be great if you came home, Meg, even if you just came for a week or two, but I don't expect you to do it. Why should you? You did it for years, and now you've got your own life to live. Adam will survive. I'll get in lots of biscuits and stuff before I leave—stuff he can open by himself. But I've been wondering about this bed-wetting business. Can kids put on their own diapers? 'Cause that's going to be a tricky one."

"I'm going to kill him," Megan said. "It would be worth going home just to kill him."

Annabelle said, "Megan, we can manage here, you know. Janet's very capable. Why don't you go for a week or two?"

"There are three adults in that house. There isn't a single thing I could do that they couldn't do just as easily. I am not going."

"He's trying to blackmail me," she said to Andrew. "He's trying to make me so worried about Adam that I'll have to go home."

"I get the feeling he's succeeding," Andrew said.

"No, he isn't. He is not."

"That's okay, then," Andrew said. "Anyway, I thought you said he said he didn't expect you to come."

"That's because he's smart. Tom is very smart."

"You could go just for a week or two. For your own peace of mind."

"It wouldn't give me peace of mind because I'd see how *useless* they all are and I'd never be able to leave."

"Buy a return ticket. Tell them from the outset that you aren't staying. Go for two weeks, sort things out and then come back . . . Megan, are you crying?"

He got up and came around the table and put his arms around her, the first time he had ever done such a thing, and she was too upset to savour it.

"I'm just so mad," she said between sobs. "The idea of Adam sleeping for *weeks* in a soaking wet bed. And being actually *hungry*. I'm just so *furious* with them all."

"I'll meet you at the airport when you get back," Andrew said. "You can come home and have a nap and then in the evening we'll go out for dinner and you can rage about them to your heart's content."

"I'm not going," Megan said. "I am *not* going."

CHAPTER SEVENTEEN

Edward

Struan, March 1969

I've just had a visit from Reverend Thomas. I was on my way upstairs to bed—the rest of the household had retired long ago—when there was a knock at the door. Needless to say I was reminded of his non-visit a couple of weeks ago and sure enough when I opened the door there he was in his big black coat, looking so ill I thought he might collapse on the doorstep.

Before I had time to open my mouth he said, "I'm sorry to trouble you, Edward. I know you don't relish my company but I'm afraid I must talk with you."

I invited him in, of course. I took his hat and coat and hung them up and led him through to my study. When we were seated I asked what I could do for him. He didn't reply for a moment; just sat, looking vaguely at my desk. It crossed my mind that he might have had a turn of some kind, a small stroke perhaps, and I wondered if I should call John Christopherson. But then he pulled himself together.

"I won't keep you long," he said, finally raising his eyes to mine. "There are only two things I need to say. The first is an apology. Some years ago you and I had a disagreement about Joel Pickett. I expect you remember."

I nodded. There was no danger of my forgetting.

"Subsequently I used my position—my pulpit, you might say—" there was a trace of that smile I dislike so much— "to . . . vent my anger against you. What I implied about you was untrue and did you damage. It was wrong of me and I am sorry. I hope you will accept my apology."

That was something I had never expected to hear. Given the man's overwhelming pride and arrogance, it must have cost him a great deal to say those words.

"Thank you," I said. "I do accept it."

He nodded, and then looked away again and sat for a bit studying the titles of the books in the bookcase behind me. I imagine his home is full of books too. In another life Reverend Thomas and I might have found we had something in common.

"The second thing is harder to say," he said finally. "Harder to tell. I need to make a confession and I have decided that you are the right person to confess to."

That startled me, I have to say—I would have thought I'd be the very last person he would want to confess anything to—but he certainly had my attention.

He drew his gaze back from the books. "You remember my son, Robert's, trial."

"Yes."

"You remember he was given a very light sentence. The sentence, as I'm sure you know, is decided by the Crown attorney. In Robert's case, a term in jail was expected, but instead he got off with three months' service to the community."

I nodded. The sentence had been particularly surprising because the current Crown attorney is known to be very tough on the drink and drive issue, particularly where young men are concerned.

"He is a friend of mine," Reverend Thomas said. "The Crown attorney, Gilbert Mitchell. We have been friends since university. Several weeks before the trial I went down to North Bay to see him. I told him Robert had suffered enormously for his crime already, which was true. I said that he was a sensitive boy, which was also true, and that he would be utterly crushed by a period in jail, that he would be destroyed by it. Which was not true. Robert was desperate to atone, he would have positively welcomed a prison sentence. I knew that. The truth is . . ."

His voice was shaking and he stopped. He swallowed, the sound of it painfully loud in the silence of the room. I couldn't look at him. I focused on a splatter of ink on the blotter on my desk. I was so alarmed by the thought that he might break down in front of me that I found I was holding my breath. I could hear his breathing shuddering with the effort of control, and I willed him to achieve it. Gradually, he did.

"The truth is," he said finally, his voice steadier but harsh with the effort of forcing out the words, "I could not stand the idea of a child of mine going to jail. The idea of everybody knowing that my son was in jail.

"So justice was not done and the child's mother could not bear it and said things to Robert that he could not live with. And he killed himself. But the truth is, I killed him. For the sake of my pride."

He stopped again. I think he expected me to say something, but I was so shocked, so appalled, I couldn't speak. After a moment he carried on.

"It has destroyed my wife and I know it has harmed your son as well, Edward. I don't know if he has been blaming himself in any way, but I want to be sure he knows that he could not have prevented Robert's suicide. No one could have. I would be grateful if you would tell him that and apologize to him on my behalf. I would do it myself but I think he might find that . . . painful, and I don't want to add to his burden. Whereas you would know how to put it."

I have to say I felt the most profound admiration for him at that moment. I couldn't imagine how he had managed to say what he had just said, how he had brought himself to come here. That previous night when he had come to the door, it must have been to say this. He had knocked and waited, but I had delayed so long in answering that his courage had failed him. I thought of the weight he must have been carrying for the past year and a half; it must have been like being crushed by rocks. It struck me as astonishing, in such circumstances, that he'd still been able to think of what Tom was going through and had come to try to put it right.

Finally I managed to look at him. "Thank you," I said. "Thank you very much. I will tell Tom."

He nodded but didn't reply. After a minute, knowing that nothing I could say would make any difference but having to try, nonetheless, I said, "I've always understood that the Christian god is a forgiving god, Reverend. Surely if we're supposed to forgive others, we're also supposed to forgive ourselves."

He looked away.

"God has been silent on the subject," he said after a minute. "He has been silent on all subjects since the day Robert died."

I imagined him, alone in his house, waking each day to the knowledge of what he had done, listening for some message—any message—from his god, hearing nothing but the howling of his own mind. Here is a strange thing: I found myself *loathing* his god for abandoning him at such a time. Hardly a rational thought for a non-believer.

We sat for some time, not speaking. Finally, with an effort, he got to his feet. I would have encouraged him to stay—I felt no resentment towards him anymore; what had happened between us years ago seemed utterly trivial now—but it was clear he had said what he had come to say and wanted to go.

As he was leaving, he held out his hand and I took it. He said, "Thank you for listening, Edward. I wanted you to know."

When he'd gone I returned to my study. After a moment the floorboards creaked above me and then I heard someone coming downstairs and knew it would be Tom.

"Come in," I said when he appeared in the doorway. "Sit down."

"Was that Reverend Thomas?" he said.

"Yes, it was."

He sat down. "What did he want?"

I told him what Reverend Thomas had said. How he had fixed the trial, how he felt he was to blame for Robert's suicide.

Tom put his head in his hands. "Oh God," he said when I'd finished. "Oh God."

I said, "He asked me to apologize to you on his behalf, Tom, for what you've been through. He was afraid you might have been thinking you could have prevented Robert's suicide. He asked me to tell you that no one could have."

He didn't reply. I got up and went out to the entrance hall and brought back a coat and draped it over him—he was wearing only pyjamas. I risked putting a hand on his shoulder, just briefly. Then I sat down again. Outside the wind had picked up and snowflakes were splattering against the window, melting and trickling down.

When he seemed to have collected himself I said, "You and I have to talk, Tom. But not tonight. You should go back to bed."

He nodded and after a moment he straightened up and left without looking at me so that I wouldn't see that he'd been crying. I sat on for a while and then went upstairs myself. I was afraid I might dream about Reverend Thomas, but when it came to it I didn't dream at all.

―――

I am glad Betty is a librarian. It means I have a reason to see her frequently, and there is something about her that gladdens the heart. She has ditched her sleeping bag. When I went to the library at lunchtime she was wearing only her coat (with three layers underneath, so she informed me), hat, scarf, boots and gloves with the fingers missing.

"Reborn, like a butterfly!" she announced, wafting her arms. "Emerging from my chrysalis. Summer's coming."

I was enjoying the idea of Betty as a butterfly—she is on the hefty side—but I urged caution. Another blizzard is forecast for this evening.

"Nonsense," Betty said. "What do they know?"

I told her that I had not had time to do justice to the books on Rome, which are due back at the library in Toronto next week, and she said she would try to get an extension for me. I hadn't known that was possible. Apparently, if someone else is waiting for them I'll be out of luck, but otherwise I can hold on to them for a while longer.

She asked how things were at home and I said better, which isn't strictly true. I considered telling her about Peter and Corey's little forays into arson but decided against it. She would suggest that I talk to them. I've got as far as imagining knocking on their bedroom door but I can't imagine what comes next.

I also thought of telling her about Reverend Thomas's visit but decided that would be breaking a confidence.

When I got back to the bank I saw in my desk diary that Luke Morrison had made an appointment to see me. I can guess what it's about: Sam Waller of the building firm Waller and Sons has been up here recruiting for the new hunting lodge/hotel, and my guess is that Luke Morrison has won the contract to make the furniture for them. I hope very much that is so. It's good to see talent and hard work rewarded.

Luke Morrison and I have a connection he is probably not aware of. His father was the senior accountant at the bank when I joined it after the war and was therefore my first boss. He was an exceedingly nice man. It was he who encouraged me to study accountancy by correspondence course and saw to it that I had time off to get the qualifications. He and his wife were killed in a collision with a logging truck about fifteen years ago. A terrible thing. Several of us from the bank went to the funeral out in Crow Lake. I remember thinking the children—there were four of them—behaved with great dignity.

But as a result of that accident, the job of senior accountant at the bank became vacant and I was given it. And then a few years later, when Craig Stewart retired, I became manager. You could say I benefitted directly from that family's tragedy, and I confess I've never been entirely comfortable with that.

So a few years later when his eldest son—Luke—came into the bank wanting to borrow money to set up a furniture-making business, I dealt with his request myself and gave him as much help and support as I could. He has done very well and when Sam Waller dropped in last week and asked what I knew about Luke, I was able to give him a very good reference. If he does get this new contract, it will set him up nicely.

In contrast to last night this has been a remarkably pleasant day. Reverend Gordon came into the bank this afternoon. I believe I said before that he has been hauled out of retirement by the church until a replacement for Reverend Thomas can be found. It seems to me unreasonable, given his age—he must be in his seventies; he was at least fifty when we were in Italy during the war—but he claims to be enjoying it.

He came in to discuss his finances. His pension is very small but so are his outgoings, and I was able to reassure him there was no cause for concern. When the business side of things was out of the way we sat on for a few minutes (his was my last appointment of the day) and talked about this and that, mostly about the new hotel and what it will mean for the town. There will be more tourists—always a mixed blessing—but it will bring money into the area and create a good number of jobs and we agreed that on balance it would be a good thing.

We didn't talk about the war. We never do. We shared what you could call an intense experience in the course of it but it wasn't the sort of thing you talk about afterwards. He sat with me during what was unquestionably the worst night of my life. About a dozen of us, myself and another badly wounded man, had taken shelter from a bombardment in a deserted villa on the outskirts of Motta in southern Italy. In the end, after a day and a night of bloody battle, our forces did take the town, but that was no thanks to me; I was out of it by then.

I have several very clear memories from that day, one of which I have tried unsuccessfully to wipe from my mind ever since. I was on a stretcher—this was shortly after I was wounded—being carried to the villa. Pain had set in, and a desperate thirst, and no one had any water. I lifted my head, looking for someone to appeal to for a drink, and what I saw instead was a flame-thrower in action, simultaneously coating its target—and inevitably the men who were manning that target—in fuel and setting fire to it. And therefore to them.

Both sides had flame-throwers, I know that. But all I knew then was that this one was being used by us. By our side—the side that God was on. I remember hearing screaming and realizing it was coming from me.

Then I remember nothing until I came around in the villa and found myself lying on a heap of blankets beside the other injured man, with a padre sitting on his rucksack on the floor between us. The padre was Reverend Gordon. I didn't know him at that stage and had no idea he was also from the North. He was the minister of the church in Struan, and Emily and I didn't move here until 1948, when I got the job at the bank, so our paths had never crossed. He was just a man in a padre's uniform, sitting on a rucksack.

We were in a large, imposing room with grand furniture and several magnificent paintings hanging on the walls. From outside I could hear the bombardment still going on. Inside, my fellow soldiers, who had discovered a wine cellar in the basement and were in exceedingly high spirits, were breaking up the furniture and throwing it on the fire. As I watched, two of them climbed onto a table, wrenched a painting off the wall and started hacking it up for the fire as well.

I guess I went a little mad. I remember shouting at them, struggling to get up and fighting savagely with Reverend Gordon, who was trying to restrain me, until eventually I was too exhausted to continue and fell back on the blankets.

Sometime after that the injured man next to me started calling for his mother and I heard Reverend Gordon say that his mother was here, right here beside him, and then he prayed with him and in the course of the praying the man died. I remember thinking that his death didn't matter, that no man's death mattered because the entire human race deserved to be wiped from the face of the earth.

My final memory from that day is of an exchange I had with Reverend Gordon in the middle of the night when the men had drunk themselves into a stupor and there was silence apart from the never-ending hammer of the guns. I was in terrible pain and certain that I was about to die. If I'd had any religious faith before that day, the flame-thrower had put an end to it, and I just wanted to depart this world as swiftly as possible. Reverend Gordon was still beside me—he never moved from my side all that night—and I remember saying to him, "Just don't talk to me about God," (though he hadn't been) and him saying, "All right."

"And don't pray for me. I don't want to be prayed for."

"All right," he said. "Have some water. It's very good—there's a well in the garden."

And then later still, feeling the warmth of his hand on my arm, I opened my eyes and saw that although he was still sitting upright, his eyes were closed, which made me suspicious, so I said, "You promised not to pray for me."

He smiled and opened his eyes and said, "I'm doing my best not to, Edward. But I'm praying a kind of general prayer and you'll have to forgive me if sometimes you slip in. Not often, though. I'm trying to keep it to a minimum."

As I say, not the sort of thing you talk about sitting in a bank thirty years later. But not the sort of thing you forget either. I hope he knows I am grateful. I have no doubt he would say there is nothing to be grateful for.

The events of that day—in particular the flame-thrower—coming as they did hard on the heels of the forest fire and my father's death, pretty much finished me off, mentally speaking. I had what they now call a mental breakdown and for several years I was not in good shape.

Physically I recovered almost in spite of myself. I spent six months in a hospital in England and it was while I was there that I received a letter from my sister Margaret telling me that my mother had died. Her lungs had been affected by smoke inhalation during the fire and she died of pneumonia. I remember the gaping chasm that opened within me when I read that letter. It—the chasm—is there still, though I am not aware of it so often.

A matter of days later I received a letter from Emily—it had been written before Margaret's but it had spent some time in Italy and was two months old by the time I got it—in which she told me I was going to be a father.

I read and reread that letter, trying to make it say something other than what it said. While I was still in Italy I'd realized that if I had ever been in love with Emily I no longer was. I'd worked out that as soon as I got home I would tell her that the war had changed me, which was certainly true, and that I no longer wished to be married and wanted a divorce. Her pregnancy made that impossible. Abandoning her with a child was not something I could bring myself to do even in the state I was in. With hindsight, of course, it might have been better for Emily if I had.

Very little account was taken of your emotional or mental health back then. When I was considered physically well enough to be moved I was transferred to a hospital ship and sent to Toronto, and after a spell in hospital there I was sent home. By the time I got there Tom had arrived. I remember Emily, delightedly, ecstatically, holding out to me this small bundle that was our son, and the way her expression changed when I made no move to take him, merely looked at him and said, "This is him, then." Hardly knowing what I was looking at.

Her parents had rented a very small house for us so that we could be on our own and I could "get back on my feet"—very kind of them, of course. We were there for two years. It felt to me like being in a steel box barely big enough to stand in, containing scarcely enough air to breathe. I circled around and around inside that box. Around and around. It's a wonder I didn't wear a groove in the floor.

It's also a wonder Emily didn't get out the rifle and shoot me, now that I think of it. It must have been very hard for her.

At one stage I thought the endless babies were Emily's way of punishing me for not loving her, but I don't think that anymore. Emily isn't vindictive. More likely she's never quite got over Henry's death. Or maybe it's simply that I don't make her happy and babies do. The problem is, they refuse to stay babies. She tries to hold on to them but one after another they slip away.

———

It is now Friday night. Another weekend in the bosom of my family. This evening when I got home there was blood on the rug in the living room. My first thought was that Emily had had some sort of post-childbirth problem. I took the stairs two at a time—there were splotches of blood on them as well—and went into her room, to find her peacefully feeding the baby. After asking if she was all right I went back out onto the landing and then, of course, noticed that the splotches led to Peter and Corey's room, from which came the usual sounds of battle.

I knocked on the door. There was instant silence. I opened the door and found them frozen, Peter with Corey in a headlock; Corey with blood dripping from his nose.

"Let go of your brother," I said to Peter, and he did so. Corey continued to drip. The two of them looked terrified. Probably they were afraid I'd summon Gerry Moynihan again.

"There is blood all over this house," I said. "You have fifteen minutes to clean it up."

I went down to my study and shut the door.

I still have no idea what to do about them. You'd think we'd know how to bring up our own young. Other animals seem to. Generally the job seems to fall to the females, but Emily, many times a mother, doesn't have the first idea, whereas Megan was seemingly born knowing everything there is to know.

I've tried to remember how my mother achieved discipline—
I don't remember her ever shouting at us, nor do I remember us
ever misbehaving. I wish I could ask her how she did it. I would
like her advice on a good many things.

I've felt her presence very much the past few days. It's as if the
past has sidled up alongside the present for a while. She doesn't
seem to be either approving or disapproving, merely there. A
bonus is that I haven't had a visitation from my father for several
weeks now. I don't know if he's gone for good—maybe he's off
on a binge like old times and will come staggering back. But in the
meantime I'm sleeping better.

I went upstairs an hour ago, thinking I'd have an early night, and
saw that the light was still on in Emily's room, so I went in. She was
asleep with the baby curled beside her. I stepped forward to switch
off the light and suddenly realized that the baby—Dominic—
wasn't asleep. His eyes, which are dark and astonishingly clear,
were open and were looking intently into my own. He seemed very
interested. His fists knotted and unknotted themselves several
times and he blew a small bubble but his gaze never wavered. I
wondered what he was thinking, or indeed if he was thinking—
it's difficult to imagine how you go about thinking without words.

There was a chair in the corner of the room. I brought it
closer to the bed and sat down, but in the moment I had been out
of his line of vision he'd fallen asleep. I sat for a while watching
him sleep beside his mother. I wondered who he was—who he
would turn out to be.

I wondered if there were any possibility that I could be a
good father to him, this late in the day.

That last thought was so unsettling that I gave up on the idea
of an early night and went back downstairs, thinking I'd leaf
through one of the books on Rome to distract myself. I pulled the

largest of them over to my side of the desk, opened it at random and found myself transfixed by a magnificent full-page photograph of a sculpture by Bernini of Apollo pursuing Daphne.

The remarkable thing is, that very photograph was on the cover of one of the books Mr. Sabatini let me take home all those years ago, and of all the works of art he introduced me to, it was the one that moved me most. When he left the school he gave me the book. It was quite literally my most treasured possession. It was destroyed in the fire and when I tried to buy a copy after the war it was out of print.

But there on my desk was the same photograph, every bit as heart-stopping as it had been the first time I saw it.

It depicts in dazzling white marble the moment when Daphne is transformed into a laurel tree. Apollo is pursuing her, mad with love and lust, and Daphne is fleeing from him, her hair flying, her back arched in a desperate attempt to evade his grasp. But Apollo's too fast, he has grabbed her, hard—you can see the indentations his fingers are making on her hip. In panic, Daphne cries out to her father, Peneus, for help, and to save her Peneus turns her into a laurel tree. You can see it happening right before your eyes: leaves are sprouting from her fingers and a root is flowing down from her heel into the ground. It is all over for her. She has escaped Apollo's advances but she will never walk the earth again.

Spellbinding.

One day, I will get to Rome.

CHAPTER EIGHTEEN

Tom

Struan, March 1969

He stood looking at the phone when he'd hung up, wondering if he'd said the right things. He thought he knew his sister pretty well, but she'd been away three years and people change; he himself was proof of that.

There was a sound on the stairs—Adam, coming down again. Tom had sent him up to their mother's room while he was speaking to Meg. Now Adam crept in and stood by the table, watching him fearfully. At least he was no longer crying.

"I think I got her," Tom said slowly, more to himself than to Adam. "But I'm not sure. But I think so." She'd been madder than hell within a second and a half, which he took as a good sign; it meant she was still the same old Meg in that respect at least, still reacted with her guts instead of her brain.

Adam was still looking fearful.

"The aim of the game is to make her come home," Tom said. "Basically that has to happen. There's no other solution."

He noticed Adam's clenched hands sliding up towards his chin.

"This is Meg we're talking about. Your sister, Meg. Nobody

you need to be scared of. The rest of us need to be scared of her all right, but not you. She's the one who sends you the cars."

The fists came down and, for maybe the first time ever, a look of cautious hope appeared. "When is she coming?"

Now he'd set the kid up for something that might not happen. Megan's final words, in fact, had been "I am not coming!" which on the face of it wasn't all that hopeful.

"I don't know for certain she is, I just hope so. Meantime we're going to have to sort you out. You can sleep in the twins' room. But you'll need a diaper at night. Don't start crying!" (Tears were welling.) "Just don't start! It is not your fault and it's not a problem—that's what diapers are for. Let's go and ask Mum about it."

Now that Meg was coming (he still thought she was—you didn't want to pay any attention to what Megan said; it bore no relation at all to what she eventually did), even the prospect of having to think about diapers didn't bother him unduly.

Their mother looked baffled but pointed to a neat pile of muslin squares. They were snowy white—evidently they still got washed, unlike everything else in the house.

Tom looked at them dubiously. "I don't think they're big enough."

"The towelling ones are in the cupboard," his mother said. "But he won't be needing them for a long time yet."

"I don't think we're talking about the same backside," Tom said, his head in the cupboard. Sure enough, there was a great stack of towelling diapers. He lifted out a foot-high pile.

"What else do we need?" he asked, but his mother had gone back to communing with the baby.

"Safety pins," Adam said. "And plastic pants."

"Do you know where she keeps them?"

Adam nodded, burrowed around and came up with the goods. It was a good thing he was smart, Tom thought, or getting through the day in this house would be completely impossible. They took everything through to the twins' room and heaped it on one of the beds.

"What does she do with the dirty ones?" Tom asked, trying not to think about dirty ones.

"There's a bucket."

"Good. When you take it off in the morning, put it in the bucket. Do you know how to put it on yourself?"

"You have to fold it first."

Tom shook out a diaper. There was no shape to it; it was nothing but a big square of towelling. "So how do you fold it?"

"There's a special way," Adam said.

"Do you know it?"

Adam shook his head.

"Right," Tom said slowly. Looking at the square reminded him of the paper-plane-making contests they'd had every year at university. Each of them would be given a single sheet of paper— just that and nothing else. No glue or tape was allowed; it all had to be done by folding. There was a prize for the longest sustained flight and another one for hitting a target. He'd won the sustained flight two years running but he was crap on accuracy.

"Wonder if we can make an airplane out of it," he said. "If we fold it like this" (taking two corners of the diaper and suiting action to words) "and then like that" (folding a previous fold in on itself) "we've got an acute-angle triangle. This is a good shape we've got here. These are the wings, see? Think of the lift you'll get when the air flows over the front edge there. This is going to be the world's first and finest aerodynamic diaper."

Adam was grinning at him, bouncing up and down on his toes for all the world like a four-year-old kid, and Tom was suddenly swamped by a tidal wave of dread and doubt. You have to come home, Meg, he thought. Because what the fuck is going to happen to him if you don't?

In the morning the air had a softness to it that had been absent for months and the snow was mushy underfoot. It smelled like spring, which was impossible—the ground was still buried under a couple of feet of snow—but still, some sense you couldn't put a name to knew it was happening; shoots were stirring down there in the dark.

When he drove past Reverend Thomas's house he saw that, apart from an inch or so that had fallen overnight, the car was now clear of snow and the driveway had been partially cleared as well. There'd been no repeat of bare feet on the porch. Maybe things were finally getting better for the Reverend too.

Out by the New Liskeard turn there was a car in a ditch. The driver was trying to shovel it out, so Tom stopped and they attached a tow rope and got it back on the road. It made him late getting back to town and when he went to buy a newspaper they were sold out, but generally someone left one lying around in Harper's and anyway so much was going on in there nowadays that the paper wasn't the necessity it used to be. The town was buzzing. The boss-guy was due to start recruiting any day and everyone wanted to get a look at him first and—more fascinating still—get a look at his wife. She'd visited twice now and people just couldn't get enough of her: the furs, the sunglasses, the makeup, the voice—the whole package was riveting.

Tom himself was not immune. The last time she was in Harper's he'd got hooked on the way she ate—each morsel taken delicately off the fork, masticated primly (eyes cast down) and finally squeezed down her gullet—as if eating were an uncouth business you'd rather not be seen doing in public. After each bite she'd wipe her mouth, twice, inwards from each corner, for fear a gross crumb might be left on her lips. Tom had watched, mesmerized. She made him want to stick a finger up his nose.

But there'd been no sign of the sea plane today and Harper's was relatively quiet, which meant that Bo wasn't rushed off her feet. She pounced on him the minute he stepped in the door.

"So where is he?" she demanded.

"Who?" Tom said. He tried to edge past her but she blocked the way.

"Why haven't you brought him with you? Give me one good reason."

"I've just finished my shift," Tom said. "And I'm hungry. That's two good reasons."

He took a step towards her and she had to take a step back or he'd have been right on top of her, so he kept that up until they reached Luke's table. Tom slid in opposite him for moral support.

"How long would it take you to go home and pick him up?" Bo said, hands on hips. "Ten minutes? If you're too lazy to walk you could've picked him up in the snowplough on your way here. Think how much a four-year-old boy would love riding in a snowplough. Just think about it."

"Any suggestions?" Tom said to Luke.

"About kids and snowploughs or about her?"

"About her."

"Nothing works," Luke said. "Just stick a couple of pieces of Juicy Fruit in your ears and get on with your life."

Beside Luke's plate there was a page torn from a newspaper. It was creased all over as if it had been crumpled and then spread out again. Luke passed it across to Tom.

"Brought this in for you," he said. "It was wrapped around some tools I had sent up from Sudbury, caught my eye when I unwrapped it. It's a couple of weeks old—there was that blizzard, newspapers didn't make it as far as here. Thought you might not have seen it."

The headline read, "The Big Bird Flies." Beneath it was a photograph of what had to be the most beautiful aircraft that had ever existed or ever would exist, sailing up into the sky. "Concorde makes faultless maiden flight," the sub-headline read.

"Holy Moses," Tom said. "Holy Moses."

He'd seen interpretive drawings and artists' impressions and photos of the prototypes and plans of the profile of those incredible wings, but the finished plane was so much more beautiful than anything he'd imagined it made him go hot and cold all over just looking at it.

"Says it only went three hundred miles per hour, though," Luke said. "Wasn't it meant to go faster than the speed of sound?"

Bo walked off, disgusted. Neither of them saw her go.

"Yeah, it does," Tom said. "The top speed's something like thirteen hundred miles per hour, but they wouldn't take it to the limit on its first flight. You need to warm things up a little."

He couldn't take his eyes off it—that incredible fusion of beauty and function. Even in the grainy photograph you could almost see the air streaming over those wings. He could see exactly how it would work.

His dinner landed with a thump on top of the newspaper. Tom looked up to warn Bo that if she splashed gravy on the photo he would tear her head off but she was already halfway down the aisle.

"She's giving you the silent treatment," Luke said.

"Hallelujah," Tom said. "Long may it last." Though the fact was, when he'd been face to face with her a few minutes ago, it had been disconcertingly difficult to resist getting a little bit closer. Ever since noticing how good-looking she was he hadn't been able to stop noticing it. Grow up, he told himself. You're as bad as the boss-guy. She must be ten years younger than you. Eight, anyway. If you want to look at something sexy, look at Concorde.

"Could I have this?" he asked Luke. "To keep, I mean."

"Sure. That's what I brought it in for." He was looking thoughtfully at Tom.

"What?" Tom said, suddenly nervous.

"I was just wondering if you really want to spend your life making furniture."

"Oh," Tom said, relieved. He lifted his plate, folded the paper carefully and set it to one side. "I don't know," he said honestly. "I've been thinking about it, but I still don't know."

There'd been moments lately when going back to it did seem possible. And just now, looking at Concorde, he'd felt stirrings of a kind of hunger he'd thought had left him forever. Imagine working on something like that. It had to be the most amazing job on the planet. But would he be up to it? It would be a challenge and he wasn't sure he was ready for a challenge. A couple of months back he'd had a letter from Simon, who'd been with him down in the ravine that day. Simon was working for Boeing now, out in Seattle, and after a cautiously worded inquiry about how things were going, he'd said that Boeing had a new project under development and in a few months' time would be taking on more aeronautical engineers.

"*Don't know if you're interested,*" he'd written, "*but there's some great stuff going on out here.*"

At the time, Tom had been unable even to contemplate it. Now, though . . .

"I need to think about it a little more," he said to Luke. "I'm still not sure."

"That's okay," Luke said. "I talked with your dad this morning and I'm going to be extending the workshop and buying more equipment, so I won't need more guys for a few weeks yet."

Bo sailed by carrying three dinners, a jug of coffee and a foil-wrapped package tucked under her chin. It seemed to Tom she stirred the air in a certain way when she passed, as if she generated a strong magnetic field. He had to resist the urge to turn and follow her with his eyes.

On her return trip she stopped at their table. Tom concentrated on his hot beef sandwich. She's too young for you, he reminded himself, forking in a mouthful.

"This is a brownie," Bo said grimly, depositing the foil-wrapped package in front of him. "It is not for you, it is for Adam. I imagine you'll eat it yourself on the way home but that's a risk I have to take."

Tom swallowed his mouthful. "I thought the silent treatment lasted for days," he said to Luke. "I was counting on it."

Luke shook his head. "'Fraid not. Half an hour's her limit. After that her mouth snaps open like it's on a spring."

———

That night, just as he was sinking into sleep, there was a knock at the front door. It wasn't loud, but nonetheless it jolted him awake, almost as if he'd been waiting for it. He heard his father answer the door, heard voices faintly. He knew it was Reverend Thomas. He stayed where he was, lying on his back, staring at the darkness, until finally he heard the front door open and close again. Then he got up and went downstairs.

Afterwards, when his father had told him what Reverend Thomas had said, he went back up to his room. He didn't go to bed straight away; instead, he went over to the window and stood for a while looking out at the night. The wind had picked up and it was snowing again, the snow creating a shifting, swirling halo around the light at the end of the drive. For a moment he saw Rob and himself staggering down the road in the wake of the snowplough, laughing like idiots, Rob clutching the hubcap he'd found in the snow.

He thought about Robert's death—allowed himself to think about it, for the first time didn't try to suppress it.

A car went by, a cloud of snow whirling up behind it. The wind caught it and sent it spiralling upwards and then it paused and drifted down.

He thought about Reverend Thomas, coming out on such a night, driven by the unendurable need to unburden himself to another mortal soul. And also to absolve him, Tom, of blame. Grateful though he was, Tom wasn't sure the Reverend was right that no one could have prevented Rob's suicide, but he could see now that it was possible; that someone might be in so much pain they couldn't even hear what anyone else said, far less be comforted by it.

You're never going to know, he said to himself, watching the snow. You're going to have to live with that. There's nothing you can do but face it, and accept it. That's all. Just let it be.

———

Late the following evening there was another knock on the door and when Tom opened it Sergeant Moynihan was standing on the doorstep.

"I need to speak to you and your dad," the sergeant said. You could see by his face that it was bad news. Tom took him through to his father's study and the three of them sat down.

The sergeant spoke heavily, directing his words at the floor. He told them that earlier in the afternoon he'd been driving along Whitewater Road. As he passed the turnoff to the ravine he saw a glint of metal through the trees and decided to investigate. The glint of metal turned out to be Reverend Thomas's car, stuck in a snowdrift. Reverend Thomas was inside.

"Wasn't carbon monoxide poisoning," the sergeant said, "'cause the engine was switched off. The doc says it could have been a heart attack. He can't say for sure until the post-mortem. He says it could have been just the cold. Got down to minus eighteen last night."

When he stopped speaking there was no sound in the room. Tom watched snowflakes hitting the windows, spearing out of the dark. The snow had been heavier still last night. He thought of it drifting silently down around the car, the old man watching it, perhaps even marvelling at its beauty, as the cold crept in.

The sergeant had been studying his boots but now he looked up.

"Haven't found a note," he said. "So could have been an accident. But he hasn't been lookin' too good lately. My guess is he just couldn't make sense of things anymore. Couldn't find a reason to go on."

CHAPTER NINETEEN

Megan

Struan, March 1969

When she arrived, Tom was standing in the middle of the kitchen eating cornflakes. His shoulders were hunched in order to shorten the distance the spoon had to travel and he looked thin and dishevelled, just as he always had. The unexpected rush of gladness at seeing him was so great that for a moment Megan didn't notice that he was eating out of the upturned lid of a saucepan. Then she noticed and, looking beyond him to the kitchen counter, saw why he was eating out of the lid of a saucepan and she almost turned around right then and there and went back to England.

"Why are you eating out of a saucepan lid?" she asked.

Tom turned and saw her and his face lit up.

"Well hey!" he said. "It's Meg! Hi! You came! How are you? How was the trip?"

"Long. Why are you eating out of a saucepan lid?" She wanted to hear him say it. She was floating in a haze of fatigue— the Toronto airport had been closed by snow and the plane diverted to Montreal, adding many hours to an already painfully long trip—and she was not in a tolerant or forgiving frame of mind.

Tom said, "There aren't any clean bowls. It's really good to see you, Meg. No kidding, it really is."

"You look terrible," Megan said, because that was the next thing she noticed. There were bruise-like shadows around his eyes and he looked about forty.

"Yeah, well. You don't look too great yourself but I imagine we'll both survive." He tipped his head back and shouted, "Adam! Come see who's here!"

Adam appeared in the doorway. Megan forgot about the saucepan lid and being tired. He had their mother's eyes and soft fair hair, and no photograph could possibly have done him justice. She forbade herself to scoop him up in her arms—he didn't know her and it might frighten him—but she knelt down to be on his level.

"Hello, Adam," she said.

"Hello," he said. He studied her gravely. "Are you Meg?"

"Yes," Megan said. "I'm Meg."

He held out a car. It was the silver Mercedes. "This is my favourite," he said.

Next she went up to see her mother.

"Hello, Mum," she said from the doorway. "How are you?"

"We're fine, dear," her mother said, rubbing the baby's back. "We're both just fine. How are you?"

"I'm fine too," Megan said, though a chill went through her. She crossed to the bed and took a look at her youngest brother (he looked exactly like the rest had at that stage), kissed her mother and sat down on the bed beside her. She wanted to hug her but her mother looked too fragile.

"I've been away a long time," she said. "Did you miss me?"

Her mother looked down at the baby.

"Mum?" Megan said.

Her mother looked up. There was bewilderment in her eyes. She searched Megan's face as if for clues.

Megan wrapped her arms tightly around herself. She looked away, fear like a taste in her mouth. Then she smiled at her mother, leaned forward and kissed her forehead. "It's okay," she said gently. "Don't worry. Everything's fine."

She went downstairs, phoned Dr. Christopherson and made an appointment for a house-call the following morning. When she'd hung up the phone she sat down stiffly on a kitchen chair and tried to talk some sense into herself. Don't start imagining things, she said silently. It could be something quite simple. Something to do with her hormones, maybe. Probably in the morning Doctor Christopherson would give her mother a pill, and she'd be fine.

From the living room came the sound of a mini pileup. For some reason Megan found it comforting. She drew a deep breath, stood up and surveyed the kitchen. Now then, she thought. From an untouched pile in a kitchen drawer she dug out two clean tea towels, summoned Tom and Adam, gave them a towel each and together they washed every dish in the house. Then she made out a shopping list and gave it to Tom.

"This is just to tide us over till tomorrow," she said, steering him towards the front door. "I'll do a proper shopping then."

Then she went down to the basement to put in a load of laundry and then she came up and gave Adam a bath.

"Do you have any clean clothes?" she asked him, towelling his thin little body. Not dangerously thin, though, she thought. He's okay. He hasn't actually starved.

"I don't think so," Adam said.

"We'll put on dirty ones for now, then."

Downstairs the outer door slammed and then the inner door.

"Who do you think that is?" she asked Adam, listening to the ruckus.

"Peter and Corey," Adam said.

"I think so too. Let's go downstairs and surprise them."

Peter and Corey had fought their way through the living room to the kitchen and were locked in mortal combat on the floor.

"Hello, boys," Megan said, standing in the doorway. "Remember me?"

"We need to talk," she said to her father, "but not tonight."

That was the second thing she said to him. The first (apart from hello) was that she was flying back to England in two weeks minus a day. "I'm tired and I'm going to bed now. But Dr. Christopherson is coming to have a look at Mum at eight thirty tomorrow morning and you're going to need to be here. Can you manage eight thirty or should I change the appointment?"

"I believe I can manage that," her father said. He had trouble meeting her eyes and Megan hoped it was because he was ashamed, because if he wasn't he should be.

"Megan," he said as she turned to go. "It's very nice to see you. And very good of you to come."

So he was ashamed, which was something. "It's nice to see you too," she said, because strangely, in spite of everything, it was.

"I'm sleeping in here with you," she said to Adam, unpacking her exceedingly small suitcase. "Is that all right?" They were in the twins' room.

"Yes," Adam said. He was looking anxious, though. She guessed it was the diaper question.

"It's your bedtime too," she said, "so we can both get ready. Do you know how to fold your diaper? I put them on the chest of drawers." She said it as if it was a perfectly normal thing for four year olds who had been dry for some time to suddenly need to wear diapers again, and it seemed to do the trick; the anxiety cleared.

"Yes," he said.

"Show me, then."

He took a diaper from the pile, spread it out on the bed, took two of the corners and folded them in, then folded one of the folds in on itself, then the other.

"Um . . . ," Megan said doubtfully.

"It's aerodynamic like this," Adam explained. "These are the wings and the air blows over the top of them like that and lifts it into the sky."

"I see," Megan said, forgiving Tom all sins past, present and still to come. "Fair enough. But how do you put it on?"

"You have to pull it apart a bit at the front and fold it down and then bring the back around and pin it, but I can't do the pinning."

"Okay. I'll do that."

In the night she heard the wind and the creaking of the house and she was back where she started. Andrew, Peter, Annabelle, the Montrose, her much-loved bedsit, her lost suitcase, the trip to England—all ghostly figments of a dream. She went back to sleep and Andrew was there but she couldn't touch him and every time she tried he disappeared.

When she woke she washed and dressed and supervised Adam doing the same and hammered on Peter and Corey's door and went down and got breakfast on the table and took tea and toast up to her mother and hammered on the boys' door again and went down to make their lunches for school.

As the boys were leaving, Dr. Christopherson arrived. He stayed for an hour. He was very kind and very gentle with her mother, and then very kind but very honest with Megan and her father. When he had gone Megan and her father sat on in the kitchen for some time, not speaking.

Early-onset dementia, he had called it. Megan had never heard of it.

"Have you heard of it?" she said to her father at last.

He stirred himself and rubbed his hands over his face. "I think it's what used to be called premature senility," he said. "Though I'm not sure." He looked very strained.

Whatever it was called, Megan couldn't reconcile it with the person who was her mother. But maybe it was something else, something less serious. Dr. Christopherson had said they'd know more once they'd seen a specialist in Toronto.

Megan pulled herself together. "We need to talk about the practical side of things. Can we do it now or do you want to wait until tonight?"

"Now will do."

"Dr. Christopherson seemed to think that she could stay at this stage for quite a while," Megan said. "If the specialist agrees, then that's really good, especially for Dominic's sake. But you're going to have to get someone reliable to do the housework and the cooking and keep an eye on Mum. What happened to Mrs. Jarvis?"

"Mrs. Jarvis?"

"She used to come in to help Mum."

"Ah. I believe she was ill."

"Oh. Well, would you like me to make some inquiries?"

"That would be good of you, Megan."

"All right, I'll ask around. Now, regarding Peter and Corey . . ."

Her father visibly flinched.

"You are all they're going to have," Megan said.

Her father picked up his pen, removed the top, put the top back on, set the pen down. Megan waited. Finally he met her eyes.

"You're all they're going to have," Megan said again, because he had to understand that, and accept it, or nothing was going to work. "They need a firm hand, they need routine and they need supervision, and you can't expect someone who comes in to cook and clean to do that. Which leaves you."

She waited for it to sink in. Then she added, gently but very firmly, "And, Dad, you won't be able to do it from your study."

She felt like the executioner with red tights in the painting of Lady Jane Grey.

"And then there's Adam," she said that night after Adam was in bed. She and Tom were in the living room. Their father was in his study while he still could be.

"Yes."

"Are you all right, by the way?" she asked.

"Yes. Things have been a little rocky. But yes."

"You said on the phone you were leaving soon. Where are you going?"

He hesitated. "There's a guy, Luke Morrison, out in Crow Lake who makes furniture—he's got the contract for this swanky new hotel they're building out along the lakeshore, so he's taking people on. He asked if I'd like a job. I might do that for a bit."

"Why?" Megan said. It was just plain ridiculous. He'd been mad about planes for his entire life; he'd just made a flying *diaper,* for goodness sake.

"Why not? He's a nice guy."

"What's that got to do with anything? You're a . . . whatever it's called, an aerodynamic engineer."

"Aeronautical," Tom said. He shrugged and looked evasive. "I might see if Boeing or de Havilland have any vacancies. I'll see how it goes."

Megan decided that meant he was going back to planes, he just wasn't going to say it out loud yet. He had always hated committing himself. He'd keep saying "I'll see how it goes" until he had his suitcase packed and one foot out the door.

"How about you?" Tom said. "You're sold on England, are you?"

"I love my job."

"You run a hotel, right?"

"Yes."

"You'd be good at it."

He scraped at a spot on his jeans with a fingernail. Shifted in his chair. Cleared his throat. "Look, I'm not saying what I'm about to say with any ulterior motive. I'm just telling you because it happens to be true. Okay?"

"Just say it," Megan said.

"Right. The guy who owns this new hotel is up here at the moment recruiting staff. There's a list of the jobs in the *Temiskaming Speaker* today and one of them is for a hotel manager. I'm just telling you, okay? It was in the paper and I saw it and I'm telling you, that's all."

Megan forgot that she had forgiven him all his sins. "I looked after this family for *fifteen years!*" she said. "And I'm *not* coming back!"

"Okay. I know. I don't blame you. Though it's a live-in job, so you wouldn't exactly be back, you'd be a couple of miles away. But I don't blame you."

There was silence apart from the sound of the wind.

Tom said, "The boss-guy of the hotel is a bit of an idiot but he seems pretty nice, pretty flexible. He might not mind if you had Adam with you." He lifted his hands. "Okay, okay. I was just thinking out loud."

"Well, *stop!*"

"Okay. I've stopped."

He arched his back stiffly. "I'm going to bed. I have to be up at five fifteen."

The wind was making whooping noises in the chimney, which meant it was from the west. Strange, Megan thought, the things you remember and the things you forget.

Tom stood up, hesitated, sat down again.

"Have you met someone over there, Meg?"

She saw Andrew. He'd be at his desk now. Fretting over a word, a comma. In a while he'd get up and stretch and wander across the hall to her room, but she wouldn't be there.

"I think that's a yes," Tom said after a minute. "That changes things all right. If you've found the right person, well . . . that's the rest of your life you're talking about. Obviously you have to go back."

He went up to bed shortly after that. Megan tidied the few things that needed tidying and listened to the wind and the creaking of the house. The sounds of her childhood. Sounds she had known long before she knew there was a world out there beyond the frozen North.

When she went upstairs to get ready for bed she left the bedroom door ajar a few inches rather than switching on the light, but Adam woke up anyway. He sat up in bed, looking at her, eyes wide.

"It's all right," Megan said quietly. "It's just me."

"I didn't know if you were real," he said.

Megan smiled at him. "I'm real. Are you real?"

"Yes."

"Good," Megan said. "I'm very glad about that." Once again she resisted the urge to pick him up and hold him to her because if she did that she'd start to cry and she didn't want him to see her cry. She closed the door and climbed into the bed beside his and reached out across the space between them and took his hand. "Let's go to sleep, shall we?"

"Okay," he said.

She waited until she was sure he was asleep before she

retrieved her hand and let the tears roll, welling up out of the great sea of grief and loss within her. She wept for her mother, who was slipping away from them all, and for Adam and Dominic—and even for Peter and Corey, nuisance though they were—all of whom were going to finish their growing up without a mother. She wept for England, for her beautiful bedsit, which someone else would move into now and paint a horrible colour, and the Montrose, and Annabelle and Peter. But above all, she cried to ease the terrible ache for Andrew, whom she would phone tomorrow and who would tell her she was doing the right thing and mean it, because it was the right thing, and who at the end of the call would ask her, quietly, if she was all right, if she would be all right. She wept for his laugh and the sound of the typewriter, which had always been the first thing to greet her when she got home at the end of the day, and she wept at her own foolishness in pretending they were right for each other and could make a life together.

When she'd finished crying she lay in the darkness, listening to the quiet rise and fall of Adam's breathing, until, finally, she fell asleep.

In the morning she got everyone up and dressed and breakfasted and packed Peter and Corey off to school and told Adam she was going out but would be back shortly. And then she went out into the billowing snow to find the boss-guy and get herself a job.

ACKNOWLEDGEMENTS

The town of Struan is an invention, but in my mind it is located at the northern edge of the vast and beautiful area of lakes, rocks and forests known as the Canadian Shield, in Northern Ontario. I imagine it west and a little north of the real towns of New Liskeard, Haileybury and Cobalt, the last of which was the site of a spectacular silver rush back in 1903.

When researching the section of the novel that deals with that silver rush, I consulted a number of books, among them *Two Thousand Miles of Gold*, by J.B. MacDougall (McClelland & Stewart, 1946); *Six War Years, 1939–45: Memories of Canadians at Home and Abroad*, by Barry Broadfoot (PaperJacks, 1974); *Ten Lost Years, 1929–39: Memories of Canadians Who Survived the Depression*, also by Barry Broadfoot (PaperJacks, 1975); *Cobalt, Ontario*, by Michael Barnes (Looking Back Press, 2004); and in particular *We Lived a Life and Then Some: The Life, Death, and Life of a Mining Town*, by Charlie Angus and Brit Griffin (Between the Lines, 1996). I am indebted to Paul McLaren, owner of the wonderful Chat Noir Books in New Liskeard, Ontario, not only for telling me of the existence of this excellent and invaluable book, but for giving me his own copy.

In a section of *Road Ends* set in England, there is reference to a painting by Paul Delaroche entitled *The Execution of Lady Jane Grey*, which hangs in the National Gallery in London. A character in the book (Megan) is very moved by the painting when she visits the gallery in 1969. Art historians will be aware that, in fact, the painting did not go on display there until 1975. My excuse is that I myself was very moved when I first saw the painting, and I so badly wanted Megan to have the same experience that I played a little fast and loose with the dates. My apologies. But after all, this is fiction.

I would like to thank the following: in Canada, Patricia Anderson of the town of Cobalt for a fascinating tour of a silver mine; Tamara Fishley and Breanna Bigelow at the Cobalt Mining Museum for their help, advice and hours of photocopying from the *Daily Nugget*, back copies of which, along with the *Temiskaming Speaker*, provided a vivid picture of life in Northern Ontario over the years; Eddie Sagle and Chris Callaghan, former snowplough drivers on Manitoulin Island, Ontario, for the lowdown on ploughing northern roads; Malcolm Loucks, formerly of Montreal, for suggesting the Sicard snowplough; and Denise Organ of Manitoulin Island for sharing her memories of life in the early mining communities.

In the UK, my thanks to Steve and Eleen Warren, owners of the fabulous Penally Abbey Country House Hotel, near Tenby in Pembrokeshire, for their memories of running a small hotel in London "back then"; Amanda Grant, for her insightful reading and sound suggestions; and Carolyn and Nigel Davies for encouragement and support through good times and bad—and Nigel in particular for all things relating to aerodynamics. The flying diaper would never have come into being without him.

Heartfelt thanks to my peerless agent, Felicity Rubinstein of Lutyens & Rubinstein, and to my wonderful editors and publishers: Louise Dennys and Marion Garner in Canada, Clara Farmer and Poppy Hampson in the UK and Susan Kamil in New York. Special thanks to Alison Samuel for her great patience, encouragement and tact, and for the remarkable skill with which she kept all the editorial balls in the air.

Last, but definitely not least, I would like to thank my family on both sides of the Atlantic, without whom I would never have managed to write one book, far less three: my brothers, George and Bill, for their meticulous reading and advice on everything from the use of flame-throwers in the Second World War to the northern limit of poplar trees in Ontario; my sons, Nick and Nathaniel, for their perceptive reading and their unwavering support; and above all, my husband, Richard, and my sister, Eleanor, who, as with both *Crow Lake* and *The Other Side of the Bridge*, were involved every step of the way. For both of them, once again, thanks are not enough.

Mary Lawson, 2013

MARY LAWSON was born and brought up in a small farming community in Ontario. She is the author of two previous novels, *Crow Lake* and *The Other Side of the Bridge*, both of them international bestsellers. She lives in England but returns to Canada frequently.